where
NORTH
meets
SOUTH

where NORTH meets SOUTH

ROSE JOHN SHEFFLER

"Lenox Avenue: Midnight" The Weary Blues (Alfred A. Knopf, 1926) by Langston Hughes. This poem is in the public domain.

POLAROID is a Trademark of PLR IP Holdings, LLC

FIRST EDITION

Cover design by Rose John Sheffler
All interior photographs by Rose John Sheffler
© Canva Creative Studio / Canva (instant photo frame)
Daydream front by NendesKombet Studio
paperback: 979-8-9926214-0-2
eBook: 979-8-9926214-1-9

for Dan—
you're my home

for Mrs. Elizabeth Gaskell—
more of the world deserves to know about you

The rhythm of life
Is a jazz rhythm,
Honey.
The gods are laughing at us.
The broken heart of love,
The weary, weary heart of pain,—
Overtones,
Undertones,
To the rumble of street cars,
To the swish of rain.
Lenox Avenue,
Honey.
Midnight,
And the gods are laughing at us.

—Langston Hughes
LENOX AVENUE: MIDNIGHT

Chapter 1

Margaret Hale arrived in Milton, Connecticut on a dreary winter's day, the gray clouds striped with smoke from the factories that rose towering up against the sky. Tired and spent, she hugged her coat around herself as she stepped from the airport, shouldered her rucksack, and looked around. She wished her stomach would settle. The flight from Rochester, Minnesota hadn't been kind to her, but air travel never was. The wind rushed by her, forcing its icy fingers into every crack and crevice in her clothing. She blinked back tears and pressed through the crowd to a line of yellow taxi cabs.

"Where to?" The cab driver stared at her as she fumbled with her bag, looking for the address. "I don't have all day, sweetheart," he said.

She shoved her bag aside. "The college then. You can drop me at the Main Building."

She watched as the city skyline drew nearer, the cab zig zagging through the busy streets. She unzipped her bag and pulled out a dusty Polaroid camera. She ran a finger over the ridges and into the grooves, wiping the dirt away. She blew on the viewfinder, ripped open the covering of a film packet, and fumbled while loading the old camera. She held it tight and stared out the window. A massive stone church loomed on the horizon as the cab came over the rise of a hill. She caught her breath and snapped her first photograph of Milton. She followed the old building with her eyes, craning her neck until it sank again into the coming twilight. The camera had been her mother's last gift to her before she left.

Capture what you love, Margaret Ann, and keep it close.

Her mother's goodbye had been cold and limp, her thin arms lying flatly on Margaret's shoulders in a weak display of affection. Margaret forgave her when she saw the pain in her mother's face. Her mother had been at Mayo Clinic for nearly a year, but she was slowly and surely slipping away. Margaret had been surprised when her estranged father had rung and invited her to come live with him again. She'd jumped at the chance to put as much distance as possible between herself and the weight of her mother's long, weary illness. It wouldn't be long, the doctors said. There was nothing more to do but wait.

Before Margaret left for the airport, Dale Dixon—her mother's long-time friend and unofficial boyfriend—had given her a large parcel and patted her shoulder awkwardly. "Maria wanted you to have this."

"What is it?"

"Open it."

Margaret had held the box tightly, raised her chin, and turned away without another word. For ten years, ever since her mother had invited him into their lives, Dale Dixon had tried to be friends with Margaret.

But he was not her father or her friend.

He never would be.

Margaret paid for her cab, and turned, scanning the buildings before her. Milton University was deserted for the holidays. It took nearly an hour to locate her father's tiny office. She rapped on the door and heard his soft "Come in,"—so familiar and yet strange, like an echo of a ghost.

Father and daughter regarded each other in an odd silence. After her parents' divorce when she was nine, there had been phone calls and a few awkward Christmas visits. But since her mother had moved them from England to America, Margaret hadn't seen her father properly in years.

"You're earlier than I thought you'd be." Richard Hale stood and walked around his cluttered desk, glancing at the clock on the wall. "Dear me, it seems the opposite. I'm running rather late."

"It's all right." Margaret smiled thinly. But when her father pulled her into an unexpected yet genuine hug, she felt warmer than she had in months.

Mr. Hale stepped back and smiled, tapping her nose like he had when she was a child, his eyes sparkling. "How was your flight?"

"Not too bad," she said.

Her father studied her face, a little skeptical, and she shrugged. "I could use a cuppa, to be honest."

"I thought as much." Her father patted his jacket pockets and smiled in triumph when he produced a set of keys. "Everything is better after a cup of tea."

This time, her smile felt real. He always said that.

A half-hour later, she sat with a large mug of good English tea, staring into a cheery fire. She had proper scones and butter and jam sitting at her elbow. She sighed. Sometimes she missed England so much it almost hurt. She'd not been there in six years, but she still longed for it, even if London had never been home. Margaret shook herself, shoving down a sharp feeling of weary loneliness. None of the places she'd lived since her parents separated had ever felt like home.

Why should Milton be any different?

SUNDAY: DECEMBER 25, 2005

"Dad?" Margaret shuffled sleepily into the cramped kitchen and stopped in surprise at the sight of her father making pancakes.

"Happy Christmas, Margaret Ann." He looked up with a smile. "Were you able to sleep?"

"Of course, I was. I'm not five, Dad, all anxious for gifts from Father Christmas."

"Do you want blueberries or chocolate in your pancakes?"

"Blueberries. They're my favorite."

"I remember." Mr. Hale sprinkled the cakes on the griddle with fresh blueberries and turned them. He glanced at her again. "Have I got flour on my face?"

"It's just," she smiled, "you're cooking. I don't remember you ever making anything but tea."

"Desperation is an excellent teacher. My first few attempts at pancakes were dreadful, if not inedible."

"If you get tired of eating pancakes, I can always cook something. I wouldn't mind, Dad."

"I can make a few other things besides pancakes."

Margaret opened her mouth to insist on helping but held back when she saw the look on her father's face. "I can't wait to try them all."

Mr. Hale brightened. "Really?"

"Of course."

There were a few presents for her under the scrawny tree, which made Margaret blush. She'd brought nothing for her father except a necktie, which now struck her as unimaginative and juvenile. After the wrapping papers were cleared away, and a pot of tea was settled on the side table with plenty of biscuits, they sat in a comfortable silence. Margaret fiddled with her camera and watched her father stuff his pipe, light it, and puff a few smoky breaths. He settled himself comfortably and picked up a large leather book, opening it to a ribbon page marker. She studied him as he read for a moment before she raised her camera and snapped his photograph, the sound cutting through the crackle of the fire. She watched the photograph develop with scrutinizing attention. She was getting better.

"Did your mother give you that?"

Margaret looked up at the sudden question and shrugged. "Yes."

"I wondered," Mr. Hale said hesitantly, "did you have a Christmas before leaving?"

"Not exactly," she said. She didn't like talking about her parents to each other. "I asked for an old quilt Gran made and this camera, but that was back when I decided to come here."

"I see." Mr. Hale took his pipe out of his mouth and studied the bowl, tamping down the ashes. "There was nothing else?"

"Well," she said, remembering the parcel Mr. Dixon gave her before she left. "There was one other thing, but I haven't opened it yet."

"Well, it *is* Christmas," Mr. Hale said.

She fetched the box from her room and sat on the couch, carefully removing the bright red paper. Tears flooded her eyes as she lifted the creamy white lid, pulled aside the tissue, and stared at the dress inside. She looked up at her father.

"Do you like it?" he asked.

"Did you and Mum—?"

"We did, but your mother chose it. I thought dark purple was a lovely color for you."

A heavy, almost suffocating, sadness pressed on Margaret's chest as she thought about her parents setting aside their grievances one last time.

Just for her.

"Thank you."

Chapter 2

"How will you spend the rest of your holiday, my dear? You shouldn't be cooped up in the house with me."

"I don't know, Dad." Margaret was helping her father chop carrots for a stew. "It's a nice city, but there's not much to do."

"I suppose not." Mr. Hale set down a half-peeled potato, staring thoughtfully at nothing. He picked up a kitchen towel and dried his hands. "Milton does have some beautifully preserved buildings dating back to the mid-1800s."

"Oh?" She looked up, curious.

"There's a charming old cotton manufacturing district that may interest you. Milton was built during the industrial revolution. Many of the old buildings are still here, being put to new use by the shipping companies. You might wander down to the truck yards."

"What for?"

"I think you would enjoy yourself."

"Enjoy poking around a truck yard?" Margaret tossed a doubtful glance over her shoulder as she transferred the carrots to the soup pot.

Her father had opened a small drawer, pushing through bits of paper and pencils, until he pulled out a battered business card.

"If you want to, you should visit my friend, John Thornton. I'm sure he'd show you as many old buildings as you like."

She took the card and studied it. "Is he a truck driver?"

"Heavens, no. John's the owner of Marlborough Shipping Depot."

Her father looked so hopeful that Margaret suppressed a sigh and gave what she hoped was a bright smile. He wanted her to go.

"I suppose I could visit this afternoon. I'd like to explore a bit before term begins."

Mr. Hale beamed. "Tell John hello for me."

It took less than five minutes for Margaret to bitterly miss the efficiency of Boston public transportation. The bus system in Milton was passable at best, but she soldiered on, determined not to be discouraged. Her father was right; the historic downtown district was full of hidden beauty. The old buildings stood proud and tall. She studied them carefully, itching to take a picture. She stepped off the bus and braced herself for the now-familiar rush of icy air. The wind in Milton was persistent and unforgiving. A large lorry, with a dark red cab, slowly rumbled by, sloshing a slurry of gray snow in its passing.

Margaret checked her camera and shouldered through the wind, following in the truck's wake. She didn't want to pop in on her father's friend, but a twinge of guilt and her own curiosity got the better of her. She was drawn to the old manufacturing building like a moth to a flame. Mr. John Thornton had changed very little of the structure of the building, blending the necessities of modern business with the skeleton of the past. She wandered down the drive, taking in every small detail. The building itself was likely the most interesting thing about old Mr.

Thornton, and she prepared herself for at least a half-hour's worth of complete boredom.

The loading dock for the lorries was occupied by a handful of rough-looking men, hustling about the newly arrived truck as the driver backed towards a square door. Margaret hesitated. She had no real business in the yard. She turned and caught sight of a tall, dark-haired man, dressed in a charcoal gray suit so dark it almost looked black. She moved closer. The man stood near a quarter-flight of stairs, watching the activity in the yard with a look that commanded the scene before him while remaining separate from it. Behind him, the words *Marlborough Shipping Depot* were painted in white on the weathered brick.

"Can I help you, ma'am?" A grizzled older man appeared at Margaret's elbow, startling her.

"I hope so." She was still half-staring at the man in the dark gray suit. She shook herself. "Are you Mr. Thornton?"

"I'm Tucker Williams, the dispatcher for Marlborough Shipping. What's your business with Mr. Thornton?"

"He's a friend of my father's. I'm Margaret Hale."

"You'll have to wait in the office, Miss Hale." He glanced back over his shoulder and nodded at the suited man. "That's him there."

"*That* man is Mr. Thornton?" Margaret openly stared at him again. He was young, much younger than she supposed, with a stern almost immovable expression. A sudden sound of shouts made her jump.

Two men, one skinny and red-faced, one large and swarthy, were shouting obscenities at each other. Then the skinny, red-faced man was shoved aside by the larger man. The red-faced man swore and took a wild swing at the man who shoved him. Margaret stared in horror, unable to move, as a full-blown fistfight broke out, the men slamming into each other with hard, unforgiving blows.

9

"Boucher!" A harsh voice thundered over the scuffle. Mr. Thornton had jumped over the rail and rushed at the two brawling truck drivers.

The large man hesitated, but the other man threw a solid punch to his chin, knocking him off his feet. Mr. Thornton walked straight at the red-faced man who threw the punch, grabbed him by the shirt, and tossed him to the ground with a firm shove.

"There ain't no problem, Master," the red-faced man slurred, swaying as he regained his feet. "Wouldn't want to dirty that pretty suit now, would we?" He threw a wide punch. Mr. Thornton moved without hesitation; in one swift motion, he stepped back, pulled a gun from under his jacket, and held it inches from the man's face.

"Oh my God," Margaret gasped, stumbling forward, fear pounding in her ears. "What's he doing?"

"If you want trouble, Boucher, I'll give it to you," Mr. Thornton said, his voice almost a growl.

The red-faced man spat, tipping sideways, his focus shifting from the gun to Mr. Thornton's face. "Wolf is always trying to snivel up to you when we both know I'm worth ten of him. I got my kids to think of, see?"

"Get out of my yard, you drunk bastard." Mr. Thornton stepped forward, forcing the man to step back. "Now."

"Stop it!" Margaret hardly knew what she was doing as she rushed up and grabbed Mr. Thornton's arm. "Put that thing away."

He glanced sideways at her, his face dark with anger. "What the hell are you doing?" He shook her off and took another step forward, the man called Boucher flinching back.

"If you don't stop this," Margaret said, ice in her voice, "I'll call the police."

"Williams, take care of this woman," Mr. Thornton called out, ignoring her. He kept walking, the firearm trained on the stumbling, red-faced man. "Get your sorry ass out of here."

Tucker Williams tugged at Margaret's coat, gently guiding her back towards the brick building. "Come with me, Miss Hale."

"He can't do that," she said. "Aren't you going to help?"

"Can I call you a cab?" He held the door for her.

"No, thank you," she said, almost spitting the words out, trembling with adrenaline. Her eyes were still fixed on Mr. Thornton. "I don't want a cab."

The red-faced man was now gone. Mr. Thornton turned and stalked back towards the yard, the gun hanging loosely in his hand. "Show's over," he said to the men loitering about. "Back to work."

"Why hasn't anyone called the police?" she demanded, turning back to Mr. Williams.

"The police?"

"He threatened to shoot a man."

"Oh." Mr. Williams shrugged, looking utterly unconcerned. "Don't worry about that. Did you still want to talk to him?"

"I—" Margaret almost bit her tongue. No one seemed to be bothered by the entire mad exchange. "No, I don't. Excuse me."

She watched Mr. Thornton disappear into the building through a side door, contempt boiling under her skin. If she never spoke to that impossible man again, it would be far too soon.

John Thornton stormed into his office, the door slamming against the wall. He pulled out the bottom drawer of his filing cabinet, set his gun down, shoved the drawer closed, and locked it. He shrugged out of his jacket and tossed it on the desk. A throat cleared.

"Was that really necessary?" Williams asked. He poured a cup of coffee—long cold—from the machine and handed it to John.

"Boucher was sweating booze." John took a drink and made a face. "He deserved to have the living shit scared out of him."

"He could press charges."

"He won't."

"Are you going to fire him?"

"I should." John looked at Williams over his coffee and sighed, feeling his temper simmer down. "How was his last drug test?"

"Clean as a whistle." Williams poured out the coffee dregs from the machine and took a long slurp. "I'll write him up, but he wasn't even on company time."

"Give his next haul to someone else. He'll get that message loud and clear."

"That won't go over well."

"I don't care. He puts one toe out of line on the clock, and he's gone."

Williams downed the rest of his coffee. "Anything I need to know about the bank meeting?"

"We got approved to refinance our loan." John shoved his coffee aside, unbuttoned his shirt cuffs, and rolled up his sleeves. He pulled out a stack of papers and began to sort through them. "Did you get that woman taken care of?"

"She left."

John shook his head, his temper rising again. The idiot woman could have gotten herself shot or worse. "Did she say what she wanted?"

"Might have. You're lucky she didn't call the police. She was angrier than a wet cat."

"I've half a mind to call them on her for trespassing. Who the hell is she anyway?"

"Miss Margaret Hale. Said her dad was a friend of yours."

"Hale?" John looked up, a puzzled frown melting through his anger. "She must be Richard Hale's daughter."

"The ex-preacher at the college? I don't recall you mentioning him having a daughter."

John shrugged and sat heavily in his chair. Mr. Hale was in his sixties, and he'd assumed the man's only daughter would be in her late thirties.

"Can't figure how she ended up in the middle of the yard," Williams continued, scratching his chin. "I ain't never seen anything like it. She was all fired up, let me tell you."

"She's a damn fool and a trespasser."

"True, but hot damn." Williams smirked and let out a low whistle. "She's mighty fine to look at."

"Get back to work," John said, forcefully turning his mind to the spreadsheet on his desk.

He had work to do, and he'd wasted more than enough of his time on Margaret Hale.

Chapter 3

Margaret sat through her first day of classes at Milton University with mild disinterest until her father's introductory ethics class. She hadn't told him that she was registered for his section. He would've tried to discourage her, arguing that it would be mildly inappropriate since she was his daughter. But he was only the lecturer, and the actual graded work would be handled by the graduate students overseeing the recitation sections. She planned to argue her point until he gave in, which he would.

He always did.

Mr. Hale took out a piece of chalk and began writing on the blackboard: *Pride and Prejudice.*

"Don't worry, you're not in a literature class," he said, underlining the words. He turned to face his students. "In this course we will scrutinize the way people think and behave, their creeds and their passions. We will examine the divisions between our convictions and assumptions, and everyday actions. The characters Miss Austen sketched for us—their pride of class and rank, and their prejudices—are still applicable today."

He glanced around the room, eyes twinkling at Margaret, smiled, and moved on. "You might assume 21st century modern man doesn't have problems with these issues of class and inequality. Or do you?"

He let his question hang.

"Yeah, we do," a blonde girl with a pixie cut said.

The class laughed.

"Some would agree with you," Mr. Hale continued, "and many would disagree. Isn't that the point? We all think differently, we experience the world differently, and this affects how we live. Now, jumping right in, how might one describe some of these common cultural divisions?"

"Rich and poor," someone said.

Mr. Hale wrote it down quickly.

"Liberal and Conservative."

"Well done." He paused. "Any others?"

"North and South," said a deep growling voice from the back right corner.

Margaret turned and stared in surprise at John Thornton as he looked up from his notes. They locked eyes. How could *that* man be here, in a college lecture hall? The class was so large, she hadn't noticed him when she walked in. But it was the same man from Marlborough Shipping Depot, with the same commanding presence, except now he was dressed in a brown canvas jacket over a plaid button-down shirt, with worn jeans and a rough pair of work boots. A faded red ballcap, with his company's name stitched across the front in dirty white lettering, covered his black-brown hair. He studied Margaret for a second, and she glared back.

"We could also compare East coast and West coast," Mr. Hale

was saying, adding the words to the board. "The ideologies encompassed by words like *North* and *South*, have less to do with the physical locations, even if that's where the ideas originated. The culture clash, however, is still present. Like Elizabeth Bennet and Mr. Darcy, I hope to help you explore what you believe, why you believe it, and where you might possibly be wrong."

John stood as soon as the class was dismissed, his eyes skittering over the crowd and coming to rest on Margaret Hale again. He pulled out his phone, switched it on, and dialed the office. There were shipments to check, and he was burning daylight. He weaved his way through the tangle of students milling about the halls and stepped around the corner by the water fountain. "Williams, did Boucher show up today?"

"I sent him home. Got his haul covered like you asked."

"Who'd you pull in?"

"Slick. Boucher was spitting nails."

"Serves him right."

"When are you coming in?"

"Soon." John heard his name and glanced over his shoulder. Richard Hale waved. "Half an hour." He disconnected the call, shoving the phone into his back pocket. He turned and shook Mr. Hale's hand.

"How are you, John? How's business?"

"Good."

"I'm delighted you're joining us again this semester. Are you taking any other classes?"

"Just the one."

"Excellent. You've met my daughter, haven't you?" Mr. Hale turned to Margaret, who was studying the floor in front of her with a fierce determination.

"We met yesterday. She stopped by the Depot." John removed his hat and took the opportunity to really look at her this time. Margaret Hale was a petite but sturdy young woman with wavy dark brown hair, pale skin, and a large pair of blue-gray eyes. Those eyes were like ice as she finally looked up and stared defiantly back at him.

"How did you like Marlborough Shipping, Margaret?"

"I didn't." She continued to stare at John, almost in a challenge.

He cleared his throat. "I had to break up a fight between two of my drivers while she was there."

"You threatened an unarmed man with a gun," she said coldly.

"Did you really?" Mr. Hale asked, startled. "Goodness."

"I did what I had to do."

"Had to?" She looked at him without any attempt to hide her disgust. "A decent person would never use violence against an innocent man—"

"There's nothing innocent about Ben Boucher," John interrupted. "He's a coward and a bully, and he was blind drunk. I don't tolerate substance abuse or violence in my workplace."

"So, you threatened him instead?"

"I stopped it from getting ugly." John folded his arms. "I wouldn't shoot unless I had to."

"Is that supposed to make me think better of you?"

"Think what you like. How I choose to manage my business is not your problem."

"He's not the only one who's a bully."

John narrowed his eyes, but his retort was cut off by a short, insistent ring from his phone. "Excuse me." He nodded to Mr. Hale, tugged his hat back on, and pulled out his phone, glancing at Margaret. "Miss Hale."

She drew herself up and walked past him without a word. He watched her until she turned the corner. Williams was right—she *was* a damn fine woman to look at. More than fine, if John were being honest, which he wasn't inclined to be right now. But Margaret Hale was also a firecracker with a short-ass fuse.

If he didn't watch himself, he'd get burned.

SUNDAY: JANUARY 15, 2006

On her nineteenth birthday, Margaret spent most of the day on the phone. The first call came from Henry Lennox, at 9:05 a.m. She tried to be friendly and kind. She appreciated his thinking of her, but his manner was strained and awkward. Henry was mildly interested in her, but she wondered how much of his interest was cultivated by her cousin Edith, who also happened to be dating Henry's brother, James Lennox.

♥

Edith's call came shortly after Henry's. They talked for nearly four hours, chatting, laughing, and bickering like they used to when Margaret had lived with her aunt and cousin in London. Margaret brushed the tears from her cheeks, trying to force her voice to be steady when her cousin said how much they all missed her. Edith was happy to share all the London gossip and demanded Margaret repay her in kind.

"Milton doesn't have much gossip, Eds."

"Wherever there are people, there's gossip."

"I don't know anyone, except Dad."

"Surely you've met someone we can talk about," Edith wheedled. "Any single, dishy men yet?"

Margaret snorted. "You said I was too boring for a boyfriend."

"You are, darling, but this is America; the land of the scoundrels and cowboys and all that. Even you have a chance for a little romance."

"I think all the scoundrels and cowboys are in the South. Or is that in the West? I can never remember."

"Southern men are delicious. Their accent alone is swoon worthy, don't you think?" Edith giggled.

"Well, the accent may be all they have in their favor. So far, the only southern man I've met is completely awful."

"Do tell."

"His name is John Thornton, and there isn't a single person on the planet I dislike more." Margaret proceeded to thoroughly abuse him to her cousin, who was more than happy to listen.

"He sounds horrid. But Migs, darling, is he handsome?"

"I hadn't noticed." Margaret was glad Edith couldn't see the blush flaming on her cheeks. "Not much, anyway. He's all right."

"Henry will be pleased. Did he ring?"

"Yes." Margaret sighed. "Because you told him to."

"Why would I do that?"

"Edith Shaw, you're a terrible liar."

Aunt Shaw telephoned for exactly one minute and fifteen seconds. "Margaret Ann, this is your Aunt Shaw."

"Hello, Aunt."

"Happy Birthday, Margaret."

"Thank you, Aunt Shaw."

"Is your father well?"

"He's well, thank you."

"Indeed," Aunt Shaw said without enthusiasm and coughed. "I expect it's quite cold where you are."

"Yes."

"Is there much rain?"

"No, it doesn't rain here in the winter. It snows."

"How dreadful."

"I like the snow when it's newly fallen," Margaret added, almost as an afterthought. "It's lovely."

"Never mind. Has Henry rung?"

Margaret rolled her eyes. "Yes."

"Edith mentioned you haven't met many people."

"No."

"Well, be certain the people you do meet are the right sort of people, Margaret Ann."

"I'll try."

"You must tell your mother to visit London this summer. I simply cannot do without her any longer."

Margaret swallowed the burning lump in her throat. "She can't."

"Yes, well, if she would exert herself—"

"She's ill."

"Yes, of course, but my sister must come and see me soon. She can stay with me if she wishes."

Her aunt always spoke about Margaret's mother as if she wasn't dying. Nothing Margaret said helped.

She admitted defeat with a quiet, "I'll tell her."

"That's good of you."

"Yes." Margaret sat and allowed the silence to stretch out between them. Silence always made her aunt uncomfortable.

"Do give your father my regards."

"Yes, of course."

"Goodbye, Margaret Ann."

"Goodbye, Aunt Shaw."

Fred didn't ring. She didn't expect it, but Margaret always hoped. She marked a red X in her planner. It was the third year her birthday had passed without any news from her brother. Her mother didn't ring either. When Margaret saw Dale Dixon's number on her caller ID, she let it go to voicemail. She stared out of the window, watching the sunset, wrapped in her gran's old quilt. Later, her father brought up tea and they sat together in the silence.

Once it was dark, he handed her a small, square parcel.

"Happy birthday, Margaret."

It was a package of Polaroid film.

Chapter 4

"Bloody hell," Margaret muttered. She was certain she had the worst luck on the planet. Not only was John Thornton in her ethics recitation section, but he'd also been assigned as her peer review partner for the entire semester.

She shoved herself away from the library table, a disgusted taste in her mouth. She'd just finished reading his persuasive paper on gun control. Naturally, he was against it. It had taken her almost an hour to read, not because it was poorly written, but because every word rankled her. She was certain he'd chosen the topic to spite her. She blushed at the thought of her own topic choice and glanced back at the paper lying on the table.

It almost mocked her.

"Ignorant, impossible man." Margaret rubbed her aching forehead and decided she could mark it later. She stuffed the paper into her bag and walked out of the library, bracing herself against the Milton wind.

WEDNESDAY: JANUARY 25, 2006

John leaned against the painted cinderblock wall outside Mr. Hale's classroom, reading over Margaret's persuasive paper arguing for strict gun control. As a rule, he hated any kind of group activity, but this peer review was something else. He pulled the pencil from behind his ear and made a mark. Margaret Hale was a real pain in the ass and couldn't write worth a damn. So far, they'd managed to butt heads on every single topic discussed in class. It wasn't too surprising, since he managed to butt heads with almost everyone he knew.

This was different. She was different.

He'd spent his twenty-six years mostly ambivalent to every girl he'd met. It worked for him—he was too busy to bother about women or seriously date. But now there was Margaret Hale. He didn't know what to do about her. He didn't like how he knew the precise moment she stepped into the lecture hall, even when he wasn't watching for her, which he usually was. He also didn't like how his attention always returned to her, as if she was a damn magnet.

He grunted to himself and made another mark. He hadn't decided if being paired with her for peer review was bad luck or a lucky break; either way, he now had her cell phone number. John smiled as he finished reading and scribbled a final note.

Whatever happened, this was still going to be fun as hell.

FRIDAY: FEBRUARY 3, 2006

"Dad, must you always side with John Thornton?" Margaret blurted after the classroom emptied for the weekend. "It's not fair."

"What do you mean?" Mr. Hale looked confused.

"Every class ends in a blow-up argument, with him in the middle of it all, and you always take his side. For such a calm person, you certainly enjoy a good row."

"I like my lectures to be lively. It helps people engage on a personal level. Don't you agree?"

"I suppose." Margaret followed him glumly.

"How did your first assignment turn out?"

"Rubbish. I got an A."

Mr. Hale paused and turned. "Why is that bad?"

"Because my peer review partner is entirely responsible for it."

"Who's your partner?"

"John Thornton."

"I see." Mr. Hale's eyes twinkled. Margaret was too proud to deny her grade was significantly improved because of John's help. His comments, though biting and rude, focused on grammar, spelling, punctuation, style, and ways to tighten her argument. He was, unfortunately, quite a good writer. The only comment he had about the subject of her paper had made her furious.

You don't know jack-shit about guns.

"Mother, Mr. Hale has invited you and Frannie for tea tomorrow," John said. He sat down on the parlor sofa and opened the newspaper.

"To tea?" Mrs. Thornton asked with a sarcastic edge. "What exactly do you mean?"

"Mr. Hale invited you and Frannie to visit his house, meet his daughter, and have tea," he repeated flatly. "It's a drink British people like."

"What about British people?" His younger sister Frannie came flouncing around the corner and sat, leaning in to read over his shoulder. "What are we talking about?"

"Tea." He raised his elbow, forcing her to sit back.

"You're such a dinosaur," she said in her soft, lilting drawl. "Why do we even get a newspaper? You know they have that stuff online. You can read it for free."

"Nothing is free, Fran."

"What time are we expected tomorrow?" Mrs. Thornton picked up her book, continuing as if Frannie hadn't interrupted.

"Four-thirty."

"Who is *we*, and what are we doing?" Frannie asked.

"We're going to have tea with the Hales." Mrs. Thornton glanced at John, but he kept his focus on the article he was pretending to read.

"Do we have to?" Frannie huffed. "He's nice and all, but I've never even met his daughter."

"I imagine that's the point," Mrs. Thornton said. "Mr. Hale's daughter is young and doesn't have any friends in Milton."

"Whatever the point is, I'm asking you both to go," John said. "Try to be nice."

"Why don't *you* go, if it's so important to you?" Frannie poked his shoulder. "Why do you care anyway?"

John put the paper down, losing his patience. "Richard is my friend. Margaret is his daughter. That's why."

"John, Fran, please try to act your age." Mrs. Thornton set her book aside. "I'll call Mr. Hale tonight."

Frannie sighed dramatically, dragged herself off the couch, and left the room. When she'd gone, Mrs. Thornton turned to John and stared at him until he lowered the paper again.

"What?"

"Why are you so insistent that we visit Margaret Hale?"

"Mr. Hale wants her to meet you and Frannie."

"So do you." She held his stony glare, unbothered by his brooding irritation. "Why?"

He shrugged.

"Is this Hale girl pretty?"

"Mother," John warned.

"That's a yes if I ever heard one."

He rolled his eyes and raised the newspaper. "Are you done?"

"For now."

SATURDAY: FEBRUARY 4, 2006

Mrs. Hannah Thornton sat in the Hales' living room holding her cup of tea. She watched Mr. Hale prepare his own drink and settle back, perfectly at ease. His shabby blazer needed elbow patches, and his rumpled shirt needed a good iron. Her eyes shifted to Margaret, who sat across from her in reserved silence. Dressed simply and neatly in a light-colored blouse, dark sweater, and a brown skirt, Margaret drank her tea with a cultivated self-awareness, commented on the weather whenever the conversation lagged a little too long, and didn't speak more than was necessary to maintain a comfortable sense of civility.

Mrs. Thornton nudged Frannie with her foot, but her daughter kept rambling on about the current Broadway shows in New York City she was obsessing over, her latest boyfriend among the never-ending Watson brothers, and her interest in design and fashion. Margaret listened to it all, with polite, but obvious, disinterest.

After an appropriate amount of time, Mrs. Thornton rose and made her excuses to return home, reciprocating the tea invitation with one for dinner. Mr. Hale smiled pleasantly. "We would be delighted to come, wouldn't we, Margaret?"

Margaret smiled thinly and nodded. "Of course."

Mrs. Thornton thanked them both for the tea and left, her lips pressed closed, her mind full.

Margaret Hale was *not* a pretty girl. If she were only an attractive face, Mrs. Thornton would dismiss her without much consideration; but Margaret was a striking thing, with blooming confidence, self-possession, and a maturity far beyond her years. She had a fiery sort of steel to her that Mrs. Thornton couldn't help but like. Within five minutes of meeting her, she knew exactly why John wanted her to visit, even if he didn't quite know why yet himself.

For now, he seemed indifferent to the Hale girl. Whether or not that changed was up to him. Margaret was a little young but not an absolute impossibility if things between John and Lana Lancaster continued to rapidly sour.

Mrs. Thornton sighed. She had heard all the outrageous gossip about his behavior at the Lancasters' New Year's Eve party a month ago. John still refused to talk about it and disappeared whenever the Lancasters visited. Mrs. Thornton wondered what he'd do if she told him the Hales were coming to dinner.

She decided not to tell him.

Chapter 5

"Do I know you?" The short blonde girl Margaret was following turned abruptly and folded her arms. "Or do you always weirdly follow random strangers around?"

"You don't know me, but I'm not a stranger. You're in my ethics class," Margaret explained. She tried to sound more confident than she felt. "I saw you come out of the library, and I've been wanting to introduce myself. Sorry to be weird."

"I've seen you. I've heard you too." The girl smiled. "I'm Bess Higgins, and you're Professor Hale's daughter."

"How did you know?"

"Your accent." Bess stopped at the corner and glanced up the street where the number twelve bus sat at a red light. Their stop was next. "That's my bus. See you in class tomorrow, Marg."

"Could I come along with you?"

"To my house?" Bess frowned. "You don't even know me."

"I literally have no friends, and I have a feeling you'll make a good one, Bessie. May I call you Bessie?"

"Call me whatever you want."

"Thanks." Margaret climbed onto the bus after her, and they took a seat near the back.

"You're really going to follow me home."

"I won't stay, I'd just like to chat. I've got time, if you do."

Bess gave her a long, almost suspicious look, then shrugged. "Sure."

"Brilliant." The bus shuddered as it pulled away from the curb and rumbled over the pitted streets of downtown Milton.

"So, how do you normally start off awkward conversations with people you don't know?" Bess asked.

"The weather?"

Bess made a face. "Boring. Where in England are you from?"

"Near Oxford originally. Then I lived in London with my cousin, before we came to America. Now my mum lives mostly in Boston."

"Mostly?"

"She's been in Minnesota for a bit. At Mayo Clinic."

"Oh," Bess's voice softened. "And you came here for college?"

"Yes, but I'm a year behind. My parents divorced when I was little. Dad moved to Milton when my mum's health took a nasty turn, about three years ago. He says it was a job opportunity, but I think he did it to be near me."

"Did your dad teach at Oxford?"

"No," Margaret said quietly. "He was a vicar for a while."

"Lost his faith?"

"Not exactly."

"Do you miss it? England, I mean."

"Sometimes, but I've got Dad now, and that helps."

"You don't look like him at all."

"No." Margaret smiled. "I don't look like either of my parents. I

29

once asked if I was adopted, and my mum was furious for three weeks."

"I'll bet she was. You don't have much of a filter, do you?"

"What do you mean?"

"Well," Bess grinned, "look at you and John Thornton. All you ever do in class is argue with him because you can't keep your mouth shut."

"Me? He's the one who can't keep his opinions to himself," Margaret shot back. "I simply refuse to give in to his bullying rhetoric."

Bess raised her eyebrows. "Even if you risk being a bully yourself?"

"I—" Margaret stammered, her face growing warm. American bluntness would never cease to amaze her.

"I won't lie, it's kind of refreshing seeing you give Thornton as much hell fire as he gives you, even if it's exhausting. It takes guts to boss around the boss."

"I'm not bossing him around," Margaret muttered. "He's the world's most stubborn human being."

"Takes one to know one," Bess said with a laugh.

"I wasn't aware you knew Mr. Thornton."

"My dad trucks for Marlborough Shipping." Bess signaled her stop and stood. Margaret followed. "He drives mostly cross-country hauls."

"For John Thornton?" Margaret demanded.

"Sure." Bess walked quickly down the street, hunched against the wind, her coat pulled close around her. It was thinning in more than one place. "Is that a problem for you?"

Margaret was saved from making a reply as they reached the Thomas Street apartment buildings. Bess paused, glancing over the car park, before she stepped inside the musty building. "My dad's home. I forgot he'd be back today. He'll be sleeping."

"In the middle of the day?"

"Trucking takes it out of you. When you're at home, you sleep."

"Maybe he should work for someone else."

"He could. There're manufacturing plants or half a dozen other shipping companies that call Milton home. But if you're lucky, you truck for Thornton. At least, that's what Dad always said."

Margaret rolled her eyes. "You couldn't pay me to work for that man."

"I'd rather work for him than Slickson or Hamper. Watson's quarry would be my second choice."

"You don't drive trucks for Mr. Thornton, do you?" Margaret asked, a little out of breath, as they reached the third-floor apartments.

"Dad doesn't want me to. Not yet anyway."

"Sensible man. I like him already."

The Higgins' apartment wasn't grand or tidy, but it welcomed Margaret in a comfortable way she'd yet to find in Milton. "It's not much," Bess said. She tossed her rucksack onto the table, shucked off her coat, and threw it at a nearby chair, half missing. The coat slowly slid to the floor.

"This is cozy."

"Cozy?" Bess looked skeptical. "You don't have to lie—it's a dump."

"I'm not lying," Margaret insisted. "I think it's very homey."

"Sure." Bess was already busy digging a large stack of files out of her bag. She set them on a rickety table and began to sort through them.

"What are those?"

"Paperwork I've got to get done before tomorrow for Thornton. I'm the office manager at Marlborough Shipping."

"You're his secretary?"

"It's a job." Bess turned and folded her arms defiantly. "Can't afford school without it."

"Sorry, I just—"

"Think I can do better than secretarial work?" Bess chuckled humorlessly, as if at a private joke. "Are you sure you still want to be my friend?"

"Why wouldn't I?"

"We have about as much in common as oil and water. You believe in a lot of pretty sounding nonsense. Maybe all that social utopian shit works for you in England, but nothing is that easy to fix. Especially not people."

"Are you a pessimist?"

"No, just a realist."

"I know life can be hard," Margaret said defensively. "I want to help make it better."

"You think I want to be Thornton's secretary?"

"I think you could be anything you want."

"No, I can't," Bess said, a defiant look sparking in her eyes. "Life is too damn hard for me to be picky. You can't change people with shiny ideas that only work in your head. People don't change."

"I think they can, if you give them a chance."

"See? I told you we don't have much in common."

Margaret almost laughed and shook her head. "You're trying to scare me off on purpose."

"I doubt I could scare you. I just want you to know exactly what you're getting into."

"Look, I need a friend, and I want that friend to be you. I like you."

Bess shrugged again and knocked her shoulder gently against Margaret's. "Don't say I didn't warn you, and don't think I won't call you on your goody-two-shoes act when you deserve it."

"Likewise."

Bess smiled, but it was different this time. "You hungry? I can make dinner."

"No, thanks." Margaret felt as if she'd passed some sort of test. "But I'd love to come back sometime, if I could."

"Come anytime you like, Marg."

"I will, Bessie."

Chapter 6

John sat heavily in his favorite armchair and closed his eyes. His body sank into the cushions, the day draining away. Spring break had officially started, but he was drowning in a mountain of paperwork for next week's shipments, a long list of tax preparation, and another paper to write for Mr. Hale's class. Right now, it could wait.

"You need a shower." Frannie walked past, bumping his feet, before flouncing onto the couch across from him.

"Hello to you too," he grumbled. He didn't even crack an eye.

"I'm serious, John. You better get your butt cleaned up."

"Why?"

"You smell like an ashtray."

"You're the only one who cares," he said, pulling his hat lower over his eyes. What he needed was a whiskey, a book, and a quiet room.

Or his own home.

"We have company coming for dinner."

"Company?" He stood.

"It's not the Lancasters, if that's what you're worried about,"

Mrs. Thornton said, stepping into the room. "I invited the Hales."

He paused, suspicious. "You invited the Hales for dinner?"

"She didn't invite them for tea," Frannie said, snorting.

"Both of them?"

"I thought you'd be pleased." Mrs. Thornton sat and picked up her book. "He's your friend."

"You couldn't bother to tell me about this earlier?" He shook his head. "When are they coming?"

"Six-thirty."

He glanced at his watch. "Ten minutes. Great."

"You needn't dress up." Mrs. Thornton turned a page, but he knew she wasn't reading. "A shower is enough."

"You should shave," Frannie said. "You look like John the Baptist with all that scruff on your face."

"I hadn't noticed," he said sarcastically.

"You best hurry," Mrs. Thornton continued, "if you plan to shower before supper."

John shrugged out of his jacket, grumbling under his breath, and took the stairs two at a time. He hated it when his mother sprang company on him. When he reached his room, he swore loudly. His shower head had busted two days ago, and he'd planned to spend part of the weekend fixing it. He grabbed his razor and a towel before heading back downstairs. The shower next to the mudroom would have to do.

"Dearest, you're very quiet."

"Am I?" Margaret glanced at her father and tried to smile. "I'm just a little tired."

"Exert yourself a bit, my dear. The Thorntons aren't all bad."

"Yes, of course," she said with a sigh and stared out of the car window again. The city had many faults, but downtown Milton was oddly charming.

"So, what's bothering you?"

"This dinner. Mrs. Thornton is so severe, and her son is worse. All he ever does is growl and snap at people, and I'm his favorite target. I don't think I can handle them both at once."

"John likes to have a go at anyone with enough brains and spirit to keep up. You should take it as a compliment."

She raised her eyebrows.

"Besides, he might not even be there tonight," Mr. Hale continued. "He's a very busy man."

"Let's hope so." She crossed her arms, watching the sky sink into a murky gray that promised rain.

When she saw the Thornton's house, Margaret wished she'd brought her camera. It was a large, historic stone building with lingering Victorian architecture that artfully blended history with modernity. Mrs. Thornton ushered them down the hall and into a smaller set of rooms towards the back of the old house where Frannie sat flipping through a magazine. The interior of the house was as fascinating as the exterior, although the decor was a bit spartan for Margaret's tastes. She gave it grudging approval.

"Perhaps the house makes the Thorntons a little less intimidating?" her father teased in a low whisper.

"A little."

Mr. Hale winked.

After offering them a hot drink, Mrs. Thornton sat down on the sofa, stiff and stern as a statue. "I apologize my son isn't here to welcome you both."

Margaret gave a small sigh of relief.

"We're sorry to have missed him," her father was saying. "Perhaps we can chat later this evening when he comes home."

"Oh, he's here," Frannie said, yawning. "He's powdering his nose."

"My son works hard," Mrs. Thornton said, ignoring Frannie. "He only returned home an hour ago. He'll join us shortly."

Margaret tried not to slouch. Frannie continued paging through her magazine, humming a tuneless song. Margaret glanced at her, annoyed. The entire evening was shaping up to test her patience and civility. "Excuse me, Frannie," she said. "Where's the toilet?"

Frannie stood, flounced out of the library, and down a short hall, pointing to another adjoining hallway near the back staircase. "It's that last door on your left."

Margaret nodded and escaped down the long hallway, her footsteps muffled by the thick carpet. She didn't want to be here having supper with people who clearly didn't like her and whom she didn't like. But John Thornton was her father's favorite student, so there was nothing for it, except to keep calm and soldier on. She opened the last door on the left, stepped inside, and closed it firmly behind her.

It took less than a second for Margaret to realize the bathroom was full of steam; at the same moment, a very surprised, and very naked, John Thornton stepped out of the shower. They stood there in shocked silence for far longer than was appropriate.

"Oh my God." Margaret slapped her hands over her face and stumbled backwards, bumping into the door. "I'm sorry." She turned, her hip knocking hard into the marble topped sink.

"Miss Hale—"

"I'm sorry, I'm going." Muscles, skin, and dark hair. *Oh God.* "I'm so sorry." She fumbled for the doorknob. It slipped with condensation and refused to turn under her trembling fingers. She'd seen a man with his kit off before but never quite like—

"Bloody hell!"

"Miss Hale," he began again, the amusement in his deep voice making it even harder for her to compose herself. "Hand me that towel before you open the door."

Margaret peeked carefully to her right and saw a large white towel sitting on the sink next to his razor. She grabbed it and thrust it behind her, her heart beating so loud she thought the house would come down around her ears. *Don't look again. Don't look at all.* She frantically tried the knob again. Why wouldn't the bloody thing open?

"The doorknob sticks."

"What?" She turned, froze, and blushed furiously. His black-brown hair stuck out at all angles, and he was still quite wet, clad only in the towel hanging low on his hips. Besides that, the man was practically made of lean, lanky muscle.

"Move." He took her by the shoulders, and she jumped as he slid around her. He leaned his shoulder into the door and turned the knob with a sharp flick of his wrist. She looked quickly away as he glanced at her with a curious expression.

Then he was gone.

She stood in the steamy silence, catching her breath. After a minute, she ran the tap and splashed cold water on her face. She wiped some of the steam from the mirror. John's amused face burned in her memory. *Impossible man.* Of course, he thought this was funny. As she turned to go, her foot caught on something, and she glanced down at a pile of clothes. His clothes. Her face grew hot, and she flinched away, a fresh image of a naked John Thornton lingering in her mind. Of all the awful things that could have happened today, this was the worst.

38

John straightened his jacket and walked towards the library, slowing when he saw Margaret come around the corner from the bathroom. She stumbled when she looked up and caught him staring. The corner of his mouth twitched at her obvious discomfort. He would never forget the look on her face when he'd stepped out of the shower.

"After you." He gestured to the library. She glared haughtily and darted past him.

"Hello, John," Mr. Hale said, standing to shake his hand.

"Richard."

Mrs. Thornton quickly led the way into the dining room. John's stomach ached at the smell of food. Their part-time cook had outdone herself. "How was your shower?" Frannie teased, glancing over her shoulder. "You sure took long enough."

"Crowded," he said, keeping his voice disinterested. Margaret quickened her pace, putting a few more inches between them. He grinned to himself, enjoying his new advantage over her. When they reached the table, he surprised himself by taking the seat next to her. She looked as if she might get up and move, but Mrs. Thornton had already bowed her head to bless the meal, forcing Margaret to stay put.

Once all the food was served, Mrs. Thornton turned to Mr. Hale, starting the dinner conversation with a question about the history of the manufacturing in Milton. John looked at his sister. Frannie was pretending not to text her latest boyfriend. This time she was dating his best friend, although Watson hadn't officially told him yet. John had Margaret all to himself, and he wasn't even annoyed. Forced civility wasn't his favorite activity, but even he knew how to be a gentleman.

He slowly unfolded his napkin and stole another glance at Margaret. Her eyes flicked over to him at the same moment, her cheeks coloring. She let out a small breath. "Mr. Thornton," she said in a hushed tone.

"Please excuse me for earlier. I didn't realize you were—your sister said I could use the loo."

"Next time, knock."

She stiffened and stared at him. "Excuse me?"

"You heard me." He put a roll onto his plate and held out the bread-basket. "Knock." A muscle in his jaw twitched from the effort to keep his face expressionless. He knew he should back off, especially since the Hales were guests, but John couldn't help himself.

Margaret took the basket from him with an angry swipe and handed it to her father, who was still engrossed in his impromptu history lecture. "Are you always this rude?" she demanded, keeping her voice low.

He gave her a smug smile. "Only to you."

Margaret's mouth closed with a snap, and she turned back to her food. She snatched up her fork, took a small bite, and chewed vigorously as if to stop herself from speaking.

"How do you like Milton, Margaret, now that you've had a chance to see all its finest sights?" Mrs. Thornton asked.

John coughed a little, and Margaret choked, grabbing her napkin. He handed her a glass of water, forcing her to look at him, his eyebrows flicking up ever so slightly. She flinched when he deliberately let his fingers brush along hers.

"Of everything I've seen, I can't say any of it has been particularly notable or exemplary."

"Are you sure?" he muttered under his breath.

Mrs. Thornton looked at Margaret and then frowned at John. "I hope we can change your mind about Milton."

"How could she like anything about this pokey old city when she's lived in Boston and London?" Frannie said, suddenly interested. "I can't wait to leave." She tossed back her curls. "Does Milton even come close to places like that?"

Margaret sat, thoughtful. "Most cities are all rather similar, and I could be as content with Milton as any other place, I think."

"What's stopping you?" John asked. It wasn't a secret she wasn't exactly happy in Milton.

"London," Mr. Hale said with a sigh. "The old city holds her heart, and nowhere else can really be home, eh, Margaret?"

"Lord, I would give my eye teeth to see London," Frannie gushed, her face brightening. "What's it like?"

"I don't remember it very well," Margaret said. "It's been ages since I've lived there."

"I've never been anywhere that exotic," Frannie said. "My brother thinks travel is a waste of time and money."

John opened his mouth to defend himself, but his mother cut him off. "You and my son are in class together," she said, looking at Margaret. "Do you like it?"

Margaret took another slow sip of water. "Which part?"

Mrs. Thornton's face quivered the tiniest bit, and John wasn't sure if it was in frustration or amusement.

"It's not a fair question, Hannah. I'm her teacher," Mr. Hale said with a mild laugh. "She could hardly answer honestly with me sitting here."

"She's more than capable of saying what she thinks," John said, "no matter who's in the room."

Margaret set her fork down with a sharp clank and even Frannie looked up. "What's that supposed to mean?"

"Exactly what I said."

"I only say what I believe to be true. Is that a problem?"

"The only problem is sometimes, when people throw around the word *truth*, it's simply their opinion." John poured himself a cup of coffee. "Believing something is true doesn't make it true."

"Is that your opinion then?" she replied, returning his superior look.

"Yes. It's also true."

♡

When the Hales had gone, Mrs. Thornton sat in the library, her book lying abandoned on her lap. John lingered after dinner only for a minute or two before escaping upstairs. She was surprised he'd let himself get so engrossed in the conversation, to the point of rudeness. It wasn't like him to care so much. She doubted he noticed how much he cared.

Ever since her tea with the Hales, she'd had a nagging curiosity to observe her son in Margaret's company. What she saw were sparks, the instant the two got near each other.

Every movement, every look, and every word crackled with an intense chemistry. Mrs. Thornton sighed. John would put the pieces together soon enough and when he did, Lana Lancaster—or any other girl who wasn't Margaret Hale—would cease to exist.

For better or for worse.

Chapter 7

As she predicted, Margaret liked Bess's father, Nick Higgins, tremendously. She enjoyed sitting in their cramped living room, studying with Bess and her younger sister Mary, or chatting about social issues with Nick when he was home. They were a private family, yet they welcomed her into their life with a blunt, but genuine, hospitality.

A staunch union man, the passion closest to Nick Higgins's heart was opening a trucker's union chapter for the regional shipping companies in Milton. He talked about it whenever anyone gave him a listening ear. Within weeks, Margaret learned far more about the commercial shipping industry than she'd ever wanted. Nick was a fiery man, and his enthusiasm was catching.

"What's today's discussion topic, Professor?" Margaret teased. "Fair wages or health benefits?"

"A strike."

The three girls all looked up from their homework. "Is your union planning a strike?" Margaret finally asked.

"No." Nick winked. "Not yet. But we've got to have a plan ready. If there's an angle to strip money from drivers, the carriers will do it."

"Thornton doesn't angle or scam," Bess said with a dry smile. "The Depot might not be unionized but Thornton's up front and straight with all of us from day one."

"Well." Nick sighed. "I'll give him that. I'd give him a piece of my mind, too, if I thought he'd listen. Thornton could do a load of good if it were worth his while."

"He doesn't think the wellbeing of his drivers is valuable?" Margaret asked.

Nick shook his head. "Only so far as it's good business. He doesn't believe in unions. He's fought us tooth and nail every step of the way. To be fair, he doesn't play games with us, and he's honest about his wages, even if they do scrape the bottom of the barrel. That don't stop him from handing out a bad DAC."

"A what?"

"A DAC is a driving report. You screw one of those up, and you're shit out of luck."

"Thornton's never blacked a driver, Dad. Not unless he had to," Bess said. "You know he hasn't."

"Why're you defending him?"

"He's the best of them all," she replied, "and you know it."

"Thornton's still an owner and a hard bastard," Nick said sharply. "But he's the same hard bastard to everyone. I'd take him over any of the other owners."

"Surely you can make him see the benefits behind a union."

"That's where you're dead wrong," Nick said with a grim smile at Margaret. "Nobody makes Thornton do anything he doesn't want to do, and once he's made up his mind you might as well try to change the stars in the night sky."

"He's not *that* stubborn," Bess said to Mary as she set down a plate of sandwiches to share. "If anyone's got half a chance in hell of changing Thornton's mind about anything, it's Margaret."

"I refuse to talk about this again," Margaret announced.

"Talk about what?" Nick asked, half chewing his bite of bologna sandwich.

Bess and Mary exchanged a loaded look.

"Your daughters think Mr. Thornton is," Margaret made a face, "that he's fond of me."

"Sure," Bess snorted. "That's one way of saying it."

Nick set his sandwich down, giving his daughter a hard look.

"Watch him and you'll see, Dad," Bess said. "He likes her."

"John Thornton hates me."

"If he doesn't realize how much he likes you now, he will," Bess insisted. "Eventually."

"You keep saying that, and I think you're mad as a hatter."

"I watch you two go at each other three times a week. Thornton enjoys a good fight."

"Is that all I am, then?" Margaret glared at Bess, not bothering to control her temper anymore. "A bloody conquest? Another woman to be put in her place by a strong man?"

"Pull that stick out of your feminist ass. He wouldn't bother if that's all you were. You're pure fire, Marg, and once he gets a little taste, he'll keep coming back for more. You won't be able to stop him."

"Leave her alone, Bess," Nick scolded and returned to his food. He finished his supper in less than five minutes and stood, grabbing his coat off the back of the couch.

"Are you leaving already?" Margaret asked. "I thought you had another day of home-time."

"My auntie is coming round with her kids," Mary explained. "Dad hates the noise."

"I didn't know you had an aunt."

"Two floors up. Six kids. Loud as hell," Nick said, zipping his jacket. "Don't wait up for me."

Nick Higgins drove across town, lost in his thoughts. Bess was perceptive, a good judge of people, and not often wrong. Like his mother had been. He'd learned to listen to his daughter's intuitions the hard way. She'd told him her mother would leave him. Nick hadn't listened. All that was left now were his two girls. They were good to him, keeping him honest and sober—most of the time. He tried to do right by Bess and Mary, keeping both girls in school and out of a truck cab. It was a harsh business to the few women who made it their livelihood. But he couldn't blame Bess for wanting to try her hand at it. She'd practically been raised in a truck cab. It was in her blood, and she would have her own way. She always did. At least she'd work for Thornton and that was good enough. For now.

Nick parked his car at the Depot, stashed his coat in his locker, and checked on his rig. He wasn't due in until the morning, but he needed to know if Bess was right about John and Margaret.

It could change everything.

"How's the old girl, Williams?" Nick asked. Tucker Williams was going over the truck with a fine-tooth comb, making sure it met specs for another long haul. Nick, of course, would be required to run his own checks tomorrow per industry regulations.

"Slick? What the hell are you doing here?"

Nick turned and nodded to John. "Master, I wanted to ask you about the trouble with Ben."

"There's nothing to talk about. Keep him sober and out of my way." John flipped a page on his clipboard and glanced up at him.

"What else, Slick?"

"Thought I'd hang out here for a piece." Nick scratched his cheek, watching him from the corner of his eye. "I've got womenfolk coming out of my ears. Bess brought home a friend of hers from school. You might know her, being in the same class and all."

"Margaret Hale?"

"That's her."

"I've met her." John took off his hat and roughed his hair. "She's a spicy one. Don't get on her bad side."

Nick couldn't help the amused smile that broke over his grizzled face. "Guessing you have?"

"Every damn day." John half smiled and tugged his hat back into place. He turned back to his clipboard. "Get out before I kick you out."

Nick left satisfied. There was a chink in the Thornton armor after all. Of course, Bess had seen it. He couldn't pass up an opportunity like this. If he ever needed it, Nick might have a winning ace up his sleeve after all.

MONDAY: MARCH 20, 2006

When Margaret finally reached the library for her second peer review, it was obvious John was tired of waiting for her. He held his hat in one hand, pacing back and forth, his hair sticking up at odd angles. He gave her a dark look. "Do you own a watch?"

"Yes. Why?"

"You're late."

"Technically the bus was late. I was on time."

"Then get a car."

"Here's my paper." She tossed it onto the nearest table, ignoring his sarcastic remark. "Happy reading."

"Pro-choice?" He gave her a tired look. "How original."

"Why should freedom of choice bother you, Mr. Thornton?" she asked. "You're American."

He pulled on his hat and held out his own paper.

She made a face as she read the title. "Defending traditional gender roles? Are you serious?"

"What do you have against tradition? You're British."

"Sorry?"

"Your country still has a Queen."

She stared at him. This man was impossible. She knew she should keep her mouth shut and leave, but she couldn't let him have the last word. "Are you always like this?"

"Like what?"

"I hoped you were a clever man; difficult and stubborn, possibly a little ignorant, but clever all the same. Then you open your mouth, and I'm forced to think otherwise."

"Excuse me?" His voice dropped, a hard warning, but it only made her more determined not to be bullied by him.

"I don't have to read this to know it will defend a value system we've spent ages trying to reform." Margaret shook his paper at him. "No one lives this way anymore."

"Last I checked, I'm still alive."

"Then you're delusional. The rest of the world has moved on, thank God. Your silly, southern ways aren't relevant."

"My southern ways?" He snorted. "Like standing when a woman walks into a room, or showing up to a meeting on time, and knocking before going into a bathroom?"

She flinched, her face suddenly hot with anger and embarrassment. "That's not what I mean."

"Explain it to me then," he rolled his eyes, "and be sure to use small words so I can understand."

"I apologized for interrupting your shower. I won't do it again."

"Interrupt my shower or apologize?"

"Both."

"Pretty sure I'll need an apology after this semester."

"I'm not ashamed of what I believe, and I won't apologize to the people who use old traditions to smash everyone else underneath them. If people like you had your way, women would be subservient to men and dependent on them for money, protection, and—"

"No," he interrupted, rolling his eyes. "If I had my way, men would be men again and women would be women."

"What do you even mean?"

"Read my paper and you'll find out."

"That you're a misogynist?"

"Just because I'm not your brand of feminist, doesn't mean I hate women. I like them. A lot."

"Feminism provides a platform for equality of the sexes."

"Most so-called feminism is a platform for man-bashing."

"Do you live under a rock, or do you make this stuff up?"

"I live in the same world you do, and I've been here a lot longer."

"Is that supposed to intimidate me?"

"No, but it might make you pause long enough to stop talking and try to live in the real world, even if it doesn't always agree with you. But you're just running around with your fingers in your ears."

"Are you trying to win *Asshole of the Year*?" Margaret asked fiercely, her temper boiling over. "Or do you simply enjoy insulting everyone?"

She turned and marched off, not bothering to wait for his answer, but she still caught his growling response.

"Stubborn ass woman."

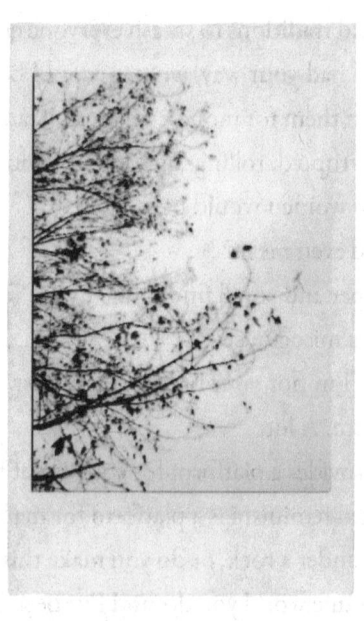

Chapter 8

John stopped as he stepped from the loading bay into the hallway. Margaret Hale stood in the reception area of the Depot, talking to Tucker Williams. What the hell was *she* doing here?

Yesterday, in their ethics class, the discussion topic was ethical business practices. He took the side of employers, Margaret took the side of employees, and within seconds, they'd practically been at each other's throats. But then, they usually were. He knew better than to poke her again, but he couldn't help his curiosity. He closed the door to the bay, and Williams paused, waiting for him. Margaret shrunk back a little, her arms folded around herself.

"Miss Hale," John said. "I didn't think I'd see you here again so soon."

Or ever.

"Neither did I," she said tightly. She shifted a step behind Williams. "I'm here to meet a friend. She gets off work at six and I thought I'd walk her home."

"You mean Bess Higgins," John said. "Follow me."

"I can wait right here, thanks."

"The office has chairs."

She glanced back at the empty reception area and Williams coughed. "Excuse me, Master, I've got a few calls to make."

John nodded. Margaret watched Williams go with a look of resignation. Then she turned, a hard glint in her eyes. "Master?" Her voice dripped with disdain. "Your employees call you Master?"

John forced himself to unclench his teeth. This woman was forever misunderstanding him. "It's my handle. Like a nickname. Every truck driver has one."

"You chose yours a little too well."

"You don't choose your handle; it chooses you."

"But you Southerners have always liked being the masters, haven't you?"

It was a cheap shot and they both knew it, but she would never admit it to him or apologize. Not that he needed her to.

But the remark still stung.

"Let's skip the self-righteous lecture for today," he said. "Some of us work for a living."

"Mr. Thornton—"

"No." He stepped closer, cutting her off. He hated it when she refused to use his name. He should let it go, and walk away, but for some reason he couldn't resist the temptation to throw her own rudeness back in her face. "You can bitch at me all you like but at least have the decency to use my name."

"You are incalculably rude." Her face was red from her temper.

"Yeah, I'm not the only one."

"I didn't come here to be insulted."

"You shouldn't have come here at all." His own temper was now blazing, a sharp energy charging between them. "I don't care if I'm your punching bag in class, but when you're here, mind your own damn business, and leave me to mine." He pointed towards the front entrance. "If you've got a problem with me, there's the door."

"The only real problem is that you have a red-hot poker jammed so far up your own arse, you couldn't find it without help."

"Are you offering your services?" he shot back at her. "I'm currently taking applications."

"Of course not." She stepped closer, looking like she might slap him, which he probably deserved.

"Then leave." He turned away and strode towards the office. "I didn't invite you here, and I don't have time to waste on you."

"I came to see Bessie," she hurried after him, taking two steps to his one, "not you."

"Really?" He turned sharply, and she ran right into him. He caught a whiff of a soft floral smell as she pushed herself back, wiping her hands like she'd touched something nasty. He shook himself and kept walking. "Then why are you still following me?"

"I happen to be walking in this direction."

"Walk somewhere else." John slammed through the office door, and Bess Higgins jumped up as they came charging inside. He was vaguely aware that they now had a rapt audience consisting of Bess, Williams, and Wolf, but he frankly didn't care. His limited patience was gone.

"I'll walk where I jolly well please," Margaret was saying. "I won't be bullied by you or anyone else."

"I'm not bullying you." John took off his hat and tossed it onto his desk. "You're a pain in the ass and this is my private office."

"Are you going to throw me out then?"

"In the spirit of gender equality, I'm considering it."

53

"By all means, treat me as an equal."

"Fine." He folded his arms and bent until his face was inches from hers. "Get out."

"With pleasure."

John scowled as Margaret marched off. *Crazy-ass woman.* And yet, he admired her spunk. It was the only way to describe her. Well, maybe *ballsy*, too. He grinned begrudgingly. Margaret Hale was sharp as hell and wasn't afraid to say what she thought without fear or guile. He found himself weirdly enjoying every minute of it, for all she was a giant pain in his ass.

"I'll be damned." He liked this fiery British woman. He didn't see that coming. He ran a hand through his hair and glanced out of the office window, but she was long gone.

"You're an asshole, John Thornton," he said to his reflection.

Williams and Wolf, who were still loitering about the coffee machine, both snorted. Loudly.

"Shut up." John grabbed his truck keys and headed for the door. He needed to think about this.

"What the hell was that?" Bess called, jogging after Margaret. "Wait up."

"That. Man!" Margaret couldn't remember the last time she'd been this angry. "I have never met a more rude, vulgar, offensive person—"

"Yeah, yeah, he's the worst man ever. You've said."

"He is." Margaret whirled on Bess and made a sharp, frustrated sound in her throat. She yanked herself free from Bess's grasp and kept walking at a furious pace.

"He lives under a God-forsaken rock, on the farthest planet from the sun. And then he has the audacity to spout off the most backward opinions, expecting all the rest of us to fall in line, growling and snapping with his ridiculous deep voice, like he's God's bloody gift to all mankind."

"Wow." Bess said flatly. "You two should just get a room."

"What?" Margaret almost shouted. She felt as if Bess had tossed a bucket of icy water in her face.

"You and Thornton, in a bedroom, alone. Preferably naked."

"Have you lost your sanity?"

"It would be hot. Orgasmic, even."

"No." Margaret hurried towards the street, trying very hard not to think about Bess's suggestion. She failed. "I'm seriously questioning our friendship, Bessie Higgins. Why would you say that?"

"There's so much sexual tension, I could choke on it."

"All of you Americans are insane."

"Someone has to be." Bess paused when they reached the gate to the street. "So, who started the fight this time?"

"He starts everything. I swear on a Bible, there's no reasoning with him. He would try the patience of Mother Theresa."

Bess's eyes flicked over Margaret's shoulder and her grin widened.

"Why are you smiling?"

"Exhibit A." Bess pointed, and Margaret turned. John had just stepped out of his rusted blue pickup truck which was parked outside the Depot's machine shop. He stripped off his shirt, threw it into the truck, and stuck his head under the bonnet.

Margaret's mouth fell open. "Oh."

It came out soft and unbidden, followed by a furious blush.

"I don't know about you," Bess knocked her shoulder against Margaret's, "but I'd totally hit that."

"Have a little self-respect."

"Thornton is hot."

"He's also old."

"Since when is twenty-six old?"

"When you're nineteen."

"You're nineteen?" Bess looked at her in surprise. "No way."

"People are forever assuming I'm older than I actually am. Dad says it's my old soul."

"It's your accent."

"Maybe." Margaret glanced back at John again, annoyed. The man was irritatingly fit.

"Do you think he knows how old you are?" Bess teased. "I hope he likes his women young."

"I'm getting nauseated at the thought." Margaret almost laughed at the absurdity. "Could you imagine the gossip?"

"They'd just be jealous. Thornton is one of the more desirable bachelors in Milton, and it would eat them alive if you swooped in and stole him from them.

"Milton women find misogyny attractive?"

"He doesn't hate women," Bess rolled her eyes. "I think you willfully misunderstand him because you're attracted to him."

"I am not—"

"Personality flaws aside, he's still smoking hot."

"You can have him then, with my blessing."

"Nah," Bess winked. "You like your man-cake way taller than I do."

"No, I don't."

"Everything about your body language says he lights you up like the Fourth of July."

"He's a bit too intense for my taste. Please stop."

"Tell the truth, and I'll leave you alone."

"Fine." Margaret thought for a moment. No one could lie to Bess and get away with it. She could always tell. But what could Margaret say about John without embarrassing herself? She'd have to comment on something nonsexual. Was there anything nonsexual about a man like that?

"He has very nice eyes," she said, hesitating. "They're a lovely shade of blue." She glanced at John again and allowed herself to look him over, once more. He slammed the bonnet of his truck, took off his hat, and ran a hand through his hair. It was doing that funny thing again where it stuck straight up. Was it as soft as it looked?

She shook herself. "I like his hair too."

Bess was staring at her, bewildered. "You've got six feet and four inches of beautiful man flesh, and you go with his hair and eyes?"

Margaret shrugged. Their bus shuddered to a stop, and they climbed on, grateful for a respite from the wind.

"Okay, if all you can say is that he has lovely eyes, then you deserve to have someone else snap him up."

"Go on then." Margaret grinned cheekily. "Shall I plan on a summer wedding?" she teased. "Can I be maid of honor?"

"I'm not his type."

"Which is what? Subservient, sweet, and silent?"

"Spicy." Bess looked sideways at Margaret. "Like Lana Lancaster."

"Who is Lana Lancaster and where do I send my condolences?"

"She's the it-girl among the upper crust of eligible Milton women. I almost feel sorry for Thornton, the way rich single women throw themselves at him, hoping he'll bite."

"Yes, I'm sure it's a great pity," Margaret said sarcastically.

"No, listen. Something happened between Thornton and Lana at the Lancasters' New Year's Eve party. My sister worked the event as a server, and she said they disappeared together sometime around midnight." Bess dropped her voice to a conspiratorial whisper. "But Mary says his truck was gone by the time she left, less than an hour later. Lana was a hot mess the next day and wouldn't speak to anyone."

"Could we talk about something else, please?" Margaret said. She felt oddly uncomfortable.

"Like why you're so determined to hate him?"

"I don't—"

"Lying is a bad look for you."

"No matter what we discuss, he has the nerve to accuse me of spouting ignorant positions. I'm sick of him and his old-fashioned nonsense. Our last paper he was all in a fit about the topic I chose," she scoffed. "Ignorant, impossible man."

Bess sat thoughtfully, then said, "His old-fashioned nonsense runs a lot deeper than ignorant opinions."

"What do you mean?"

"Have you met his sister?"

"Yes. She's a bit silly and talks too much, but she's nicer than he is or his mother. I could like her if she'd talk about something interesting."

"When Frannie was fifteen, she met some loser from out of town and climbed into the back of his truck. He disappeared and left her pregnant. She didn't tell anyone and made a desperate choice. It was a rough time for them, and John felt responsible for what happened to her."

"Bloody hell." Margaret felt like someone had knocked the breath out of her. No wonder her last paper had made him so irritable. She hadn't realized it was because of his sister. It made it harder to be angry at him, but not enough to stop her.

"Frannie was in a bad way, so Thornton cut a deal with his biggest investor to get her out of South Carolina as fast as possible. That's when they moved back to Milton. I'm not saying he's right about everything, but I'd say he has a right to have his own opinions after the hell they lived through."

"How exactly do you know all this?"

"Frannie and I went to the same middle school. Dad started working for Thornton in Blanding, South Carolina. After my mom ran off, we moved up here to be closer to my mom's sister, Rosa."

"Rosa Boucher? Ben Boucher's wife?"

"One and the same."

"She's your aunt?"

Bess nodded.

"And yet you all work for John Thornton."

"Sure." Bess frowned. "What's that have to do with this?"

"He threatened Ben with a loaded firearm. Remember?"

"He wasn't going to shoot him."

Margaret stared at her, stunned. "I can*not* understand you people. A gun, Bessie. A bloody loaded gun, and—"

"Uncle Ben was lucky Thornton didn't fire his sorry ass," Bess interrupted. "He showed up drunk at the Depot during his home-time. He was so wasted, he tried to take Wolf's truck."

"And that somehow makes it all right, does it?" Margaret asked sharply. She signaled the bus for their stop, and they stepped back into the unforgiving cold. "It's madness."

"It's the way things are around here."

"No, it's how *your* people do things."

"My people?" Bess's face clouded over. "Poor, working class, American people?"

"No, Bessie, I didn't mean that."

"For someone who shits so damn hard on John Thornton for being biased and ignorant, you're not that much different from him."

"I—" Margaret broke off. She felt like she'd been slapped.

They stood there awkwardly until Bess coughed. "I've got to go. Dad's expecting me."

"I'll see you in class Monday?"

"I might have to work."

"I'll take notes for you."

Bess gave her a funny look, then shrugged. "Don't bother."

Chapter 9

Bess didn't come to class on Monday. Margaret kept glancing around the room, hoping to see her hidden behind another student, even though it was silly. John Thornton was also absent for the first time, and her eyes continually strayed to his usual seat. She was so used to him watching her from the corner, waiting for him to pounce. She turned back to her notes, trying to focus on the lines. When the lecture finally ended, she sighed with relief, unaware of how tense she'd been until it was over.

Her father caught her eye as the class dispersed. "Stay a moment, if you would."

She nodded, studying the tiled pattern on the floor.

"Did something happen?" her father asked after the room emptied. "You seemed quite distracted today."

"I think I had a row with Bessie Higgins. It was all weird, and she's not been herself lately."

"Does it have anything to do with her job at the Depot?"

Margaret nodded. "She knows I don't approve, but I can't help it.

She should be in school full-time, not working a mind-numbing desk job for the likes of John Thornton."

Her father gave her a look and she sighed. "Sorry, Dad, I know he's your friend."

Mr. Hale collected his papers, stacking them haphazardly and sliding them into his briefcase, before replying. "Margaret, this may not be right for me to say, but Miss Higgins informed me a week ago that she's withdrawn from Milton University."

"She—what?" Margaret studied a loose thread on her father's lapel, her eyes stinging. Why hadn't Bess told her?

"Are you all right, my dear?"

"I'm fine. I have somewhere to be, yeah? I'll be home for dinner."

Margaret shouldered her rucksack and took the city bus down to Thomas Street. She walked the two blocks to the apartments and ran up the three flights of stairs. Mary Higgins answered the door, a toddler on her hip and another little boy clinging to her leg.

"Is Bessie in? She wasn't in class, and I brought her my notes."

"Bess is studying for her CDL," Mary said gently.

"Her what?"

"A commercial driver's license. She quit school. Didn't she tell you?"

"I heard something like that. I thought maybe—" Margaret paused, pulled the notes out of her bag and held them out. "Here."

Mary looked at the pages and sighed. "She won't need these."

"Give them to her, please."

Mary nodded, shifting the little boy on her hip.

"Is this one of your cousins?" Margaret asked, stuffing her hands into her coat pockets.

"This is Pete. My aunt's working a double shift today. And this troublemaker is Joey."

The other little boy hid his face in Mary's jeans again.

"Where's your Uncle Ben?"

"Driving a long haul. Won't be back for another two weeks."

Margaret brushed Pete's chubby wrist with her finger. Her thoughts rushed over her, crushing and heavy. She dropped her hand. "Make sure Bessie gets my notes."

John looked up from his spreadsheet and frowned at the full cup of coffee steaming on his desk. He glanced around the room. Empty. Time to take a break. He pushed back his chair and stretched out his long legs and arms, feeling his joints groan and pop. He stood, picked up his coffee, and walked out into the hall. He caught sight of Bess Higgins standing by the copy machine.

"What do you want, Higgins?" he asked, taking a long sip.

"Sir?" The girl didn't look up.

"I appreciate the coffee." He took another swallow. "I appreciate brevity more. What do you want from me?"

"I'm nearly done with my CDL certification."

He studied her. Short, stocky, blonde, and smart. Like father, like daughter. "I've had enough trouble with your dad trying to bring in a union chapter. Why should I let you drive for me?"

"Because I'm a trucker, born and bred." She looked up. "Because I love the road, and I hate Milton. I have to get out of here somehow."

He thought for a minute, leaning his shoulder against the wall. "You know my zero-tolerance policy on substance abuse."

"That's Dad's problem. Not mine."

"Runs in the family, though, doesn't it?"

She looked down, her face red. "I was sixteen and stupid."

"You also know my policy on excuses."

"Yes, sir." She nodded. "It won't happen again. All I'm asking for is a chance."

"Fine." John grunted, drained the rest of his coffee, and sighed. "One chance, Higgins. No more."

FRIDAY: MAY 5, 2006

Margaret flung herself down on the sofa and kicked off her shoes. Term had finally come to an end, and she was looking forward to a long, hard-earned, summer holiday. Her anger at Bess had faded in the last few weeks. Not seeing her at all helped too, she supposed.

Her father shuffled around the corner, a stack of books in his arms. "How was your final exam?"

"Rubbish. I hate literature. Give me maths any day."

"I could have helped you prepare." He began shelving the books with an absent-minded air.

"That would be an unfair advantage. You're my teacher, you know."

"Only your ethics teacher, my dear. And I'm not that anymore."

Margaret shifted her feet so her father could sit and set them in his lap. She was surprised at how tender he could be at moments. He was never overly affectionate when she was small, but she'd never spent more than a few weeks with him at a time.

"Do you like living here?" Mr. Hale asked, as if he'd guessed the direction her thoughts had taken. "With me?"

"Of course, Dad. I wouldn't stay if I was unhappy." She sat up and put a hand on his arm. "I'm glad I have you."

He nodded again and patted her hand, pleased.

"What shall we do with ourselves in the summer months?" she teased. "We'll be shamefully lazy and useless without some sort of project to occupy us."

"Oh, I have work already lined up for most of June."

"I said a project, Dad, not work."

"Aren't those the same?"

"No, it's summer."

"I must take summer students, my dear. Weren't you saying you wanted to get a job?"

"That's different. You deserve a proper holiday."

"I do allow myself most of May for a rest. After that, it's back to the books. I wouldn't charge you a thing if you had a mind for some summer reading. You should join us."

She frowned, crossed her arms, and stuck out her tongue. "I do not like literature."

"We study any number of things, not just literature."

"Who is *we*?"

"John Thornton, mainly. There are others here and there. I give lectures downtown as well. That's mainly architecture and art history, if you're interested."

She pulled her legs against her chest. "Mr. Thornton comes here to study? Weekly?"

"Yes, of course. Is there something wrong?"

"No. I just thought I'd have a break from him, now that term is finally over."

"You two seem to enjoy having a go at each other."

"Are you taking the mick, Dad? He hates me."

"Smart men like smart women." He tapped his finger on the bridge of her nose. "I think John enjoys your spirit. You're quite passionate, and it's very refreshing."

"I'm not the only one who's passionate," she mumbled.

"Certainly not. Although, you could both try to be a bit more civil."

"I *am* civil."

Mr. Hale made a noise that sounded very much like a snort and retired to the kitchen to make tea.

Chapter 10

Margaret stared at the wall phone as it rang. It must be Bess. Not many people had their home phone number. When it stopped ringing, she felt a wave of fresh anger. Bess would be leaving for her first haul any day now. Margaret couldn't stand the awkward goodbyes that etiquette required. She hated herself for letting the phone ring out, for cutting off her friend because she was afraid. She jumped when the phone rang again and grabbed the handset. "Bessie?"

"I'm about to leave town, and you were going to let me go without saying goodbye," Bess said. She sounded angry and relieved. "You're being a real bitch right now."

"I know. I'm sorry."

Bess was silent for a moment. "Marg, remember what I said about your shiny ideas? This is one of them. I'm doing the best I can with what I have. Try to understand. Try to give a damn about my choices." She paused, then said, "I knew I'd never have more than this."

"But you *can* have more, if—"

"Take care of Mary and Dad while I'm gone. Don't let my cousins eat them out of house and home."

Margaret sighed. "See you later, Bessie."

FRIDAY: JUNE 2, 2006

Margaret opened the front door after the two sharp, insistent knocks. John Thornton's face immediately hardened when he saw her. She stared at him, equally surprised, stiff, and silent.

"Miss Hale."

"Mr. Thornton."

They stood for a moment. She stepped back and motioned him inside. "Won't you come in?"

He ducked through the door, looking large and out of place in the tiny space. She shrank back, keenly aware of how close they were standing, and willed herself to be civil. Her father's gentle rebuke still stung in her memory. "To what do we owe the pleasure?"

"I have a lesson with your dad." He set his hat on the corner table and tossed his keys and wallet inside. He pulled his mobile from his back pocket and switched it off.

"Right. I'll go fetch him."

John nodded and Margaret escaped upstairs. She was about to knock on her father's door when she heard his voice, speaking quietly. She held her breath when she caught her mother's name. Her heart felt tight, and she leaned closer, listening, but the floorboards groaned traitorously under her weight.

"Thank you, Dale, but I must be going."

Margaret knocked quickly. "Dad? Mr. Thornton is here."

The door opened. Mr. Hale was smiling but his face was drawn and closed. He patted her on the shoulder. She waited for him to tell her about his hushed phone conversation, but he slipped past her and started down the stairs.

"Who was that, Dad?"

"What's that, Margaret?" He paused halfway down.

"Just now on the phone." She was right behind him. "It was Mr. Dixon, wasn't it?"

His shoulders dropped a bit. "It was Dale Dixon, yes."

"Mum?" The choking word felt raw in her mouth.

"She's all right. She had a bad scare last night. It won't be long now."

Margaret nodded. She'd come to Milton because her mother was dying, but they never talked about it. Mr. Hale's face was etched with fatigue and regret as he studied her. She pulled herself in and straightened her body. She wouldn't cry, wouldn't let him be weighed down by her grief. "It's all right, Dad. I know."

"Why don't we make some tea?" He smiled but it didn't reach his eyes. "Everything's better with a cup of tea."

"Yeah, all right." She followed him quickly, forcing a smile. Her father's posture slowly reflected her own cheery mood.

It made her want to cry.

"I'm not sure Mr. Thornton will want tea."

"If you make it, I'll drink it." John's deep voice startled her, and she looked up to see him leaning against the kitchen doorway, casually reading a paperback book.

"How are you, John?"

"Busy." The two men shook hands.

Margaret decided to make tea after all, because she knew her father would if she didn't, and he always over-steeped the bags.

"What are you reading?" her father asked.

"Historical Fiction. Victorian." John ducked his head, narrowly missing the low-hanging chandelier with a practiced ease and followed them into the kitchen. How many times had he done that? He looked comfortable here, and it unnerved her.

She set the heavy kettle on the tiny stove top and lit the gas burner with a match. The igniter had stopped working sometime in early February. She took a breath and decided it was her duty to try some civil conversation, for her father's sake. "How long have you been studying with Dad one on one?"

"Three years."

"Really?" She turned, frowning. "That's quite a long time, isn't it?"

"What do you mean?"

It was more of a demand than a question.

"I'm curious why a successful businessman would spend his time and money on college classes when he doesn't need them."

"Being successful in one thing doesn't mean I don't have more to learn." John tossed his book onto the counter beside her, and she jumped, her jaw tightening in annoyance.

"True." She pulled down her father's old, chipped tea pot, cups, and saucers, grateful to have something to do with her hands. "But you have a reason," she said, poking around the cupboards for biscuits, which her father didn't have. "You always do."

"I do." A pause. "I'm trying to finish my college degree."

She turned again, unable to hide her surprise at his admission. "You never graduated?"

"Not yet." A fact which clearly bothered him. He shifted and ran a hand through his hair. "I had to quit college in my second year."

"What was your course?"

He tapped the book laying on the countertop. "Double major in English literature and business with a minor in history."

"You?" She stared at him, standing there in old jeans and

a plaid shirt, hair rumpled and untidy. "You're an English literature major?"

"John's a fairly decent writer as well," Mr. Hale added, packing his pipe. "Always has top marks."

"I'm aware of that," she said, rolling her eyes. "What's all this private tutoring have to do with your trucking business?"

"Nothing. And everything," he said. "There's more to education than sheer utility."

"So, you admit higher education has merit in itself?"

He frowned. "I never said it didn't."

"But heaven forbid you actually help your employees improve their own education." She couldn't help the sarcasm that found its way into her reply. They had argued about this in class several times. Neither of them had succeeded in changing the other's opinion.

"Dearest, that's ungenerous," her father scolded gently, looking at her over his glasses.

"Is it?" she asked. She poured the hot water into the pot and set the cups on a tray while the tea steeped. "I think Mr. Thornton likes having uneducated people work for him. It gives him the upper hand."

"I don't insist on a college education," John said, "and I'll admit a commercial driver's license isn't difficult to get, but people make their own choices. I couldn't care less what they do or don't do with their lives, so long as it doesn't hurt me or innocent people."

"You still take advantage of them and the broken system." She turned and handed John a cup of tea. "Not everyone wants to drive trucks for the rest of their lives."

"Other people aren't my problem."

"Of course they are," she replied sharply. "You're partly responsible for the vicious cycle they're caught in."

John frowned. "How?"

She took a slow breath. "The sorts of people you hire start with financial disadvantages. Maybe they're poor, maybe they never finished school, or maybe they're simply too desperate to do anything else. They put off higher education and work simply to survive, but they have no opportunities or resources to better themselves. They barely make enough to pay the bills let alone set aside money for their education or their future."

"They set aside plenty of money for their booze, drugs, and cigarettes." He crossed his arms, and the movement infuriated her with his devil-may-care posture. "But again, so long as they don't bring that shit into the workplace, it's not my problem."

"Don't you think that's a bit harsh?" Mr. Hale asked. If her father weren't sitting there, the conversation would've already got out of hand. Everything between them always spiraled out of control so quickly.

"No," John said. "Opportunities are there for anyone who wants them."

"What opportunities?" Margaret demanded, abandoning her tea. "These are real people with real struggles. They aren't cogs in your giant Capitalist machine."

"Throwing gobs of money at people doesn't solve anything. It makes it worse. It doesn't change minds."

"Education can. You can't make choices without knowledge. Have you ever considered what a scholarship program or even decent nutritional education could do for your drivers?"

"I run a business, not a charity. What drivers do with their money, their home-time, and their lives, is their business and none of mine. I expect them to do the job and do it well. They expect me to pay them a fair wage. That's it."

"And yet, here you are, improving yourself."

"Because it's *my* life," John said tightly. "Nobody tells me what to do with it or how to live it."

"How very American," she said waspishly, folding her arms.

"It's not American, it's human. If other people won't take the initiative to get what they want from their life, that's their own choice. I won't waste my energy, money, or time on something that's not my problem."

"Some people aren't as lucky as you've been."

"Excuse me?" His expression hardened. "Lucky?"

"Margaret, that's not fair," Mr. Hale said, but she barely heard him. She was too angry to care about civility anymore.

"You're already in a position of opportunity and means, far above those of your workforce. Everything you have was given to you—"

"You don't know what the hell you're talking about," John interrupted, his voice razor sharp.

"Don't I? My friend Bessie Higgins dropped out of college for your stupid trucking company. She drives for you because her father doesn't make enough money to support their family on a single income. I haven't seen you driving a truck for weeks on end, struggling to make ends meet while your family waits at home with next to nothing. You've had good luck and other people have nothing but bad circumstances."

"You want to talk about luck? Bess Higgins is lucky I gave her a job," he said, his voice hard with anger. "I'm the one giving Boucher and Higgins a chance."

"You'll do it because it's profitable for the moment. What happens when they start costing you?"

"They get fired."

"Exactly," Margaret snapped. "If you thought about something other than money for once, you might see people as human beings instead of a profit or a loss, but that requires you to care about someone other than yourself."

"Margaret—"

But she ignored her father, turned on her heel, and escaped out of the back door before he or John Thornton could say anything else, her frustration boiling over. The door slammed with a dull thud.

"Impossible man," she growled at the night sky.

Everything felt too big and too much—her grief for her mother, hundreds of miles away in Minnesota, waiting to die, her frustration with Bess, and her anger at John with his stupid, heartless approach to life. It all melted together into hot burning tears. She couldn't carry it any more today. She turned and walked aimlessly down the street, not caring where she went.

John was in a foul mood when he got home. He strode past his sister without a word, hearing nothing she said, ignored his mother, and charged up the stairs to his room. He would have to apologize to them tomorrow. He threw his hat and keys on his dresser and swore. Loudly.

He hadn't expected Margaret to be there tonight, and it caught him off guard. He raked his hands through his hair and crossed to the window, yanking it open. He took a deep breath of the cool night air. Her sharp words had stung like a bitch.

It wasn't like him to let another person's opinion of him matter so damn much. He shook himself and collapsed into bed. He would also have to call Mr. Hale tomorrow and apologize for losing his temper.

"Dearest?" Mr. Hale knocked gently on Margaret's bedroom door. She sat on the bed, nestled in her gran's old quilt her mum had given her. He sat next to her. "It's not like you to be so harsh or rude as you were tonight."

"If I was rude, I'm sorry." She drew the quilt tighter around her shoulders. "I doubt Mr. Thornton cares what I say or think."

"Margaret," Mr. Hale said slowly, "John knows much more about miserable circumstances than you give him credit for."

"Does he?" She was almost too tired to care anymore.

"Yes." He hesitated. "When John was fourteen his father killed himself. There was a terrible scandal."

She turned, stunned and confused. "What?"

"The Thorntons were a wealthy family, but John's father left a massive financial mess behind him when he died—a mess John was forced to sort out. His mother did what she could, but it was John who repaid every creditor, rebuilt his family, and his life, with his own hard work."

Margaret looked away again, her face burning with shame. All of her clever words suddenly felt ugly and cruel.

"He's been anything but lucky. He knows exactly how unforgiving, brutal, and cruel life can be. His opinions are hard, but they're not entitled nor are they ignorant; perhaps a bit unyielding, but that's just how he always is."

"If he knows what it's like to suffer, why doesn't he care?"

"John has a heart, no matter how well he hides it." Her father paused, laying a hand on her arm. "So many people allow life to beat them down. They give up when things are too hard, and then they turn bitter and resentful. John never let himself become one of those kinds of people."

"Not everyone can be that strong."

"I know. His father wasn't, and that weakness forced John out into the world much earlier than he deserved."

"You think I was wrong to say what I said."

Her father didn't answer, which was all the answer she needed.

"You think I should apologize to him."

"Life hasn't been kind to John Thornton. I think you ought to consider that and try not to judge him so harshly."

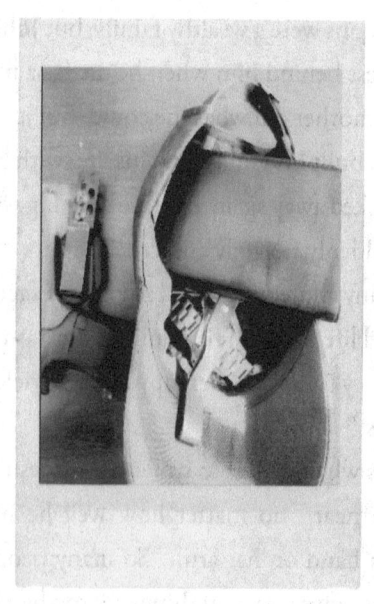

Chapter 11

Margaret studied the thumb-sized grainy photograph on her new work badge as the number twelve bus grumbled along the downtown Milton streets. The picture could literally be any number of other girls. Getting a job at the computer maths lab had originally been Bess's idea, before she quit school. Margaret had applied as an afterthought, but discovered she thoroughly enjoyed the coding and computer work. The money wasn't bad either. Her boss was a little bit strange, but she was used to men being a little intimidated by her.

Except John Thornton.

She frowned and glanced up as the bus slowed for a stop. Marlborough Shipping Depot loomed down the street. She felt a twinge of guilt, her conscience rearing its ugly head yet again. She had repeated a dozen different reasons why she shouldn't feel guilty. It had been nearly a month since their fight, and she'd managed to avoid John entirely. She worked during his weekly lessons, met Bess outside the gate at the Depot, and sat in the back pew in church when her father dragged her along. None of it made her feel better.

If anything, she felt worse.

The bus shuddered. "Wait, please." She jumped up and hurried forward. "I'm getting off here." Once the words were out of her mouth, she almost regretted them. The bus driver smiled and paused, opening the door with a nod.

"Thank you." She walked slowly away from the bus stop, fighting the temptation to go back and wait for the next bus. The last time she apologized to John Thornton, she swore she would never do it again. It was humiliating, yet she knew it was also necessary. She'd been cruel and unkind, and she was better than that.

Margaret straightened her shoulders and walked faster. It didn't have to be a dramatic thing. She would say she was sorry and leave.

"What's a pretty thing like you doing here?" a leering voice called.

She glanced across the lot. Three truck drivers stood around a truck being unloaded, all staring in her direction. She recognized Bess's uncle Ben and waved hello. Ben Boucher lit a cigarette and said something she couldn't hear. The men all laughed, their eyes fixed on her in a way that made her skin feel clammy.

"Hello, Mr. Boucher. I'm Margaret Hale. Remember?"

"Who'd forget Master's firecracker?"

"Firecracker?"

The men all laughed again.

"Are these your friends?" She tried to smile politely. The blacktop radiated a stifling heat, sweat gathering along her forehead and neck.

"This here's Bean and Lancer." Ben Boucher pointed to an impossibly skinny man and a large black man. They grunted hello.

"How are your children?"

Ben took the cigarette from his mouth and spat. "What's it to you?"

"I wondered how they were getting on. I know Timmy's been

wanting to get his learner's permit."

"I don't see them anymore than you do. So what?"

"Boucher, leave the nice girl alone." Bean winked at her. "You'll scare her away."

"We wouldn't want that," Lancer added.

Margaret shifted awkwardly. "How's the driving?"

The three men moved fractionally closer, and she stepped back, bumping into the man called Lancer.

"Lonely."

"Think you could help a man with that?" Bean added. He ran his grimy fingers down her arm, and she flinched. They laughed again.

"Excuse me." She turned, trying to slip by.

"Don't go yet." Bean caught her wrist, his eyes traveling over her. "We're gettin' acquainted and all."

"Let go," she said coldly, glaring back, and tried to pull her arm free.

"Say please, like a good girl." Bean moved closer, then stopped, his attention now fixed on something behind her.

She turned, still tugging at the vice-like grip on her wrist. John stood less than three meters away, arms crossed, his face as dark and threatening as a thundercloud. He locked eyes with Ben Boucher.

"Go."

The word was like a gunshot. The men scattered, swearing under their breath. Ben's face turned angry, red, and dangerous, but he backed off with the others. "Thank you," Margaret said when they'd gone. She shivered, rubbing her arm.

"Did he hurt you?"

"No, I—" she paused, surprised, as John took her hand, running his fingers quickly over the red mark on the skin around her wrist. His hands were rough, calloused, and scarred. But gentle.

"I'm fine," she said, trying to steady her voice. "Everything was fine."

"Fine?" He snorted and let go of her. "For a smart person, you're really dumb." He turned and walked away.

"I—What?" Margaret hurried to catch up, following him into the machine shop where his pickup truck was parked. She stopped abruptly, staring as he stripped off his shirt and tossed it on top of his truck. He grabbed his tool bag.

"Wait a minute, please."

"The office is that way," he said, and pointed towards the main building. "In case you forgot. Stay out of the yard."

"But I'm here to see you."

"Me?" He sighed, pulled a rag out of his back pocket, and wiped his hands. "Make it quick."

"Well, I—" she stopped. She wasn't keen to apologize to him, especially not half-dressed. Her eyes traveled over him, and she blushed, trying not to think about him naked. Or wet. Or at all. "I brought you something," she said a little too loudly, remembering the paperback novel he'd forgotten that night. She took it out of her rucksack. She didn't know why she'd carried it around with her for a month. "You left this at the house."

"I know."

"You know?" She stared, feeling silly. "Brilliant. Now you can have it back, yeah?"

"Did you read it?" he asked, his attention on his truck.

"No." She pressed her lips together. His muscles shifted under his skin just enough to be attractive, annoying, and distracting.

She let out a sharp huff. "I don't like novels."

"Then why'd you keep it?"

"I didn't keep it. Look, I'm trying to be nice to you and return your silly book—"

"No, you're not." He looked at her for a second, a ghost of a smile hovering at the corners of his mouth. He slid under the car, leaving only his long legs still visible. "You should read it. It's all about the Industrial Revolution in the North and South of England."

"I'm sure it's riveting," she said flatly. She turned a few pages, glancing over the printed words. A handwritten note at the bottom of the page caught her eye.

I think you're hot. Love, Nora Jean.

Curious, Margaret turned a few more pages. There was another note in the right-hand margin.

Thinking of you, babe. Love, Nora Jean.

"Maybe I *will* read this," she said, smiling, and flipped through the remaining pages. The book was littered with cringeworthy notes. "But only if you tell me about Nora Jean."

"Who?"

"The girl who *swims in the depths of your cobalt orbs*," she quoted and made a face. "God, who says things like that?"

"What the hell?" He stuck his head out from behind the tire, his face smeared with grease. She held up the book and he grabbed it, scanning the page quickly. He swore.

"Well?" Margaret raised her eyebrows. "Who is she?"

"My girlfriend."

"You have a girlfriend?" she asked incredulously. "Forgive me if I don't believe you."

"Had." He rolled out from under the truck, sat up, and rubbed his face with his rag. "Back in high school."

"You let her write in your book?"

"No." He shoved the novel into his back pocket and ducked under the car bonnet. A moment of awkward silence stretched between them. "Why are you really here? Try not to lie this time."

She scowled. He waited, face expectant. The man was like a bulldog—he never let a thing drop. Apologizing to him would have been much easier if he'd been wearing his shirt.

He sighed heavily. "Look, I don't have all day to wait."

"I'm sorry," she blurted. "I'm sorry for what I said to you. I didn't know about your father. I was nasty and prejudiced and rotten, and I'm sorry."

"Okay." He looked at her for a moment before he slammed the bonnet closed. "But you haven't changed your mind."

"Why would your father's death change my mind? Your employees are still people who deserve respect and decent treatment. I also think you deliberately choose to ignore that fact for profit."

"I don't think you heard what I said at all." He grabbed his shirt and pulled it on. "I pay them, they work, end of story. They're not my friends, and they're not yours."

"How would you know?"

"What do you think would've happened to you if I hadn't seen you come into the truck yard today?"

She hesitated and looked away, unwilling to admit that she didn't know, but it wouldn't have been good. "Do you have so little faith in basic human decency?"

"I never had much to begin with. Neither should you."

"I choose to see the best in all people."

"Does that include me?"

She would've been amused by his remark, but it pricked her conscience. She shrugged.

"You only have grace for people you like, and I'm not one of them.

Because I don't fit your damn narrative," he said. "It's hypocritical."

"You're bloody difficult to like."

"And Boucher isn't? What makes him so special?"

"He's like any other man."

"Exactly." John sighed, his face hardening. "Like most people, he isn't worth it."

"That's a terrible thing to say," she said. "Look, I'm sorry about your father, but that doesn't give you the right to disparage the rest of humanity. Cruelty is a choice."

"So is weakness."

"Mr. Thornton—"

"Not this again," he grumbled and sighed heavily. "Let's skip the part where you get all worked up and call it a day."

"I don't—" she flinched in surprise when he slid his hand under her elbow and led her gently around the truck. "What are you doing?"

He opened the passenger door. "I'm taking you home."

"I can get the bus, thanks." She pulled her arm free. "Excuse me."

"The next bus won't come for another forty-five minutes," he said stubbornly. "I don't feel comfortable leaving you here knowing your dad will worry about you."

She scrambled for a reason to refuse, but he was right. Her father *would* worry. "Fine." She hauled herself into the truck, ignoring his offer to help her up.

He climbed in after her and started the engine. "Don't hurt yourself with happiness."

"What did you expect? Accolades and jubilance?"

"A polite *thank you* would be nice," he muttered and steered the truck out of the shop. "I do have feelings."

"I wouldn't have guessed."

"Your fault, not mine."

"What's your actual problem with me, Mr. Thornton?"

"You sure you want me to answer that?"

"I asked, didn't I?"

He glanced at her and shrugged. "I think you're shallow and too damn naïve for your own good."

"Shallow and naïve," she repeated, his honest words cutting her pride deeper than she expected. She turned in her seat to face him. "Do you really think that?"

"You talk like you've got all the answers, but you don't. You can't have all your shit figured out at nineteen, and you throw a fit when people like me disagree with you. What makes you think you can tell me how to live better than I can?"

They sat in a tense silence for a moment.

"So that's it then?" she asked angrily. "You tell me I know nothing, and I have to agree with you or else I'm throwing a fit."

"That's bullshit, and you know it." He raised his voice, his face stony and hard. "I want you to give a damn about opinions you've never considered before, even if you don't like them. When you start doing that, we can have a conversation worth having."

"You just want the whole world to think the way you do."

"Yes." He shrugged. "And no."

They pulled up to a stop light and sat in another tense silence. When he spoke again, his voice was oddly soft and cold. "The only good thing my dad ever taught me was to tell the truth, because he never did. I'm not always right, but at least I'm trying to live as honestly as I can."

"Are you calling me a liar?"

"I think you lie to yourself, and it pisses me off."

"Why do you care?"

84

"Because you're better than that, Margaret. You're smart as hell and you're not really thinking."

She sat, stunned. "I don't understand you."

"You don't *want* to understand me," he said, smiling grimly. "That's the problem."

"You're right." Two words Margaret never thought she'd say to this man. "I don't understand you and I don't want to."

She unbuckled her seatbelt and let herself out of the truck, slamming the door just as the traffic light turned green. The warm sooty air hit her face with its dirty sewage smell. She shook her hair back and headed towards the nearest bus stop. When she reached it, she groaned. She'd left her bag and camera in John's truck. She turned and spotted the blue truck pulling into a vacant lot.

He got out and walked toward her, his expression stern and unmovable. "What the hell was that?"

"Do you think you can change my mind by insulting me?" she demanded before he could say anything else. "You want me to live a little more, but I'm not a child. I have my own share of suffering, not that you care, and I've seen enough to know what I think right now. Maybe that's not enough for you. Maybe you think I need a few more hard knocks from life. But you don't understand me either, Mr. Thornton."

She marched past him back to the truck. He followed and opened the passenger door for her.

"I'd rather walk."

"It's getting dark."

"It's not that dark, and I know where I am."

"But it's three miles, Margaret."

She ignored this remark and set off down the street. Of course, walking home was ridiculous, but she wouldn't admit it. John's words lingered in her mind like a stinging itch she couldn't scratch.

Impossible man.

♡

John locked up his truck and silently caught up to Margaret, keeping pace with long-legged ease. His damn conscience wouldn't let him leave her to walk home, alone, in the growing dark. He sighed. Her apology surprised and irritated him. Mr. Hale must have told her about his dad at some point, but John didn't need her misplaced pity or her forced apology.

Except, it wasn't forced. He knew it wasn't. She was a terrible liar, and he could always tell when she did. He took off his hat and scratched the back of his head. Margaret Hale brought out the fiery side of his temper, but damn it, there was something about her he couldn't shake off, like a burr stuck in his boot.

It took almost an hour and a half before they reached the Hales' small home. He followed her to the door and waited as she dug her keys from her bag. It was now or never.

"Margaret." He paused. "You were right."

"Was I?" Her tone radiated fury and impatience.

"I don't understand you, and I haven't really tried to. Maybe we can both start there."

She pulled her keys from her bag and looked up, her expression haughty and unyielding.

"At the very least, I'd like to be civil." He held out his hand. "Friends, even, if you think we could manage it."

"Do you think we can be in the same room without sparks flying?"

"Depends. Do you actually want to try?"

She studied his outstretched hand, dubious, struggling to turn the key in the temperamental lock. The bolt finally slid back. "Good night,

Mr. Thornton."

The door shut and the lock clicked sharply back into place.

"Shit."

It came out louder than he intended. He shoved his hands into his pockets and sighed heavily. He probably deserved that, but her snub still stung. More than he expected.

Then the door opened again.

"Wait, please." Margaret stepped onto the porch, her cheeks red. "I've changed my mind."

He raised his eyebrows.

"If you're willing to try to be friends, then so am I." She held out her hand and looked at him with fierce determination. He gave her a crooked grin and took her hand, pleased at her strong handshake.

"Right," she said. "Civil."

"Here." He slowly let go, pulled the book out of his back pocket, and held it out. "I left it on purpose. For you."

"You did?"

He nodded. "Read it."

"I hate novels."

"Read it anyway."

She stared at the book for half a beat before she took it and stepped into the house without another word.

"I'll be damned," he said softly and flexed his hand, curling it into a fist. He wasn't sure what had just happened, but whatever the hell it was, he liked it.

Chapter 12

Margaret sat on the porch steps and panted, her clothing sticking uncomfortably to her skin. The smoggy August heat was unbearable. She hated Milton summers, she decided. The air conditioning was out, turning their home into one of Dante's circles in hell. The phone rang inside but she closed her eyes, ignoring it.

University would start again in three weeks, and it was a relief to be moving into a new school year. She had finally decided on a maths major with a minor in art history. She closed her eyes, praying for a hint of air which didn't come. The phone was ringing again. "Bloody hell." She hauled herself to her feet, headed into the kitchen, and snatched the handset off the wall. "Hales' residence."

"Margaret, it's me."

"Dad? Was that you ringing this whole time? Sorry. The AC broke down again, and it's hotter than Satan's arse in the house."

"Margaret, please—"

"I know, I shouldn't swear, but it's so hot."

"No, that's not it."

"Shall I call the handyman? Can we afford it again so soon?"

"Margaret," Mr. Hale said. But he didn't finish.

"Dad, what is it? What's happened?"

"Mr. Dixon rang. Your mother—she's gone."

Margaret felt the phone slide from her hand and settle on her shoulder as she sat abruptly. Gentle tears slid down her cheeks as she returned the phone to her ear and half-heartedly listened to her father explain the brief details of her mother's death. It felt like a great weight had been cut from her heart, and the pain it left behind was both unbearable and an immense relief. After her father finished, promising to be home within the half hour, she stumbled to her room. She dug her planner from her bag. In the back was a phone number written in bold red ink.

She dialed.

"Mr. Dixon? It's Margaret."

Bess Higgins jumped from her truck. Tucker Williams met her at the bay and together they walked through the post-haul procedures. She was glad to be home even if the heat threatened to suffocate her. Milton felt that way, more and more, even when it wasn't ninety-three degrees. Her father stood by the lockers and gave her a nod. "How are you, girl?"

"Tired. What's up?" She immediately noticed the strain on his face. She frowned when he didn't answer. "Is it Aunt Rosa? She's gone."

"You always know, don't you?"

Bess swore and slammed her fist against her locker.

"Rosa disappeared a week ago. No one's heard from her since. Ben's drunk through his home-time, and I took over his haul for the week to keep him off Master's radar. I'm headed out now."

"Bastard." Bess took her hat off and shook out her short hair.

"Is Mary with the kids?"

He nodded. "Timmy too, but school starts soon."

"Have you called social services?"

"We can't do that."

"You call them, or I will."

"They're kin. We can handle it."

"Like you're handling your strike?"

He grabbed her arm and jerked her back, glancing around sharply. "Keep your mouth shut about things you don't know."

"Or what?" She shook him off. "I think you're all bat-shit crazy as it is. This strike won't work. We'll all get fired with a black DAC and then what do we do?"

"I'm warning you, girl. The plan will work, but we need every driver with us. You understand?"

She stared at him glumly.

"Look after the kids while I'm gone."

"Drive safe." Her words were empty, and she said them like an apology. But it never seemed to matter.

Nick grunted and left.

THURSDAY: AUGUST 10, 2006

The funeral was held in Boston. The drive hadn't been pleasant in the heat, even with the windows rolled down. The air conditioning in her father's car had died the summer before. Her father was resting in their hotel room while Margaret worked out the details of the funeral. Dale Dixon had been appointed executor of Maria Beresford-Hale's estate, making the arrangements for her funeral and all her assets his responsibility. Her last will and testament couldn't legally bar Richard Hale from attending her funeral, but it excluded him in every possible fashion. Margaret was furious.

"She cut Dad out?"

Henry Lennox nodded. As her mother's lawyer, and a close friend of the family, Henry had flown to America for the funeral and for the reading of the will. They sat in a conference room of a chain hotel outside the city.

"And now some man she didn't have the courage to marry or even to take as a lover is in charge of her estate?"

"I'm truly sorry, Margaret. But as your mother's lawyer, I can't interfere with her final wishes. Mr. Dixon will be the executor," Henry continued. "You will inherit, of course, but your father—"

He left the sentence unfinished.

"He's to have nothing," she said bitterly. "And I suppose I can't give him anything?"

"Your inheritance is in trust with your Aunt Shaw until you come legally of age."

"How old do I have to be?"

"Twenty-five."

"Brilliant." She sighed, defeated. "Thank you for your time, Mr. Lennox. What a bother this must be for you."

"Margaret." He laid his hand on hers. "Don't be angry."

"I'm not. Not with you."

"I believe your Aunt Shaw arrives tonight. Would you care for some supper?"

She shook her head and pulled her arms around herself. The mere thought of her aunt made her head and stomach hurt. There would be little time for her own grief.

"Let me take care of you tonight."

"No, Henry. I'd like to be alone, please."

SATURDAY: AUGUST 12, 2006

The morning of the funeral was bright and sunny and terribly hot. Sweat trickled down Margaret's back as they stepped into the church. Her father hadn't spoken since their arrival. He'd grown more and more withdrawn the closer they came to the old church building. She knew he wasn't looking forward to crossing paths with Mr. Dale Dixon, and she didn't blame him.

The service was plain and sparsely attended. Her Aunt Shaw hadn't found sufficient energy to attend her dear sister's funeral after all. No one regretted her absence. Uncle Shaw and Edith had sent a sumptuous floral arrangement that looked out of place among the white lilies and ferns. Margaret stared at it, the wooden pew biting into her legs, cold and hard against her skin. She sat tall and unmoving—Mr. Dixon on her left, her father on her right—absorbing the despair and rejection and loss each man emanated. Dale Dixon was a soft, rotund man, large without being obese, with mousey hair and a very red face. He'd cared for her mother, that much was obvious, but he wasn't family.

She stood as the hymns were sung, bowed her head for the prayers, and tried not to cry. The priest gave a brief message on the pain of death and the mystery of eternity. She soon grew listless, longing for it to end, to be over and done, even as guilt pressed in on her. She clutched the edge of the pew, her gaze wandering over the sanctuary. She didn't know these people and they didn't know her mother, she thought angrily. If they'd been in London, or in her father's old parish near Oxford, the church would have been full. The congregation stood for the final prayer.

"I can't stand this." She slipped past Mr. Dixon, hurried down the side aisle, unseen and unheard, and escaped through a side door. She stepped into the sunshine, blinded by its sudden brightness. The burning light held back the tears threatening to break her. She took a deep, heated breath.

A moment later the main doors opened, and the mourners began to trickle out. Margaret nodded to each one that stopped and offered her their sympathy. She held her breath when the casket was carried out, and watched the six somber men take her mother away for the last time.

"Almost over." Henry placed his hand above her elbow and guided her to the waiting car.

Maria Beresford-Hale was laid to rest in a corner of a small cemetery close to the home of Mr. Dale Dixon. Margaret kept her eyes closed as the final parting words were said and the casket was lowered into the earth. It was done. When everyone had left, her father sat heavily, fresh tears dropping into his lap. She turned away and wandered through the headstones. So many lives stood there with nothing but cold rock to remember them. She clutched at one of the markers, the stone rough under her hand.

"Margaret?" John Thornton stood a few meters away, his head lowered, hands in his pockets, watching her. She stared at him, confused and oddly comforted.

Why was he here? Had he been here the whole time?

His usual plaid shirt, jeans, work boots, and ball cap had been replaced with the same dark gray suit he'd worn the day they'd first met. His black-brown hair was combed, and his face was clean-shaven. Neither of them spoke and neither looked away. There was an unexpected but gentle understanding in his eyes.

He stepped closer and held out a white handkerchief. She brushed self-consciously at her cheeks. They were wet. His face softened.

Something in that look snapped the heavy cord holding her together. She sank to her knees, covered her face with her hands, and wept like the child she was. Her mother was dead. She knew the yearning ache in her heart that demanded God return her mother to this earth was utterly selfish. But it didn't make it easier or better. Nothing ever would.

John crouched and held out his hand. Somehow his steady presence helped her control the rage of grief inside her. She was grateful for his silence, which was more comforting than the mountain of empty words she'd endured today. She took a deep shuddering breath and took his hand. He helped her stand and waited.

"Thank you," she whispered.

He nodded.

She walked back and sat by her father, taking his soft hand in hers. He needed her to be strong for them both.

"Is it over, dearest?"

"It's over." Her voice shook and he patted her hand.

"Let's go home."

Home. The word almost itched, as if mocking her, but she squeezed his hand reassuringly.

"I'm glad, you know—" he broke off and looked away. "It's all done for Maria now, all that pain—I'm glad."

"I know." She laid her head on his shoulder and set the handkerchief on his knee.

He took it and wiped his eyes and cheeks. He blew his nose, folded it up, and gave it back to her. "This isn't yours."

"John Thornton lent it to me." She studied his initials embroidered in the corner. His mother must have done that. She wondered what the 'S' of his middle name stood for. "He was here the whole time."

"He's a good friend."

"He is." Margaret's heart lifted when she saw a little brightness in her father's face. She looked back to where she'd left John standing among the headstones.

But he was gone.

Chapter 13

MONDAY: AUGUST 14, 2006

The house was unbearably hot when they returned. Margaret sighed and went to plug in the two large box fans she'd found in the attic. She left her bag in the cramped hallway, looking around at the clutter. She didn't think she had it in her to tidy up. The air conditioning was still broken, the mail spilled out of the basket on the corner table, the bins needed emptying, piles of dirty clothes littered the upstairs, the lock on the front door still needed to be replaced, the toilet had started leaking right before they'd left—the list went on and on.

"I'll have a lie down," her father said. He climbed the stairs with heavy footsteps. "Don't mind me."

"Leave your bag, Dad. I'll do the washing later."

"You needn't bother today."

"How about a cuppa?" she called after him. His door closed. She sat on the bottom step and laid her forehead on her knees. The clock in the living room ticked loudly against the constant whir of the fans.

Be brave, Margaret Ann.

But she didn't feel brave anymore.

She sat up in surprise at the sound of three sharp knocks. A man in a blue HVAC uniform greeted her and asked to be shown the broken unit. "I'm sorry, you have the wrong house. We didn't call."

The man repeated their address, and she frowned. Had her father finally rung and forgotten to tell her? She let the repairman in, still puzzled. Within the hour, the man finished his work and wrote up the ticket. She held out her hand for the bill, but he shook his head and folded the paper neatly. "I've been paid."

"I don't understand."

"It's all taken care of." The man smiled and handed her a copy of the company's card. "Call us if you have any more trouble."

"Thank you." She was too tired to argue anymore and too relieved to feel the cool air blowing through the vents. After seeing the man to the door, she wandered into the kitchen, flipping the light switch, but nothing happened. The bulbs had blown weeks ago.

"I'll make tea," she told the empty room, holding back a wave of overwhelmed defeat. "Everything is better after a cup of tea."

She filled the kettle, pulled down the cups and saucers, and put the tea bags in the teapot. While the it brewed, she found some white crackers in the corner of a low cupboard and a little butter and jam in the fridge. Her father hadn't been to the grocery store in a week and a half. Margaret sighed, adding it to her list of tasks. She arranged a tray with the tea and crackers and carried it up to her father. "I've brought tea, Dad," she said, nudging the door open.

He sat in a large chair in the corner of his room, staring out of the small window. She set the tray on his bed and fixed him a cup. "Thank you, dearest," he said, but he didn't take it.

She pulled his little bedside table closer, buttered and jammed several crackers, and arranged them on a plate near his elbow, next to the tea. "Do you want anything else?"

"Hm?" He turned towards her, not really seeing her.

"I'll be downstairs tidying up. I'll leave the tea."

He didn't answer.

She poured herself a cup and left him to his thoughts, carrying his suitcase in one hand, her tea in the other. Two knocks sounded at the door, and she dropped the bag with a little gasp of surprise. She stumbled over it and yanked the front door open, spilling her tea all down her shirt.

"Oh, sod it all." She stared at the spreading stain, forgetting the open door, and sat down on the bottom stair, trying not to cry.

"Margaret?" John took off his hat and ducked into the house, stepping over the bags tossed about in the cramped hallway. "Are you okay?"

"I'm fine." She set down her cup and rubbed her eyes. "It's been a very long week."

"I know."

"Sorry." She wiped her face and finally looked up. "Did you need something?"

"I brought food." He held up two paper grocery bags. "Chicken casserole, bread, and green beans."

"Oh." She leaned against the wall. "Thank you."

"Do you want this in the kitchen?"

She nodded but didn't get up. He headed down the hall and flipped the switch for the overhead floodlights. He frowned, flicking the switch back and forth. Mr. Hale was a brilliant scholar, but he wasn't good for much else; his house was proof. John had called the HVAC company a week ago when Mr. Hale mentioned it wasn't working again. The Hales' unit was on its last leg and would need to be replaced before next summer. John made a mental note to make sure it happened.

He set the bags of food on the table and rummaged around the cabinets and drawers until he found a clean plate and fork. He didn't like the drawn look in Margaret's face or the dark circles under her eyes. He filled a glass with water, dished out some casserole and green beans, and set the plate on the table. Next, he searched until he found a pack of light bulbs stashed in the high cabinet over the fridge. It was a miracle that Mr. Hale had bulbs in the house. John slit the plastic and, standing on tiptoe, unscrewed the three blown-out bulbs.

"What are you doing?" she asked as she sat down at the table.

He pointed to the food on the table. "That's for you."

She was quiet for a moment. "You don't have to be nice just because my mother died."

He paused and looked at her. She sat with her head in her hands, staring at the plate of food, completely exhausted. The last time they had argued, she'd said she had her own share of suffering. Everyone did. He knew that, but knowing and *knowing* are two different things. "I'm not being nice," he finally said. "You need a ladder to reach these, and I don't. It's easier if I do it."

"And the food?"

"My mother sent it."

"That's kind of her." Margaret raised her head from her hands and started picking at the casserole. As John watched, a surge of unexpected satisfaction swept over him. He never saw her eat enough. When he finished with the light bulbs, he fixed another plate for himself and sat across from her. He knew how hard it was to eat alone.

"It's not bad," she said. "For a casserole."

"There's some banana bread too, although I'm not sure how good it is. Frannie made it."

"It doesn't matter," she said, her voice breaking. "I hate bananas."

He looked up. She'd buried her face in her hands again, her shoulders shaking. "Are you laughing or crying?" he asked.

"Both, I think." She pulled out the handkerchief he'd given her at the funeral and wiped her face. "Please don't laugh at me."

"Never." He smiled a little when she put the handkerchief back in her pocket. They ate in silence until Margaret pushed her plate away, only half finished. He scraped her leftovers onto his plate, quickly finished them, and took their dirty dishes to the sink. It was full to the brim. The countertops were a mess too. He glanced back at Margaret. She'd laid her head on her arms.

He set the plates aside, walked over, and slid his hand under her elbow, helping her to her feet. "Come on."

"Sorry?" She started up and looked confused as he took her hand. "What are you doing?"

"Trust me."

She followed him hesitantly, and he smiled, enjoying the warmth of her hand firmly grasped in his.

"Where are we going?" she asked.

He opened the passenger door of his truck, helped her in, and closed it with a grin. "Shooting."

Margaret stared horrified at the black metal gun John laid on the table at the firing range. "You can't be serious." She shot a sideways glance at him. "You realize I've never touched a gun in my life, yeah?"

"Yes." He handed her a pair of safety glasses.

"And now you want to give me one to shoot?"

"You can't keep it. It's my mother's. My dad bought it for her."

"Bloody hell," Margaret mumbled. She watched carefully as John showed her how to check the chamber, load the magazine, and set the safety on the weapon. She picked up her gun gingerly, almost expecting it to bite her the moment she touched it. She was surprised at its sheer weight. It took both hands to hold it steady. With his supervision, she loaded the nine-millimeter herself.

"Keep your finger off the trigger," he said, his face serious. "Always treat a gun like it's loaded and don't touch the trigger until you're ready to fire. Is that clear?"

She nodded, and he stepped behind her. "Let her rip."

"You can't actually expect me to do this."

"It'll help." He adjusted her grip, his arm brushing along hers. "Remember to squeeze the trigger, don't pull."

"That doesn't seem too hard."

"That's what she said," he said, grinning.

She felt a surge of butterflies in her stomach, and her pulse quickened in her ears. "I can't. This is ridiculous and mad and dangerous."

"Trust me, Maggie." There was a sudden gentle look in his blue eyes. He laid a hand over hers, holding her steady. "You can."

She swallowed, straightened the gun, and took aim at the paper target. He stepped behind her, close enough she could almost feel his heat at her back. She took a deep breath, held it, and squeezed the trigger. She yelped as the gun jerked back sharply with a satisfying crack.

"Keep going."

Her hands and arms shook with adrenaline as she emptied the entire magazine at the paper target. When she finished, she carefully took her finger off the trigger and laid the gun down. Her whole body was trembling. She slipped her ear protection around her neck as he hit the target recall. The paper was pocked across the top.

"Not great, but it's not bad for a first try."

"I was aiming for the middle," she said dryly.

"Kickback. You get used to it."

"I can promise you I will never do that again."

"That bad?" He smiled wide, a bright flash of genuine pleasure.

"Well," she said slowly, "it wasn't as bad as I expected."

"Do you feel better?" He was looking at her like he had at her mother's funeral. His face became almost kind and handsome.

She blushed a little and looked at her feet with a nod. "It seems poking holes in an object with an explosive weapon is quite therapeutic."

"It's a long-kept secret." John reset the target. "You're sure you don't want to go again?"

"Absolutely."

He pulled out his own firearm and set it on the shelf in front of him. Margaret watched, fascinated. He handled his gun as if it were alive, but she didn't doubt for a moment he could make it do anything he wanted. He was confident, careful, and oddly respectful of the horrible thing in his hand. He put in his ear plugs, twisted his neck from side to side, and rolled his shoulders, loosening them. "Ready?"

She nodded and put her ear protection back on as he picked up his weapon and took aim.

Watching him shoot, she felt lighter, almost carefree. It wouldn't last, but for now, life and all its sorrow could simply wait. She pulled out her camera and took his picture. She decided not to care that she'd let John Thornton take her shooting. Three months ago, she wouldn't have thought it possible, but she'd accepted his odd olive branch of civility, even if the first olive had been a little hard to swallow.

Chapter 14

Everything in the house was quiet—too quiet. Margaret leaned against the wall outside her father's bedroom, listening. He hadn't come out for two weeks.

She had watched her mother dying, slowly and surely, for the last eight years, but she hadn't expected her death to be like this. She felt empty and listless, the heavy weight of her father's grief overshadowing her own. She leaned closer to the door and pressed her ear to the paneled wood.

Nothing. She sighed and walked back to her room. She angrily shoved aside the stack of magazines, Polaroids, and mathematics books off her bed and flopped down, rubbing her eyes. She had to get her dad out of his bloody bedroom, but nothing she tried so far had worked. School would start soon, and something had to be done. Margaret sat up and began tidying the mess she'd made. She paused and picked up a familiar, worn paperback. It was the book John had given her at the beginning of the summer.

I left it for you.

She still couldn't understand why. She'd told him she wouldn't read it, and she hadn't. She flipped the book open, read the first paragraph, and paused. She set it aside and pulled open the little drawer of her bedside table, rummaging through the bits of paper, abandoned pencils, and other office supplies until she found the wrinkled business card her father gave her that first week in Milton. She quickly dialed the number on the front, trying not to think about the conversation she was about to have. The phone rang five times before the answering machine picked up.

You've reached the offices of Marlborough Shipping Depot...

She closed her phone a little too sharply, frowning. Surely, John was at the office. He always was. She dialed again, chewing her thumbnail. The phone rang four times, then—

"What?" a gruff voice demanded.

"Mr. Thornton?"

A pause. "Margaret?"

"Am I interrupting you?"

"Yes."

"I—" she paused, caught off guard by his blunt honesty. "Should I call back when you have a free moment?" she asked crisply. "I had a favor to ask you. But if you're too busy—"

"What kind of favor?" he interrupted. She could almost hear the amused look on his face, imagining the way his lips would twitch into that stupid, sarcastic smile of his.

"I was wondering," she said and took a breath, "if you would like to come to the house for supper."

"Tonight?"

"Yes, tonight."

"Why?"

"It's my father. He's been a bit low since Mum passed. He could use some company, and he likes you."

"What about you?"

"What about me?"

"How are you?"

She swallowed past the lump in her throat. "I'm worried about Dad."

"And your mother died."

"Yes, thank you for reminding me," she said sharply, too tired to be polite. "I'm fine."

"Are you sure?" It was a gentle challenge, like he knew she was barely holding it together. "Maggie?"

"I'm really fine." She would *not* cry. "Can you come tonight?"

"I'll be there in thirty minutes."

"Right." She hung up the phone and hurried downstairs. Should she tidy up? She shook her head, smiling at her own nonsense. John wouldn't care if the bins were full or if the countertops were littered with dishes and clean linens.

She filled and started the dishwasher, picked up the novel he'd given her, carefully reading through the first chapter while the oven pre-heated. It wasn't bad; a bit slow in the beginning, but she suspected older Victorian novels always were. The oven beeped. She unwrapped a frozen pizza and set it on a baking sheet. Once that was done, she set the table and started on a salad. There wasn't much veg in the crisper, but they did have tomatoes, celery, and a dying head of cabbage. It would just have to do. She kept pausing to glance at the clock and almost sliced her finger open when John's two firm knocks broke through the silence.

"I've lost my bloody mind," she muttered and opened the front door. John stood with his hands jammed into his back pockets, a crooked grin on his face.

"What are you smiling for?"

"Does this qualify as a date?"

"That's not funny."

"You asked me to have dinner with you." He stepped inside, tossing his hat and keys on the hall table. "It's kind of a date."

She glared at him, her cheeks hot. "I asked you here to visit with my father, Mr. Thornton."

"I have a name, Margaret." He followed her into the kitchen, ducking around the hall chandelier. "Would it kill you to use it?"

She resumed her salad preparation with ferocious precision, ignoring him. He reached over to the fruit bowl, plucked up an apple, and took a bite. "Think of it as an exercise in civility," he said.

"Why do you care so much?"

He chewed slowly and swallowed. "Because you do it on purpose. It's really annoying."

"I—I'm sorry."

He shrugged. "Where's your dad?"

"He's upstairs." She tossed the celery she'd been chopping into a bowl and rubbed her forehead. "For two weeks he's done nothing but sit in his armchair, staring out of the window." She brushed away the threat of tears with the back of her hand. "I don't know what to do."

"That's why I'm here."

"Exactly." She looked up and smiled a little. "Fingers crossed, yeah?"

He nodded, finished his apple, and tossed the core into the bin. "Let's do this."

She hurried upstairs and knocked gently on her father's bedroom door. "Dad?" She opened the door and peered in. "John is here. He's come for supper."

Mr. Hale turned and blinked. "Supper?"

"I've made pizza." She took his hand and tugged gently. He didn't move. "Change into something clean and come downstairs."

"Why is John here?"

"I asked him to come."

"But you don't like him."

"I didn't before, but he grows on you, doesn't he? He's lent me a book to read," she added hastily, "and I thought we could all discuss it together. Won't that be nice?"

"Really?" Mr. Hale almost smiled. "Well, that's good of you." He looked around, patting his dressing gown pockets. "Where's my pipe?"

"In your sock drawer. There's a fresh shirt and jacket in the closet."

"I'll be right down. You go on, my dear." He stood and she breathed a small sigh of relief.

She returned to the kitchen and found John sitting at the table, his chair balanced precariously on its back legs, reading the book he'd lent her. He didn't even glance up. She moved to the stove to put water on for tea, enjoying the new silence he brought into the house. It was an easy quietness that simply was there and demanded nothing from her. She sighed softly, feeling more comfortable than she had in weeks. "Would you like a coffee?" she asked.

"Please."

When the coffee machine beeped a few minutes later, she filled a large mug, walked over to where he sat, and held it out. John reached to take it, eyes still on his book, his hand closing around hers.

"Sorry." She slowly pulled her fingers free, not wanting to drop the cup, her skin prickling. She glanced up. He was watching her with a strange look. She stared back, caught by the intensity in his blue eyes. They really were quite lovely and—

"Go on then," she blurted. The tension between them broke.

He took a large swallow and promptly spit it back into the cup. "What the hell did you do?"

"Is it really that bad?"

"Yes."

"It was my first try."

"It was shit. Like most first tries." He walked to the sink and poured it out. He tossed the rest of the coffee down the drain and threw the coffee grounds into the bin.

"That's rude," she said, annoyed. "Must you always be so blunt?"

"Only to you." He winked.

"Next time, I won't make you any."

"Next time, you'll do it right." He gestured for her to join him at the counter. "Because I'm going to show you how."

"Shall I take notes, Professor?"

"If you want." He grinned and cracked his knuckles. "Are you ready for this?"

"Shut up and show me, please." She gave him a dark look but watched carefully as he filled the pot with water, replenished the reservoir on the machine and portioned out the grounds.

"It's not rocket science. Just a rounded scoop for every two cups of water. I personally like double, but that shit takes paint off a car."

"And a layer of your stomach lining."

"Margaret? John?" Mr. Hale shuffled into the kitchen. He smiled. "What are you two doing?"

"I'm learning how to make coffee the American way." She smiled back, her heart leaping at the sight of her father looking so much like himself. He was dressed in a shabby blazer, a wrinkled blue oxford, brown trousers, and his favorite slippers.

He shoved his hands into his pockets and peered at the mess of coffee grounds and water in the sink. "I see."

"Richard." John reached out and shook his hand. "How are you?"

The two men began to chat easily, as if nothing had changed. Margaret checked on the pizza, her smile widening. "Supper's nearly done."

Once the food was on the table, John filled two cups with coffee and set one in front of her. "Bottom's up."

"Oh." She shook her head. "No, thank you."

"Try it." He sat down next to her and took a long noisy slurp from his own mug, his eyes dancing with mischief.

"No," she repeated and handed him a plate of pizza. He gave her that same challenging look that always crawled under her skin and made her want to smack him. She raised her chin and stared back. His expression changed, the same odd tension from earlier building between them again. Then the kettle whistled.

She quickly stood and began to prepare her tea. When she returned to the table, the mug of coffee stood a little closer to her plate. She looked at John accusingly. The man never let a thing drop.

"Give it a try," he said. "I dare you."

"You're such a bully," she said. She picked up the cup and sniffed it. "Will my esophagus melt?"

"One taste won't kill you."

She sighed, sipped carefully, and managed to choke down a small mouthful.

"What's the verdict?"

"Poisonous tar."

"You get used to it." He took another noisy slurp of his coffee.

"Shall I say grace?" Mr. Hale asked, bowing his head without waiting for them. Margaret took her father's outstretched hand and gave it a squeeze. John shifted next to her, and held out his hand, watching her again with that same burning look from before. She told herself she was being civil and slipped her hand into his. His skin was warm and rough and oddly comforting. She quickly pulled her hand free after her father's soft *amen* and shook the feeling away.

"So, John," Mr. Hale said with a smile. "Tell me about this book you two are reading."

Chapter 15

John knocked on the Hales' front door. No answer. He frowned and knocked again, louder. The car was in the driveway, so Mr. Hale must be home. John tried the doorknob. It was open and he stepped inside.

"Hello?" he called, tossing aside his hat and keys. He walked through to the kitchen and found Mr. Hale in the tiny mudroom off to the left, staring at the clothes dryer. "Richard?"

"Hello, John," Mr. Hale said with a sigh, shaking his head at the dryer. "I can't get the blasted thing to work. The clothes are still wet, even after an hour on the highest setting. See?"

"Let's take a look." John crouched and soon discovered the drum wasn't turning. "I can fix it," he said and rolled up his sleeves. "Give me an hour. Two at most."

"Are you sure?" Mr. Hale asked, patting his pockets absently. "I don't want to trouble you."

"It's no trouble."

Mr. Hale wandered into the living room while John ducked outside and grabbed his tool bag from his truck. He didn't have time to spend fixing the dryer, but he couldn't leave either. When he returned, Mr. Hale was sitting in his usual chair, holding his pipe, staring at the empty fireplace. "You're worried about me," he said. "You and Margaret. She asked you to check on me while she's in class."

John didn't say anything. Mr. Hale hadn't been himself since his wife died, and Margaret wasn't the only one who was worried.

"I miss my wife." Mr. Hale lit a match, ignoring the flame as it ate the small wooden stick in his hand. When it reached his fingers, he barely flinched and tossed it into the grate. He sighed, pulled a photograph from his inside jacket pocket, and held it out. John took the Polaroid and studied the tired looking woman. It was probably the last picture Margaret had taken of her mother before she moved to Milton.

"I loved Maria and yet I hurt her the most." Mr. Hale took the picture back and stared at it. "I've lost her, and it was all my fault."

John cleared his throat. His mother had grieved for his father in her own stoic way, but the emptiness was too damn familiar. "I'm sorry, Richard."

"Don't be. I'm a foolish old man." Mr. Hale looked up at him and gave him a small smile. "Don't let your pride steal what you love." He stood and stuffed his pipe back into his pocket. "I'd like to take a walk before supper. Tell Margaret, would you?"

"Mr. Thornton?"

John pulled his head out of the dryer drum and looked up at Margaret. She stood with her arms folded and her head tilted to one side. "What are you doing?"

"Fixing your dryer." He was sprawled out on the Hales' tiny kitchen floor, pieces of the old machine littering the space around him. He'd been there almost two and a half hours.

"I wasn't aware you were an expert on household appliances," she said and shrugged out of her backpack.

"I'm not."

"If you break it, we can't afford a new one."

"I won't break it." He grabbed a wrench from his tool bag and winked. "I'm *very* good with my hands."

She made a face and began filling the kettle with water. "You shouldn't let Dad talk you into playing handyman."

"It needed doing, and I was already here." He greased a bolt and tightened it back into place. "I'm good with machines. Always have been."

She made a noise, not really listening, and set the kettle on the stove. He heard her rummage about, looking for the matches to light the gas burner.

"I fixed that," he said.

She paused and then turned the knob, the tiny *snap-snap* of the igniter making him smile. "Did Dad ask you to do that too?"

"Nope." He grunted as he set the dryer drum back into place. He rubbed his hands on his jeans and picked up his screwdriver. "I noticed it was broken weeks ago." He screwed the dryer cover over the innards of the machine and tossed the screwdriver into his tool bag. "Good as new."

"If it blows up, I'll blame you."

"Have a little faith." He shifted the machine onto an old towel and pushed it into the mudroom. He glanced at his watch and sighed. There was still a pile of paperwork waiting for him at the office, and he couldn't put it off much longer. He needed to hire a new office manager. After a little coaxing, and cursing, he managed to hook the dryer back up to the wall. He flipped it on to make sure the drum turned and ducked back into the kitchen to gather the rest of his tools.

His tool bag sat on the table next to a steaming cup of coffee and a sandwich. The floor was cleared, and Margaret was sweeping away the last of the dust he'd kicked up. He frowned. "Is that for me?"

She nodded. "You should eat something besides coffee."

"You didn't have to do that."

"Don't you have somewhere to be?"

He sat down, stretched out his legs, and picked up the coffee. "I always have somewhere to be."

"Doesn't your mother ever worry?"

"I'm a grown man."

"Who still lives with his mother." She sat next to him, flipped open her Calculus textbook, and began making notes in the margin. "I've always wondered why you still live at home."

"It's complicated." He picked up the worn-out novel he'd given her months ago. She was about a hundred pages into it, one of his wrinkled business cards marking her spot. "I thought you didn't read novels." He chuckled as she snatched the book from him.

"I told my father I was reading it, so now I have to."

"Wait until you get to chapter twenty-four." He picked up his sandwich and took a bite. "That's when things get interesting."

"I can't decide if I'm more irritated with the heroine, her love interest, or with your Nora Jean."

He snorted. "Nora was a nice girl."

"You still dumped her."

"I never said that."

"She wrote ridiculous love notes in your book." Margaret looked up. "In sparkly pink pen."

"Fair." He grinned and finished his sandwich. He was enjoying the delicate civility they'd established in their joint effort to keep her father afloat. They still argued, but it was different now, more understanding and more fun.

"It's still a great book." He drained his coffee, chewing on the grounds. "The author was a genius."

"Genius or not, I hate literature."

"I bet I could persuade you to change your mind."

"And ruin all our progress?" She raised her eyebrows. "We're very nearly friends."

His eyebrows shot up. "Are we?"

"Well, even if I did sit in on another one of your discussions with Dad, you know we'd just bicker the whole time."

"Maybe." He shrugged. "The best book discussions happen when smart people disagree with each other."

"Careful. You're starting to sound nice."

"It'll pass. Thanks for the coffee and the sandwich." He stood and picked up his tool bag. "I'll see myself out."

She followed him to the door, like she always did, and handed him his hat and keys before he could grab them. "Mr. Thornton—"

"Margaret," he interrupted, pulling on his hat as he stepped closer. "My name is John."

"I know, I'm sorry." She blushed and quickly took his hand, giving it a gentle squeeze. "Thank you, John."

Chapter 16

"You're such a dork," Bess said, eyeing a large stack of National Geographic magazines Margaret had tossed into a large box marked *Donate*. She was emptying out her closet and the Higgins sisters were supposed to be helping, but Bess and Mary were too busy lolling about on Margaret's bed, digging through a box of old photographs.

"How do you have any normal friends?" Bess demanded.

"Be nice," Mary said, flipping through a stack of pictures. "Your mom was such a stunner in college, Marg."

"Too bad I look nothing like her."

"Who do you look like?"

"My great-great grandmother." Margaret walked over and dug down to the bottom of the box, pulling out a pasteboard envelope. Inside was an old black-and-white photograph. She smiled. "Mary Ruth Barton. I'm practically her twin."

"What a babe," Bess said and blew the dust off the picture. "She's a solid eight."

Mary and Margaret groaned, but Bess ignored them. "Hold the

phone." She held up a picture that had been tucked into the back of the same envelope. "Who's this hottie?"

"That's Fred."

"Who is Fred and is Fred single?"

Margaret hesitated. "He's my brother."

"You have a brother?" Bess sat up. "Since when?"

"We don't talk about him."

Mary and Bess exchanged a loaded look.

"What did he do?" Bess asked.

"A lot of things." Margaret shrugged. "Hales are quite good at ignoring our skeletons. Like Fred."

Mary took the photo from Bess and studied it carefully. "Is he still in the US Navy?"

Margaret shook her head and sat next to them on the bed. "That, like so many other things, wasn't right for Fred."

"Is he still this hot?"

Margaret snorted and pinched Bess. "You're as bad as my cousin."

"That's gross." Bess looked incredulous. "Your cousin definitely shouldn't have the hots for your brother."

"She doesn't," Margaret said, rolling her eyes. "Besides, she's *my* cousin, not Fred's."

"Wait, what?"

"He's my half-brother. Dad's son, not Mum's."

Bess let out a low whistle.

"He looks like your dad," Mary said. "A lot."

"Yeah, he does. He hates that."

"Enough about wayward brothers." Mary took the picture, tossed it carelessly into the box, and slapped on the lid. "We need to talk about Halloween." Mary gave Bess and Margaret a scathing look when they both groaned. "Our cousins will be crushed if we don't take them Trick-or-Treating. We promised them."

"I might have to work," Margaret said.

"If you asked Terry, he'd get Dr. Martin to give you the night off, and you know it, Margaret Hale," Bess said. "Terry's got it bad for you."

"Gross. He does not."

"It's true," Mary insisted. "He does."

"How am I supposed to go back to work now with *that* thought invading my brain?"

Mary and Bess high-fived each other, staring at Margaret with identical smug looks.

"I hate both of you." She turned back to the mess in her closet. "I don't have a costume, and I hate being dolled up and stared at."

"No one will see but the kids," Mary argued. "You need some fun in your life, and I need help."

"I do fun things."

"Geometry does not count as fun," Bess said. "Who even does that?"

"I like it." Margaret sighed. "I'll help with Halloween but only if Bessie does too."

"I am *not* dressing up—"

"I'll introduce you to my brother the next time he's in town," Margaret countered, winking at Mary.

Bess considered this. "Give me his picture too, and it's a deal."

"Creeper," Margaret muttered.

But she gave Bess the picture anyway.

WEDNESDAY: NOVEMBER 29, 2006

"This came in the post, Dad." Margaret set her rucksack down and held out the thick red envelope to her father. Mr. Hale laid aside his book and gripped his evening pipe between his teeth as he carefully opened the envelope. The fire crackled, pleasant and warm. She sat in her chair, stretching her toes out towards the flames.

"It's an invitation to the Thorntons' Christmas party." Mr. Hale turned over the heavy, cream-colored cardstock covered with delicate calligraphy. "I missed it last year."

"Why?"

"You'd just come home to Milton. Remember?"

She blinked, her eyes heavy and sleepy, and shrugged.

"We ought to go this year. You'll like that, won't you?"

"Me?" She laughed a little. "Like going to a fancy dinner party?"

"Of course, dearest."

She pulled her legs towards her chest and hugged them for a moment, thinking. She and John got on well enough now, but Mrs. Thornton still didn't like her, and Frannie was all but ambivalent.

"I've nothing to wear, Dad. Nothing proper."

"What about that dress your mother and I bought you last Christmas?" Mr. Hale asked quietly. "I'm sure that will do."

"That's so formal. I'd be terribly overdressed, don't you think?"

"Nonsense." He pulled his pipe from his mouth and smiled. "I've got my old three-piece dinner suit. With your dress, we'll make quite the dashing pair, you and I."

She was a little surprised. Her father so seldom insisted on anything, but she hadn't seen him quite this animated about a social event since before her mother died. So, she pushed aside her misgivings and smiled. "I'll send your suit out to the dry cleaners, shall I?"

"Please do." He beamed. He picked up his book and returned to his reading with a contented sigh.

"Is that one new?"

"Marcus Aurelius's *Meditations*. John lent me this. Isn't it a beauty? Will you be joining our discussions again?"

"No, I think I've had my fill of reading for pleasure," she teased.

After a little cajoling from John, she had sat in on a few of their weekly book discussions. It had been lively and exhausting. But Mr. Hale had finally settled into his normal, quiet routines again, the sadness of the summer all but a memory. Margaret knew her father's steady improvement was as much John's doing as hers, and she was grateful. Neither of them could've done it alone.

"All right there, Margaret?"

"I am, just, it's been a while since I've seen John, that's all. Tell him hello from me," she added, almost as an afterthought. "I've missed seeing him."

It was a soft admission that was as surprising as it was true.

She missed him and didn't quite know why.

SATURDAY: DECEMBER 2, 2006

"Thornton invited you to his Christmas party?" Bess squealed in excitement, her brown eyes sparkling, when Margaret told her about the party. She threw herself onto Margaret's bed with a sigh. "I knew it! He totally likes you."

"His mother invited my father, Elizabeth Higgins," Margaret said, tossing a shoe at her. "It's her party."

"But you're going, right?"

"Apparently, it's the social event of the season, and Dad missed last year." Margaret sat with a little flounce. "He's rather excited to go."

"He won't be the only one," Bess snickered. "If Little John's not excited to see you—"

"Bessie!" Margaret interrupted, blushing hotly. "I'm not going to this party to be ogled. I'm accompanying my dad to a dull evening of rich, old men in ill-fitting suits, smoking and talking and eating."

"You literally have no sexual imagination. Do you think Thornton will care about anyone else at that party if you're there?"

"Isn't his Lana Lancaster going to be there too?"

"Probably. We need a plan." Bess jumped up, opened the closet, and began flipping through Margaret's clothes. "Do you own anything that doesn't scream crazy cat lady? My grandmother would wear stuff like this." She held up a light blue blouse. "We've got to take you shopping."

"I'm not wearing that." Margaret snatched the garment from Bess. "I already have a dress." She pulled down the box from the top of the closet and opened it.

"Oh, Marg," Bess breathed. She bounced on her toes, more excited than Margaret had ever seen her, touching the dark purple fabric with her fingertips. "Where did you get this?"

"My parents bought it for me. It's a Hale family tradition, sort of a coming-of-age gift or a graduation thing. It's silly."

"You're going to look so hot, I might even be into you."

"I'm flattered."

"I want to do your hair, and Mary can do your makeup." Bess grabbed her hands and spun her around.

Margaret giggled, her excitement growing. They collapsed in a heap on the bed and Bess sighed. "This is going to be the best Christmas party ever."

SATURDAY: DECEMBER 23, 2006

The day of the party dawned crisp and bitingly cold. Snow fell heavily in soft white drifts, turning the dirty, smoky city into a gilded ghost town. John looked out of the window and scowled.

"Don't frown like that, John-John, your face will get stuck," Frannie said. "Isn't it wonderful? It's like a fairy tale land."

"I hate snow."

"It's perfect for the party."

"I hate parties."

"Really, John, the way you go on." His mother turned from her desk and gave him a disapproving look. "Leave your sister alone."

He grunted and sat heavily in his armchair. "Who's coming this year?"

"The Hampers, Slicksons, John Watson and his endless catalogue of younger brothers, the Collingbrooks, the MacPhersons, the Stephensons, the Browns, and the Lancasters, of course. Mr. Bell declined, as usual."

"Good." John couldn't stand the man.

"The Porters, Mr. Young, Mr. Tucker Williams, and the Hales."

He sat up straighter.

"Why did you invite the Hales?" Frannie asked.

"We invite Mr. Hale every year, Fran," John said.

"He didn't come last year, and Margaret will be bored out of her mind. She's too young for all your stuffy business friends."

"That's the pot calling the kettle black," he muttered.

"How old is she, Frannie?" Mrs. Thornton asked, turning back to the notes on her desk.

"Nineteen? Maybe twenty."

"She's almost twenty-one," John said.

His mother and sister turned to look at him. "How do you know that?" Mrs. Thornton asked, carefully searching his face.

"Richard mentioned it." John didn't add that Margaret wouldn't be twenty-one for almost another year. What he'd said was technically true, but not exactly. And he didn't know why he'd said it.

"I don't think I like her," Frannie said dismissively. "She's always walking around with that camera, acting like she's better than everyone, always talking like she knows everything."

"Nobody asked you, Fran," he said sharply. He stood and walked back to the window where snow was falling again. Frannie marched from the room in a temper, and he heard his mother move closer.

"You're too hard on your sister."

He sighed. "I'd appreciate it if you and Fran would try to get to know Margaret better."

"Why?"

He turned. "Because I like her."

"She's not even twenty-one yet. You're twenty-seven."

"Almost twenty-seven," he corrected. "And her birthday is two weeks after mine."

"Is that supposed to make me feel any better about your obvious romantic interest in her?"

"Not exactly." He took off his hat and scratched the back of his head. "I don't care how old she is. She's an adult, and so am I." He looked out at the snow again, growing more and more uncomfortable. He could feel his mother's steady gaze on his back.

"What are you going to do?"

And just like that, two important facts smacked John in the face. First, he had expected to have this exact conversation about Margaret with his mother at some point. Maybe not this soon, but he'd known it was coming. And second, his mother wasn't surprised, which meant she'd expected this to happen too.

"Holy shit," he whispered.

His mother laid her hand on his back in a gesture of uncharacteristic affection. "John?"

"I need to shovel the walk." He marched from the parlor to the garage, dazed by his own realization. He jammed his feet into his boots, tugged on his gloves, hat, and coat, and stood. Shoveling snow was exactly what he needed to get his tangled thoughts and emotions back into order. He grabbed the shovel and pushed himself hard, the cold wind biting his skin. The work beat him down while he tried to figure out what the hell he was going to do about Margaret Hale.

John burned with restless energy. He was wearing his best suit and tie, trying to hold still under his mother's sharp, unforgiving scrutiny. Mrs. Thornton picked a small thread from his shoulder seam and brushed at imaginary lint on his sleeve. "Do I pass inspection?" he teased.

"Did you use the cologne Frannie bought you last year?"

"Yes." He rolled his eyes. "I changed my boxers too, in case you're wondering." His mother shot him a scolding look and he grinned. Every muscle in his arms, legs, and back ached from shoveling snow, but the work had put him back in possession of himself.

"You're strutting like a rooster in a hen house," Mrs. Thornton said in a low voice. "Does this girl even know you've got your sights set on her?"

"She has a name." He bent forward at the waist, so his mother could pin the customary white rose to his lapel. "Please use it."

"I'll try to like her for your sake," she said, looking as if the words tasted bitter. "Are you sure about this?"

"I said I liked her. I never said she liked me."

"As if she could do any better than you."

"I appreciate your motherly confidence," he said. He glanced in the hall mirror and frowned. He brushed at his dark hair, dislodging it until he thought it looked more natural. "But I wouldn't hold your breath."

Chapter 17

When the Thornton's house came into view, all buried in purple-tinted snow, Margaret felt oddly excited and nervous. She'd remembered to bring her camera this time, but the light outside was too low for a decent photograph. The house was still a grand old place, and the festive season lent it a touch of magic, making it grander still.

They were among the last guests to arrive, and Mr. Hale hurried off to deposit their jackets, leaving Margaret by herself for a moment. The rooms glowed with candlelight and the soft sound of murmuring voices. Little knots of people were slung across the ground floor rooms, drinking and talking. She was tempted to slip away and explore the house in solitude, but dinner would be served within the next half hour. Her chance would come, she was certain. She smiled to herself and resolved to knock at every closed door, just in case.

Mr. Hale returned, and they were greeted by Frannie and Mrs. Thornton. Margaret made certain not to look for John, despite her burning curiosity to know where he was. "Mr. Hale, Margaret." Mrs. Thornton shook their hands firmly. "I hope the snow wasn't too inconvenient for you."

"Oh, not at all," Margaret said. "It's quite whimsical, and it's perfect for Christmas. I love snow."

"John hates it," Frannie said. "He spent all day fussing about it and even shoveled all the walks and driveway himself."

"I don't think our guests care about your brother shoveling snow." Mrs. Thornton nodded to the Hales, stiff and proper, making certain they were comfortable and had something to drink, before returning to her other guests.

"Goodness," Mr. Hale said to Margaret with a sheepish smile. "I didn't think to shovel or salt the walk."

"I'll do it later." Margaret patted his arm and pulled it through her own. "I'll play I'm Fred, shall I?"

"Oh." He dropped his eyes, paling a little. "I suppose."

"Dad, I didn't mean—"

"It's all right," he said quickly. "Shall I get us more punch?"

She sighed as he wandered away, staring down at her full cup of punch, embarrassed by her heedless words. She didn't know what had gotten into her, except she'd fallen into the habit of talking about Fred with Bess and Mary. Margaret straightened her shoulders and took a deep breath. She would not sulk.

She was grateful her father had insisted she wear the dark purple dress, with its low-cut neckline and full skirt that nearly brushed the ground. All the Thorntons' guests were similarly dressed. She felt elegant and a little exposed, but held her head high as she stood alone, her fancy dress a sort of armor against all these strange people. She soon found a quiet corner, gathering and smoothing the fabric of her skirts.

It was going to be a long night.

♥

"Thornton," Matt Hamper said, interrupting John's conversation with Jerry Slickson. "Who's the tasty treat at my three o'clock? In the fancy purple dress."

John glanced at where Hamper was pointing and almost joined him in a low, appreciative whistle. Margaret Hale stood by herself, watching everything with a curious expression that looked both bored and amused and—something else. She sighed, her shoulders slumping a little, and fiddled with her skirt. He frowned and quickly scanned the room. Her father sat alone near the fire, distracted and aloof.

Something had happened.

"Excuse me."

He cut across the room, and her face brightened when she saw him. She held out her hand. He chuckled to himself and took it, giving it a firm shake. "I believe we've successfully managed to acquire some civility, Mr. Thornton," she said brightly, her accent thickening.

"Except," he said, still holding her hand, "you've forgotten to use my name, Miss Hale."

"Tonight, you're Mr. Thornton again. It fits the grand festivities. Don't you think?"

"I guess." He slowly let go of her hand. "Thank you for coming."

"Dad wouldn't miss this for the world."

"How is he?"

"Much better, thank you."

"Are you sure?" John studied her face, seeing a tinge of embarrassment rise in her eyes. "Maggie, what happened?"

"It's nothing, just a little misunderstanding, and you've got guests." Her gaze flicked behind him, and he turned. George Lancaster, his wife, Carol, and his daughter, Lana, stood with wide smiles.

"Who's this vision of loveliness?" Mr. Lancaster asked. "A friend of yours, Thornton?"

John quickly made the introductions, and Margaret smiled. "So, *you're* Lana Lancaster," she said, looking almost mischievous. "I've heard so much about you."

"What's John been saying about me?" Lana laughed, her hand sliding around his arm. He forced himself not to pull away.

"Oh, he hasn't mentioned you." Margaret gave him a quick side look. "You're well-spoken of in general."

Everyone laughed politely, and John held in a frustrated snort. He hated how women always talked about him, even when he was standing right there. He also wondered exactly what Margaret knew about Lana and where she'd heard it.

"I'm very happy to meet you all," Margaret continued, still the picture of courtesy. Her eyes narrowed a fraction. "I hear your family hosts a marvelous New Year's Eve party."

John swallowed a curse and coughed. Did she know anything about what happened last year?

"We do," Lana replied, a hint of color rising to her cheeks.

Margaret was looking right at John again. *Oh shit.* She knew.

"Come see for yourself, Miss Hale," Mr. Lancaster added after an awkward pause. "We'd be delighted to have you. Can we expect you again this year, Thornton?"

"Daddy, you know John doesn't like parties."

"He seems to be enjoying this one," Margaret said to herself.

Before John was forced to reply, his mother mercifully announced dinner. Lana hadn't relinquished his arm, and he was obliged to escort her into the formal dining room. Margaret brushed past. She glanced at him and winked, her smile sharp and knowing. John's eyes followed her all the way to her seat. He didn't notice the crooked grin on his face until he seated Lana, and she poked him. "What was that all about, John Thornton?"

"Hell if I know."

But he was going to find out.

Dinner was a dull affair. The talk almost immediately turned to the rumors of a factory workers' strike. John only half listened, mildly sympathetic to the threat the factory owners faced. They droned on about the ungrateful working class and their damned unions until he was sick of it all. He hated parties.

"What do you think, Miss Hale?" Lana Lancaster's clear voice cut across the conversation.

Margaret flinched a little and looked up from her plate. Usually, she was in the thick of any controversial topic but tonight was different. She'd spent the entire dinner carefully listening, and while John was enjoying watching her observe the conversation, he was eager to hear her opinion. He'd missed their heated arguments.

And her.

"Well," Margaret began thoughtfully. "I think it's best to try to understand both sides of any issue. Factory workers are people too." One of the factory owners, Mr. Porter, laughed, but she was unphased. "It's easy to forget that every person, no matter how inconsequential, has a story," she continued. "If we try to see things from their perspective, we'll treat them differently."

"A pretty idea," Matt Hamper added in a low voice. "Pretty stupid."

John frowned at him.

"What about you, John?" Mr. Hale asked. "What do you think about a factory strike?"

"I've got enough of my own problems to worry about without borrowing other people's."

"At least a strike isn't one of them," Mr. Lancaster said.

"Why wouldn't the truckers strike, if necessary?" Margaret asked.

"Most smaller shipping companies have no union chapter in Milton. It would be financial suicide for truckers," Slickson sneered.

"What if all the truckers in Milton agreed together to support the factory strike?" Margaret asked, turning to Mr. Slickson, her blue-gray eyes flashing. "What would happen then?"

"Would you support a trucker's strike?" Lana asked sharply, not waiting for Mr. Slickson's reply. "Aren't you pretty friendly with the union man who works for John?"

"You mean Nicholas Higgins."

The table fell silent as the men turned their full attention to Margaret. John knew she was friends with Bess Higgins, and he wasn't surprised that friendship included the old trucker.

"Slick Nick," Matt Hamper muttered. "We all know him."

"He's my friend," Margaret said. "I've talked to him at length about a trucker's union."

"And a strike?" Lana looked from Margaret to John.

"Yes," Margaret nodded, without embarrassment, "and a strike."

"You'll do no one any favors encouraging them," John said. "A strike hurts employees and employers alike."

"How else are they to be heard, if no one listens?" Margaret demanded, steel in her voice.

John held her steady gaze, her words making him uneasy. His mother cleared her throat and swiftly changed the subject. He excused himself as dessert was served, nodding at Tucker Williams. The two men ducked into the hallway. "You don't think there's anything to it, do you, Master?" Williams asked, once they were out of earshot.

"I hadn't even considered it until tonight."

"What's got you all jumpy?"

"Margaret's been talking with Slick." He paused. "I think we should listen. We'd be stupid not to."

"What do you want to do?"

"How fast could we get new drivers if ours strike?"

"What, not all of them?"

John nodded. "If they all strike—all the drivers, not just at Marlborough Shipping, but all of them—we would be hard pressed to replace them on such short notice."

"It'd be one ballsy move." Williams shook his head. "I can start making calls the day after Christmas."

"You do that." John watched as the guests trickled out of the dining room, his face grim. "I want a working list on my desk by Wednesday."

After dinner, Margaret settled her father near the fire again and waited until he was completely absorbed in conversation before taking the opportunity to slip away. She stole up the great front staircase, careful to stay on tiptoe. The Thornton house was enormous compared to her father's tiny home, and she wanted to explore the grand splendor alone. She laid her head against the wall and listened, almost as if the house would tell her its secrets. So much history echoed in the very stones. The ambient sounds of the party below wafted through the house while she wandered into the open rooms, enjoying the solitary respite.

John endured almost an hour of dull after-dinner chit chat until he couldn't stand another minute of it. He slipped out the front door and took a deep breath of the cold, biting air. The sky looked purple and ominous. More snow was coming. He allowed himself fifteen minutes of blissful solitude before finding his mother. "The weather is looking bad," he said quietly and handed her a glass of wine. "Time to send people home."

"Are you sure it's the weather," Mrs. Thornton asked, "or your personal distaste for company?"

"It's snowing again. Hard."

She looked over his shoulder towards the windows and sighed. Great flakes cascaded from the purple-yellow sky. "No sign of clearing up?"

"Not for a while."

The party was quickly dispersed, each guest saying how disappointed they were to be going so soon. John shook hands all around, eager to be done. Mr. Hale lingered in the hall, one of the last to leave. He was alone. "John, have you seen Margaret?" he asked, tugging at his coat sleeves. "I seem to have misplaced her."

"I'll find her."

Margaret silently scolded herself for being so nosy. She opened a few doors and poked her head into the rooms, enjoying the story the house was telling, wondering about the people who'd once lived here. It was easy to imagine John Thornton among them, taking his place as a distinguished occupant in its long history. She opened yet another door and stepped inside a small room stuffed to the brim with pictures and stacks of books. She smiled, poking through the pictures.

"Miss Hale?"

She jumped and turned. John stood in the doorway, hands in his trouser pockets, watching her.

"How long have you been standing there?" she asked.

He ducked into the small room without answering and glanced at the picture she'd been examining. The space closed in on her with him to fill most of it. He raised his eyebrows.

"I'm sorry. I couldn't help myself when I saw all these photos," she said, blushing. "I hope you'll forgive my snooping about your home."

"Did you enjoy it?"

"The snooping or the house?"

"Both."

"Yes," she said simply, looking at her hands. "I like old things."

"Even me?"

"You're not old." She turned towards the door, brushing past him. She paused when she felt his hand on her arm, her skin rippling and the hair standing on end. She didn't pull away, and he moved closer.

"Is that a compliment, Miss Hale?"

"I suppose it is. We're friends now."

"Are we?"

"Of a sort. Don't let it go to your head."

"What kind of friends?"

"The usual kind." She took another step towards the door. He stepped with her. She stepped backwards, and he moved with her again, as if they were dancing. "What are you doing?" she asked.

"Talking to my friend."

"Really?" She moved to the side again, grinning as he moved with her. "Do you always dance about when you talk to friends?"

"If the occasion calls for it."

"You know how to dance?"

"I do."

"Are you any good?" she walked towards the staircase, smiling as he followed, his hand shifting from her arm to rest on her lower back.

"Yes."

"When was the last time you danced?"

"College. I was forced."

"Who would dare?"

"My mother." At the top of the stairs, he offered her his arm, and she took it. "It was for Frannie's prom."

"And you were her date?"

"I was dance practice." He shot her a sly smile. She almost didn't believe it. She wanted to say more, but they'd reached the landing where her father stood talking with Frannie and Mrs. Thornton.

"Thank you for tonight." Margaret pulled on her coat and nodded to John's mother and sister. "I had a lovely time. Happy Christmas."

John insisted on walking them to their car, which was parked down the icy street. Margaret smiled to herself. It was one of his old-fashioned habits that had slowly become less annoying when she realized it was a quiet, genuine curtesy. She slid a little on the newly formed ice and shivered as his large, firm hands steadied her.

"Careful."

"I'm fine," she insisted, but he didn't let go, one hand resting on her waist. Perhaps it was the snow or the festive season, but she was enjoying the warmth of his touch.

"You know, it's a shame you don't like dancing," she said.

"Why is that?"

"Because," she leaned closer, smiling, "a tall handsome man in a suit ought to be danced with. Otherwise, it's a tremendous waste."

"Would you dance with me?"

"No. I'm rubbish."

"So, what would you do with me?"

"You're assuming I'd want to do something."

"We could have dinner."

"We just ate."

His eyes flicked over her. "I could eat again."

"Are you flirting with me, John Thornton?"

He opened the passenger door for her and raised his eyebrows. "Are you flirting back?"

Margaret pressed her lips together, but she couldn't stop the smile that forced its way onto her face. She wasn't certain what this new thing was exactly, but she liked it. Maybe a little too much.

John joined his mother by the fire in the parlor. She silently handed him a glass of whiskey. He glanced at the clock, frowning as it ticked out the hours and minutes and seconds. He loosened his tie and slung it over his shoulder, sipping from his glass.

"Tread lightly, son. That girl has a fiery temper on a hair's trigger."

He took another sip and leaned back in his chair, stretching out his legs. "I like her anyway."

"We all know that. You might consider showing a bit more discretion with that girl."

"Her name is Margaret."

"Well, you know what they say about playing with fire."

"What do they say?"

"If you're not careful, you're going to get burned."

Chapter 18

John leaned against the back wall of the largest room in the Lancaster's mansion, his suit jacket tightening as he crossed his arms. He was a damn fool for letting Frannie talk him into coming to the Lancasters' New Year's Eve party again—especially after last year's disaster. What the hell was he thinking?

The second he'd walked in, Mrs. Lancaster had cornered him with a wide smile. "John Thornton, I didn't know you were coming tonight."

"Carol." He had forced himself not to grimace and nodded to her husband. "George."

"Lana is here somewhere. You wait right there while I find her." Mrs. Lancaster pointed at him, common courtesy gluing him to the spot. He had swallowed a sigh and a curse while Frannie quickly made her escape. He was forced to wait for Lana, listening to George Lancaster detail the recent home improvements his wife was undertaking. After a grueling hour and a half, John had managed to disentangle himself from the Lancasters long enough to find a quiet corner in the back of the ballroom, where he'd been counting down the seconds until he could leave. For three damn hours.

He should've known better. He *did* know better. Yet he was here anyway. He sighed and checked his watch. He'd let his sister drag him here for one reason; he hoped Margaret would be here too. Ever since the Christmas party, he couldn't make himself think straight when it came to Margaret Hale. He glanced back over the crowd to where she sat sipping water, talking to her mother's lawyer, Henry Lennox.

"John!" Frannie sprang out of the crowd, grabbed his arm, and pulled him towards the dance floor. "Stop hiding from Lana and come dance with me. It's salsa."

"Fran, don't," he said. His dark expression visibly deflated his sister's enthusiasm.

"You're such a dinosaur." She stomped her foot. "Why can't you enjoy yourself like a normal person instead of glowering in disapproval all the time?"

"I'm here. Isn't that enough?"

"I wish you weren't."

"That makes two of us."

"Then leave." She shoved his arm and took a shot of something bright pink from a passing server. The young man winked at her, with a stupid, shit-eating grin. John sighed, chasing the boy off with a glare.

"You're the absolute worst. Let the rest of us enjoy ourselves."

"I'm your designated driver," he said, "unless Watson is home early from his holiday trip to California."

Before his sister could answer, Lana appeared at his elbow and held out a drink. He hesitated for a split second, then took it with a sigh and said a gruff, "Thanks."

After three hours of nothing but his own stupid thoughts, he deserved a drink. Lana followed his gaze across the room. "Do you know anything about Margaret's date? He's super cute."

"He's her mother's lawyer," John said stiffly.

"And?"

"And nothing."

"I think they're enjoying themselves, don't you, big brother?" Frannie teased, swirling her drink. She'd noticed he was staring at Margaret, but he didn't care.

When he didn't answer, she turned to Lana. "They've spent the whole party cozy as two peas in a pod. He's positively adorable *and* he's from London. His accent is to die for, honestly. He could read me the phone book and I'd be in heaven. I heard he's an old flame of Margaret's and—"

"Nobody asked you," John interrupted. He swallowed the large whiskey whole and handed his empty glass to a server.

"You should loosen up a little more," Lana said. "You might enjoy yourself if you try. Isn't it your birthday?"

"Who told you that?"

"If you want any fun out of John-John, you've got to get more alcohol in his system." Frannie winked at Lana and finished her shot. "Even then, it might not work. He's a regular killjoy."

"Shut up, Fran."

"Make me." She handed John her empty glass with a wink. She shook back her hair, turned on her heel, and danced happily back into the crowd.

11:40 PM

Margaret tried not to look bored, but the flicker in Henry's face told her she'd failed. The urge to yawn was almost overpowering. They'd been sitting at this table for nearly four hours and talked about absolutely nothing. Her bum was numb, and she squirmed. Henry Lennox was nice enough in theory, but he kept showing up at all the wrong times.

When she opened her front door that evening, she'd half hoped to see John standing there. The Thornton Christmas party lingered pleasantly in her memory, making her wonder what exactly had happened between them to make John act as he did. Margaret had frowned at Henry without meaning to and taken a step back.

"Henry? What are you doing here?"

"I was in town finishing up the final details of your mother's estate and thought I'd say hello to your father."

"Really?" she asked. She wasn't fooled for a moment. "Just thought you'd pop down to Milton from Boston?"

"Quite." His eyes traveled over her knee length, dark red dress. "I'm interrupting your evening. I apologize."

"Henry, is that you?" Her father came down the stairs with a delighted smile. "This is a surprise."

Henry explained his being in town and Mr. Hale nodded, his face turning grave at the reminder of his wife's passing. "Why don't you take Margaret to the Lancaster's? You two can make an evening of it. I should like a quiet night in."

"Are you sure, Dad?" she asked, worried at his sudden gloominess. She wanted to kick Henry. "John might be there, and you know you always enjoy talking to him."

"I'm sure he would much rather see you."

"Who's John?" Henry asked, moving to stand closer to her.

"You must take Henry and introduce him to John, my dear. Have a good time for me, won't you?"

She had nodded, stifled a heavy sigh, and submitted herself to an evening of Henry's tedious company. Now, four bloody hours later, she was sipping her fifth bubbly water as he continued talking.

In all her summers spent with her Aunt Shaw, her cousin Edith continually threw them together in every way possible, hoping *something* would happen. Nothing did happen or ever would. He wasn't entirely unpleasant, but she didn't like the weight of expectation hanging upon their every encounter.

"Margaret, are you listening?"

"No, I'm not," she said, astonished at her own sudden frankness. "I find estate law to be achingly dull conversation."

"Yes." Henry blinked, surprised. "Perhaps we could talk of your interest in pursuing mathematics as a career."

"I'm sorry, but I'd rather not discuss school while I'm on holiday." She glanced around. "This is a New Year's party, Henry. It's supposed to be fun, you know."

His eyes followed her gaze towards the back of the room, and he cleared his throat. "Shall I get us something naughty to drink?" He stood and walked towards the bar, without waiting for an answer.

She sighed, watching him go. She felt far too young for this party but also far too old. There was dancing, and drinking, and gossip, but it was all within such a restrained demographic of the young wealthy professionals that counted themselves among the acquaintances of the Lancasters. Margaret might have been invited as a courtesy, but she felt far from welcome. What on earth was she even doing here?

She picked up her mobile and checked the time. Quarter to midnight. If she slipped away now, she might shake Henry for a while. Her eyes traveled the room again, lingering on a tall shadow at the back—a shadow she thought might be John Thornton.

She'd seen him earlier when the first round of cocktails was served, but with Henry hovering at her elbow and John pinned between the three Lancasters, it had been impossible to get near enough to talk to him. Henry had noticed him immediately. She wickedly enjoyed his discomfort when she explained that the tall handsome man was her friend John Thornton.

She sighed again, her attention flicking between John and Henry. If Bess were here, she'd tell her what she should do. Margaret frowned a little and stood. She could jolly well do what she wanted, and she wanted to talk to John. Even if he wasn't in the mood to talk, she infinitely preferred his glowering silence to any more of Henry's banal conversation. And if John's mood was anything like it was at the Christmas party, she was certain to enjoy herself. She smiled. He had been downright flirtatious, and it had been nice to be teased and admired like that.

She wove through the press of people, pleased to see it *was* John in the very back corner. He was dressed in a smart navy suit with a white shirt and a burgundy tie. He leaned casually against the wall, hands stuffed in his pockets, looking irritated and bored. When she got closer, her smile dropped. Lana Lancaster stood next to him, sipping on wine, attentive and beautiful. A strange twist in her stomach made Margaret veer away and slip through the first door she came to. It turned out to be a broom cupboard. She slumped against the wall, pulled out her mobile, and dialed Bess.

"Hello?"

"Bessie, it's Margaret."

"Yeah, Marg, I saw," Bess said, her words slurring a little.

"Are you drunk?"

"Nah, just having a drink. It's New Year's. I'm having a damn drink. Deserve it too, Marg. I deserve this drink."

"Bessie," Margaret started, but then stopped when she heard something grainy and echoey over the phone. There was a crackling static, and a new voice said, "Slick to Milker. What's your twenty? Over."

"What's that?" Margaret asked.

"Nothing. Just Dad and my stupid handle. Milker, my ass."

Margaret heard a clank, and then—

"Milker here. Sitting at Jellico, Slick. Over." Bess's voice sounded further away.

"Third strike you're out. Over."

"ETA, Slick? Over."

"New Year, New Day. Over."

"Ten four. Over and out."

"Bessie?" Margaret called. And again, louder. "Bessie!"

"God, quit yelling. I have ears."

"What was that all about?"

"Nothing. It's nothing. Marg, I've got to go. I'll see you soon. Maybe Wednesday."

"But I thought you weren't due back until—"

"Happy New Year's, okay?" Then Bess hung up.

Margaret stepped out of the closet, confused and a little annoyed. She hadn't been able to ask Bess about Henry or John. It didn't make sense, but neither did Bess when she was drunk. And she *was* drunk. Margaret sighed and pushed it from her mind.

"There you are." Henry appeared at her elbow, his free hand settling on her lower back. "What were you doing in there? It's nearly midnight. I've brought your drink."

She groaned. Was there no escaping him? She didn't want to talk to him or anyone else. All she wanted was some peace and quiet and time to think. She took the glass of champagne he held out, and walked away, not knowing where to go or what to do, only that she had to get away.

11:55 PM

John watched Margaret wander around the perimeter of the room, Henry in tow. Lana had fallen silent, but she wouldn't leave him alone. He knew she found his own stubborn silence deterring, like most people did. He could wait all night long in complete silence if he had to. "It's almost midnight," Lana finally said.

He glanced at his watch. Two minutes. Lana continued to linger, and he finally realized why when the crowd began watching the clock and cheering during the last minute of the year. She was waiting for a New Year's kiss. Just like last year.

"Oh, hell no." He pushed himself away from the wall and escaped into the tangle of bodies. He didn't care if he was being rude. He'd rather kiss a stranger than Lana Lancaster. But his eyes found Margaret again and once they did, his body moved toward her like a damn moth to a flame.

11:59 PM

"Would you please stop for a moment?" Henry reached out and turned Margaret towards him. "I've been trying to ask you a particular question all night and you're making it quite difficult."

"Am I?"

"Yes." Henry paused awkwardly as the people around them began to cheer, the final minute of the year ticking down. "Margaret—"

"Please don't." She stepped back, bumping into the crowd that pressed in around them. She finished her champagne and handed him the empty glass. "Whatever you're going to say, I don't—"

"Let me finish, please." He set the glass aside, took her hands in his, and pulled her closer. "You would make me incredibly happy if you would—"

"Would what?" she interrupted again.

"I thought I made myself clear." He looked taken aback, his face flushed. "I flew all the way from England to see you."

"Henry." She pulled her hands free. "Don't."

"Margaret Ann Hale," he spoke haltingly, raising his voice as the crowd shouted the last ten seconds. "I would like you to be my friend, my partner, and eventually something much more intimate, if that pleases you. It would please me enormously."

She flushed, desperate and uncomfortable. He was looking at her with his usual self-satisfied smile that always made her skin crawl, as if he knew what she would say and do.

"No." She shook her head, turned, and almost collided with John Thornton. She sucked in a sharp breath and steadied herself against him, her hand shaking. He was looking at her with a strange burning intensity. She couldn't look away, his gaze holding her like a magnet.

"Margaret?" Henry's voice got lost in the sounds of cheering as the clock struck the hour. She glanced back at him for a half second, then turned to John, moving before she could change her mind—one hand grasped the lapel of his jacket, the other slid up towards his neck as she stood on tiptoe and pulled his face to hers in one fluid movement.

She kissed him, hot and hard.

Margaret felt John's breath on her face, his large hands resting on her waist. The look of elated disbelief in his blue eyes drowned out every protesting thought screaming at her. Henry would get the message after this. She should let go of John right now and walk—no, she ought to *run*—away. She laid a hand against his cheek, fingering the stubble he hadn't bothered to shave yet. Her fingers moved slowly and brushed over his lips.

He tasted like whiskey and peppermint.

She didn't know which of them moved first. All she knew was that she was kissing John Thornton again, and this time she had no intention of stopping. Maybe Henry said something more. Maybe he didn't. She couldn't be bothered with that. Then John picked her up, still kissing her, and they were moving awkwardly through the crowd until the noise faded, and they were alone in a small, private study.

"Maggie."

It was a deep, throaty rumble.

Bloody hell.

Technically, she'd been kissed before, or so she always assumed. But none of those scattered, awkward attempts from her younger years could compare to this. This was heat and silk, madness and sanity, awkward and perfect. It was everything. Every place he touched her, nerves and skin crawled with heat. The air around them almost crackled. If she'd been struck by lightning, she wasn't certain she could tell the difference. Perhaps it was just the champagne she'd drunk, but the more he touched her, the more she wanted him to. Where he hesitated, waiting for her permission, she dragged him after her, his grumble, velvety sounds of complete enjoyment drowning out any rational restraint.

John was air, and she could finally breathe.

Chapter 19

John didn't start his evening expecting to make out with Margaret Hale. His escape from Lana was rude and necessary. There was no way in hell he was going to repeat last year's disaster. As he'd moved through the boisterous crowd, everyone shouting out the last ten seconds of the year, he'd seen Margaret standing in the middle of the room, locked in conversation with Henry Lennox. Even when he'd felt a tug on his sleeve, he kept moving, until he was nearly on top of them, his hand at Margaret's elbow to keep her from stumbling. She stepped closer to him, the air charged for a moment before a determined look crossed her face. When she grabbed his jacket, he bent down instinctively, his hands on her waist, letting her press her lips against his, the contact a hot, searing force.

It was one kiss, one short electric moment, but it was everything.

He was surprised he could still breathe. She pulled back and looked up at him, still clinging to his jacket. "You taste like a peppermint stick."

And then she'd kissed him again. Or he had kissed her. He couldn't tell which. Her mouth was heaven, sweet and velvety. He didn't know how long this insane moment would last, but he knew he couldn't stop kissing Margaret if she didn't make him. Only she didn't. She kissed him again and again and *again*, until he was drunk with the honeyed taste of her.

"Maggie."

He'd lifted her off the floor and managed to weave his way out of the press of people without much of a pause. He'd only been in the Lancaster's house a handful of times, but he remembered a small study tucked away at the west corner. It had taken him a minute to find it, but now there was no going back.

He shouldered the door open, only letting go of Margaret long enough to shrug out of his jacket and toss it aside. He pulled her down onto the leather sofa with him, his hands sliding over her shoulders and neck, into her hair, catching at the pins. He swore in frustration, and she laughed against his lips, a low, throaty sound that sent heat crawling down his spine.

"Take them out, if they bother you."

He slid the pins free, one by one, sending the brown mass of curls tumbling to her shoulders. She sat back and shook her hair out. He tangled the silky stuff around his fingers, a helpless guttural sound catching in his throat.

"Do you like that?"

He couldn't answer.

An aching, gnawing hunger he'd spent most of his life ignoring, uncoiled itself inside him, like a wild animal long asleep. It wanted to touch and taste, to consume and be consumed, until there was nothing left. He shuddered as she shifted closer, gently running her fingers through his hair until it stood on end. "Maggie, I—"

She leaned in and kissed him again. "Shut up, John."

"Yes, ma'am."

John kissed Margaret as if he'd done nothing else his whole life, every brush and breath charged with the singular burning focus of his being. And she was the center. Everything melted into the maddening softness of her lips, her skin, her hair. He couldn't get enough of her, like a dying man in the desert who'd finally found the sweetest, purest water, he drank long and deep.

For the next hour—was it an hour? or only seconds?—his entire world flipped upside down. His lips moved slowly, enticingly, over her neck, shoulders, mouth, and face, followed by his hands. She tasted like champagne and smelled like some soft purple flower his mother grew every summer. Lavender? Whatever it was, it was heaven on earth, hidden in the soft curves of her skin, and he found each spot, determined to make them his. He should've known once he started kissing her, he wouldn't stop. He couldn't, until a sudden ring of a cell phone jerked them both back to reality.

"Damn it—"

She stood hurriedly. "I should go."

"Wait, Maggie. Don't—"

His phone kept ringing, and she slipped away, leaving him in the sudden silence as the call went to voicemail. It was probably his mother.

He sighed, swearing, ran a hand through his hair, and tried to think. The clock in the corner ticked loudly, intruding on the silence, almost scolding him. He needed to pull himself together. He needed to find Frannie and get her home. But he couldn't get past the feeling of Margaret's hands and lips on him, the smell of her skin and hair, the sweet, heady taste of her mouth, and the growing hunger she left behind now that she was gone. He checked his watch.

There would be no going back to how things had been. Not for him.

1:13 AM

Margaret stood outside in the cold, staring at the cloudy sky. Henry had rung her mobile twice, but she'd missed both calls. He'd left her here, and she couldn't bring herself to care. The wind blew fresh snow into her face, stinging the sensitive skin where John's stubble had rubbed her cheeks. She cupped a hand to her face and breathed in the lingering smell of his aftershave.

Maggie.

She knew she ought to ring Henry and apologize. She should be ashamed of her behavior, but there was no going back now. She hugged her coat closer, remembering the warmth of John's arms around her. It was a delightful sensation she didn't expect to miss.

The front door opened behind her, and Frannie Thornton stumbled out, bumping hard into her. Frannie laughed uproariously, and fell, pulling them both down into the snow.

"I am so drunk," she sang. "My brother is furious."

John appeared a moment later. He rolled his eyes and hauled his sister and Margaret out of the snow. Frannie was swaying and laughing, and her brother scooped her up like a small child. Margaret brushed the snow off her own dress.

"I can walk by myself, thank you," Frannie said, trying to extricate herself, but John kept hold of her. "Happy new birthday year, big brother."

Margaret laughed quietly and followed him as he carried Frannie to his truck. She opened the passenger door and helped him arrange his sister in the seat. She handed Frannie her purse, which she had dropped.

"Thank you." John leaned his arm on the passenger door and gave her a soft, crooked smile. Her cheeks and neck flushed when he reached out and gently pushed her hair from her face, tucking a bit behind her ear. She shivered under his touch, her skin prickling.

"Where's Henry?" he asked.

"I think he left quite a while ago."

"Need a ride home?"

"Yes, please."

1:42 AM

John followed Margaret to her front door, ignoring her half-hearted protests. "I'm safely arrived, as you can see," she said, rummaging for her keys, waiting to see if he would go.

He didn't, and she tried not to look at him. He stood as if he had all the time in the world, hands in his pockets, watching her with that same burning intensity, a ghost of a smile making him far too handsome. She pulled out her key and unlocked the door, pushing it open. He didn't turn to go, and neither did she. "Can you come in for a minute?"

Her words hung between them. He raised his eyebrows.

Why had she asked him that?

She cast about for some explanation. "I have your book."

He ducked in behind her. She moved quickly, picked up the shabby paperback from the front table, and held it out to him. "Here."

His hand closed gently around her wrist instead. "Did you finish it?" he asked.

"Not exactly."

"Why not?" He pulled her closer.

"Too much arguing," she said, her voice hushed and soft, "and not enough kissing."

"You like arguing." His face was inches from hers. "And kissing."

"It depends." Whatever madness had possessed her earlier flared to life again, and she stood on tiptoe. "If it's you, I do."

His laugh rumbled against her lips. She pressed herself closer, relishing the slow, burning kiss he gave her, letting go of whatever rational thought she had left. That kiss became another and another, all heat and tongue and teeth.

She laughed, a little breathless, when he lifted her onto the tiny hall table. "You should probably go."

"Make me."

"Are you always this rude?"

"Only to you."

She sat back, a little dazed. "If this is you being rude, I can't imagine you being nice."

"Trust me." His eyes glinted with a fierce longing that sent a jolt of something new and delicious along her skin. "I'm just getting warmed up."

She blinked.

You and John should just get a room.

Bess Higgins's suggestive remark echoed in her mind. Part of her viciously rebelled against it, but a strange part of her wondered how nice he would be if he stayed. The two opposing thoughts raged against each other. He kissed her again, so softly that she shivered, and leaned his forehead gently against hers, his hands cradling her face.

"Maggie—"

A loud, sharp blast from the truck horn broke through the night stillness. Margaret jumped and smacked the back of her head against the wall, the clear harsh sound shattering her thoughts. She stared at John. What on earth were they even doing? Was she completely mad?

He sighed and ran a hand through his hair, making it stand on end.

He looked over his shoulder and then back at her as she slid off the table. "I should take my sister home."

"You should." She grabbed the still-open door, holding it between them like a shield, terrified of the mad thoughts she'd entertained a moment before. She raised her chin and straightened her shoulders. "Good night, Mr. Thornton."

He smiled, his blue-black gaze sliding over her one last time. "Good night, Miss Hale."

6:46AM

"What happened at the Lancaster's party last night?" His mother stood by the kitchen table the next morning, disapproval written in every line of her face. She waited impatiently as John lazily sipped his coffee, pushed his hat back, and stretched out his legs, forcing her to step out of the way.

"What have you heard?"

"Mrs. Lancaster called this morning. Your foolish behavior is now the tittle-tattle of Milton. Again."

"Gossip is a waste of your time."

"Are you going to tell me what I want to know?"

He shrugged and took another sip of coffee.

His mother tapped her foot. "Have you settled things with that Hale girl yet?"

He pretended to consider this for a moment, swirling the remaining contents of his cup before finishing it. There was something between him and Margaret, that was for sure, but he had no clue what the hell it was yet. He stood, kissed his mother on the cheek, and headed for the door.

"John Thornton."

"It was just a kiss."

Mrs. Thornton's frown sharpened. "You kissed her?"

"More like she kissed me." He chose his words carefully, allowing himself a small grin. Mrs. Lancaster knew more than he'd like, but she couldn't know everything. He'd made certain of that. "And I kissed her back."

His mother rolled her eyes.

TUESDAY: JANUARY 2, 2007

Margaret gasped and swore when Bess Higgins burst into her work cubicle. "Margaret Ann Hale." Bess grabbed her by the shoulders, face blazing with triumph. "I'm gone for less than two weeks and when I come back all of Milton is in an uproar over you and John Thornton."

"Don't be so melodramatic."

"Tell me everything."

"We shared a New Year's kiss."

"That's not what I heard."

"Did you flirt with Terry to get in here?" Margaret asked. "You shouldn't lead him on."

"Don't change the subject. You *kissed* John Thornton."

"I—" Margaret flushed again, but she didn't know whether it was from shame or pleasure. She had kissed him, and he'd kissed her. Quite thoroughly, too. "I did."

Bess's smile widened. "Details, Marg, I need details."

"Mr. Thornton is delightful, as you've always insisted."

"What are you going to do now?"

"Nothing. It was nothing."

"Eating his face for two hours is not nothing."

"I was caught up in a momentary lapse of judgment. We had a bit of fun. Now it's back to real life for us, yeah?" Margaret shoved away the nervous stirring feeling in her stomach, her heart beating a little harder. She still wasn't certain why she'd done it, or what to do now. "Like I said, it's nothing. I'd rather not discuss this anymore."

"Were you drunk?" Bess demanded, sitting heavily on her desk. "Even a little bit?"

"I had one glass of champagne."

"Was he drunk?"

"Not that I recall."

"Then I will swear on a stack of Bibles blessed with holy water that whatever happened was *not* nothing. Did you sleep with him? Please say you did."

"For Heaven's sake, Bessie," Margaret snapped, flushing. She felt the weight of her friend's words as a challenge. She pushed her off her desk. "Why aren't you at work? Does this have anything to do with a strike?"

"There you go, changing the subject again." Bess jumped to her feet and headed for the door. "Go ahead and keep lying to yourself about your make out session with John Thornton. I'll see you later."

WEDNESDAY: JANUARY 3, 2007

The next morning, Williams was waiting for John at his desk. John tossed his keys aside, bracing himself. "What is it?"

"I got a call this morning from Porter."

"A strike?"

"All the factories. Every one of them."

John swore, and sat heavily, his shoulders sagging.

"That's not the worst of it." Williams paused and John looked up, waiting. "Our entire fleet is unreachable. I can't raise any of them on the band. Same for Hamper, Slickson, and Stephenson."

"Shit," John growled. He paced the room. "You made that list like I asked?"

Williams nodded.

"How long until we can get new drivers in?"

"We have enough to replace about a dozen guys. The rest could take up to two weeks at least. Maybe three."

"Son of a bitch." John kicked at the trash can, sending it flying. "I'll wring their necks, I swear to God. What about the trucks that were out on delivery?"

"Best assume they've been abandoned."

"Track our trucks down. You write off those drivers. I don't want any of them to haul freight ever again. I'll start making calls, see if I can smooth things over with our distributors."

"And the rest of the fleet?"

"Pull their files. They get one week before I fire their asses."

"What if we don't have drivers to replace them?"

"Fire them anyway."

"All of them?"

"I don't negotiate," John snapped. "Do it."

"You got it, Master."

John swore again and slammed his fist hard on his desk. He did not need this right now. He sat, threw his hat on the floor, and began sorting through the paperwork he'd abandoned the week before. Williams lingered, poured himself some coffee, and took a long, noisy slurp. John looked up and saw the old man staring at him over his cup, an amused glint in his eyes.

"What?" John demanded.

"Heard you had a mighty fine birthday with a certain British firecracker. You want to share with the class?"

"Get out."

"It's about time you made a move." Williams chuckled, and slipped out of the office before John could say anything else.

Chapter 20

Ben Boucher was drunker than Nick had ever seen him. The call had come from Marlborough Shipping, as Nick expected, except Thornton had given them only one week to come back to work, no questions asked.

That was it.

"He's bluffing. Thornton can't replace you in a week, Ben." Nick shoved him into a large easy chair. "He'd have to know our plans, which he doesn't. We stick together. We stand with the working class, and we'll show them we mean business."

Ben shrunk down in the chair, his face red and slick with sweat and tears. "It's been four days, Nick. If I don't go back, I'll have nothing. I haven't heard from Rosa in weeks. I can't lose this job. My kids need me out there working."

"You go back, and you'll screw over everyone else taking the same risk with you. We're in this together, as brothers. I said I would take care of you and the kids, and I will."

"And what happens when we all lose our jobs?" Ben demanded,

tears streaming from his eyes. "What then?"

"He can't replace all of us in a week. No way in hell." Nick began pacing. "No one can. Thornton will cave, like the others. We have the power now, Ben. You mark my words."

"That's bullshit." Ben stumbled into the filthy kitchen. "You fed us a load of shit and damn you if we didn't eat it from your hand."

"Shut up. You stay put and let the union handle this."

"I hate you." Ben pulled a beer from the fridge. "You and your damn union. I hate you all."

FRIDAY: JANUARY 12, 2007

"Have you heard the news?" Mr. Hale sat before a cheerful fire, loading his pipe.

"What news?" Margaret took her shoes off and tucked herself into John's favorite chair. She didn't remember when she'd begun thinking of it as *his*, but he always sat there when he visited, and it always smelled faintly like him.

"Milton is on strike. All the factories shut down last week."

"I heard."

"The truck drivers went on strike as well. They've effectively gone off the grid."

"But I saw Bessie a week ago."

"Have you heard from her since?"

"No, I haven't, but I thought she had another long haul." Margaret bit her lip, putting together the odd pieces from the last few weeks in her mind.

"It won't last much longer, you know."

"What do you mean?"

"Strikes get ugly rather quickly, especially when they're desperate.

I'm afraid nothing but trouble will come of it."

SATURDAY: JANUARY 13, 2007

The days crawled by, and each morning John woke, feeling older. Most nights he stayed at the office, sleeping when he could. Everything was a mess. He knew logically he couldn't fire his entire fleet, no matter how much he wanted to. There was also the question of Nick Higgins. If he could prove he'd had a hand in the strike, John would send the man packing without a second thought. Besides Williams, Nick was John's oldest and best employee. He'd been with John since the beginning, and he would hate to lose the clever bastard. But Nick had disappeared.

Then there was Margaret.

Two weeks had passed since New Year's Eve. John ran a hand through his hair and sighed. Like everything else in his life, she had to wait too. He stretched his aching limbs, stood, and looked out of the office window. The sky was cloudy, but the usual smoke from the factories was absent. Williams walked in, holding a clipboard.

"What is it?" John asked.

"I've got enough staff coming in by Monday that we can resume statewide deliveries with the trucks we have. I had to suspend all our current out-of-state contracts until next week."

"What about the abandoned trucks?"

"All are accounted for, except two. We've got locations on them and I'm in touch with the state police for both; one in California and one halfway through Canada. Just waiting for verification and other red-tape shit. We've got pickups arranged, but it will take time."

"How much time?" John leaned his hands on the windowsill.

"Depends."

"This strike might put us under. If we can't get off the ground by

Monday, we're fucked."

"Don't be so cheerful. We're doing better than anyone else."

John turned. "I'll take care of the locals today. Send Hanley out on pickup and see if we can't get an extension on the canceled orders."

"I already tried that."

"Try again."

SATURDAY: JANUARY 27, 2007

It had been too long since Margaret had heard from Bess or Nick, and she was getting worried. The longer the strike stretched, the more Milton hummed with tension. She took the bus to Thomas Street and hurried up to the Higgins' apartment building. Her buzz was ignored.

"Hello?" she called, buzzing in again. "Mary? Bessie? It's Margaret." The wind whipped down her neck and she waited, shivering. She looked up when the door opened, and Timmy Boucher motioned her inside. "Timmy? Where's Bessie?"

"I'm not supposed to let you in. They're all upstairs."

Margaret climbed the stairs quickly, her heart racing faster at the sound of muffled shouts. She stepped into the Higgins' apartment and gasped. Nick shoved Ben Boucher against the wall. Ben sagged to the floor, his face bloody and bruised. Mary was crying in the corner, her arms wrapped around Bess.

"You little piece of shit," Nick growled. He kicked Ben, who crawled towards the door. "You sniveling, conniving, son of a bitch."

"Stop it," Margaret said sharply. "Nick, what's happened?"

"I'll kill him." Ben lunged for the door, grabbing Margaret's coat. "I swear, I'll put a bullet in Thornton if it's the last thing I do."

Margaret stared at him, horrified.

"You do that, and we're done." Nick grabbed Ben's shirt and

slammed him against the apartment door.

Ben took a wild swing at him, clipping his nose. Nick dropped him, and he scurried out of the apartment.

"You're a liar, Nick Higgins," Ben shouted, stumbling down the stairwell. "I'll kill that Thornton son of a bitch."

Margaret didn't move as Nick barreled after him, snarling obscenities. She turned to Mary and Bess, staring in shock at the ugly bruise on Bess's cheek. Her stomach twisted. "What the bloody hell happened?"

"Uncle Ben went to see Thornton today. He tried to break the strike," Mary said. "He told him everything, begging for his job back."

"What did John say?"

"He fired him." Bess wiped the back of her hand over her eyes. "Told him he'd never drive trucks again. We're all screwed. Thornton's already started hiring new drivers."

Bess moved to the door.

"Where are you going?"

"The Depot. Someone's got to put food on the table for these kids, politics be damned."

Margaret glanced around the room, the smaller Boucher children's faces peeking around a bedroom door, their eyes wide and frightened. "I'm coming with you," she said.

♥

John frowned when Margaret marched into his office, her face a storm of dark determination, dragging Bess Higgins behind her. He would've smiled if it had been any other day. He stood and offered them a seat.

"I prefer to stand," Margaret said.

Bess Higgins kept her eyes on the floor, but he could see she'd been crying, a fresh bruise on her cheek. His frown deepened and he folded his arms. "What can I do for you, Higgins?"

"I need my job," Bess said, "if you'll take me back."

Margaret was silent, but she held on to her friend, watching John like a hawk.

He sighed. "Margaret, excuse us for a minute."

"No, you'll not excuse me."

"You need to leave," he said sharply.

"I will not be ordered from the room like a child—"

"Go on, Marg," Bess said, cutting her off. "I don't need you for this."

Margaret went in furious silence. John closed the office door behind her, ignoring her fierce scowl, and focused on the problem at hand. He took a deep breath. "Give me one good reason why I shouldn't kick your ass out of here."

"You should," Bess said. "I made a mistake. I'm here, and I'm asking for a second chance."

"Nothing would make my day more than to fire every last one of you." He bit the words out. "But I need you. You start right now, and we'll come back to this another time."

Bess nodded.

"Go talk to Williams," he said, sitting heavily. "Keep your head down. This isn't over."

Bess left, and Margaret stepped back into the office.

"In the future," John said without preamble, "don't interfere with my employees. You had no right to march in here making demands."

"Bessie is my friend. She needed me."

"She's an adult." He took off his hat and roughed his hair before settling it back into place. "This has nothing to do with you. I'm asking you to stay out of it."

"This strike isn't her fault."

"Maybe not, but Bess played her hand."

"That's not fair."

"What's fair got to do with anything?"

"She's got bloody bad cards to play," Margaret insisted, raising her voice. "Why do you keep punishing her for it?"

"I'm trying to help her."

"So am I."

"You can't save everyone, Maggie." The soft endearment slid out easily. "And you shouldn't try."

She swallowed hard and didn't answer him.

"Where'd you find her?" he asked, weariness finally breaking through his anger.

"At home."

They were silent for a moment, and she shifted uncomfortably under his frank stare. She cleared her throat and said, "I heard you fired Ben Boucher."

"It was a long time coming." John felt fifty years old, his shoulders slumping. He would bet money it was Ben who'd hit Bess. "He's a mean bastard, and this was the last straw."

Margaret didn't argue with him. She continued to hold his stare, a slow, pink flush crawling onto her cheeks.

He almost smiled, but he was too tired. "It's late." He glanced at the wall clock. "How did you get here?"

"I should go," she said, ignoring his question. "Dad will worry if I'm much later."

"You need another car, Maggie."

"Dad can barely keep up the one we have."

John stood, stretching, picked up his keys, and grabbed his jacket off the back of his chair. He motioned to the door. "Come on."

"Are you going to make this a habit?" she asked quietly when they reached his truck.

He finally smiled. "Only if you keep wandering around Milton in the middle of the night."

John walked Margaret to her front door. The drive had been silent and weirdly easy, almost peaceful. They needed to talk about New Year's Eve and now wasn't a good time. But he couldn't let it go. She paused a fraction of a second at the door before slipping inside. He stood for a moment, the memory of their kiss easing the tension in his shoulders a little. He'd thought about that night every day for two weeks, even with the insanity of the strike.

He should've known she would be in the middle of this mess, and he didn't like it one damn bit. He had to make sure she stayed out of it until the whole thing blew over. Bess Higgins was one of a dozen of his drivers that had called him that week. The trucking companies were finally grinding forward, but the factories were still at a stalemate. The strike would fail, and when word got out, things would only get worse before they got better. John didn't want Margaret anywhere near it.

Chapter 21

The strike ended with a gunshot. John rubbed his eyes and stared at the clock in the hospital waiting room. He leaned against the wall and immediately shifted, his ribs on his right-side throbbing. The nurses had said he was lucky they were only bruised. *Lucky, my ass.* He should have a bullet in him. Margaret hadn't been so lucky. He straightened and began pacing again, nervous energy pouring off him, making it impossible to keep still. He'd never felt as helpless as he did right now, but there was nothing to do but wait. And worry.

Almost an hour later, Dr. Rick Donaldson walked down the hall, and John stopped pacing. He'd been grateful to see him working the ER tonight. Rick Donaldson was an old friend of his father's, and the only doctor he trusted. John rubbed his palms over his jeans, folded his arms, and nodded, trying to keep himself calm.

"You look like death warmed over," the doctor said.

John glanced at his shirt, stained and stiff with dried blood. He looked back up and cleared his throat. "How is she, Doc?"

"She's fine. The bullet wound was superficial. Barely a graze."

Dr. Donaldson shoved his hands into the pockets of his white coat. "Cuts to the head bleed like little devils, even when they're small. It's never like you see on TV."

John wasn't prepared for the heavy wave of relief and exhaustion that pressed him against the wall. His knees buckled, and he slid slowly to the floor. She was fine.

"Are you all right?" Dr. Donalson asked. "Can I get you something to drink?"

"No." John scrubbed his face with his hands. She was fine. He let out a sharp breath. "You're sure she's okay?"

"Margaret took a nasty blow to the back of her head when she fell. I'm more concerned about her concussion than anything else. It could've been much worse."

"Yeah." John felt sick.

"They're stitching her up now, and I've ordered a CT scan to monitor that concussion. She'll need further treatment to make sure she heals properly, but I promise she's going to be fine." Dr. Donaldson reached out a hand and helped him to his feet. "Get yourself a coffee while you wait."

John shook his head. "I want to see her now."

"Coffee first," Dr. Donaldson said. "The police still need to take your statement. There's no rush."

John followed him to the cafeteria and drank the worst cup of coffee he'd ever had. But it gave him something to do.

"Margaret didn't want her father contacted," Dr. Donaldson said, finishing his own coffee. "We'll keep her for a couple of hours for observation to be on the safe side, but I assume you'll take her home."

"I'm not going anywhere."

"I've got rounds to make. Call if you need anything."

"Thank you, Doc."

Dr. Donaldson waved it off. "Get some sleep and change that shirt."

John hurried out to his truck, grabbing his cell phone and the spare shirt he kept in the small duffle bag in the back seat. He needed to call Mr. Hale before the older man had time to worry. He slung the clean shirt over his shoulder and dialed. He didn't know what to say, but he had to do something. "Richard, it's John. I'm calling for Margaret."

"Oh, thank goodness. I heard there was some trouble down at Marlborough Shipping, and I was worried. Is everything all right?"

"It is now." John paused, choosing his words carefully. "Margaret said she'll be home pretty late. I'll make sure she gets there safely."

"May I speak to her? Is she there with you?"

"Not exactly."

Mr. Hale sighed. "Have her call when she gets a chance."

"I'll take care of her." John felt his throat tighten. "I promise."

Margaret gripped the blue plastic vomit-bag and fought against the waves of nausea rolling through her. A nurse rubbed her back and waited until she stopped dry heaving. Tears slid from Margaret's eyes, but she kept them shut. The lights were too bright, and she couldn't focus her vision. The world kept tilting and spinning, making the nausea worse. The tugging and pulling on her scalp didn't help either.

"You're a lucky girl," clucked the nurse stitching her up. "I never saw a gunfight that ended without someone hurt or dead."

"Where's John?" Margaret asked, pushing their hands away. "Is he all right?" She had to make sure he was all right. Someone wanted to hurt him. "Where's John?"

"Hold still for a little longer, okay?"

"I have to find him."

"He's all right."

"Where's John?" Margaret asked again, her voice shaking. Had they told her? Why hadn't they told her yet? She had to find him. Why wouldn't they answer her? Her head swam, and she retched again. "I need to find him," she whispered, tears sliding down her cheeks.

The nurses exchanged a look, and the one holding Margaret's shoulders nodded. "Wait here."

John stripped off his dirty shirt and tossed it into a trash can, the motion pulling at his sore ribs. He forced himself to move slower as he buttoned the clean shirt over the ugly bruises starting to form on his torso. When he finished, he saw a large nurse eyeing him with a cheeky grin. "You don't have to hurry for me, baby." She folded her arms. "Take your time."

"Can I help you?"

"Are you John Thornton? The man who brought in Margaret Hale?" He nodded and she motioned for him to follow her. "She's been asking for you, sugar."

The nurse turned and walked down the hall, John at her heels. She opened the door of a small exam room. His stomach plummeted when he saw Margaret huddling on a gurney, face pale, her cheeks stained with tears. He stared at the nasty gash that snaked back from her forehead, through her hair.

His fault.

"She's very confused right now, and we need to finish her stitches," a second nurse was explaining.

"Your job, Mr. Handsome, is to keep her calm and still." The first nurse nudged him towards Margaret. "Don't be shy."

"Maggie." He sat on the bed and gently pulled her into his lap, his hands shaking. He felt his body finally relax as her thin arms circled around his neck.

"John?" She was crying.

"It's okay. You're okay." He stroked her back, keeping his voice low, until she stopped trembling. "I've got you."

"If she feels sick again, here's a bag." The first nurse laid a small blue plastic bag next to them. "Keep her as still as you can."

He watched the second nurse as she worked, deftly cleaning and stitching up the nasty gash with efficient movements. He couldn't tell if she was doing a crap job or not. He still glared at her when she pulled too hard. It was over sooner than he expected.

"All done." She patted Margaret's shoulder. "One more on the back." The nurse cut away some of the hair around the gash and quickly administered the local anesthesia.

Margaret flinched with a small whimper.

"Careful," John growled.

"I'll be quick," the nurse said. "Keep using that boyfriend magic."

Margaret shivered, fresh tears on her cheeks. "I want to go home."

"I know, Maggie," he said gently and held her a little tighter. "We'll go home soon."

"Do you promise?"

"I promise." He tucked her head under his chin, waiting until she was still. He nodded at the nurse. She was done within five minutes.

"We'll be moving her out of the ER for her CT scan as soon as we can." The nurse peeled off her gloves and tossed them into the biohazard bin in the corner. "You two sit tight."

"Thank you."

They were finally alone. John let out a breath. Margaret stirred and tried to sit up, but she winced and closed her eyes again. Her face was pale, almost gray. "What's wrong?" he asked.

"The light's too bright."

He stood, still holding her, and took one step to the light switch, flicked it off, and sat in a chair by the door. "Better?"

She nodded, still shivering.

"Are you cold?" He glanced at her flimsy hospital gown. "Do you want a blanket?"

"I'm tired." She hugged her knees, leaning her head against his chest. She was half asleep. "Where's John?"

"I'm right here, Maggie," he said, frowning. He sat in the silence until he was sure she'd dozed off, listening to the sound of her breathing, and feeling the warmth of her body.

She was fine.

But he wasn't.

Chapter 22

Running. Time was running out. *Tick. Tick. Tick.* Where is he? Running. Hurry. *Tick. Tick. Tick.* Find him. *Tick.* Hurry. *Tick.* Too late.

Crack! Crack!

"John!" Margaret sat up in bed with a gasp, shaking, the dream slowly fading. A light flicked on, and a nurse appeared.

"How are we doing?" the nurse asked in a low soothing voice.

Margaret blinked and flinched away from the sudden brightness.

The nurse checked her pupils, her temperature, and her blood pressure. "Do you remember what today is?"

"Today is—" Margaret stopped. She didn't know what day it was. "I don't—" she frowned, her head pounding, and looked around. She was in a hospital. What was she doing here?

"I need to go home."

"I'll page Dr. Donaldson." The light flicked off. "The police want to speak with you about what happened, Miss Hale," the nurse added before she left. "Whenever you're ready."

Margaret's frown deepened. What had happened? She tried to

think. There was the riot. She had gone to the Depot earlier and—

Flashes of memory came slowly, so slowly, in jagged pieces

—Ben Boucher and his desperate bloodshot eyes.

I'll put a bullet in that son of a bitch, I swear to God.

She shook her head, trying to make herself remember more.

—Bessie screaming.

Oh my God, he's shot!

"Not John." Margaret clenched the bedclothes, her breaths sharp and shallow, her heart slamming against her rib cage as adrenaline hit her blood stream. "He can't be—"

Had Boucher *shot* John?

No. She remembered the sharp sound of the firearm and pain. But she had jumped between John and Boucher, her feet tangling with John's as he tried to pull her away. He'd lost his footing. Bess had grabbed Boucher's arm as he shot at John, the terrible sound splitting the night. Margaret raised her hand and brushed the bandage along her hairline with her fingertips. "Oh my God."

She'd been shot.

So how the bloody hell was she alive?

"Just tell me what you remember, Mr. Thornton." The police officer turned to a fresh page in his notebook and waited.

John stared at his paper cup of coffee. "I was at work. It was maybe six-thirty. I got a call from my dispatcher, Tucker Williams. He told me a group of the factory strikers were headed my way."

"What is it, Williams?"

"I caught Nick Higgins in the loading bay. He said he came to get his daughter out of here."

"Why?"

"He thinks trouble is brewing on the north side of town. A lot of hands from the factories have been meeting at The Stray Stone, drunk as hell, hollering on about the strike breakers."

"Bess?"

"One of them. Nick thinks Boucher's getting dangerous."

John took a swallow of coffee. "I've fired almost a dozen men in the last month. Add that to some of my drivers helping break the strike, I knew nothing good would come of it. Williams tends to worry, but I don't like borrowing trouble."

The officer nodded, making a note.

"I was locking up. Thought I'd go home early. Everything was fine until Maggie showed up."

"Is anyone there?"

John quickened his pace towards the front door. Margaret stood, looking puzzled. "Go home, Maggie. You can't be here."

His eyes flicked behind her, where he saw movement. He felt his skin go cold, a shivering dread threading up his spine. A crowd of people were coming down the drive. "Shit." He pulled her inside, locking the door behind her. "We're in trouble."

"Trouble?"

He grabbed her hand and dragged her after him. "Come on."

"Did your girlfriend say why she was at Marlborough Shipping?"

"No." John stared at the officer, his jaw tightening. The word *girlfriend* sank in his stomach like lead. "With that riot on my ass and Margaret in the building, I got my gun and called the cops. We went to the locker room to wait, but I didn't figure on a late truck pulling in."

"That was Elizabeth Higgins?"

John nodded. "She was a strike breaker out on a long haul. Got back a day earlier than scheduled. Those idiots surrounded her truck before she could come to a full stop."

"Were any of them your former employees?"

"I recognized about six or seven guys. Only three were mine. I couldn't name the rest."

"How many people were there?"

"Thirty to forty."

"How would you describe their behavior?"

"Drunk as hell, all red-eyed, and looking to blow off steam. Bess Higgins was smart and stayed out of sight. The mob crowded around the cab, beating on the windows."

The officer scribbled some more. "What time was that?"

"Maybe seven, seven-fifteen?"

"And then what?"

John rubbed his eyes. "Maggie was scared. Bess Higgins is her best friend. She wanted to help her."

"Oh my God, John, it's Bessie! We have to do something. We have to tell them to stop."

"They won't listen."

"They have to. They have to stop!"

"Help is coming. The police will be here any minute."

"But they'll arrest everyone. No, you can't wait. We can't."

"Maggie—"

"We've got to do something now. They're going after Bess. Be a man and do something! Please!"

"I went outside."

The policeman looked up sharply. "You did?"

John glared at his coffee. "I figured if I could stay in one piece for five minutes, the police would do the rest."

"Did you have your firearm?"

John nodded.

"Did you discharge your weapon at any point?"

"No," John said. "I didn't want to pull it if I didn't have to."

"How did your girlfriend get in the middle of the altercation?"

"She followed me outside." John picked at his paper cup, swallowing hard. "Maggie got herself between me and the mob. I don't know what she thought she could do. They had rocks, bricks, and baseball bats. She didn't even flinch."

"Please stop. Please! All of you listen!" Her voice carried over the shouts. They died down at her unexpected appearance. The mob hesitated as Margaret wedged herself between them and John, her hands outstretched in a placating gesture. "Please don't do this. He's one person. This isn't his fault."

"That's some kind of stupid." The officer shook his head.

John glanced up, glowering.

The officer cleared his throat, the smile fading from his face. "Sorry. Then what happened?"

"She told them to go home."

"This is madness." Margaret held her ground. "Use your bloody brains. You think the police aren't coming? Stop this nonsense and go home before you do something unforgivably stupid."

"Master has to answer for this."

"It's not his fault." Margaret drew herself up and glared into Boucher's red face. "I swear to God, Ben Boucher, if you lay a finger on John, I'll report you myself."

176

John stopped, the words catching in his throat. The officer waited, his pen poised.

"That's when Ben Boucher pulled out a gun."

"Didn't I say she was on his side?" Ben spit his words out, swaying. "Master's little bitch."

"Can you tell me how your girlfriend was injured?"

John breathed out slowly. He didn't want to think about it again, didn't want to relive that terrible moment. "It happened all at once."

"Take your time. Tell me what you remember."

John's hands moved instinctively towards his own weapon, his eyes glued to the firearm Ben held. He hesitated. Too many people. Too dangerous. And Margaret was right there.

"Maggie." The word came out in a desperate plea. He grabbed her arm and tugged her close. "Inside." He had to get her inside. "Now."

"I started to push Margaret back into the building. Bess Higgins was there—I don't remember how she got there—and she grabbed Ben's gun. Everyone was shouting." John closed his eyes, remembering. "Maggie jumped back in front of me, and my feet got tangled with hers. I tripped hard into a handrail right as the gun went off." He paused and fought back a wave of nausea. He'd felt her body warm against him as he fell; then it jerked, her head snapping sharply to one side just as the harsh *crack!* of the gun rang in his ears.

"Maggie went down, and I couldn't catch her."

Margaret hit the concrete next to him with a sickening smack and lay still—too still. John scrambled over to her and brushed his fingers over her face. Blood was everywhere. "Maggie?"

"I thought she was dead."

John didn't hear the police as they came barreling through the mob.

"I've got you." He scooped her off the pavement and held her tight. Bess followed on his heels. He had to get help.

"You're fine." He didn't realize he was speaking. His shirt was wet and sticking to his chest. He looked down and saw the rapidly growing red stain had soaked his jacket and shirt.

"John," Bess whimpered. "Is she dead?"

"She's fine," he barked.

Margaret's body was limp in his arms, like a rag doll.

"Look at me, Maggie. You're fine." He leaned down and brushed a kiss on her forehead. "You're fine."

Her skin was cold and pale. Bile burned at the back of his throat. "Please, Maggie, look at me."

"I didn't wait for an ambulance or the police. I drove her straight to the ER." John cleared his throat and tossed back the rest of his coffee. "That's all I've got."

The officer closed his notebook. "Thank you for your time, Mr. Thornton. We'll have to confiscate your firearm as evidence. Once it's cleared, it'll be returned to you."

"It's in my truck."

The officer nodded and held out his card. "We'll keep you informed of the investigation."

By the time John got back to the room where he'd left Margaret, it was long past midnight. He opened the door and stopped. The bed was empty. He stormed out and cornered the first nurse he saw. "Where's Maggie?" He was almost shouting.

"What room number?"

He told her and she tapped her keyboard. "Margaret Hale's gone home."

"Home?" He shook his head. "That's not possible."

"Checked herself out about a half hour ago. Dr. Donaldson signed the discharge papers."

John swore and jogged out to his truck, quickly dialing Dr. Donaldson. "You let her go home alone?" he demanded when the doctor answered. "What the hell are you thinking?"

"Hello to you too, John."

"Give me one good reason not to beat the shit out of you."

"That's a bit melodramatic, especially for you."

"She was shot, and you sent her home *alone*."

"I didn't know she left alone. Margaret needs rest, but her scans all came back normal. I saw no reason to keep her overnight when she wanted to leave. What did you expect me to do? Chain her to the bed?"

"You should've called me."

Dr. Donaldson chuckled. "Get some sleep, John. At least six hours. Doctor's orders." He hung up.

John swore again and tossed his phone aside, slumping down in the driver's seat. He knew the doctor was probably right, but it didn't make him any less pissed off. Or less worried. He straightened and started his truck, the grumbling engine tearing into the quiet night.

There was nothing left to do but go home and wait.

He wouldn't sleep.

Chapter 23

When she woke the next morning, Margaret frowned and glanced around, confused. She was lying on the sofa in the living room, but she didn't remember how she'd got there. She sat up slowly and raised her hand to her aching head, wincing when she brushed her left temple. She gingerly fingered what felt like a bandage. She shuffled to the hall mirror and stared at the mess reflected there. She had medical dressings on her temple and the back of her head, and her hair was all tangled, looking like she hadn't slept in days.

"Bloody hell." She grimaced, pulling the gauze off. She hissed and brushed the neat row of tidy black stitches. She walked to the kitchen in a daze, spotted a blue folder, flipped it open. Inside were hospital discharge papers. She stared at them for a moment, overwhelmed and disoriented, her head pounding. What had happened to her?

She decided to make tea and call Bess. If anyone knew what was going on, it would be her best friend.

"Oh my God, Marg, oh thank God." Bess began crying as soon as she picked up.

"What did I do?"

"That's not funny."

"Bessie, I'm not trying to be funny. I was in the hospital yesterday and I know I have a concussion because that's what my discharge papers tell me, but everything else is a bit fuzzy."

"Do you remember being shot?"

"Shot?" Margaret paused, a slight ringing in her ears. "I guess I do remember." She took a long sip of tea. "The riot, right? I think I was hoping that was all a bad dream."

"Are you crazy?" Bess shouted, cutting her off. "What the hell were you thinking, jumping in front of a loaded gun? You could've died, and I would've had to watch." Her voice broke. "Do you have any idea what it would do to me to watch my best friend die?"

"I'm sorry, Bessie."

"You should be sorry. You should be fucking sorry."

"I said I was."

"Well, I'm still pissed at you."

"Yeah, I know."

"So," Bess was starting to calm down, her voice settling into its familiar teasing sarcasm, "how come you can't remember being shot? Things like that tend to stick with a person."

"Apparently, memory loss is a common symptom of a Grade 3 concussion," Margaret read from the hospital handout, trying to sound casual. "It says here that many patients report little or no memory of the trauma, or the events occurring immediately afterwards, up to twenty-four hours."

"You have amnesia?"

"Don't be ridiculous. I don't have amnesia."

"But you don't remember going to the ER last night?"

"Not really. Thank you for getting me there and back again."

"I didn't take you," Bess said quietly. "I was held for questioning."

"Then who did?"

"John."

"Oh." Margaret shivered, a vague memory of a tender, deep baritone lingering at the edges of her thoughts.

I've got you.

The skin on her back prickled. "I didn't know."

"Has he called you?"

"No," Margaret scoffed. "Why would he?"

"Because," Bess said. She sounded confused. "You really don't remember any of it?"

"I don't know. I don't even remember what I was doing at the Depot." Margaret frowned, rubbing her forehead. "I think I had something to give someone. Or meet someone." She felt dizzy at the effort, and her stomach rolled. "I don't know, Bessie."

"Margaret? Is that you?" Mr. Hale called from the stairs. "You came home late last night."

"I've got to run."

"Marg, wait—"

"Chat soon." Margaret quickly hung up the phone and swept the discharge papers into a pile, tossing them into the recycling. She pulled her hair down around her face, hoping the stitches wouldn't show too much, and grabbed her tea.

"How is Bess?" Her father opened the refrigerator. "I heard about the riot at Marlborough Shipping. Nasty business. I do hope everyone involved is all right."

"Bess is fine."

"What happened to you yesterday evening? I rang."

"I misplaced my mobile," she answered, slowly and as truthfully as possible. "I ran a few errands and got a bit delayed."

"Oh?" Mr. Hale turned around and frowned when he caught sight of her. "Margaret, what's happened?" He went pale as he brushed her hair aside. "You're hurt."

"It's fine, Dad. It was an accident, but it looks far worse than it is. I swear I'm fine."

"But what happened?"

"I fell and hit my head." She tried to sound casual. "It was stupid and embarrassing. Nothing to worry about."

"Why didn't you call? I would've fetched you home."

"But you would also fuss like a mother hen, all worry and wringing hands," she teased, trying to hide her dizziness and pitching stomach. She felt awful. And she didn't like lying to her father.

She smiled and patted his arm. "I promise I'm all right."

John sat at the kitchen table, watching the sun rise. He turned when his mother walked in, a few hours later, and sat down. "You're up early," she commented, paging through the newspaper.

He didn't answer. She'd waited up for him the night before and peppered him with questions until he told her everything, in short concise answers—about the strike, the riot, the ER—everything. She was watching him now, her sharp eyes seeing everything. "Did you get any sleep last night?"

He shook his head.

She sighed. "If Dr. Donaldson sent her home, I'm sure everything was done properly. Getting all worked up for nothing won't help."

He checked his watch. It was his father's, the one thing his mother had saved for him. The newspaper rustled as his mother turned the page. She glanced sideways at him, but he ignored her, turning his coffee cup in his hands.

He'd been on tenterhooks ever since he'd left the hospital, pacing the house like a caged animal. His thoughts were a tangled mess, and he was too tired to sort them out. He had called Margaret a half dozen times, but she wasn't answering her phone. He didn't trust himself to try the home phone. She rarely answered it, and he didn't want to talk to Mr. Hale yet.

"Stop worrying, son," his mother scolded.

"I can't. I need to talk to her."

"What do you have to say that can't wait a few hours?"

He lifted his head and looked at her. She'd always been able to read him like a book.

Her shoulders sagged. "You can't be serious." Her expression hardened. "She's too young, John."

"I can't wait."

"You would if you had any common sense in that foolish head of yours." She sighed. "You're always sprinting ahead without thinking."

"What are you talking about?"

"I suppose you should marry her, after everything *else* you've done with that girl."

He stiffened. "What's that supposed to mean?"

"Nobody's forgotten New Year's Eve, except Frannie."

"When have I ever cared what the Milton gossip mill thinks of me?" he interrupted. "It's none of their damn business."

"She's barely twenty years old. Everyone, including your investors, knows what happened or has guessed. And there's still talk about last year and what you did with Lana Lancaster. This town is having a field day with your reputation."

"I don't care." He picked up his coffee, trying to hold down his temper. "Maggie almost died yesterday. I have to ask her."

"I don't know why you're so worked up about it."

"Mother—"

"That girl rushed into an angry mob and saved your life. If that's not love, I don't know what is. I might even like her for it."

He didn't answer. He couldn't.

Mrs. Thornton sighed and laid the paper on the table. She stood and walked out of the room, returning a moment later. "After our conversation at Christmas, I called Mr. Bell." She set a small square box on the table and laid a hand on his head. "She may as well have it since you're hell bound and determined to have her."

He picked the box up and turned it over in his hand. "You should've let me ask for this."

"I might be a proud woman, but I'm not too proud to ask a favor for my only son."

"Thank you."

"When will you go?"

"This morning."

"Wait until tonight. Try to get some rest."

"I can't."

His mother bit back her retort as a yawning Frannie came sauntering into the room, her pink silk bathrobe shimmering. "Margaret Hale's here to see you, John-John." Frannie opened the fridge, pulled out the orange juice, and poured herself a glass. "She's waiting for you in the library. Get off your butt and go talk to her."

He sat and stared at Frannie for a moment, then stood so fast he knocked his chair over. He grabbed the box off the table, and walked out, feeling his mother's eyes following him.

"What's gotten into him?" Frannie asked.

But he didn't hear his mother's reply. All he could think about now was Margaret. What was she doing here so early? His pulse thundered in his ears.

If that's not love, I don't know what is.

Shit. This was it for him. This was really happening, and he wasn't ready. He paced the hall in front of the library door, unable to stop long enough to open it. He rolled the square box between his hands, every nerve, every muscle, on edge, his body singing with adrenaline, tension, and exhaustion. He needed a plan, but—

As he neared the library door again, he forced himself to stop and rested his hands on either side of the wooden frame, his body drooping with fatigue. Image after image of the night before flashed through his mind, relentless, insistent. There was no time to think about what had happened, no time to understand the struggle raging inside his chest and stomach, no time to wait for tomorrow or for sanity.

His father had died in the blink of an eye, leaving too much unsaid, too much left to do. John had sworn he would never let himself live with regret like that. He had to do something *now*, before he lost her for good.

The door to the library suddenly opened, and he straightened. Margaret stared at him. He stared back and folded his arms to stop the wild seesawing of his stomach, to keep from pulling her close in a rib-splitting hug of relief and wonder.

She was here.

And she was fine.

Chapter 24

Frannie Thornton had deposited Margaret in the dusty library with an exasperated huff. Margaret didn't know why she'd come over so early or why she'd come at all—but now that she was here, she couldn't leave. When the heavy tread of footsteps approached, she felt her head swim with a fresh wave of dizziness. Her vision wavered. She leaned against the closed door, listening to John pace in the hallway.

She was sure it was him; his heavy purposeful tread was so familiar to her now.

I've got you.

Memories of last night washed in and out with hazy uncertainty, clamoring for her attention. She hugged her arms tight around herself, a sinking feeling of dread expanding in the pit of her stomach. *Why* was she here? What would she even say to him?

The footsteps stopped, the floor creaking on the other side of the wood paneled door. All at once, she knew she was tired of waiting and pulled the door open. John stood there, closer than she expected, looking wrinkled and exhausted.

"Oh." She took an awkward step back, and they stood staring at each other for a long, silent moment.

She took another step, hating how uneasy he made her feel, with just one stupid look. "I'm sorry to bother you so early."

"Maggie."

His voice sent a fresh wave of goosebumps over her skin. She felt like she was falling. "I brought you something," she said hastily. She began to rummage in her bag. "The book Dad borrowed at Christmas. I forgot to give it to you yesterday, with everything that happened and—" her voice trailed off.

"A book?" He tilted his head a little to one side, almost smiling. "You're here to give me a book?"

"Yes." She held out the thin leather volume. "I also wanted to thank you for all your help yesterday."

He frowned. "You don't have to thank me." He sounded offended.

"Of course, I do." She held the book in front of her like a shield and stared at the floor. "Dad didn't say if you had anything new so—"

"Maggie." He raised his hand and carefully pushed back her hair, revealing the line of stitches curving along her forehead towards her left temple. "Does it hurt?"

"I'm fine."

"Hey." His hand was still in her hair. "Look at me."

She lifted her chin and finally met his gaze. She clutched the book to her chest. "About the books—"

"Forget the book. I have something for you too." He pried one of her hands free and set a small black box on her palm, brushing her skin with his thumb. She felt a surge of panic at the strangely soft smile that brightened his tired face, even as a rush of heat crawled up her cheeks.

He was still holding her hand.

"Please stop," she whispered.

Why wouldn't her voice cooperate?

"What?"

"Stop." She jerked her hand away and stepped back. "You're making me uncomfortable."

He looked confused. "You weren't uncomfortable with me last night."

"I don't remember last night."

It was a lie, but she wasn't certain what she remembered, if anything. She wasn't even sure she wanted to remember. "I don't know what you're talking about."

"No." He stepped closer. "You're lying."

She flinched further back. "Excuse me?"

"I held you for every one of those stitches." He reached out again and lightly traced the place where the bullet had raked its angry fingers. His hand slid through her hair, holding her, firm and gentle. "And you held on to me."

"I appreciate what you did," she said, her voice shaking.

"You have a strange way of showing it."

"I've said thank you," she snapped. "What else do you want me to say?"

"Say yes."

"Yes?" There was a pause, and then her eyes widened as she glanced quickly between the black box and his face. "Oh God." She stumbled backwards, almost tripping on her feet until she bumped into the shelf behind her. "No!"

She flung the box away, as if it had bitten her, turned, and stumbled out of the door.

"Maggie, wait." John caught up to her in two steps and grabbed her hand. "Please wait."

"Are you out of your bloody mind?" She jerked her hand free. The panic and horror in her eyes was like a slap in the face.

"No. I'm not, I—" he stiffened and shook his head. No, no, *no*. This wasn't right. Nothing was coming out the way he wanted. He couldn't find the words he needed to say to make her understand. "Maggie, I—"

"I *barely* know you. Why the bloody hell would you think I'd marry you?"

"Because we—" he broke off. His mind raced through the last few weeks, each memory taunting him. "Yesterday. Maggie, we—"

"Whatever you think I did for you at the Depot," she interrupted, "I did as one civil human being for another. I would have done it for *any* man there. You're not special."

"Really? What about New Year's Eve?" he asked, his voice stony, each word hot as his temper rose. "Would you do that for any man there?"

"It's a tradition." She blushed, but her voice remained cold. "I was being polite. One kiss does not entitle you to behave in such a presumptuous manner, Mr. Thornton."

"One kiss?" He clenched his fists. "That's bullshit."

"Stop swearing—"

"You can't blame me for thinking we're something more. Not after we made out. Hell, I almost stayed the night."

"You did *not*." Margaret bit out the words as if they were poison. "My kissing you once doesn't mean anything."

"No," he said harshly. "Don't lie to me."

This whole damn year had meant everything.

"Haven't you ever made a foolish decision in a heated moment that you bitterly regretted later?" she demanded. "I imagine you'd be offended if Lana Lancaster inferred some special connection between the two of you based on your stupid mistake last year."

"Mistake." John felt sick. He did regret what happened with Lana last year, but Margaret wasn't Lana. She wasn't a mistake. "Is that what you think I am? A fucking mistake?"

"You're my father's friend, and he likes you. I don't. There's nothing about you that's remotely romantic or tempting. Trust me."

He flinched, hurt and disappointed, every word a barb, goading his temper. But she didn't stop. "You're rude, unfeeling, and make a mockery of people who are less fortunate than you."

"Don't you dare." He took one step, closing the distance between them. "Don't drag the strikers into this."

"Why not?" she scoffed, a hard, mocking sound. "Your behavior to those men was reprehensible from the beginning."

"They made their own hell. They don't deserve a damn thing from anyone."

"If you would've talked to them, listened to them, they might not have—"

"This isn't my fault," he growled. "I'm not going to waste any more of my time on them."

"A civil and decent man would care. So, what does that make you?"

"I was more than decent." He grabbed her arm, turning her so she had to look at him. "They came after me and my drivers."

"Because they were desperate."

"They were drunk and too lazy to get the hell back to work."

"They wanted fair work. You're the one who fired Boucher."

"He deserved it," John shouted. "He's had it coming for two years. I'm the only one who kept him on the road."

"But now you've ruined him. He won't get any work after this. He might even go to jail."

"I did what I had to do to make sure that son of a bitch doesn't hurt anyone else."

"What about his children? Would you make them suffer for their father's decisions?"

"They're his problem, not mine."

"My God." Her eyes widened in shock. "You don't care at all, do you?"

"I care." His hands and voice shook, memories flooding over him. "I thought you were dead."

She took a sharp breath.

"I don't give one fuck about the man who shot you, and I won't apologize for that. Maggie—"

"Don't," she interrupted, pushing past him. "I don't want your twisted version of affection, John Thornton, and I never will."

He stood there like an idiot, her last words swimming around in his head. The desperate truth tumbled out of him before he could stop it. "Maggie, I love you."

But she was already gone.

♡

Margaret rushed out the front door, her head aching, her temper boiling, tears stinging her eyes. The memory of John's face and her own harsh bitter words refused to be pushed aside. She clung to her anger like a life preserver. She drove her father's car around aimlessly, not knowing where she was going until she found herself in front of the Thomas Street apartment buildings. Mary Higgins mercifully said nothing when she let her into the apartment. Bess took one look at Margaret and dragged her into the bedroom.

"Something's wrong." Bess shut the door firmly behind them. "What is it?"

"I went to the Thorntons' house this morning."

"I thought you might."

Mary pushed the door open and handed Margaret a cup of tea, lingering in the doorway. "So, what happened?" she asked.

"Nothing." Margaret stared at the cup.

All the confusion and anger and fear pressed up through her throat. She set the mug down on the chest of drawers and looked away from Bess and Mary, fighting tears. "Everything."

Mrs. Thornton watched her son walk slowly down the street, looking as if he didn't care where he was or where he went. She didn't understand what went wrong, even though the shouting match between John and Margaret was plain enough. Even Frannie had heard every word. After Margaret left, John locked himself in the library for almost an hour. When he finally emerged, he looked broken in a way that she hadn't seen since his father had died. He left without a word.

Mrs. Thornton would've admired the Hale girl's fortitude and fiery spirit, if she hadn't used it to crush John at his lowest and most vulnerable moment. That girl was harsh, proud, foolish, and headstrong. And John would pay the price. He'd never loved anyone like he loved Margaret Hale. He'd been too busy to bother with it before. Now that he did love her, he would keep loving her.

Mrs. Thornton almost hated him for it.

But she hated Margaret more.

"You're kidding me, right?" Bess folded her arms and sat heavily on the bed. "You said no?"

"What was I supposed to do?"

"Marry him. Duh."

Margaret stiffened. "How can you say that? We don't even get on."

"You get it on just fine, so don't pull that crap with me. It's a little fast, but it makes a lot more sense than you telling him to fuck off."

"I did *not* say that."

"You might as well have," Bess replied. "You don't flirt with a man for a year, tongue wrestle at a party, and then tell him you never even liked him. That's a new level of low. Anyone with a few brain cells and half an eyeball can see you two have it bad for each other."

"That's not fair."

"What's fair got to do with it?"

"Why are you defending him? You know better than anyone how he treats people. You should've heard him talk about the riot. It's awful, and he's awful, and he doesn't care. He says he cares about me but—"

"Margaret," Bess interrupted, her face darkening. "I'm his employee, not his girlfriend."

"He didn't ask me to be his girlfriend."

"Just his wife," Mary said quietly.

"No, he didn't actually ask that either. He didn't *ask* at all."

Bess rolled her eyes. "Maybe Thornton didn't go down on one knee, but we all know what he meant."

Margaret shook her head. "A decent, normal man would've made his intentions clear ages ago and dated me for at least six months. He wouldn't jump in like this, with no warning or hint of his feelings."

"You're kidding, right?" Bess looked shocked. "He's been flirting with you for over a year. Anyone with eyes can see how he feels about you. You keep lying to yourself about it."

"John Thornton is rude, arrogant, and—"

"Loyal, hardworking," Bess interrupted again, "and honest. He's also human. You're both impossible." She made an exasperated noise and shook her head. "God, you deserve each other."

"Even if he thinks he's in love with me, I'm sure after today, he'll find a way to stop."

"No, he won't." Bess walked to her closet, grabbing her boots and jacket. "I've never seen him like this with anyone. You're it for him."

"You can't know that, not even with your stupid Higgins witchery."

"John loves you." Mary again. "You know he does."

"Sometimes love isn't enough. My parents married for love. So did his parents and look how well that turned out." Margaret couldn't stop the words spilling out of her. "We can barely manage two civil words between us. What kind of hell would we make if we did get—" she choked. She couldn't bring herself to say the word *married*.

"You and John aren't your parents." Bess sat again, shoving her feet into her work boots. "Their marriage might have been hell, but that doesn't have to be your life."

"I would rather die alone than become my parents."

There was a long pause as Bess tied her laces. She and Mary exchanged a look. "You said no because you're scared," Bess said, her voice low. She looked at Margaret with hard pity. "I get it. But did you even think about John and what he wants, before you took his heart and bulldozed him over like a worthless piece of shit?"

Margaret looked away, shame burning in her stomach.

"I've seen the way you love, Marg."

"That's not enough." Margaret felt desperate, clutching her mug of cold tea in both hands. She shook her hair back from her face, fighting the tears that formed against her will. "I'm not in love with him."

"You're lying again," Mary said gently. "You've got all the proof you need."

"What proof?"

"You took a bullet for John Thornton," Bess said.

Margaret closed her eyes, as if to shield herself against the truth, but she still saw Boucher's gun pointed at John whenever she did. Paralyzing fear coursed through her at the memory, making her mouth dry and her breathing shallow.

"Truth bites like a bitch." Bess hugged her. "I'll see you later."

Margaret sat on her bed and stared at her hands, her vision blurry with anger and dizziness. Bess was wrong. It wasn't love. She would've done what she did for any man. John Thornton was just another man. She did *not* love him. She didn't even like him. Still, an awful twisting feeling clawed at her insides, half-formed memories echoing with a soft, strong baritone.

I've got you.

She clenched her hands into fists, forcing them to be still, but her body continued to rebel, tears crawling down her cheeks and dropping onto her lap.

Maggie, I love you.

She uncurled her hands and pressed them against her mouth, stifling the sob that tore out of her. What had she done?

John sat and listened to the roaring stillness of the old church. The sanctuary almost breathed, like a living thing, the creak of the wood and stones filling the empty spaces. The crucifix hanging above the altar was lit with the flickering glow of candles burning their silent prayers. He took off his hat and set it on his knee. He ran his hands through his hair and leaned his elbows on his knees, resting his aching head in his hands. He shut his eyes against the weary, cutting defeat that pressed onto his shoulders and held him down.

"John? Is that you?"

He raised his head. Mr. Hale stood behind him, looking pleasantly puzzled. John blinked, confused. He slid over and made room for the older man to sit down.

After a moment, Mr. Hale said, "This is the last place in the world I would ever think to find you."

"That's the whole point."

Mr. Hale leaned forward, rested his arms on the pew in front of him, and studied the altar. "I left the church fifteen years ago, and yet I always find myself coming back."

The two men sat in silence for a long time. The sun shifted and slanted through the stained-glass windows, bright fingers dancing across the room. "John, are you all right?"

John couldn't answer. He was too tired, and he had nothing left. No words, no explanation, nothing.

"If I can help, you'll tell me."

He nodded.

Mr. Hale stood, shuffled out of the pew, and left.

Chapter 25

The sharp rap at the office door interrupted John's concentration. He glanced up, then back down at the stack of files on his desk. "What is it, Williams?"

"It's almost nine."

"Go on home." John scribbled a note and shuffled through another stack of papers.

Williams didn't say anything. John looked up again when he pulled up a chair and sat heavily. The older man set down a half empty bottle of scotch and two plastic cups. "I've been with you nearly ten years, Master. You've been more than fair with me. It's time to return the favor. I'm going to pour us a drink, and you're going to tell me what the hell's the matter with you."

John leaned back in his chair, frowning while Williams poured two modest drinks, took a sip of his own, and settled himself. "Start at the beginning. Don't leave anything out."

John sighed and picked up his own cup. "Define *the beginning*."

"Margaret Hale."

"It's complicated."

"Women always are."

John emptied his cup in one swallow. The old dispatcher refilled it. He sighed and told Williams everything, starting with the first day he'd met Margaret and ending with his train wreck of a marriage proposal. When he stopped, the bottle was almost empty.

"Damn." Williams poured the remaining scotch into his cup and took another sip. "You've got yourself one hell of a mess, don't you?"

"Looks that way."

They sat for a moment, then Williams said, "I've been married three times. I don't know much about staying with a woman, but I do know that's *not* how you ask a woman to marry you. I don't blame her for saying no."

"No shit." John finished his drink and shook his head.

"Did you ever think," Williams said slowly, "that romancing a fiery thing like Margaret Hale might take a little work? Considering your stunning personality, maybe a little extra work?"

John didn't answer. What could he say? Williams was right.

"Think about that before you shoot your shot again."

"I'm not that stupid."

"Yes, you are. You're so far gone on her, you won't be able to stop yourself. If it were me, I'd sure as hell try again. Maybe after some real, honest romancing." Williams shrugged. "Lucky for you, she likes you more than she likes me."

"She hates me."

"Maybe." Williams stood. "Maybe not."

"You're drunk."

"Here's another two cents for you, son, since I'm feeling mighty generous tonight. She's worth it. You know it, and I know it. Untuck your tail, dust yourself off, and try again."

John took off his hat and roughed his hair, glaring at the smiling old man. "Go home," he muttered.

"I'll see you on Monday."

WEDNESDAY: MAY 2, 2007

The Higgins' apartment was strangely quiet. Margaret sat on the sofa, trying to study, glancing at her mobile every so often. Bess always checked in every day she was gone. This was her fifth long haul, and she would be fine. Margaret sighed. The only other sounds were the ticking of the clock and the squeaking of Mary's pencil. With the flurry of final examinations, every spare moment was spent either working or studying. There shouldn't have been time to worry or ruminate.

After the failed strike, Ben Boucher was still out of work and barely sober. Nick was constantly on edge. Mary and Bess were determined to keep life as normal as possible for their cousins, even if it meant working themselves to death. Margaret checked her mobile and sighed again.

"We should take a break," Mary said. She set aside her flashcards. "I can make tea."

"No, thanks." Margaret managed a thin smile. "The children will be home soon, and we can't study when they're here."

"What's bothering you then?" Mary asked, flipping through her notes without reading them. Margaret tried to conjure up a decent answer. Mary was quieter and more thoughtful than Bess, but she was still a Higgins, and Margaret didn't want to think about what she really meant. It really was just like a Higgins to ask all the wrong questions when they already knew the answers.

"Life's not fair," Margaret finally said. "Bessie and your dad are both working so you can scrape by, and your uncle's nowhere at all. Who's got to keep the kids, yeah? You have school. It's all a mad mess."

"You're still angry at Bess." Mary looked up. Her eyes were sad. "No one forced her to do this."

"I could think of a person or two," Margaret said, her voice hard.

"Do you want to talk about John now?"

"Absolutely not."

Ruddy Higgins witchery.

♥

Nick Higgins didn't have the foggiest clue where Ben Boucher went these days. After the riot at Marlborough Shipping, Ben was in and out of their apartment and the bars. Nick's temper boiled every time he had to collect the useless bastard. Ben was also under investigation by Child Protective Services, ever since Rosa Boucher disappeared, and a neighbor found baby Pete wandering down the street in nothing but a diaper. Bess didn't have to call them after all. God only knew why the state granted temporary custody to Nick, and the extra mouths to feed, the extra noise, and the stress was pushing him to his breaking point. He hadn't seen or heard from Ben since the kids moved in two weeks ago.

"This is stupid, and you know it."

Nick glanced over at his oldest nephew. Timmy Boucher was too young for this. "He's your family, boy," Nick grumbled. "You remember that."

"He's a loser, and I'm so sick of this. I want to go home."

"What's your hurry?"

"Nothing." Timmy slouched in the front seat. "Margaret promised to help me with my homework."

"You care about homework now, do you? Or maybe you care more about her pretty face."

Timmy blushed and Nick allowed himself a grim chuckle. "We keep looking until we find your dad."

The boy fell silent, and Nick gripped the steering wheel a little tighter. He still couldn't think about Margaret Hale without a mixture of anger and shame adding to his pit of guilt. All his hopes for the strike had been crushed because of her. His carefully laid plans tumbled down around him the moment she went to Marlborough Shipping and got herself shot. Nick had thought he could force John Thornton into a corner, but he hadn't counted on Margaret being as much in love with John as he was with her.

"Try down by the river." Timmy said. "There's an old garage where people go to get high all the time."

"Do I want to know how you know that?"

Timmy shrugged. "Everyone knows, Uncle Nick."

Nick turned the car towards the river. He didn't miss having teenagers. If Ben couldn't get himself together, he would have another set of them. He wasn't sure he could keep his own shit together if it came to that.

♥

When Nick finally found Ben in the garage down by the river, he knew the bastard was dead. The man's body was an unnatural shade of pink, and his glazed-over eyes stared at nothing. Nick shuddered, covering his mouth against the urge to vomit. The son of a bitch had locked himself in the abandoned garage, sat by the exhaust pipe of his car, and suffocated himself. Nick shoved the man's heavy, worthless body aside, swiped angrily at his tears, and tried to calm his stomach.

This was a coward's way out.

He pulled out his phone and dialed the police, his mind reeling. Timmy hovered outside the door, and Nick tossed the cell phone aside, grabbing the boy before he stumbled into the shop.

The kid shouldn't see this. "Get back in the car."

"Uncle Nick, why's he pink like that?" Timmy's eyes widened in horror, and he scrambled backwards. "Is he dead? Is Dad dead?"

Nick half carried, half dragged Timmy back to the car. The boy fought back, screaming and lashing out in sudden anger, tears pouring down his face. "I want to go back. Let me go!"

"You'll be all right," Nick muttered under his breath. He wrestled him against the car and hugged him tight as the kid sobbed. "It's going to be okay, son."

The words felt thick and heavy.

Because Timmy Boucher *was* his son now.

Three days later, Mr. Hale hung up the phone feeling a new weight settle on his shoulders. Ben Boucher was dead. He glanced at his sleeping daughter. Margaret had returned home, tired and triumphant after completing her examinations and promptly collapsed in a heap on the sofa. He wouldn't trouble her with this yet. He walked quietly to the kitchen and put on water for tea. He set out biscuits, grimacing when he tasted one—rather stale.

Margaret would feel the loss of the surly truck driver deeply. She had a tender heart and had taken all the Boucher children into it. Mr. Hale returned to the sitting room and set the tea tray quietly on the side table, moving the shoe box of her photographs aside. He poured himself a cup of tea and sat in his chair, watching his daughter sleep.

Trouble would keep.

It always did.

Chapter 26

The phone rang, jolting Margaret awake from a dreamless sleep. She rubbed her eyes and picked up her mobile. "Eds?"

"Oh, Migs, darling, I've so much to tell you."

"It's six in the morning." Margaret slumped against her pillow. The sky was a grayish pink, hinting at the coming dawn. "What's so bloody important it couldn't wait until a decent hour?"

"I'm engaged," Edith squealed. "I'm sorry, I know it's early, but James just asked me, and I had to tell you. I know you're not much of a morning person, darling, but—"

"Eds, breathe."

Her cousin took a gulping breath and continued her squealing. Margaret blinked slowly. Her eyes felt like sandpaper. She'd fallen asleep crying again. She couldn't remember the reason why this time, but reasons to cry seemed to fall like rain. She'd lost track of them all.

"Dearest, are you even listening?"

"Yes, I'm here."

"So, will you?"

"Will I what?"

"You weren't listening. I want you to be my maid of honor. Do say you will. It would be perfection."

Margaret took a resigned breath. "Yes, of course, I will."

"Oh Migs, now everything is settled. I can't wait for June."

"June?" Margaret sat up. "You're getting married in June?"

"You really weren't listening, were you?"

"June is next month."

"Yes," Edith said, exasperated. "You don't think I'd wait a whole year, do you? How droll. It's all been planned for ages anyways. It was simply a matter of waiting for James to find the courage to ask me."

"Bloody hell," Margaret whispered. But she wasn't surprised. This was Edith Shaw. She'd probably begun planning her wedding the day after James Lennox first asked her out. *Poor James.*

Edith was still chattering away.

"Eds," Margaret interrupted. "I'm happy for you. Truly. But I want to go back to bed. I'll ring in a bit."

She hung up and sat silently for a moment before she slipped out of bed, her gran's old quilt tucked around her. She made her way downstairs and settled on the couch, staring absently at John's chair. The sun rose too quickly, flooding her eyes with blinding, rosy-golden light.

FRIDAY: MAY 18, 2007

John sat in his truck, drumming his fingers on the steering wheel. He glanced at his watch. Five more minutes and he'd be late. He was parked a block from the Hales' house. He hadn't seen Margaret since that awful day after her accident, and he wasn't sure he wanted to see her now. She clearly didn't want to see him, and there was no reason for her to be there, especially on his usual night for meeting with Mr. Hale.

She had a job, and friends, and—

John sighed in frustration at his own stupidity. He hated shit like this. It turned him around in circles, just like her. He muttered a curse, put his truck in gear, and pulled away.

Margaret stared stupidly at the three suitcases, all packed to the brim. It was simply ridiculous. A sane person didn't need three suitcases' worth of clothing for a little trip. She stood, jerked one open, and began removing the contents. When she finally pared down her belongings to fill only one suitcase and her rucksack, she felt better. Her Aunt Shaw would want her to stay in England for a while, but Margaret would fight back by wearing the same eight outfits for four weeks straight if need be.

A light knock came at her door. "Are you ready, my dear?" Her father stepped inside her room.

She squared her shoulders and nodded.

"Only one bag?" Mr. Hale eyed the suitcase and the rucksack in the middle of the floor.

"Yes." She raised her chin and began to maneuver the large suitcase through the door, her father following behind with her rucksack.

"Are you sure you don't want a ride to the airport?"

"Quite sure," she said, straining with the effort of lifting the heavy bag down the stairs. "Mary will take me and—" she stopped mid-sentence at two familiar sharp knocks.

The front door opened, and John Thornton stepped inside.

"Hello, John," Mr. Hale said brightly. "I'll be a moment after I see Margaret off."

John nodded and glanced at her. His face darkened into a hard frown. They hadn't seen each other in months. There was an awkward pause, then he stepped forward and took her bag in one hand, lifted it down over the railing, and set it outside on the porch.

She hurried past him into the living room. She still needed to find her passport before she left. She rummaged through the drawers of the small secretary, unable to concentrate as he came in behind her.

"Where are you going?"

"Greece." She didn't turn around. Her hands kept shifting stacks of envelopes, bills, and bits of scrap paper. "For a wedding."

"Do you have everything, my dear?" Mr. Hale entered the room, patting his jacket pockets.

She nodded and held up her passport and polaroid camera. Her father sat in his chair and began loading his pipe, humming like he always did when he was distracted. "I'm afraid you'll be my only company this summer, John. We must manage as best we can, I suppose."

"Dad, I won't be gone all summer," she said for the tenth time.

"We both know the moment your Aunt Shaw gets hold of you she'll be hard pressed to let you go again."

"It's just a wedding."

"In Greece." John's tone would've made her smile if everything was the way it had been before he'd told her he loved her.

"Apparently Corfu is all the rage." Her face burned as she felt his silent scrutiny, but she couldn't look at him. "My cousin Edith is marrying James Lennox. He's Henry's brother."

"Do you remember Henry Lennox, John?"

"I remember him."

Margaret's eyes flew to John's face. He was still watching her. Why was he here after everything she'd said, after all the awful things she'd done? She felt a sudden pang of desperation to do something.

"Can I take your picture?"

The words hung in the air. She turned quickly to her father, adding, "Please, Dad?" She was rambling. "Just to have while I'm away. It'll be a little piece of home, so I won't miss you as much." She glanced back at John. "Please."

"Of course. Shall I stand somewhere or sit here?" her father asked.

"I'd like one of the both of you," she said slowly, nodding to include John, "just as you are there."

Mr. Hale smoothed his hair and his clothes. She smiled. "Dad, go on talking as you would, yeah?"

Of course, the two men remained awkwardly silent and stiff. She sighed, stepped closer, and gently positioned her father, smoothing his jacket. She brushed his forehead with a sudden kiss, whispering, "I'll miss you."

When she turned towards John, he immediately looked away. She stepped closer, carefully removed his hat, and held it out until he took it. He tossed it on the floor and ran a hand through his hair, a bit in the back standing straight up. She wanted to smooth it down but didn't dare. She wanted to ask for forgiveness but instead stepped back to a good distance and snapped their picture. Outside, a horn honked twice, and she fled the room.

Once she'd settled herself comfortably in the back of the cab, Margaret tucked the picture into her passport. When she turned in her seat to look back at the house, she sucked in a small breath. John stood in the open doorway, watching her go.

SUNDAY: JUNE 17, 2007

Margaret wrenched the fake bejeweled flower pin from her hair, wincing as she accidentally pulled out several strands of hair. *Ridiculous.* She tossed it aside and sat heavily in a corner of the veranda. Edith and

James danced with the wedding guests. The alcohol flowed freely, increasing the laughter and well wishes the longer the evening continued. She watched the festivities like a theatrical.

"You're allowed to enjoy yourself." Henry Lennox sat next to her, a glass of champagne in each hand. He held one out, and she was obliged to take it.

"I'm trying," she said. She tried not to gag on the sickly-sweet taste. Her memory of New Year's Eve would always taste of champagne, whiskey, and peppermint. "I don't like weddings."

"Is that why you're hiding?" he asked. His tone was hard but not rude. "Edith won't be pleased."

Margaret didn't blame him. They hadn't spoken since he'd left her at the Lancasters' party with John Thornton. But Henry was trying to be nice, in his own British way.

"I won't run off, if that's what you're worried about," she said.

He had the decency to look embarrassed. "About that—"

"Never mind," she interrupted and stood, handing him her glass. "Excuse me, please."

She wandered through the dancing crowd and allowed herself to be swept into a salsa by a handsome usher who'd flirted with her earlier, dancing until she couldn't feel her feet. She left without telling anyone and took a cab back to the hotel. She collapsed onto the curb and was promptly sick in the grass. Sick with weariness, sick from the travel, sick of herself.

She wanted to go home, and feel comfortable again, but even her father's house didn't feel quite right anymore. All she wanted now was a cup of tea, a long hot shower, and to crawl into her own bed, where no one would bother her or ask her questions or need her. Margaret stumbled up to her hotel room, exhausted and sad, trying to forget how

John Thornton had tasted when she kissed him.

FRIDAY: JUNE 29, 2007

John popped the hood on Mr. Hale's car and listened to the engine for a moment. The thing was a piece of junk. He took off his hat and scratched his head. The problem sounded like a spark plug or an ignition coil, or both. From the looks of things, the coils were on the back side of the engine. He sighed. This model was always a pain in the ass to repair. He swore, spat, and checked his watch. It would take an hour or two, but he owed Mr. Hale. John still came for tutoring and did odd jobs around the house in exchange. The old-fashioned arrangement suited both men.

He grabbed his tool bag from the bed of his truck and stripped off his shirt. He set his hand-held radio in the grass and turned it up loud as he got to work. But three hours later, he was still fiddling with the damn engine. He sat up, grabbed a rag, and wiped his hands. The sun was starting to sink but it was still muggy and hot. He turned his hat around backwards and inched under the front of the car. His hands were too big for this job. He jerked back as a sharp piece of metal bit into him.

"Shit." He scooted out from under the car, walked to his truck, and rummaged in his glove box until he found an adhesive bandage and slapped it over the small cut. He'd clean it later.

The front door opened, and Mr. Hale came out, smiling. "Any more progress?"

But before John could answer, Mr. Hale hurried past him. "Good heavens, Margaret, what on earth are you doing here?"

John's head snapped around. Margaret sat in a rumpled heap on the curb, her bag and backpack next to her. She looked up at the sound of her father's voice. When she saw John, her face turned gray and she doubled over, retching violently into the grass.

"Foolish girl." Mr. Hale knelt, pulled a handkerchief from his pocket, and gently wiped her forehead and her mouth. "Why didn't you let me know you were coming home so soon? Does your aunt know?"

"No."

"Margaret."

"I don't care if it was rude." She laughed bitterly. "I'm an adult, and I wanted to come home."

He helped her to her feet. "Can you walk?"

"Don't be silly. I'm fine."

"Let's get you inside, and I'll make a cuppa."

John grabbed her bags and followed without a word. He left the suitcase by the stairs and ducked into the kitchen, setting the backpack on the table.

"Thank you." Mr. Hale set the kettle on the stove. "Poor Margaret. There's no stopping her once she makes up her mind."

"Is she okay?"

"She's not good with air travel. Never has been, but she'll be fine in a day or two." He handed John a glass of water. "How's the car?"

"It'll hang on for a while."

"Thank goodness for that."

That night, John slept soundly for the first time since Margaret had left, almost four weeks ago.

Chapter 27

John stared at the police report on his desk, the lines blurring together as he read it for the third time. The truck had lost traction on the icy Canadian road, the trailer had shifted too far to one side, causing the whole vehicle to tip. The cab slammed into a line of trees and the engine ignited on impact. It took hours to put the fire out. The driver was helicoptered to the closest hospital.

"She's dead?" he asked, even though his gut told him the answer. He still hadn't read the last page of the report. He didn't want to.

"Dead on arrival." Williams stood leaning against the counter where the coffee machine sat and shook his head. "She didn't have a chance."

"Shit."

"One more thing."

John looked up, bracing himself.

"The preliminary autopsy report said her blood alcohol was over the limit. Driving over her time too."

John rubbed his eyes with one hand. He'd lost his first driver in his second year in the trucking business. Mac Muller's semi-truck had flipped on the interstate and another car had plowed into the cab, unable to stop in time. John had delivered the news to Mac's wife and kids himself. He would never forget that day. After Mac's death, he'd purchased the best cabs available with the widest sleeping berths, enforced strict hours on and off the road, penalizing his drivers heavily for working even one second longer than the law allowed.

But now it had happened again.

"The police need a family member to confirm identity." Williams handed John a cup of coffee. "Her body will arrive at the hospital morgue today or tomorrow."

John took a burning gulp and nodded. "Call Slick."

Williams hesitated. "What about his shipment from Texas?"

"His daughter is dead. Get him home."

"I'll take care of it."

SATURDAY: OCTOBER 20, 2007

Margaret stood in the basement of St. Anne's Hospital and stared at a pair of cold, brushed metal doors. She held Mary Higgins' hand in a viselike grip. She couldn't make sense of this madness.

"I can't, Margaret." It would've been a wail except Mary barely made enough sound to be heard. She clutched Margaret's hand and arm tighter. "I can't do this."

"I know." Margaret felt dead inside. Nick should've been here to do this grisly task for his daughter. But he was inconsolable, drowning his grief in alcohol. She held onto Mary until the younger girl found the courage to push open the morgue door.

The room was chilly and smelled strongly of lab chemicals and cleaner, an oddly sanitized smell trying to mask the horror of death that seeped into everything. The doctor explained what was expected. A police officer waited in the hall to take Mary's statement. She trembled and shrunk back into Margaret when she saw the table where her sister's body lay concealed under a sheet.

"Whenever you're ready," the coroner said. "It won't take long."

Mary closed her eyes, squeezing Margaret's hand.

"Deep breaths," Margaret murmured. "I'm here." She didn't want to see Bess like this, but she couldn't leave Mary to do this alone.

Finally, Mary nodded. The coroner pulled back the sheet until the body's head was visible, and Mary choked out a terrible sob.

Elizabeth Lorraine Higgins, age twenty-three, died of blunt force trauma and smoke inhalation. There were cuts and bruises and blackened skin. It was a violent death. Margaret knew that, despite the vague details the officer shared. Her heart stuttered when she saw the relaxed look on her friend's face. How could Bess look like that and be gone? But she wasn't there anymore.

The only thing left was pain.

The body on the table was just a fading echo.

Margaret took Mary home. She stood and looked helplessly at the small crowd of Boucher children waiting for them. "Where's Nick?"

Timmy shrugged. "He left."

"Right." Margaret took the two youngest children by the hand. "Timmy, make Mary something hot to drink. Laney and Rob, make us all ham and cheese sandwiches."

"What about me?" Lilly asked.

"You, Lilly-love, will help me put the babies to bed."

"I'm not a baby," Joey protested. "Pete's the baby."

"Of course, he is. But you must help him get to sleep."

Once the younger children were cleaned, fed, and tucked into bed,

Margaret sat with Mary long into the night, waiting for a call from Nick. Timmy grumbled his way through his homework. Rob didn't breathe a word to anyone, bouncing a tennis ball against the kitchen wall until Timmy yelled at him to stop. The intercom finally sounded, and Mary got up, buzzing in whoever it was. Margaret held her breath. Mary waited at the door until the knock came. She let in the police officer and, to Margaret's surprise, Mr. Hale. The two men were half-carrying a very drunk Nick Higgins. Mary cried silently as the officer spoke. "I'm sorry to bring him like this."

Mary only nodded.

"Miss Higgins, are you sure it's all right to leave him here?" The officer looked around. "I can keep him at the station until he sobers up if you'd prefer."

"We'll be fine." Margaret was surprised to hear her own voice speaking so calmly. "Would you put him in the back bedroom, please?"

When the policeman had gone, Margaret sank into her father's warm hug. "We found him at the tracks on the north side of town," he explained. "I'll stay the night, if you don't object, Mary. I'll look after your father. You and Margaret can sleep at our house tonight."

"But the kids?" Mary asked, her face etched with concern.

"Laney and Lilly will manage." Margaret laid a hand on Mary's arm. "We can't all stay here. There isn't room."

Mary reluctantly agreed. They didn't talk while Margaret drove or when she quietly made up the guest bed.

"I'll never forgive my dad for this," Mary finally said, staring at the cup of tea Margaret had made for her.

Margaret nodded, her own heart almost bursting with the heavy weight of anger and loss.

"How do you do it?" Mary asked, her voice barely a whisper. "How do you wake up the next day and keep living?"

"You carry on because you must." Margaret sighed, feeling old and weary. "Because life doesn't wait for anyone to feel like living again. It marches on and you must march with it."

Margaret sat with Mary until her friend fell asleep, then slipped into her bedroom, pulled her gran's quilt from the foot of her bed, and shuffled back downstairs. She wrapped the blanket around herself, breathing in the memories of happier times. She held her box of photos in her lap, rummaging through them, lingering over her favorite picture of Bess. She'd taken it right before last Christmas, the snow falling in wet, chunky blurs. Carefree laughter lit Bess's whole face in a bright smile.

"Bessie."

Margaret pressed the picture to her chest and wept.

SATURDAY: OCTOBER 27, 2007

It took a week for the body of Bess Higgins to be released for the funeral. Mr. Hale and Margaret were hard pressed to keep Nick sober and lucid, while balancing all the other legal details. Margaret kept Mary and the Boucher children busy and away from the turmoil at home.

They buried Bess on a rainy day under an old oak tree that stood on top of the hill in St. Michael's Cemetery. Mr. Hale stayed close to Nick, lending the truck driver quiet strength. It wasn't a fancy funeral, and the service was as brief as possible. The Boucher children were tired and cross after the whole affair, and they left as soon as it was over.

"Margaret?"

"You go on, Dad."

Mr. Hale nodded.

She lingered long after he left and wandered over the muddy paths between the headstones, the chilly wind dragging across her face and hair. She didn't understand how her best friend could be gone. Her mind grasped the bare facts, but her heart refused to stop hoping and waiting. Perhaps her mobile would ring, perhaps it would all be an awful joke. Margaret choked back a sob. She wanted to go back, to be warm again, and simply live without having to try so bloody hard all the time.

She walked around a curve in the path at the bottom of the hill and stopped. Even though his back was to her, she recognized John as soon as she spotted him. A sharp ugly anger blazed in her stomach. He'd given Bess the job that killed her, and for what? He could've stopped this, but he didn't.

John turned slowly and looked at her.

"Hello," she said.

It was disgustingly civil. His face hardened into its usual expression as she marched closer. She glanced at the black headstone in front of them and blinked. "That's your name."

"It's my dad." He shoved his hands into his pockets. He was wearing a black suit.

"Going to a funeral, are you? I've already been to one." Her words were acid. "Bessie Higgins died. We buried her today."

"I know. I came to pay my respects."

"Did you?"

"I know you think I'm incapable of human decency," he said, ice in his voice, "but I'm sorry for what happened."

"You're sorry?" Her voice almost broke. For what happened to Bess? Or to them? She stared at his father's gravestone, trying to harden herself against his simple apology. "For a drunk's drunk daughter?"

"Yes."

"I think I hate you." She blinked away her tears, her conscience stinging even as she spoke the awful words. His whole body tensed and guilt flooded into the empty hole inside her.

"Do what you want, Maggie." The low rumble of his voice made her skin prickle uncomfortably and the tired defeat written on his face caught the breath in her throat.

He crouched down and brushed away a few fallen leaves from a smaller headstone next to his father's grave. It bore only a single word.

Taylor.

This headstone must be for Frannie.

Margaret shivered, suddenly ashamed and angry with herself. This wasn't his fault, and she was being terribly cruel. She couldn't hate him, and even if she could, it wouldn't change anything. "I shouldn't have said that," she said softly. "You don't deserve it, especially not from me."

Some strange impulse made her lean down and press a soft, lingering kiss to his cheek. The spicy smell of his aftershave and shampoo filled her nose. "I'm sorry, John."

She quickly turned away, heat crawling up her face and neck. Half-way up the hill, she paused and looked back. He was watching her. The setting sun, all brilliant gold and flaming light, turned the gravestones and John Thornton into dark silhouettes. It was haunting and beautiful. She swallowed hard, absently brushing her fingers over her lips that still remembered the feeling of his skin.

Chapter 28

John spent most of Christmas Day at his office, buried under stacks of papers—filing, sorting, shredding, and other mind-numbing office work Bess Higgins once did for him. He still hadn't found the time to replace her and that meant he spent a few days every month wading through menial paperwork. Today it was a good excuse to avoid the holiday festivities. His mother would show up looking for him soon enough. On top of everything else, ugly rumors in the business world were blazing across the country. Things were not looking good for the economy.

He sighed and poured himself more coffee. The day was almost over. The last task was writing personnel reports for his truckers. When he reached Nick Higgins' file he stopped, his temper simmering. The man was a piece of work, and John had never been more tempted to fire him. He swore and threw the file aside.

Nothing good came from Slick Nick and his games. He'd worked for the Depot since the business began, and John couldn't toss him out. Not so soon after losing Bess. He decided to put Nick on long hauls for the rest of his miserable life and leave it at that. If he quit, so be it. That should keep the meddling down to a minimum, and John's conscience clear.

He wrote out the report as fast as possible, shoving the file into the drawers with the others when he finished. Sometimes he hated giving a damn. Since meeting Margaret, he cared a lot more than he used to. He stood and picked up the forest of cups littering his desk, carried them to the break room, and dumped them into the utility sink. He swiped at his cheek, the skin prickling with the memory of Margaret's lips. He'd wanted to kiss her back. He *should've* kissed her back.

But that didn't work out well the last time he tried it.

I don't want your twisted version of affection, and I never will.

He shoved the biting memory away and tried to focus on something else. But his mind refused to listen.

"You're a damn fool, John Thornton."

SUNDAY: DECEMBER 30, 2007

"Got any plans for New Years Eve?" Nick asked. Margaret and Mary were packing away the remaining Christmas decorations at the apartment. His daughter paused, a strand of lights loosely wound around her neck, trying to sort out the bad bulbs. He sat staring at his trembling hands. Mr. Hale was trying to help him get sober again. Maybe it was working. Maybe it wasn't.

"I'm talking to you, Margaret," he said, too sharp, too harsh.

"Have I got plans for New Year's?" Margaret shrugged. "Not unless you count studying for a maths examination."

"What about the Lancasters' party?"

"I'm not too fond of parties like that," she said, dropping her eyes. "I never have been."

"You seemed pretty damn fond of it last year." Nick shot a defiant look at her, bitterness lacing his words. He'd thought he knew how to play this game, but it had all been wrong. His Bess was gone now too.

"If you're going to sleep with the enemy, you might as well go ahead and do it, girl, and leave us be."

"Dad," Mary said sharply.

Margaret's face turned ghostly white. "I don't know what you're talking about."

Her hurt expression crawled over Nick's skin, and he shoved himself away from the table. He should've kept his stupid mouth shut. He should've known better than to trust her. He should've done a lot of things. But it was too late now.

TUESDAY: JANUARY 1, 2008

Margaret stared at her bedroom ceiling, listening to the *tick, tick, tick* of her clock. There were still random pops and shrill bursts of fireworks ushering in the New Year, even at two in the morning. She'd allowed herself to be talked into a work party, and Terry Hopkins had tried to steal a midnight kiss. She'd slapped him hard and didn't apologize.

"Bloody wanker," she muttered. She hoped he wouldn't tell Dr. Martin or try to get her fired. It wasn't even a nice kiss.

She rolled over onto her stomach and pulled out her new mobile, trying to distract herself. It was a late Christmas gift from Dale Dixon. She'd refused to set it up, a small, petty revenge against his continued attempts to be her friend. She tossed it onto her bedside table, trying to ignore the sudden rush of memories.

—Strong hands, rasping breath, soft hair, rough stubble, and a warm mouth tasting of champagne, whiskey, and peppermint.

I'm just getting warmed up.

Margaret swallowed hard and pulled her quilt over her head.

—Angry shouts, red faces, gunshots, white pain, a warm voice, and strong arms.

I've got you.

She shook herself, flicked off the lamp, and stared into the dark.

—Burning blue eyes, a tired smile turned to a sharp scowl, hope crashing, and a broken, gruff voice.

Maggie, I love you.

MONDAY: JANUARY 7, 2008

John picked the newspaper off the front porch, sat down in the open doorway, and glanced through the headlines, oblivious to the biting wind whipping around him. He frowned as he skimmed the front page. The largest mortgage lender in the country had gone under, and the media was predicting the worst decline in the economy since the Depression. If big businesses weren't immune, others would suffer, especially small independents with no overhead and no government buyouts. He swore softly.

"What are you doing out here?" His mother marched up behind him. "You'll catch your death of cold."

He stood and closed the front door, finally feeling the chill on his skin. "Morning, Mother." He tucked the paper under his arm and walked to the kitchen to have his coffee.

"What's happened?"

"Don't worry about it."

She raised her eyebrows, plucked the paper from under his arm, and sat at the kitchen table. He rolled his eyes. He knew better than to try and pretend for his mother's sake.

"It's not doomsday," she said, after reading over the article.

"No." He took a swallow of coffee and spread the paper out on the counter, eyeing the stocks column. "But it's trouble for everyone."

Especially us. The truth hung between them, unspoken, but there, all the same.

"How much trouble?" his mother finally asked.

"I don't know," he said truthfully. "We're struggling as it is, with the aftershocks from the strike. We lost a lot of contracts when we couldn't catch up. The Depot is barely keeping her head above water."

"If you're smart about it, you might consider using some of your capital to trade on stocks."

"I don't have free capital. It's all tied up in the new trucks."

"What about the payroll?"

"No," he said coldly. "I won't risk other people's money."

"Is it really so risky?"

"If I lose the payroll, I'm no better than the dirty cheats Dad rubbed shoulders with. I won't take what isn't mine and lose it. I've lost too much as it is."

"Could you trim the fleet then? Nick Higgins deserves to be cut loose. Wolf too. They're both union men. Their meddling could very well be what breaks the Depot if you're too stubborn—"

"I said no," he interrupted. He stood and finished his coffee, chewing on the grounds. "I won't throw my drivers and their families under the bus to save anyone, least of all me."

"Even if they tried their hardest to pull you under for being better than them?"

"If I fail, I'll fail honestly." He grabbed his hat, keys, and jacket. "I'm not done fighting yet, and I don't plan on losing."

"No one ever does."

He kissed her cheek. "Don't keep dinner for me."

TUESDAY: JANUARY 15, 2008

For her twenty-first birthday, Margaret invited the Higgins and the Bouchers for a simple meal. Her father fixed a roast and a mountain of potatoes. Mary baked a cake, surprising her with it after dinner was cleared away. "I've not had a birthday cake in ages. I'm rubbish at baking. You shouldn't have."

"Not everyone does what you think they should do, Marg," Mary teased, cutting large slices of cake for the children. "I was happy to make it for you."

"I helped," added Lilly.

"Would anyone like tea with their cake?" Mr. Hale asked.

Nick and Mary nodded, shooing the children from the room.

"Put on coffee too, Dad. We've got that new machine I bought you for Christmas. You should use it for someone other than John." Margaret blushed when Mary nudged her under the table with her foot.

"I'll take that coffee." Nick gave Margaret an embarrassed nod, running his hands over his jeans. "We got you something." He pulled out a small brown package and pushed it across the table. "Thought you could use more."

"You shouldn't have spent the money. The children—"

"Just say thank you." he interrupted gruffly. "I wanted to."

"Thank you." Margaret opened the box of Polaroid film and smiled. "You're both very good to me and I don't deserve it. I know things have been a bit tight."

"Don't trouble yourself about that. We do all right."

"How are things, Nicholas?" Mr. Hale sat at the table and began to stuff his pipe.

Margaret stood, tending to the forgotten tea and coffee. Her father's easy tone reminded her of his days as a vicar in England. He still had the same manner about him whenever a person talked of their worries and cares.

"Not good, Mr. Richard. I've six kids to feed and no help but Mary and Timmy. They've got school, and I'll not pull them out unless I have no other choice."

"Dad—" Mary tried to speak but he shushed her.

"Bess and I made enough money trucking, but with her gone and me driving for weeks on end—" he shrugged. "Those kids need more than I can give them."

"Aren't there local deliveries you could do instead of long hauls?" Margaret asked. She set down his coffee.

"That's a powerful coveted job. No one in town would give it to me," Nick said. "Not without a sparkling recommendation, and that's assuming there's an opening. That's about as rare as a unicorn in this crumbling economy."

"Why is that?" Mr. Hale asked. "You're an experienced driver. Surely, if you explained your situation, John would give you the chance or a recommendation, at the very least."

Nick chuckled darkly and shook his head. "Not after my involvement in the strike. I'm lucky he didn't fire my ass, as it is. Master has me driving long hauls nonstop. It's not looking like I'll get anything better. I was thinking of taking other work, maybe in a factory or something like that, but none of them seem too interested in me either." Nick scratched his chin. "I could always move further south. Living costs are cheaper. Maybe take a job with a tow company."

"Oh, no you couldn't," Margaret said. "The children need stability after their father's death."

"Those kids need food, and they need me around." Nick pushed his coffee aside. "What else can I do?"

Margaret sipped her tea slowly, choosing her words carefully. "Talk to John. Ask him plainly, and I know he'll help you."

"You sure about that?"

She hesitated and smiled softly, surprised by her own answer. "I am."

Chapter 29

The next morning Nick stood in the Depot office, hands in his pockets, waiting. He eyed Bess's old desk in the far corner, ignoring the grating sting of guilt and tears. He needed a drink. He crossed his arms, fingers fidgeting. When John finally showed up, it was almost four.

"Slick, what the hell are you doing here?" He stripped off his jacket and tossed it on his chair.

Nick took a deep breath. "I need a favor."

"That's rich coming from you, after what you did."

"I've got no other choice."

"You had a choice before you convinced Milton truckers to strike."

Both men stared at each other for a heavy moment. Nick finally dropped his eyes, which was as good as admitting his involvement in the strike, but he had nothing left.

"That's what I thought." John pointed to the open door. "Get out."

"I'm not asking for me." Nick kept his eyes on the cement floor. "I've got kids to feed."

"What kids?"

"My nieces and nephews. I need work here in Milton. I don't have to drive trucks; any work will do. No one else in this city will take me."

John narrowed his eyes. "I fired a third of my best drivers because of you and your damn union. The answer is no."

"Yeah." Nick shook his head, defeated and angry. It didn't matter what Margaret said. John Thornton would never help him. "I knew better than to ask. A fool woman told me to ask you anyway."

"Tell your woman to mind her own damn business and stop wasting my time," John growled, "and yours. And if I ever see you in this office again, for anything other than a long haul, I'll fire you."

Nick stalked out, swearing under his breath. He could've told John it was Margaret who sent him, but he wasn't sure the younger man would take the bait anymore. Nick was out of options.

John watched Nick Higgins amble across the snowy yard towards his beat-up car. He had a gut feeling that Margaret had sent the old trucker to see him, but Nick hadn't mentioned her by name. He was slippery as an eel and just as clever. If he had an advantage, he would use it. Except now John wasn't so sure. He opened his filing cabinet and pulled out the personnel file on Bess Higgins, flipping through it slowly. She'd been at the same high school as Frannie in South Carolina, before moving to Milton, but he barely remembered her then. He read a few lines and frowned. He pushed the file aside and picked up the telephone.

FRIDAY: JANUARY 18, 2008

Nick yanked open the apartment door and glared. He looked even older and more worn out since they last spoke, almost as old and tired as John felt every damn morning.

"I should slam this door in your face," Nick said.

"You should, and I won't stop you."

"What do you want?"

"May I come in?"

Nick grunted and reluctantly moved aside.

John took off his hat and stepped into the room, his eyes sweeping over every detail of the cramped space. The two youngest Bouchers sat on the couch, watching TV, while two others struggled with homework at the rickety table, overseen by Mary. A lanky teen boy slouched on the floor, staring at his phone, headphones in. That would be the oldest, according to the social worker. "Are these your kids?"

"They're mine now, thanks to the state of Connecticut." Nick folded his arms. "You didn't believe me."

"No," John said. "But I called your social worker yesterday. She told me all I needed to know."

"Ben is dead, his wife is gone, and I'm sorry for it. That doesn't change hungry mouths and not enough adults to go around. Mary doesn't complain, but she'll have to quit school to care for the younger three."

John nodded. "She told me."

"Did she now?" Nick looked surprised. "When?"

"I have a proposal, if you're interested."

"What's that?"

"You can have the office job and drive the local deliveries. I pulled a few strings and got Clay a position more to his wife's liking. It's the best I can do to keep you closer to home for these kids, and keep the older ones in school, where they belong."

"I can't afford a pay cut." Nick was stubborn, and John didn't blame him for his bitterness, not after all the shit they'd been through.

"I also came to offer that one a job." John pointed at the oldest Boucher boy, who was eavesdropping. "What's your name, kid?"

"Timmy."

"How old are you?"

"Stand up, boy," Nick grumbled. "He's nearly seventeen."

The kid clambered to his feet. He looked the picture of Ben Boucher, but with darker hair, and his mother's darker skin and brown eyes.

"You need a job," John said. "And I'm offering you one."

"So what?"

"You're the man of your family now." John crossed his arms and studied the sullen boy. The despair he saw in Timmy's face reminded him of how he felt, almost fourteen years ago, when his own dad died. "Like it or not, it's your job to see they have food, clothes, and a place to sleep."

"You don't want me. I'm a Boucher, and we're trouble."

"I knew your dad." John pinned him with a hard stare. "He was an asshole. Doesn't mean you have to be."

Timmy rolled his eyes, but he flinched as John stepped closer. "Look, kid, I've stood in your shoes. No one is going to fix this for you, except you. It's not fair, but it is what it is." John turned back to Nick. "I figure between you and Tim, there'll be enough to go around so Mary can graduate."

"Can I think about it first?" Timmy muttered.

"You won't need to think about it, boy," Nick said. "We'll take it. And what's more, I'll thank you, and that's a lot from me."

"And this is a lot from me." John held out his hand. Nick shook it with a wry smile. When he offered his hand to Timmy, the boy hesitated before giving him a firm shake. The kid had spirit, and if he could put honest fight back in him, Timmy Boucher might have a chance.

"Mind you come sharp to your time, kid. If I catch you making trouble for me, you're done."

The boy nodded.

"Same goes for you, Slick." John turned. "I'm not wasting time with either of you."

"Do you think we can manage to get along?" Nick asked. "Me being trouble and you being a hard ass?"

"We don't have to get along to get work done." John nodded to Mary and tugged on his hat. "I'll see myself out."

Nick opened the door for him, and John hesitated. "Did Margaret tell you to talk to me?"

The older man smirked. "Maybe she did."

"You could've said something before."

"And you'd have been a bit more decent?"

"Maybe," John admitted. "It's not like you to miss an opportunity to get the upper hand."

"People aren't cards to play with. I've learned that the hard way." Nick chuckled. "Miss Margaret's a good card though, ain't she?"

John skewered him with a dark look. "No more games, Slick."

"Don't worry, Master. I'll be keeping my games at home."

"You do that."

♥

Later that evening, Margaret brought dinner to the Higgins' apartment. She picked up the baby and entertained him so Mary could study for exams, losing herself in his chubby sweetness. She enjoyed chasing the younger ones to bed, with hugs and kisses all around. Once that was done, she checked their rucksacks for the next day and joined Mary at the kitchen table. "There." She leaned her elbows on the table with a happy sigh. "All done."

"Thank you and thanks for the food."

"I'm happy to help. How is everything?"

"Better," Mary said quietly, turning a page. "A lot better, now that Mr. Thornton offered Dad a new job. He'll run the office on the weekends and make the local deliveries. It took a bit of convincing, but I think we'll be all right. John even gave Timmy an after-school job sweeping the lot and washing the trucks. Dad says Thornton plans to train Timmy as a mechanic."

"Mary," Margaret smiled broadly, a wave of pride and affection sweeping through her, "that's bloody brilliant."

"It's all thanks to you."

"Well, I don't know about that." Margaret blushed, doubly pleased. "I had very little to do with it."

Mary looked up with a strange smile on her face. "I think Bess would say you had everything to do with it."

"I miss her," Margaret said. "Even if she was terribly meddlesome."

"She was such a pill." Mary laughed softly. "I miss her too."

"I ought to go." Margaret checked the time on her mobile. Thinking about Bess always made her body feel heavy and old. "Dad will be all fussy and worrying himself silly, like a mother hen."

"You shouldn't go alone. It's dark."

"It's not too dark yet." Margaret gathered her things and winked. "Don't tell him."

"John wouldn't like it either."

"I'll ring when I'm safely home," Margaret said, pretending not to hear Mary's quiet remark. She trotted out the door and down the stairs, a smile tugging at her lips. Somehow, she felt both heavier and lighter, her thoughts and feelings all jumbled together. She'd hoped John would understand and give Nick a chance. He hadn't let her down. She smiled again, softly content.

John Thornton had *never* let her down.

She walked the block to her car and drove home, her smile working its way from her face deep into her heart, easing the heavy weight that always rested there.

Chapter 30

When Frannie Thornton's boyfriend unexpectedly proposed, the news spread across Milton like a spark in a cotton mill. Almost everyone who mattered knew by the end of the week. Margaret and Mr. Hale were standing in the fabric store, waiting for the clerk to return. Her father had finally agreed to recover his favorite reading chair. She insisted they purchase the fabric before he could change his mind. She stood, perusing the bolts of lace displayed next to the upholstery, when she heard Frannie's excited voice.

"Margaret Hale, have you heard the news?" Frannie bounced up to her and grabbed her hands in excitement. "It's simply wonderful to see you here. Do you remember my friend Lana Lancaster?"

"Hello." Margaret nodded at Lana politely, a flush of embarrassment heating her cheeks. She tried to smile, feeling as stiff and fake as Lana looked. They hadn't seen each other since New Year's Eve last year.

"I hear congratulations are in order, Miss Frannie," Mr. Hale was saying. "Mr. Watson is a lucky man."

"Thank you." Frannie beamed and stuck out her left hand for them to admire. "Watson asked me a week ago, and it was so romantic. There were candles and roses and champagne."

"It's a beautiful ring." Somehow Margaret managed to keep her voice polite. "It looks vintage."

"It was my great-great grandmamma's ring, on my daddy's side. John was such a sneak, offering the ring to Watson, and I had no idea. It was supposed to be John's, you know."

"Oh." Margaret's face grew uncomfortably hot, and her tongue felt thick. This was the ring he tried to give her when he proposed. She hadn't even bothered to open the small box before throwing it back at him. Her fingers twitched, wanting to grab Frannie's hand to look at the ring again, but she forced herself to smile politely.

Frannie was currently divulging her plans to have a dress custom made by a small designer back in South Carolina.

"You mean from Blanding, of course," Mr. Hale said. "Is that near Helstone?"

"How do you know about Helstone?" Lana asked.

"John told me about his childhood home many times. A Mr. Bell owns the estate now, if I'm remembering correctly."

Frannie nodded with an easy smile. "Mr. Bell bought it a long time ago, but he lets us visit any time we like. He promised to let John buy it back someday, if he wants. But who knows if that will happen now." She winked at Lana, giggling as if at some shared secret. "John's a Milton man, like my daddy and my mama. And I'm sure never going to live in that poky old town again."

"I always thought your brother seemed rather fond of the South," Margaret said, frowning.

"My brother's such a dinosaur, bless his heart, and I know his southern manners rub you the wrong way. We'll train it out of him somehow." Frannie shared another knowing smile with Lana. "He's a stubborn ass on his best days."

Margaret shifted awkwardly, feeling very out of place.

"Lana's going to be my maid of honor," Frannie continued. "We're spending Spring Break at Helstone to work on the wedding plans. I need to get a start on my dress."

"Of course—"

"Oh my God," Frannie interrupted, grabbing Margaret's arm. "I've had *the* best idea. You should come with us and see real southern hospitality for yourself. It'll be perfectly divine, with all three of us girls together."

"That's generous of you, Frannie, but—"

"It would be my pleasure, Margaret Hale. The South is like a different planet. You have to experience it firsthand."

Lana was staring open mouthed, stunned into silence. Margaret didn't know why Frannie was inviting her, but a small, wicked part of her enjoyed the frustrated bewilderment evident in Lana's expression. It almost made her want to agree, right then and there. "I don't know," she said, the picture of courtesy. "It's very last minute."

"Mr. Bell wouldn't mind at all, trust me. He loves company. The more the merrier. Promise you'll think about it?"

"I'll think about it."

MONDAY: MARCH 10, 2008

"So, my dear, have you considered Frannie Thornton's invitation?" Mr. Hale asked. Margaret sat at the kitchen table, helping Mary with her Pre-calculus homework. Mary made a strange sound in the back of her throat, which strongly resembled a snort, and nudged Margaret's foot. "Dad," Margaret said, ignoring Mary, "you know Frannie and

I aren't friends. More like civil acquaintances."

Mary threw a glance at Margaret. She clearly was dying to know what Frannie had invited her to do.

"I'm sure she's only being polite."

"Very likely." Mr. Hale stuffed his pipe and lit it, his face thoughtful. "Still." He drew the word out as if he had something more to say but let it hang in the air.

Margaret sighed. "Go on then. Say it."

"You need a holiday. I've been thinking of taking a small holiday myself, you know."

"Have you?" Margaret asked, surprised. "I'm not sure I want to take a holiday with Frannie."

"Helstone is a remarkable place. The house and land belonged to the Thornton family for generations before it was sold to Mr. Bell."

"Frannie invited you to visit Helstone?" Mary asked.

"She did, but I don't know how she has permission to invite me to another person's home. Who is this Mr. Bell anyway?"

"Adam Bell is an old friend of the late Mr. Thornton," Mr. Hale said. "He bought the Helstone farmland and estate as a favor when things were at their worst for the Thorntons. In many ways, he was a Godsend."

"That was kind of him," Margaret said.

"He's rich as the king of England too," said Mary, looking up. "Dad told us Mr. Bell kept an eye on John after Jonnie Thornton died. He let him buy several heirlooms his mother wanted, once he had the cash."

Margaret thought of Frannie's engagement ring. Had John purchased it from Mr. Bell?

This is for you.

"It was Mr. Bell who helped John start Marlborough Shipping too,"

Mary was saying.

"How is it you Higgins's know so much about everything?" Margaret demanded dryly.

"We listen more than we talk."

"Helstone seems a bittersweet place." Mr. Hale looked up from his newspaper. "But worth the visit, I think, even if you're reticent about the company."

"I don't know," Margaret hedged. "It's sure to be an all-day drive, which I can't stand, and flying makes me sick."

"Still, I would consider it."

"This isn't about my taking a proper holiday, is it?" Margaret shot a look at her father. "What are you on about?"

"I think," Mr. Hale said slowly, "you could try to be better friends with Frannie. She seems lonely and so are you."

Margaret looked down, ashamed and missing Bess with a sudden fierce sharpness. "Frannie's lovely, I simply don't like her all that much."

Not like Bess.

"Have you tried?"

"No," she admitted. "Not really." Trying to like Frannie Thornton would put her in the vicinity of Frannie's brother. "I would feel so awkward at Helstone."

Mr. Hale took his pipe out of his mouth, his soft eyes twinkling. "I'm sure Frannie would enjoy the attention. She doesn't get enough, the poor girl. It would do you both a world of good."

"But for a whole week?"

"Lana Lancaster would burst a blood vessel if you went," Mary said, giving Margaret a small, sly smile. "So would Mrs. Thornton."

"You're rotten," Margaret said. "Both of you." She couldn't blame Lana Lancaster for hating her, but the idea of ruffling a few feathers, including Mrs. Thornton's, was sorely tempting.

"John won't be there," Mr. Hale added, almost to himself.

Margaret flushed. She wondered if that was part of his urging her to go on this trip. Her father didn't know the particulars, but he knew something had happened between them. He certainly wanted her to try and make amends. But he would never quite say what he wanted her to do. He never did. Sometimes, she wished he would.

"You're tempted," Mary said. "Admit it."

"Maybe a little." Margaret pulled her planner out of her bag and flipped through it. She had the time. Dr. Martin had given her all of Spring Break off because she'd volunteered to work Christmas when no one else would. There was also the temptation of Helstone itself. The history alone would almost be worth the trip. She couldn't deny her curiosity to visit the place that had made John Thornton into the man he was now.

"Bess would tell you to go," Mary added quietly.

Margaret sighed. "Maybe I'll ring Frannie and see if you can come too. We'll make it a proper girl's trip, yeah?"

Mary gave her a funny sort of look, but she smiled. "Sure, Marg. A girl's trip sounds like fun."

FRIDAY: MARCH 14, 2008

"Why are you going with Frannie to Helstone?" Mrs. Thornton put down the newspaper and looked at her son. "There's something you aren't telling me."

He sat heavily in his favorite chair and leaned forward, resting his elbows on his knees. "I'm closing the Blanding office."

Mrs. Thornton watched him carefully, absorbing this news with characteristic stoicism. Businesses all over the country were hurting. If he was closing the Blanding office, things must be worse than she'd thought. At barely nineteen, he had built his business from a crazy idea and hard work. He'd been so proud when he opened the second location for Marlborough Shipping in Milton.

This would be a terrible blow.

"I'm sorry, John," she finally said.

"It is what it is."

"Couldn't you let Bailey manage it?"

"Bailey could do it, but I'd rather be there myself to get things moving. There's also the Blanding University Business and Career Conference this week. I was invited to speak again, and it might pull in some new shipping contracts, or investors, or both." He ran a hand through his hair. "It probably won't, but I already agreed."

Mrs. Thornton reached forward and brushed his hair until it lay flat. "When do you go?"

"Tomorrow."

"Lana will be there too."

"And?"

"It may be a good opportunity."

"Mother." John usually let her say what she liked about his life, but now his tone turned cold and hard, a firm warning. "Don't."

"She's a good woman, she's well connected, and her father's your banker." Mrs. Thornton wasn't romantic, not like her husband. They'd married for practical reasons, but they hadn't been unhappy—not always. The Lancasters were a well-established family, and John could use the money now more than ever. She hated seeing him unhappy. If not for that Hale girl, she thought bitterly, John might consider Lana a reasonable option. He might still.

"You could love her, if you tried."

He stood and tugged on his hat. "I don't care about Lana. I never did, and I never will. Don't mention it again. Please."

She frowned, sighed in the way only disappointed mothers can, and returned to her newspaper.

"I'll have Williams come by the house and check in with you while I'm gone."

"Don't bother."

But he would anyway.

SATURDAY: MARCH 15, 2008

John flat out refused to fly with his sister. He didn't like planes, and he preferred to drive. Frannie huffed and even begged, but he stood his ground. In the end, Frannie and Lana booked themselves tickets, and he drove. Eight hours in the car alone was a mini vacation for him. He had space to breathe and think, in peace. When he finally crossed the South Carolina state line, he rolled down the windows of his truck and took a long, slow breath.

It was damn good to be home.

Chapter 31

Between her own petty pride, her father's encouragement, and Mary's treachery, Margaret now stood outside the airport in Blanding, South Carolina, alone. She was sorely tempted to step right back on the next plane for Milton, but that would waste even more of her father's money.

Frannie had been ecstatic when Margaret rang to accept her invitation, chattering about how much fun they would have. Her father's gentle scolding about trying to make friends with Frannie still smarted.

"This has nothing to do with her brother," Margaret muttered, straightening her shoulders. "You're here to be friendly with Frannie and to visit the Business and Career Conference at the university. You will enjoy yourself and pick up a college application for Mary."

It was a load of rot, but she clung to it, fierce and determined.

"You're a bloody idiot, Margaret Ann Hale."

Mary was supposed to have come along with her. Frannie generously extended her invitation to include the younger Higgins girl. It was the only reason Margaret allowed her father to purchase the plane ticket in the first place. But several nights ago, Mary had caught a case of strep throat from the Bouchers. She was in no condition to travel, and Margaret felt certain she'd done it on purpose.

"Little git."

She checked herself into her hotel and immediately began exploring the city. The conference wouldn't start until tomorrow, but she wanted to be prepared. The walk to the university campus was pleasant, almost picturesque. She was pleased with the feel of the city. Blanding was charming and cozy, in a way larger college cities never managed. But it wasn't Blanding John had in mind when he defended the South all those times before—it was Helstone. She'd researched the estate online, instantly impressed by the pictures and history. It was a working horse farm and historic Victorian Era house, sitting on over two hundred and fifty acres of land. She was keen to see it in person.

When she grew tired of the campus grounds, she caught a bus and rode around, nauseous and tired, trying to avoid her mildewy hotel room. At the next stop light, a warehouse caught her eye. *Marlborough Shipping Depot, established 1999* was blazed in bright red paint across the old brick building. She stood and quickly abandoned the bus.

This was where John Thornton had begun. He would've been only twenty. She smiled a little at the thought. She could almost imagine it. She pulled out her camera, checked the viewfinder, and snapped a photo, lingering in the shade while the picture developed. Two rough looking men, in jeans, plaid shirts, and work boots, stepped out of the building. Margaret chewed on her thumbnail and blew out a sharp breath. She was here, and she had nothing else to do. Why not indulge her curiosity a little bit more?

She stepped out of the shade and pulled open the door.

"Excuse me, Master." Mitchell Bailey stuck his graying head around the door, interrupting the heated debate between Adam Bell and John Thornton.

"Not now, Mitch."

"Thornton, be polite," Mr. Bell scolded in his crisp English accent, smiling at Mr. Bailey. He was enjoying rousing young Thornton, but he was getting more than a little weary. The younger man had far too much energy and was much too clever to be useful.

"Come in, Mitchell," Mr. Bell waved him in, "we're finished for today."

"The hell we were."

"There's someone to see you, Master."

"Fine." John sighed. "Who is it?"

"She didn't say. But she's real pretty."

John swore and shrank down in his seat. "Tell her I'm busy."

Mr. Bell watched John with a bemused smile on his face. He was well aware of Hannah Thornton's designs for her son and the daughter of his wealthy Milton banker. Lana Lancaster was a deliciously attractive woman, if Mr. Bell remembered correctly.

It had been his devilish idea to invite Frannie and her friend to come to Helstone the same week John planned to initiate the closure of the Blanding office. He relished the romantic tension like a sommelier relishes a fine wine. Now thoroughly bored of the business they'd been arguing over for the past two hours, Mr. Bell decided he deserved a little reward in the form of some jolly good entertainment at John's expense.

It was, after all, his favorite kind of amusement.

"Bring Lana in, Mitchell."

John shot him a black look, but Mr. Bell smiled jovially. "I haven't seen Miss Lancaster since she returned from that absurdly expensive finishing school in Europe."

He stood as the young woman stepped into the office but stopped short in surprise. The regal goddess standing before him was *not* the lovely Lana Lancaster. He was even more surprised when John glanced up and jumped to his feet, as if struck by a bolt of lightning.

"Margaret?"

"John? You're here." She paled and glanced down, but Mr. Bell's sharp eyes caught her look of panicked embarrassment. "I'm so sorry. I'm interrupting."

Mr. Bell allowed the awkward silence to hang in the air, before taking a deep breath and coughing. "Thornton, do stop standing there like a skewered trout. Introduce me."

John cleared his throat. "Margaret, this is Adam Bell. He's the largest investor in my company."

If John was any less enthusiastic, he'd probably collapse. Mr. Bell twisted his fingers in delight. Oh, this was delicious.

"Mr. Bell, this is Margaret Hale," John continued. "She's the daughter of my friend, Richard Hale."

"Oh yes, the Oxford man. I think we were in the same year. When you mentioned him, it somehow slipped your mind to also include a description of his young and stunningly beautiful daughter." Mr. Bell beamed at Margaret as he took her extended hand. He kissed it gallantly, enjoying her blush of surprise. "Welcome to Blanding, my dear woman."

"Thank you. It's a pleasure."

"Do you know, Margaret—may I call you Margaret?—I am simply in awe of you."

She blushed a becoming shade of pink. Easily embarrassed.

"What a glorious sight you are." Mr. Bell smiled. "Blush again, for it truly suits you. Don't you think, Thornton? Doesn't Miss Hale look ravishing?"

"Mr. Bell," John warned, his voice razor sharp.

Protective. Now that was *very* interesting.

"Frannie told me about you," Margaret said quickly and pulled her hand free.

"All good things, I hope."

She nodded. "I didn't know you'd be here, and I'm interrupting your meeting. I'm sorry."

"But aren't you here for a visit with Frannie?" Mr. Bell asked. "You see, I too have heard a few things from our dear Miss Thornton. I was hoping you'd say yes to her impulsive invitation. I do so enjoy company of the female variety."

"A visit with Fran?" John's posture stiffened.

"Yes, and the conference too," Margaret said hesitantly. "Mostly the conference, actually."

"Oh yes, the event at the university," Mr. Bell interrupted. He had the sudden desire to have John Thornton and this bewitching woman in the same room as much as possible. "Never mind that or Frannie. You must come to Helstone and visit *me*, Miss Hale. I'm quite taken with you, and I'm determined to have you all to myself."

"Oh no, I couldn't. I have a hotel room and—"

"That's easily settled. You must stay the week at Helstone as my personal guest. I insist, and furthermore, I swear upon my honor to be deeply offended should you refuse me. Thornton, tell her I'm not a man to be refused."

"Margaret doesn't like surprises," John said gruffly, "and she really doesn't like being told what she should and shouldn't do."

Mr. Bell studied his face. There was a hard sort of bitterness about him. Margaret's cheeks had flushed again at John's words, but this time Mr. Bell thought he saw more than embarrassment. Discomfort. Regret too, edged with sadness. There was a story between these two, and he was determined to lay it bare.

"If she won't be told, perhaps you ought to ask." Mr. Bell's eyes twinkled. "And do ask nicely this time, Thornton."

He excused himself and strolled to his waiting car, rubbing his hands in anticipation. He was going to enjoy this week immensely.

John stood stiffly, his hands curling into fists, as Mr. Bell sauntered off, leaving them in the awkward wake of his eccentric bullshit. Adam Bell was the last person John wanted digging around in the mess he'd made with Margaret, but it was too damn late to stop it. All he could do now was damage control. He turned and cleared his throat. "I'm sorry about all that."

"Please, don't apologize." Margaret looked up from her feet and smiled warmly. "I think I like him."

"You would."

"But you don't." She raised her eyebrows. "Why not?"

He frowned, considering what he should say. "Will you stay?" he finally asked. He was Mr. Bell's guest, and if the old man wanted Margaret at Helstone, he wouldn't argue. John hadn't seen her in months and the prospect of spending an entire week with her was too damn tempting.

"You didn't answer my question."

"You didn't answer mine." He gathered his keys and hat from his desk.

"I asked you first."

John looked up at her. Her reply didn't feel like the accusation he'd expected. "I don't like Adam Bell," he said slowly and tugged his hat into place. "He's a meddlesome old bastard who enjoys making other people dance for his own amusement."

"And you hate dancing."

"Yes."

"Should I stay away then?"

"Do what you want." He crossed his arms and waited, suddenly enjoying himself. "I won't stop you."

"How generous," Margaret said, a hesitant smile spreading over her face. She was teasing him, like she had on New Year's Eve. "I don't like to dance either."

"I guess we have that in common."

"A bloody miracle."

"So," John hesitated, uncertain what to say next. "If you're coming to Helstone, you'll need a ride."

"There's always the bus."

"You know I'm not going to let you ride the bus, right?"

"Yeah, all right." She smiled a little and walked quickly past as he held the door for her. When they reached his vehicle, she turned. "You know, I've always wanted to drive your truck."

"Why?"

"It's just," she shrugged, "so bloody American."

He studied her for a moment and almost smiled. "Okay." He couldn't help himself, not when it came to her. He held out his keys. "You drive."

She blinked. "Are you serious?"

"You break it, you buy it."

John knew this week was going to be hard even before Margaret turned up. It was only the first night, and he'd never been so glad for a meal to end. Margaret had kept her eyes on her plate for most of dinner, politely listening to the constant chatter of Frannie, Mr. Bell, and Lana Lancaster. John said nothing at all. He wasn't rude, but he was toeing the line. Between Mr. Bell and Frannie's inane conversation topics and Lana's constant flirting, it was a miracle he'd managed to be civil at all. There would be five more evenings of this. He sat, waiting for the right moment to excuse himself, stealing glances at Margaret. She looked as uneasy and annoyed as he was. He sighed and folded his napkin onto his plate.

"I never like these awful desserts Cook makes." Mr. Bell sighed, scraping his plate clean and pushing it aside. "Very bad for the waistline, you know."

"What's your vice of choice?" Lana asked.

"I'm rather fond of American sweets with peanuts. Peanut butter pie is my Achille's Heel. How about you, dear Margaret?" Mr. Bell turned to her. "What do you think about peanuts in sweets?"

"I don't mind them."

"What's your favorite, John?" Lana asked, lightly brushing his arm with her fingertips.

He was saved from answering when Frannie snorted loudly. "He doesn't like candy."

"Yes, I do," he grumbled and glared at his sister.

"Since when?" She tossed her curls, pointing at him with her fork. "I never see you eat any."

"Do you even eat?" Lana asked with a smile. "Daddy says you're all work and no play."

"He's eating now," Margaret said softly, picking at her apple pie.

"You must have a favorite dessert," Lana persisted. "Tell us."

"Why don't we all take a guess, eh?" Mr. Bell said.

"Don't bother." John pushed his plate aside and stood. He should've kept his mouth shut. Rude or not, he wasn't Mr. Bell's conversational plaything, and he'd had enough for one night.

"I'll guess first," Lana was saying. "Chocolate fudge?"

"No, it's got to be ice cream," Frannie insisted.

John swore silently and willed himself not to roll his eyes.

"Come, come, Thornton, indulge the ladies," Mr. Bell waved him back towards his seat as John scooted his empty chair closer to the table, took his hat from his back pocket, and yanked it on.

"Thornton, I insist you sit and tell us."

"You're such a spoil sport, John-John—"

"Candy canes."

They all fell silent and turned as Margaret spoke. She looked at John, her blue-gray eyes almost sad.

"What?" Lana glanced between them.

Margaret continued to hold his gaze. "You like candy canes best."

"How did you even know that?" Frannie asked.

"Dad keeps a jar at the house, and John's the only one who eats them."

John frowned, and Margaret's face and neck suddenly turned bright red. What she'd said about the jar of candy at her father's house wasn't technically a lie. But it wasn't the entire truth, and they both knew it.

"Well, Thornton?" Mr. Bell asked, his expression expectant and calculating. "Is Miss Hale correct?"

John allowed himself the smallest hint of a smile but didn't answer. "Excuse me."

As soon as his bedroom door closed, John collapsed onto the

mattress and lay staring at the ceiling.

You taste like a peppermint stick.

He hadn't let himself think about New Year's Eve or the perfect hour they'd shared. The world had shrunk to the two of them, tasting of skin and heat and candy canes. Now, he couldn't stop the memories. Honey sweet lips on his, the soft, purple smell of her hair, the tangy taste of her skin, and the achingly perfect curves under his hands.

He sat up, pulled off his boots, and set them aside. He tossed his hat, shirt, and jeans into the corner. He yanked the window open and took a deep breath, the night noises mingling with the sound of his pulse as it pounded in his ears. He needed to get a grip. He had a job to do, which didn't involve Margaret Hale.

She'd said no.

But she still remembered the way he tasted. He smiled, smug and satisfied. It wasn't much, but it was something.

Chapter 32

John's good mood lingered the next morning. He stepped out of his truck onto the college campus and glanced around. Each year Blanding University hosted a weeklong career conference to promote the local economy and small businesses, with high profile alumni and business leaders descending on the city in droves. It attracted attention from all over the state and beyond. He was lucky to be invited, having never officially graduated from any university—yet. Still, he was a Blanding native, and his presentation was packed.

His topic was on small independent businesses versus big national names, the challenges that presented, especially in the recent financial crisis. He looked out over the crowd and took a deep breath. He was about to speak on building a successful startup, and the irony of his own recent struggles almost made him laugh.

Margaret stood in the back of the hall, listening to John lecture with growing interest. She'd only ducked her head into the auditorium out of mild curiosity when she saw his name on the program for the day.

Every seat was occupied, but she decided to stay anyway, wedging herself into a comfortable corner. The last time she'd seen John in a suit was on New Year's Eve at the Lancasters' party. It was a guilty pleasure she didn't ever expect to be repeated.

She watched and listened with growing admiration. There was a charisma about John she'd never understood before. She'd thought he was overbearing and privileged, but here all she saw was passion, energy, and razor-sharp wit. He wasn't eloquent, not like her father, but he was compelling. He was also quite funny, now that she understood his humor a little better. The audience was fully engaged and laughing, and she surprised herself by joining in. For all his prickles and harsh personality, he was charming the entire auditorium.

"Maybe you have a great idea, but ideas aren't enough. Success requires a lot of hard work, and a lot of luck—and sometimes that's not enough either." John slid his hands into his pockets. "My best advice is bust your own ass or someone else will."

The audience laughed again. The moderator took the podium and announced ten minutes for questions. Margaret enjoyed this part too, especially his frank answers. She bit back a laugh at the barely concealed sarcasm he dished out to some of the more stupid ones.

"Last question." John looked to a woman with long red hair who stood near the back of the audience. She was dressed in a black suit and took the microphone with a flirtatious smile.

"I have two questions. First, are you single, and second, can I have your number?"

More laughter swept through the room, but Margaret's face felt hot. "Say no."

She slapped her hand over her mouth. Had she said that out loud? She shrank further back, hoping no one sitting nearby had heard her.

John made a face and shrugged. "Sure, but I still live with my mother. We're a package deal."

The crowd burst into laughter again, and the moderator ended the meeting with a chuckle. "If you didn't have dinner plans before, you do now, Mr. Thornton."

There was a decent amount of applause, and the crowd quickly dispersed. Margaret shifted in her little corner and watched as John moved down the aisle, speaking with the people who lingered. He passed out a few business cards, shook hands, and headed towards the exit. The red-haired woman waited for him at the door, smiling. A strange twinge in Margaret's stomach kept her from leaving. What would she say? What would John say back? And why did that woman toss her hair like that?

The woman stood at John's elbow, and he leaned down as she spoke again. He grinned and handed her his card. Margaret turned sharply, walked through the press of people, and stepped outside. She found a bench under a large oak tree, and sat, trying to compose herself. She pressed a hand against her stomach and breathed in the sunny fresh air.

What on earth was the matter with her?

"So, do I pass muster?"

She glanced over her shoulder. John stood behind the bench, grinning as he stared at her. "Pass what?" she asked nervously.

"I saw you watching in the back. Were you bored?"

"No, actually. I liked it."

"Yeah?" He walked around the bench and sat down. "It must be my birthday."

She straightened as he leaned back, the sun lighting his face. "If you were boring, I'd tell you, even if it *was* your birthday."

"I bet you would."

She smiled a little despite her discomfort. "Are you teasing me?"

He didn't look at her, but the corner of his mouth rose slightly. She poked his shoulder, her smile growing. "Smart ass."

"Your fault, not mine." He laced his hands behind his head. "Did you learn anything?"

"About business or about you?"

His smile grew. "Both."

"I did."

"And?" he asked, pinning her with his intense blue gaze.

"You'd like to know, wouldn't you? Want me to puff up your male ego a bit, yeah?"

"Yes." He waited, his stubborn silence daring her to be honest.

She smiled again. "I learned that a business is a difficult mistress to keep, and you're a passable lecturer, despite your propensity to swear even during a speech. You're also funny."

"Thank you." He looked satisfied. "I hate public speaking."

"So why do it?"

"Because they asked me to." He closed his eyes, and looked so relaxed, she couldn't help staring at him. She liked his cleanly shaven face and lack of a baseball cap. He looked as easy and comfortable in his suit as he did in his usual clothes.

A small group of people wandered by, and Margaret saw the red-haired woman hang back, casually studying John from head to toe. Margaret's face grew hot. "What exactly are your dinner plans?" she asked before she could stop herself. "Tonight?"

He sat up, a slow grin spreading over his face. "Are you asking me on a date?"

"No." She raised her chin, trying to look more annoyed than she felt. She didn't know what she was asking, or why, only that she needed to know. "I just wondered."

"What are *your* dinner plans?" he countered.

"Mr. Bell said the cook was making a roast duck."

"Sounds fancy."

"I think he's showing off."

John rolled his eyes. "He does that."

"Still, it would be a shame to let it go to waste, wouldn't it?"

"Would it?" He slid her a sly side glance. "Or would it be more of a shame to waste a handsome man in a suit who's asking you to dinner?"

Margaret felt hot all over, then strangely cold, with embarrassment. She opened her mouth to scold him, but the words stuck in her throat. Her shoulders slumped a little. "You don't have to be nice to me if you don't want to," she finally said, the words tasting bitter. "I've not been very nice to you."

"Yes, you have." He stood, adjusting his jacket sleeves. "We both know I'm not that nice."

"Yes, you are," she said quietly and stood, the chilly wind pulling at her clothes. She glanced to where the red-haired woman was still loitering, watching them. "Enjoy your evening."

He turned in the direction she was looking, and she hurriedly gathered her things. All she wanted was to leave with some tiny part of her dignity intact.

"Maggie."

She paused and glanced up.

He continued to stare at her, that stupid, cocky, half smile on his face. "Have dinner with me," he said, his voice grumbling low. "Please."

She looked down, her skin tingling and itchy. "Are you sure?" For some odd reason, she was enormously pleased that he was asking her again. "You know we'll only end up arguing," she said. "We always do."

"We're doing okay right now."

"Another miracle."

"I'd rather argue with you about something that matters than spend another night listening to everyone else yammer on about my favorite candy."

She snorted a little. "God help us all."

"Is that a yes?"

"I—" she stopped and swallowed, before nodding shyly. "I suppose it is."

He looked at her for a moment, as if unsure he'd heard her correctly.

"Yes," she said again.

He smiled, bright and easy. He turned, and they walked in companionable silence towards his truck. She knew he was watching her, oblivious to everything else. It was strangely lovely to have his fierce burning attention all to herself again, as if she were the only person who mattered. At least for right now. It almost made her happy, and she didn't quite know why.

"You were right last night," he said and opened the passenger door of his truck for her. "Candy canes are my favorite."

"I know." Margaret smiled at him, and it felt real.

Chapter 33

"Are you enjoying yourself, my dear goddess?" Mr. Bell arranged himself gallantly next to Margaret on the outdoor patio sofa. The sun sank steadily towards the tree line that stretched across the horizon before them, blazing gold, orange, red, and pink, in a sweeping display. The sycamore trees that flanked the house, standing like emerald-green sentinels, whipped their branches in the wind.

"Strangely, yes." She smiled and closed the photography book she'd been perusing.

"You attended Thornton's lecture the other day?"

"I did."

"And how was your dinner together after?" Mr. Bell glanced at her, his hazel eyes bright with nosy mischief. "You enjoyed having him all to yourself, selfish girl."

"His lecture was quite entertaining," she replied smoothly. Their dinner afterwards was another story, but not one she was willing to divulge. She hadn't seen John since, and she didn't know what to think about it all, especially with the lingering awkwardness that hung between them. Still, his asking her to dinner had given her a cautious sort of hope. It had been a quiet meal, lovely and confusing.

"I'm surprised at your interest in business." Mr. Bell crossed one over the other, patting her arm. "Young women ought to occupy themselves with more frivolous activities."

"That's sexist."

"It is, but you're on holiday. Don't slave away at a business conference when there's time to be wasted. Indulge yourself."

"But I'm a maths major. Mathematics and business are inexorably intertwined. I should like to be well informed, no matter where my career takes me."

"Mathematics? What on earth would you do with that?"

"I'm actually considering a doctorate in statistics."

"Good God, how exhausting," he groaned and pinched the bridge of his nose. "What will you women think of next?"

"Stop that, Mr. Bell. I'm quite as brilliant as you are, and we both know it," she scolded. "Come with me to the conference tomorrow, and you can prove it."

"No, no, I've served my time." He stood and offered her his arm. "There's only one thing to cure you. Shall we have a nightcap?"

"It's three o'clock," she said with a merry roll of her eyes as she stood and took his arm.

"Don't scold me. I usually endeavor to keep my drinking to Sundays."

"Really? And why is that?" she asked skeptically as they wandered inside and made their way towards the spacious kitchen.

"I feel the good Lord looks kindlier on me when I limit my merry debauchery."

"Today is Wednesday."

"With such an angel at my side, I'm confident I shall escape divine judgment. For now."

"Flatterer." She smiled. Mr. Bell was a shameless flirt, but she enjoyed him. The door to the library opened as they passed by, and John appeared, book in hand.

Mr. Bell paused. "Hiding as usual, Thornton? Leave your book and join us for a drink."

"Why?"

Margaret hid a smile at John's flat tone. Though scrupulously polite, his interactions with Mr. Bell were stiff and reserved. He spoke little, only when spoken to, and for once, she commiserated with his glowering silence. Mr. Bell never left anyone to themselves, and a man like John bristled under the constant barrage of his meddling.

"The lovely Miss Hale and I are on a mission to enjoy ourselves, which we simply cannot do without you."

John frowned and glanced at her. "Why?" he repeated, a tiny shift in his voice betraying his curiosity.

"You've got the longest arms." Mr. Bell walked on, Margaret in tow. "Come along."

She glanced back at John and gave him a small smile. He followed with a look of wary amusement.

♥

Lana and Frannie were chattering over pink mimosas and a mountain of bridal catalogs spread across the kitchen table. They looked up as the other three entered. "There you are, Margaret." Frannie brightened. "I need another opinion. I can't decide between roses or peonies for the centerpieces. What do you think?"

"I'm not sure you want my opinion," Margaret said slowly. "I've never given much thought to weddings or floral arrangements of any kind."

"Can it be true?" Mr. Bell gasped in mock horror. "Have you neglected the all-consuming task of planning your future wedding, goddess mine?"

"Apparently." Margaret gave him a warning look, which he pretended not to notice. "Why would I bother?"

"It's the prerogative of your fair sex to maintain fanciful daydreams of marital bliss. One must be prepared for the arrival of Prince Charming."

"If he should ever appear," she said, trying desperately to keep her attention on Mr. Bell as John brushed past her, "I'm certain there'll be plenty of time to plan."

Her eyes stubbornly flicked to where John stood. He leaned back against the counter, arms folded, his face stern and thoughtful. "In the meantime," she said quickly, "I'd rather think about other things."

"I don't believe you," Lana said. She glanced at John and turned back to Margaret. "A woman knows exactly what she wants."

"Please tell us," Frannie gushed. "We're all dying to know what your dream wedding would look like."

"I don't know—"

"As your host, I insist," Mr. Bell interrupted. "You simply must indulge our curiosity."

John stood very still. But even he looked interested.

"If I do get married, I'd like to wake up on a lovely day, not too early, and put on a lacey dress after a hearty breakfast," Margaret said softly, staring at her hands. "The ceremony would be small. A country parish or maybe even the courthouse." She folded her arms around herself, unable to stop the picture forming in her mind. "I should like it to be in the autumn, if possible, and warm enough for a walk afterwards.

Just us two, alone."

"A walk?" Frannie wrinkled her nose. "Why would you want to take a walk in a wedding dress?"

"Would you really get married at the courthouse?" Lana laughed, a condescending sound. "How unromantic."

"I don't think so," Margaret said, resolute and firm. "Anything can be romantic with the right person."

"What do you think of Margaret's prescription for a perfect wedding day, Thornton?" Mr. Bell asked John, turning her around with him so they stood face to face.

"Who cares what he thinks?" Frannie teased. "It's not like he'll get married anytime soon. Besides, who'd want a dinosaur like him?"

John's expression hardened, and Margaret felt an odd sort of dip in her stomach. He crossed the room, reached into the liquor cabinet, and pulled a large glass bottle from the top shelf.

"Surely someone would take him on," Mr. Bell said.

"Someone might," Lana murmured. "If he'd ask nicely."

"Well, it's my wedding being planned right now, not Margaret's or John's," Frannie said with a teasing pout. "And I can't decide if roses or peonies would be better."

"What are you drinking, Mr. Bell?" Margaret said, a little too cheerfully, her cheeks blazing. John had retrieved three cut-glass tumblers and poured them modest drinks.

"This is an excellent, and quite expensive, whiskey I acquired during the Kentucky Derby several years ago." Mr. Bell plucked up the bottle and added a generous pour to one of the glasses. "It's terribly hard to find, unless you know the right people."

"What kind of whiskey?" Margaret asked. "Dad usually takes a scotch, if he drinks at all."

"Bourbon, my bonnie lass, which isn't quite the same as most whiskies. A technicality, but an important one. Would the other ladies care for a libation?"

Lana walked over and picked up one of the glasses, sniffing delicately. "It smells like honey and caramel. Do you have a favorite vintage, John?"

John didn't answer, only raised his glass to Mr. Bell, and took a sip. Margaret reached for the glass Lana held, took it, and sniffed deeply. The alcohol opened her nose in a pleasant stinging way.

"Daddy loves the Derby." Lana settled herself on a high-top stool at the kitchen island and turned to John again, effectively cutting Margaret out of the conversation. "Have you ever been?"

He shrugged. Lana seemed determined to drag an answer out of him, flirting and smiling and touching him at every turn. Margaret had noticed, with uncharitable satisfaction, that John treated Lana with the same stiff politeness he extended to Mr. Bell. She shouldn't have felt so irritated, but something about Lana always rubbed her the wrong way.

"Watson wants a full bar at the wedding," Frannie said flippantly. "I told him he can have whatever he likes so long as he keeps it tucked away in a corner somewhere, since I'm not a fan of hard liquor. I prefer wine."

"I'll drink for both of us," Lana announced. She swiveled her stool back around and held out her hand for the glass of bourbon, which was supposed to be for Margaret.

Margaret had the inexplicable urge to refuse. She grated under Lana's high-handedness and barely concealed condescension. She hated herself for the ingrained politeness, embarrassment, and shame that made her give the drink to Lana.

"I've not had much whiskey myself," Margaret said, simply to fill the growing silence. She stepped towards the table where Frannie still sat but stopped when she felt a hand on her arm.

"Try it." John offered her his drink.

She held his intense stare, and he raised his eyebrows. In a challenge, or something more?

"Thanks." She took his glass and sipped. Her mouth twisted, the alcohol burning a harsh path down her throat and up into her nose. Not much of a taste, that. More like an alcoholic slap in the face. She took another sip.

"Well?" Mr. Bell asked, his eyes flicking between Margaret and John. "Has Thornton won you over?"

She wrinkled her nose. "I don't know if I like it."

"My daddy always said hard liquor is for a more cultured taste," Lana commented and took a drink of her bourbon. "Not everyone can enjoy it."

"Try it again," John said, keeping his eyes on Margaret.

She sipped a third time, smiling when the mellow taste settled onto her tongue. It was a buttery, almost nutmeggy, flavor. She took one more swallow, smiling at John. "It's a bit of a punch in the mouth at first, but lovely after you get used to it."

"Bravissimo." Mr. Bell finished his drink. "I do believe you're the lost half of my soul, Margaret Hale. If I were twenty years younger, I'd escort you to a little country church myself and marry you without a second thought."

"You're assuming I'd accept your proposal."

"Wouldn't you?" Mr. Bell waggled his eyebrows. "Or has someone more tempting beaten me to it?"

Margaret blushed and took a hurried swallow of bourbon, making a noncommittal noise.

"I think someone has," Mr. Bell continued. "Who is it? I demand to know at once. Do you know, Thornton?"

"Someone did," Lana muttered as she moved back to the table. "But she said no."

Margaret almost choked. Did Lana know about John's proposal? How the bloody hell did *she* find out?

"What's that supposed to mean?" Frannie asked, still completely engrossed in her magazines. "Who asked her?"

"Think Frannie." Lana smiled sharply at Margaret, her voice still low. "Who do you think she came to Helstone to see? It's not you, and it's certainly not me."

Margaret felt the stares of everyone in the room, her face painfully hot. Her ears were ringing with Lana's barely whispered words. How else would her visit to Helstone look but as a desperate attempt to be with John? And if Lana Lancaster thought so, what would other people think of her? What would John think?

Oh God.

"Excuse me." She escaped the kitchen and wove through the large unfamiliar rooms until she found a secluded place at the back of the house on the second floor. She trembled with mortification and anger, more at herself than anyone else. She sat down heavily on the window seat flooded with golden light and pressed her forehead to the cool glass pane. The clink of ice made her look down. She still held the glass of bourbon John gave her. Sighing heavily, she swallowed it whole, gasping as the golden-brown liquid burned a spicy path down her throat and into her stomach.

She should never have come to Helstone.

Chapter 34

"Move, you pokey old sod." Margaret shoved the heavy box up against the antique wardrobe in the corner. She hopped on top of the box. Even standing on her toes, her fingers still couldn't reach the picture album. It taunted her, perched on top of the old piece of furniture. The alcohol now raged pleasantly through her, turning all the hurt and anger and embarrassment into stubborn action. She needed that photo album, and she was going to get it if she had to locate a ladder to do it.

"Bloody hell." She jumped, reaching again, but only managed to jam her elbow into the trim as the box beneath her tilted sharply to one side, almost dumping her onto the floor. She made a frustrated sound in her throat. "I hate being short."

"Your accent gets real thick when you're mad."

"Does it?" Margaret glared over her shoulder and shoved her hair out of her face.

John leaned against the door frame, watching her. She turned back to her task. "Is that all you can say, farm boy?"

He walked over. "Farm boy?"

"You've got your own bloody accent, yeah? Forget about mine." She turned on him, her face sweaty from exertion. "I'm currently in terrible distress, if you hadn't noticed."

"I can see that."

"Are you going to help me reach that picture album or not?"

He met her stare. For once, they were almost eye to eye. "You could say please."

"I could, or you could be a gentleman and come to my rescue without requiring me to beg."

"I wouldn't mind a little begging from you."

"Fine." She rolled her eyes. "Please."

He stepped closer. She felt the hair on her arm stand up as he reached around her and pulled the album down.

"Thank you." She took it and wiped off the dust. "I was about to call the fire brigade."

"You're welcome."

When he took her hand, she didn't object. She jumped off the box, swaying a bit. He tightened his grip and placed his other hand on her waist to steady her. "Are you all right?"

"I don't think I should drink bourbon." She shrugged. "Other than that, I'm bloody brilliant."

He snorted, and she scowled at him. "Not a word, smart ass."

"Yes, ma'am." He laid on the southern accent thick with those two words. He had a smug smile plastered on his face that should've annoyed her. For once, she thought it made him rather handsome.

"Did you know whiskey makes other people more attractive?"

"Does it?"

She nodded. "You've still got hold of my hand. Do you plan to keep it?" She felt quite bold, despite the troubling accusations Lana had all but shouted. Maybe she should drink bourbon more often.

"Are you all right?" he asked again, his voice serious, his eyes softening when they caught the remaining traces of her angry tears.

"I would like to look at these pictures which I can't do without both my hands."

A corner of his mouth twitched, and he let go. She sat right down on the floor and opened the album. To her surprise, he sat next to her and leaned his long frame against the wardrobe.

"You like photography."

"Brilliant deduction, Sherlock." She leaned in conspiratorially. "The game's afoot."

"How much of that did you drink?"

"All of it." She gave him an exaggerated wink. "Can you tell?"

"Light weight."

"Rude."

"I fetched your dumb picture album."

"I said please *and* thank you. What more do you want?" she asked, turning her attention to the album. She hummed happily. The pictures were a visual history of Helstone and the Thornton family. She was thoroughly charmed, admiring page upon page of the old-fashioned black and white photographs.

"What do you think of the South now?"

She thought for a moment before she answered. "I can't believe the silence and the trees and the green. Milton is gray and black and almost dirty."

"It's not a fair comparison. They're completely different worlds." He paused. "Milton has its own kind of beauty, if you know how to look for it."

"Are you defending the merits of the North?"

He glanced down at her. "Maybe."

"I'm glad I've seen this place. I understand now why you love it and why you'll come back."

"I never said that."

"No. But you will." She flipped the page, smiling at a picture of a young dark-haired boy holding a baby. John and Frannie?

"Do you like Helstone?" he asked, trying to shift the conversation.

Margaret chewed her bottom lip, remembering her first glimpse of Helstone, the sun spilling its golden light over the great old house and barns and surrounding fields. Flanked by tall sycamore trees, pale white and green flashing in the gentle wind, the house was a glorious haven that let a person step into a different world. "I think Helstone is truly worthy to hold a place in your heart," she said.

"Would you like to visit again?"

She fingered the edge of a faded photograph of the house. The sycamore trees were much smaller. "There's too many memories here," she said quietly. "You won't come back for Helstone."

"No." He answered in the lowest register of his voice that sent a shiver running up her spine. "I won't."

She looked at him, his blue eyes clear and bright, almost burning her. "You won't stay in Milton either, will you?"

"No."

Her cheeks flushed as they continued to stare at each other. Would he have brought her here, if things had turned out differently between them? She shook the thought away, her skin suddenly hot and itchy.

She didn't want to think about that.

"Who's this?" She pointed to a grainy black and white portrait, the words *Old Jack* scribbled at the bottom. The man in the photograph was young and serious. He looked a little bit like John but with a thinner nose and closer-set eyes.

"My great-grandfather."

She pulled the photograph out, studying it carefully. "Were you named for him?"

"Sort of." He grinned. "I'm a fifth."

"A fifth what?"

"John Seamus Thornton. The fifth."

"You're kidding."

"I wish I was."

"Seamus?"

"It's Scottish."

"Oh." She made a face, replacing the picture. "I'm sorry about that."

"It could be worse." He turned the page to a picture of a Victorian couple. "That's my great-great grandfather. The first John Thornton and his wife." He cleared his throat. "Margaret Marie Thornton."

"Another Margaret?" She blushed, studying the photograph. "Good heavens," she breathed, looking at the tall man with striking eyes, deep-set under thick black-brown eyebrows, standing next to a petite pretty woman. "This could almost be you, except for the clothes."

"Thornton genes are strong."

"He's not like you." She tilted her head, studying the photograph. "You're like him."

"It's the eyebrows."

"They're quite stern, aren't they?" she said. Her finger traced the edge of the face in the photograph. "And that nose."

John leaned forward and turned the page again. His face was so close she could smell the bourbon on his breath mixing with his usual soapy, peppermint smell. She shut her eyes against the swimming feeling that gripped her stomach and the memories that flooded over her at the smell of him.

Who do you think she came to Helstone to see?

Lana's cutting words echoed in her ears, and she jerked away, feeling lightheaded and sick. Maybe Lana was right. Maybe she *was* here just to see John and—

"Excuse me." She stumbled to her feet, backing away towards the door. "I think I should head to bed. I'll be gone tomorrow morning, and I'll be quite busy with the remainder of the conference too. I—I should go now. I'm sorry."

He frowned and stood, slow and deliberate. Her words fell between them like a wall. He didn't move closer, didn't say anything, only stared at her, an unreadable expression on his face. For once she couldn't bear his piercing gaze. She ducked her head and hurried from the room.

SATURDAY: MARCH 22, 2008

Frannie insisted on a bonfire for their last night at Helstone. Margaret spent the morning alone, wandering quietly along the trails in the woods behind Helstone, avoiding Mr. Bell's company and Lana's constant scrutiny. And if she stole a peek or two at John chopping wood, she kept that to herself.

When night fell, she felt a little easier. The trees took on a bluish green golden hue, as the sun sank lower in the sky. Margaret stared at the flames, trying to ignore John as much as she was trying to ignore Frannie and Lana as their voices drifted in and out from the porch swing. All week Margaret had endured Lana's flirting and obvious posturing around John, and she was heartily sick of it. But she couldn't blame Lana for making a move.

John stood on her right with several farm hands, just outside the heat of the fire, his deep voice carrying over the crack and whistle of the flames. She was reminded of the many fireside conversations between him and her father in Milton all last winter.

So much had changed since then.

When she'd first met him, she accused John of being cruel, cold, and entirely unfeeling. She'd dismissed him as an ignorant, overly traditional man, who didn't think about his beliefs. But she couldn't anymore. She watched him pick up two small boys, one in each arm, chuckling with their father, a Mr. Jeremy Wheaton, who was groundskeeper at Helstone. Something about it made her chest ache, even as she took a quick picture.

If she'd learned anything from this week, it was that John Thornton was a puzzling collection of opposites; a completely different person here, and yet he was exactly the same. He was harsh yet quietly kind, steadfast and immovable, yet willing to concede when necessary. He cared deeply for others and yet, in many ways, didn't care at all. Were her first opinions and critiques of him accurate or even fair? She didn't know what was true anymore, and that frightened her.

She walked quietly away from the noise of the fire, uncomfortable with these new thoughts. She wandered about the garden and towards the little wooden bridge, sheltered in a grove of willow saplings, that led over the creek into the eastern pastures. She stood on the bridge and listened to the water rippling in the fading light.

"Margaret?"

She jumped and turned sharply. "John?"

"I frightened you." He leaned his elbows on the railing next to her.

"Only a bit. I didn't see you there."

"Are you hiding?"

"I—" she bit her tongue. Lying felt useless now. She felt useless. "I shouldn't be here."

"Why not?"

The familiar challenging tone in his voice made her tense, and she folded her arms against a sudden chill. He was always challenging her, always prodding her, pushing her to think harder, to be sharper, to be more. Right now, she wanted to disappear, but she couldn't hide from him. She never could.

"I don't know what I think about anything anymore." Her laugh was hard. She hoped to sound casual, but the words were bitterer than she intended. "Maybe I never did."

He didn't answer, and something about his silence was too heavy to break. She stood there, staring at the sky. She couldn't make herself walk away anymore.

♥

John stood next to Margaret in the roaring silence and watched the steel blue sky. It darkened until it was spattered with stars, the last of the sunlight melting away as if it had never been there. He sighed. The Blanding office was officially closed, the drivers relocated, or let go, after long hours of haggling and a little help from Mr. Bell's pocketbook. John hated owing him more than he already did. The meddlesome old bastard had enjoyed himself far too much at John's expense this week.

And for what?

He glanced at Margaret. Somehow, his mother had found out she was visiting Helstone and called him that morning to give him a long, scathing piece of her mind. He'd threatened to hang up on her, telling her it was none of her damn business. But nothing had changed.

"Things at the Depot are pretty busy," he said, breaking the silence. "Tell your dad I might not come by for a while."

"I will."

They were silent again, the awkwardness and wall of misunderstandings still looming between them.

"Why did you come?" He couldn't stop the question. He wondered what she might see on his face if it weren't so dark. Anger? Frustration? Or maybe stupid desperation and longing?

"Frannie asked me."

"You don't like her," he pressed. "And you don't like me."

She gasped, a soft sound, and turned to face him. "I don't think that anymore," she said, her voice barely a whisper. "I've enjoyed myself this week, and I didn't expect to."

"Because of Fran? Or me?"

"Because of myself."

He didn't say anything. He didn't know what to say.

She spoke again, so softly he used it as an excuse to lean closer to hear her. "I thought I understood you, but I don't. It's all been right under my nose, you know?" She looked up into the sky, the starlight glowing softly on her skin. "It's the same sky, the same as Milton, and yet it's more. I just couldn't see it."

He could feel her warmth, close, so damn close. He could hear the tears in her voice. "I never looked up, and I missed them," she said, clutching her arms around herself. "They're so much more than I thought, and I didn't know."

"Are we talking about stars or something else?"

"I don't know."

"Maggie." His hand moved to take hers, almost on its own, but she stepped out of reach.

It was like a slap in the face.

"Thank you. For this week." She took another small step away, falling back on the safety of civility. Another stupid wall between them. "I've had a lovely time."

He was glad she couldn't see him stare after her, like the dumb fool he was. He shouldn't, but he couldn't stop himself.

When the bonfire finally burned down to glowing embers, John was alone. He dumped two buckets of water on the smoldering pile and stomped back to the house. The clock in the kitchen ticked incessantly, slithering under his skin, reminding him how late it was. Mr. Bell shuffled into the room in his bathrobe and slippers, a folded newspaper in his hands. John had poured himself a glass of whiskey. He needed it after everything he'd endured this week. Helstone always did this to him—he loved it and hated it. Having Margaret here had made it ten times worse.

"It's been quite the holiday, eh, Thornton?"

John took a swallow, content to let the silence do his talking.

"You know, I've never liked you," Mr. Bell said.

"The feeling's mutual."

"And yet, I'm about to offer you some ruddy good advice."

"I don't want it."

"I'm not particularly interested in what you want. It's Margaret I care about."

"Excuse me?"

"You don't deserve her, but you already know that."

John glared at his drink, and finished it quickly, not trusting himself to say anything.

"You think she doesn't fancy you. I think you're mistaken."

"Adam." John bit the word out and raised himself to his full height. He'd had enough. "Fuck off."

The clock boomed in the sudden, thick silence.

"How long have you been waiting to say that?" Mr. Bell smiled wryly when John refused to answer. "I'll forgive it, but only this once, for Margaret's sake."

"I don't want or need your advice." John turned and rinsed out his glass in the sink, anger seeping up through his frustration. He'd felt the distance Margaret was desperately putting between them, like a brick wall, and he refused to make a fool of himself by begging. Not again.

"Young people are incredibly exhausting." Mr. Bell sighed. "What on earth did you do?"

"Nothing."

"And I'm engaged to Her Majesty the Queen. Blast it all, Thornton, you've clearly bungled things with Margaret and—"

"That's none of your damn business."

"Shall I guess then, since you refuse to illuminate me?"

"Good night." John turned to leave, but Mr. Bell spoke anyway.

"You're in love with her. I never supposed you were capable of falling in love." Mr. Bell chuckled. "You're also miserably unhappy, so perhaps you told her you love her, and she told you to bugger off. That would make sense, except she's not happy either. But now we come to my advice." He met John's dark glowering stare. "Lightning can, and does, strike twice."

"What's that supposed to mean?" John demanded, too angry and too tired to hide his growing confusion.

"Hang your pride, and don't waste your second chance when it comes. I doubt you'll get a third." Mr. Bell swatted his arm with his newspaper. "Godspeed, old chap."

Chapter 35

Mr. Bell escorted Margaret into Milton's oldest Anglican church, proud, preening, and peacocking, turning her this way and that. "Stop being ridiculous," she complained. "I'm not the bride."

"Nonsense. You're quite the glorious prize, my dear goddess."

"Call me a goddess one more time, and I'll pinch you. Don't think I won't."

"And I shall pretend to have won you." Mr. Bell held her hand in the crook of his arm and winked. "By the time I'm finished with you, every man here will wish you were on his arm tonight. Or in his bed."

"Stop that," she scolded. "The cheek on you. No one here cares a jot."

"I'd wager I could find at least one man here who would care very much," he said, smiling wickedly.

"Other than yourself?"

"I think I saw Thornton—"

"Shall we sit?" she interrupted.

His eyes twinkled, but he bowed in defeat. "You must learn to take a compliment, dear Margaret. A simple *thank you* will suffice. There's a good girl."

She rolled her eyes. "Are you quite finished? Because these heels are killing me."

"You're welcome, goddess mine."

Margaret allowed Mr. Bell to escort her to her seat, annoyed at his obsequious and constant flirtations. She permitted it because he was nearer to seventy than not, and it was all rubbish anyway. But whenever he mentioned John—

"Mr. Bell, you've sat us on the groom's side."

"Yes, of course, I have."

"What for?"

"Because I'm always on the groom's side, especially at the poor man's wedding."

She looked about, caught her father's eye across the aisle, on the bride's side of the church, and smiled a greeting. He brightened a bit and gave an awkward wave. When the procession began, John appeared—trimmed, shaved, and suited—and escorted his mother to her seat. Margaret's mouth opened in surprise, and she closed it quickly, with a small click of her teeth.

"I see Thornton finally got a haircut," Mr. Bell stage whispered. "I never liked him in a tuxedo. I prefer a splash of color."

"I think it's nice," she said, unable to resist clapping back at him. "I like John in black." Her eyes followed him as he circled back around the sanctuary. When all the extra relatives were settled, the guests stood with Mrs. Thornton, and Frannie made her grand entrance, John at her side. She beamed at him, and he smiled back. Margaret's stomach burned when she saw his whole heart go into that smile.

"You're staring, goddess mine."

"I thought Frannie would marry at Helstone," she whispered, ignoring his comment, watching as John helped his sister up the stairs to the altar and moved to stand as best man.

"Whatever gave you that idea?"

"Her family lived there for so long. I thought she'd want to start her new life in that happy place."

"It's hardly a family estate, my dear, whatever Frannie may have said," Mr. Bell whispered, loud enough for their neighbors to turn and give them a scolding glance. "It belonged to the Thornton family for only three or four generations. Thornton's great-grandfather bought the land about a decade after the Civil War."

"I assumed it was an old family property."

"Old Jack Thornton and his son Jack Jr.—that's Thornton's grandfather—were both shrewd men who took a gamble in America. They made a pretty profit too. Jack Jr. broke up the plantation after the Depression, once the economy fully recovered and World War I was over, selling off much of the land. He turned the rest to livestock and horses."

Mr. Bell paused as the minister asked the guests to stand for a prayer. Margaret nodded, her gaze settling on John again. He stood stiffly in his tuxedo, eyes lowered, hands clasped in front of him. She wondered about all the men who'd had a hand in making him into the man she knew. The prayer ended and the congregation sat once more.

"Jonnie, that's your John's father—God, there's too many of them—Jonnie was as slick and charming as a man could be," Mr. Bell continued in a low voice. "He didn't have Old Jack's or even Jack Jr.'s business head, but my God, that man could bloody make any person do whatever he wanted. He made his career on Wall Street, against his family's wishes. That's how he ended up in Milton. Dear Hannah had a hand in that as well."

"You met him in New York then?"

Mr. Bell nodded. "I'd never seen a more manipulative man, except for myself, of course. I'd hopped the pond about twenty years earlier to carve out my share of the American Dream. We did business together more than once. I was a little surprised when he married his pretty and rich East Coast wife. It didn't seem an American thing to do, to marry simply for the money. But they had John shortly after—very shortly after, I might add—and it made much more sense."

The audience stood again as the organ began to play. Margaret turned her program over, her eyes following the words of the old hymn.

Mr. Bell leaned closer, feigning interest in the printed hymn, but continuing to whisper. "Have I shocked you, dearest Margaret?"

"You're a miserable old gossip," she scolded. She'd never admit she was *very* curious to know exactly when John was born after his parents' marriage. She studied Mrs. Thornton's stern profile for a moment, feeling something almost like pity. Mr. Bell reached over and turned the page of the hymnal when Margaret forgot.

"The Thorntons settled permanently in Milton to be closer to Jonnie's job, spending their summers at Helstone. I think they were even happy when little Frannie made her surprise arrival."

"And then?"

"All the charm in the world couldn't save Jonnie from his own demons. He cut one too many deals that turned sour, speculated wildly, and lost everything. The family was devastated, financially, socially, and emotionally." He paused. "John was barely fourteen and our Frannie was eight."

"They were so young." Margaret glanced up, remembering the pictures of John and Frannie she'd found at Helstone. He'd been happy—truly happy—and lost it all in one terrible moment.

"Too young," Mr. Bell agreed. The music ended and they sat again. The minister began a short traditional monologue on the blessings of marriage. "Hannah did what she could, but all her money was spent, and anything left of value was sold to pay off their debts."

"Including Helstone."

"Among other things. The old southern Thorntons that were still alive were furious. Their beloved Helstone in the hands of a horrid Englishman."

"Really, Mr. Bell," she scoffed.

"Hannah burned her last bridges with that family by burying Jonnie in Milton. She's stubborn and did what she thought was best. I was proud of her for telling them off, in the end. She stunned us all when she moved her children back to Blanding and finished her nursing degree. The family barely limped along until John came of age."

Margaret's eyes drifted from John to Lana Lancaster, who stood slightly behind Frannie, magnificently dressed as the maid of honor. An expression of happy triumph flashed across Lana's face as she looked across the aisle to John. Even with her grating personality, Lana Lancaster was a beautiful and desirable woman; rich, talented, connected. A twinge of displeasure in Margaret's stomach made her turn her head away. "Why did Mrs. Thornton move back to the South?"

"Living costs are far cheaper in Blanding," Mr. Bell said. "But I suspect she wanted to protect her children. The gossip in their former circles was unforgiving after Jonnie ruined himself. There was more to it than financial ruin—drugs and infidelity and such. They were social lepers in every sense of the word, and then the poor sod killed himself."

"John never told me that." Margaret felt numb.

"He wouldn't. He hardly speaks of it at all." Mr. Bell gave her a knowing look. "He doesn't want or expect pity."

"He doesn't offer it either," she said, feeling her old anger raise its head amid a tangle of confusing emotions. It felt like an anchor against a storm she hadn't realized was raging inside her. She clung to it, hoping her face and posture showed only cool indifference as she watched Lana and John.

Mr. Bell placed a hand on her arm, arresting the nervous shredding of the program her fingers had unknowingly undertaken. "He's not his father, you know. Far from it. Jonnie cared only for himself in the end. His son is quite different."

"John told me before that he's not a nice person or particularly kind. I thought I agreed with him."

"And?" Mr. Bell waited.

"He's wrong. I've seen his kindness, and I've felt cared for. But I've also seen him be unbelievably harsh. I don't understand why." Her voice rose, and some of the wedding guests turned their heads in her direction.

She stared at her lap, embarrassed. "Sometimes I think I hate him."

Mr. Bell patted her arm in a fatherly sort of gesture. "Thornton despises duplicity. He would rather be seen as cruel and unfeeling, than manipulative and dishonest. He's not particularly kind, especially to those who don't play by the same rules. But he's a good man. Don't you dare tell him I said so. He'd land me a facer."

She swallowed a laugh, her anger fading. She wasn't sure she was even angry with John anymore. All their former disagreements felt so petty and small now. She glanced across the aisle at her father. He was listening to the wedding ceremony with a solemn melancholy.

She turned away and cleared her throat. "Why did they come back to Milton?"

"Well, there was dear Frannie's little mess. I'm sure you've heard all about *that.*"

"But why Milton?" Margaret interrupted, not wanting to discuss Frannie with Mr. Bell. Frannie didn't deserve his meddling judgement, and she felt strangely protective of her. "Why return to a place haunted by such awful memories?"

"I suppose it was pride. Young Thornton repaired what his father had broken, and he succeeded beyond anyone's expectations. Wherever you go in Milton, the name of John Thornton is known and respected, as if Jonnie never existed."

"That used to annoy me," she confessed. "I couldn't understand how a man so harsh and so—"

"Bloody backward?" Mr. Bell suggested with a smile.

"Old-fashioned. I couldn't understand why everyone respected him so much." She let out a breath as Frannie handed her bouquet to Lana, and the rings were exchanged. "He's too hard on people. Not everyone is strong enough to do what he did. But I think more people could, if someone like him would help them."

"Perhaps. At least Thornton attempts to be an honest, decent sort of fellow, whereas I myself left all that nonsense behind me long ago. I've little care for the plight of others."

"Mr. Bell, stop it."

"It's quite true, I assure you." He beamed. "I possess the rare ability of telling people to bugger off while convincing them it was their idea in the first place. They're happy to do so. Thornton does not have such a talent."

"He wouldn't consider it a talent," she said ruefully, as the organ struck up another song. "He thinks you're a meddlesome old bastard."

"He's right, my goddess."

Watson and Frannie stepped up the three stairs to the unity candle in the middle of the stage and lit it together. They bowed their heads as the minister offered a final blessing.

"Do you wish to know the real reason Thornton doesn't like me?" Mr. Bell asked. She didn't answer, knowing he would be shamelessly frank.

"When I bought Helstone, all those years ago, I promised him I'd sell it back to him. Obviously, I have no such intentions."

She frowned. "But he doesn't want it."

"Exactly."

"You lied." Her mouth fell open in shock as Mr. Bell's manipulation smacked her in the face. "You *knew* he wouldn't want it anymore, and you lied to him."

"Not exactly a lie. A gamble."

The guests stood, the new Mr. and Mrs. Watson presented, and permission was given to the groom to kiss his bride. Margaret clapped with the congregation, but her mind raced. The Watsons marched down the aisle and out of the church, followed by the wedding party, couple by couple, starting with Lana and John. Margaret watched them, her skin prickling with gooseflesh the closer they got. But John didn't see her, his gaze focused on the other side of the church.

"How could you lie and gamble with his future?" She turned back to Mr. Bell. "John was just a boy."

"I did him a favor." Mr. Bell smiled wryly. "He stood on the precipice of manhood, poised for utter ruin before he even began, thanks to his father. He needed a goal, something to work for and motivate him. I gave him that goal."

"You lied and gambled. Like his father."

"I've had my heart set on acquiring Helstone since the first day I visited." Mr. Bell offered Margaret his arm as the guests made their way out of the church. "I whisked it away from the Thorntons, a little personal payback to Jonnie, and I did it under the guise of a beneficent family friend, all generosity and kindness. My reputation glitters with philanthropy. Isn't it glorious? And to cap it all, I was the making of young Thornton, and he cannot forgive me for it."

Before she had a chance to respond, Mr. Hale joined them in the foyer. "Margaret, you look lovely. Were you planning on attending the reception?"

"I was." Margaret frowned at the fatigue and sadness hiding in the lines of his face. He was thinking of her mother. She wished he wouldn't. "But I don't have to go."

"You ought to have some fun, dearest. You'll give dear Frannie my best, won't you?"

"I'll look after her, Mr. Hale." Mr. Bell extended his hand. "Adam Bell. I'm sure Margaret mentioned me."

"Thank you, yes. She has." Mr. Hale absently shook hands and turned back to Margaret. "Tell John not to hurry back to his lessons. I know he's busy."

"A moment, old chap. Margaret's told you I'm planning a trip to Oxford, hasn't she? You should join me. We Englishmen must stick together. Do consider it."

"Of course." Mr. Hale nodded awkwardly and excused himself.

"You must help me to persuade your father."

"Dad barely knows you," she murmured, watching her father meander through the crowd. He didn't like weddings, and he only came because of his friendship with John. She still didn't know why she'd bothered to come. She wanted to think it was for Frannie, but she knew that wasn't quite true.

Chapter 36

This day couldn't get much worse. John sat crammed in the backseat of Watson's four door sedan, wedged uncomfortably between Lana Lancaster and another overdressed, overdone friend of Frannie's that reeked of perfume so strong he could taste it. He doubted he would have any more space in the front seat. He crossed his arms tighter to his chest, trying to give himself more room, and sighed. If he never had to go to another wedding, it would be too damn soon.

"Are you okay?" Lana smiled, giving him a once over. "You look uncomfortable."

"Because I am," he growled.

"You're taking up all the foot room," the other girl complained. "Could you try to shift a little to the left?"

"No."

She sighed and tried to turn herself further away. It didn't help. Why the hell Frannie insisted that the wedding party ride together was beyond John's imagination. Maybe she was afraid he would try to escape if he had his truck. She was probably right. But this was Fran's wedding, and he'd promised to be here for her and keep his stupid mouth shut. The day was almost over. He glanced at his watch, willing the hands to move faster.

The reception was held at a large historic estate on the outskirts of Milton. The older women of the family's acquaintance doted on Frannie and John in a way that was both smothering and tender. Hands were patted, shaken, kisses given, and cheeks pinched. Even Mr. Watson submitted himself happily to their elderly affection.

"Fussy old hens," Mr. Bell murmured into Margaret's ear as an older woman insisted on fixing John's tie and shirt collar for him. He'd bent down at the waist with a patient smile, letting the older woman tidy him to her satisfaction.

"I think they're lovely." Margaret smiled fondly at the nonsense, raised her camera, and snapped a picture. "You're just jealous."

"I appreciate a bit of fussing. I do think Frannie deserves as much motherly affection as she can stand, especially today." He sighed. "And Thornton deserves a little less, poor sod."

Margaret suppressed a smile, and Mr. Bell chuckled. "They all adore your John. He frowns and glowers, and they fall at his feet." Mr. Bell turned his sharp green eyes on Margaret. "Except you. You're determined to resist all his overtures, aren't you?"

"Overtures?"

"Perhaps there's a reason you're so resistant."

"Can we please sit? I'm ravenous."

"Very well. Pinched feet and empty stomachs mustn't be ignored, not even for your John."

"He's not mine," she said softly.

But he could've been.

Say yes.

The first course was soon served, and Mr. Bell scooted closer, away from the other guests at their table. "I'm curious why you think Thornton wouldn't want to buy Helstone back from me. Did he tell you that?"

"Not in so many words." Margaret sipped her wine, remembering her conversation with John in that back room at Helstone. She could still recall the spicy, bourbon smell of him and the uneasiness hanging between them. Not quite hope, not quite resignation.

"I imagine it was monosyllabic," Mr. Bell said.

She smiled a little, pushing her food about with her fork. "Yes, but I knew what he meant."

"And?" Mr. Bell pressed.

"Helstone can't be what it once was for John." She fiddled with her fork. "I think we all hope that if we can return to the places where we were happy, all those happier times will somehow come back with us. But they don't. Helstone was where John loved his father best, where they were happiest, but it's also a constant reminder of what he lost and can't get back. Helstone gave him hope he could have that happiness again, especially when he was young. He knows better now. He has to make his own way, and make his happiness somewhere else, somewhere all his own," she turned to look where John sat at the bridal table next to Lana Lancaster, "by looking to the future."

John had leaned closer to Lana, listening to something she whispered behind her hand. Margaret pressed her lips tightly together and turned back to Mr. Bell, who was smiling.

"Dear woman," he said, "you know Thornton better than anyone."

"I don't," she insisted. "Not really."

"I doubt Lana Lancaster could've answered my question."

"Mr. Bell, please." Margaret said, embarrassed, and ever so slightly pleased. "You shouldn't say such things. It's awkward and rude."

"It's the truth. If I don't say it, who will?"

"John will." It came out before she could stop herself. "He's always saying things he shouldn't."

"That he does." Mr. Bell glanced sideways at her. "I imagine he's said many interesting things to you."

"I don't know what you mean."

"I think you do."

"John's right." She took a sip of her drink. "You *are* a meddlesome bastard who likes to make other people dance."

"A badge I wear with immense pride, but you'd like me to mind my own bloody business now, wouldn't you?"

"Quite."

"As my goddess commands."

"Who are you looking for?" Lana Lancaster was seated on John's right. This was the fifth time she'd interrupted his dinner, almost shouting to be heard over the noise.

"What?" John glanced up from his plate and leaned closer. The room was buzzing with talk, laughter, and the blare of awful pop songs Fran liked. He wasn't sure how much more he could take.

Lana cupped her hand next to her mouth and said sharply, "You keep looking around like you're expecting someone. It's Margaret Hale, isn't it?"

"That's none of your damn business."

She looked stunned for a second, but it quickly melted into annoyance, and she turned back to her food. "Whatever."

"Excuse me." John wiped his mouth with a napkin, pushed

back from the table and headed for the closest exit.

He needed some air.

After Margaret's visit to Helstone, and Mr. Bell's unwelcome advice, a stupid spark of hope made him look for her wherever he went. He'd seen Mr. Hale at the ceremony, but not her, and he wasn't prepared for the stab of sharp disappointment, wearing his patience thinner than it already was. Lana's words only added more sting to his sore pride.

"John-John?"

He turned. Frannie had followed him outside.

"Where are you going?"

He studied his sister, veiled and plastered in a cloud of white fluff that looked hot and itchy as hell. He sighed. "It's been eight hours, Fran. I'm done."

"Go on then," she said with a sigh.

"Be happy." He bent down and kissed the top of her head. "Tell Watson if he ever hurts you, I'll kill him. Slowly."

"I love you too." Frannie gave him a tight hug and poked him in the ribs, smiling. "I still think you're a dinosaur."

John chuckled as she turned and flounced back inside. He walked slowly down the circling drive to a clump of large trees, leaned against one, and let the city silence settle over him. His thoughts immediately returned to Margaret. Her stay at Helstone wasn't perfect, but it was close to it. He closed his eyes and allowed himself to re-live the memory. Like the first domino in a long line of moments, their time at Helstone led him back through the last three years, each memory of Margaret turning over the next. Not all of them were pleasant, but it was all he had, and today it was enough.

♡

The cake was cut, everyone was smiling and clapping. Frannie delicately fed her Mr. Watson a perfect bite, making certain not to drop one crumb on him. Watson got some frosting on her nose, but she only smiled and ate her bite before he could take it further. There was a long awkward pause, as people waited for the toasts to begin.

"Where the devil is Thornton?" Mr. Bell twisted in his seat, glancing around the room. "He's supposed to make the first speech."

Margaret frowned, curious, as Mr. Bell glanced over to where Mrs. Thornton sat. He stood up, walked quickly across the room, and dramatically tapped the microphone, snagging a glass of champagne from a bridesmaid in the process. The crowd fell silent.

"I'm Adam Bell, and if you don't know me already, you should. I like having my own way and, on this glorious occasion, I wished to give a toast. Imagine my good luck when Thornton was gallant enough to bow out, quite literally."

The guests laughed, easily charmed. Margaret shook her head, her attention wandering around the room again. Where had John gone? She looked up when she felt someone come stand next to her. Margaret let out a small, surprised gasp.

Mrs. Thornton nodded at her. "Miss Hale." The older woman drew in her breath and pressed her lips together. "I trust you enjoyed your visit to Helstone?"

"I did, thank you. Frannie was kind to invite me."

Mrs. Thornton nodded stiffly. "Thank you for coming today."

Margaret opened her mouth to reply, but the older woman held up her hand. "My daughter means a great deal to me, whatever some people think." She glanced at Mr. Bell. "I'm not an affectionate person, but my children are all I have left. Their happiness is important to me."

"Are you going to tell me to stay away from John?" Margaret asked.

"If I did, would you listen?"

Margaret hesitated. "I don't know," she said truthfully. "Did he ask you to say something to me?"

"No." The word was bitter. "He would never ask that."

Margaret looked away, hiding a sudden flush of relief behind her glass of wine.

"He'd be furious if he knew I was interfering now."

"Then maybe you shouldn't."

"You don't know him at all; you don't value what kind of man he is. You've made your choice."

"Mrs. Thornton—"

"You took a good man, and tossed his honest affection aside like it was worthless. Have the decency to let him move on."

Margaret closed her eyes, trying to control the sudden angry tears that sprang up. When she opened them, Mrs. Thornton had gone, and Mr. Bell was finishing his toast. She stood, gathered her things, and hurried from the room, as the wedding guests toasted the new couple. Once outside, she took several deep breaths of fresh air, trying to settle her churning stomach. She walked down the curving drive towards a grove of large trees glowing in the green-golden light of the setting sun. She paused when she caught sight of a tall, familiar figure, a blush of shame rushing into her cheeks.

Did you even think about what John wants?

The memory of Bess's words made her chest hurt. Margaret hadn't thought about John at all when he'd proposed. Everything had been too much. All she'd thought of was her own confusion and fear. She had no idea what he wanted now, and part of her ached to know. Part of her hoped he still wanted her. What would he say if she asked?

Did she even want to know?

♥

"Are you hiding?" a soft voice asked. John looked over his shoulder, surprised. Margaret Hale stood there, arms folded against the chilly wind, as if his thoughts had called her up out of nowhere. He didn't answer. He simply stared as she walked over and leaned her back against the tree where he stood.

"They're doing the dances. Your mother will be waiting for you."

"I told her I wasn't dancing."

"Not a wedding person?"

He chuckled and shook his head. "Definitely not."

"But it's your sister's wedding to your best friend."

"I behaved myself."

"By abandoning them before their wedding was over," she teased. "You ought to be thoroughly ashamed of yourself."

"Don't worry. My mother will rip me a new skin later."

"I'm sure she will," Margaret said. Her smile looked forced. "I can't say I blame you for skiving off," she admitted. She placed one hand against his arm and kicked off her heels. "I don't mind the fancy dress, but the shoes are bloody torture."

"The grass is wet."

"I don't mind." She tossed her shoes aside and wiggled her stockinged toes, smiling in delight. She didn't move her hand from his arm, and he didn't mention it.

His eyes traveled over her, drinking in the slender curve of her neck and shoulders, and the silky skin of her back, the cut of her dress leaving most of it exposed. Her hair fell over and around her shoulders in soft brown waves. He couldn't help remembering what it felt like to run his hands through it all, or the fact that he wanted nothing more than to do it again.

"What are you doing out here?" she asked.

"Not a damn thing."

"Lost in your thoughts?"

"Something like that."

"Is it ever pleasant inside your head? I've always wondered."

He gave her a slow smile. "Depends on what I'm thinking about."

She dropped her hand and fiddled with her camera.

"Did you get any good pictures?"

"I think so." Her smile widened with genuine pleasure. "Would you like to see them?"

He nodded. "Why do you like polaroids? There are cheaper ways to take pictures."

"I like the challenge." She rummaged through her purse. "It's hard to wait for the right moment and even harder to capture it. But when you do," she shrugged. "I can always go back and see those moments that struck me the most." She handed him a picture. "I only take pictures of things I love."

"You love my sister and my mother?" He looked up from the photo, grinning widely.

"Look at it again, smart ass. It's more about—" she hesitated, trying to find the right words.

"A mother and her daughter."

She nodded. "That."

"You miss your mother."

"I do," she admitted. She shook herself and forced a smile. "It was a lovely day."

"It was a wedding."

"It could've been so much worse. You could be dancing right now." John rolled his eyes. "The penguin suit and forced merriment are bad enough. I hate parties. And pictures."

"Oh yes and you had to smile on purpose, too. What a tragedy." She folded her arms and leaned back against the tree again. "For what it's worth, you don't look like a penguin. You look rather nice."

"It's a rental." He shifted his shoulders. "I hate rentals."

"Was there anything about today that you didn't hate?"

"The booze."

"Liar." She shook her head. "You didn't drink anything."

John raised his eyebrows. She couldn't have known that, unless she'd been watching him. That did something to his head. He moved closer.

"At least you're not a bridesmaid," she continued, "wearing an ugly dress and shoes that cost a fortune, neither of which you'll ever wear again. The shoes are a torture device."

"I believe you."

"But?"

"But they look damn good on you." He took the liberty to freely examine her, from the front this time. The fading light fell through the trees picking up the goldish-red tint of her hair and brightened her eyes. The purple dress flowed over her like water, hugging every perfect curve of her breasts, hips, legs, and belly.

He swallowed, his mouth suddenly dry.

"So, do I pass your inspection, Mr. Thornton?" Her smile widened when he scowled. He hated it when she refused to use his name.

"You know you do. You always do."

"Is that a compliment?" She looked a little surprised and pleased, like she hadn't expected it.

He kept his eyes locked on hers, not bothering to answer. He wasn't sure what sort of dance this was, but he couldn't make himself end it. "I didn't think you'd come today."

"I almost didn't."

She didn't look away when he stepped closer. "I'm glad you did."

"Me too." She reached forward and pulled his arm towards her, pushed back his sleeve, and checked his watch. "It's late. Dad will be worried."

"You'll miss the dancing."

"I'm rubbish at it, remember?"

"You just need the right partner."

"Maybe." She hesitated, flushing a pleasant pink, and gathered her shoes. "I should go."

"I'll walk you to your car."

"It's not far. You probably have more smiling to do for pictures, yeah?"

He put his hands in his pockets and waited in stubborn silence while she slipped her shoes back on.

She sighed. "You're impossible."

He followed her as she walked away, shortening his lanky stride to her shorter one.

"It's not even that dark, you know."

"Humor me."

They reached her car, and she dug her key out of her bag. "Will you be walking Lana Lancaster to her car as well?"

"Probably. She's my ride back."

"Where's your truck?"

"At the office."

"You'll have to do some dancing and smiling after all."

"Seems like it." John shoved his hands into his pockets. "I might just walk home."

"Walk?" She turned, her face incredulous. "It's seven miles to the center of town."

"I like walking. And I hate dancing."

"John, that'll take hours, and it's getting dark."

He leaned down, resting an arm on the top of her car, with a smug grin. "It's not that dark, Maggie."

"Smart ass."

"Your fault, not mine."

She gave him a funny look. Something about it made John tense, the muscles in his shoulders and back tightening, as if bracing for something. "Maggie?"

"Impossible man." She raised her chin and unlocked her car, pointing to the passenger side. "Get in."

Chapter 37

Margaret stared at the data on her computer, her eyes glazed and stinging from overuse. Lately it felt like nothing made any sense except the pixilated numbers on her screen. She looked up at her tiny bulletin board, covered in scraps of paper and sticky notes and pictures that normally made her smile. She couldn't smile today.

She took out the polaroid of Bess she always carried, traced the edges with her finger, and hung it in the center of her bulletin board. Today, grief cut through her like a serrated knife, leaving a raw, ragged path in its wake. "I miss you." She leaned over and laid her head on her desk. "I wish you were here."

"Hey Mags?" Terry Hopkins rolled around the corner, still in his office chair.

She didn't move.

He kept chewing his pizza bagel bites too loud, smacking his lips in a wet, irritating way that was like nails on a chalkboard. "There's someone here to see you."

"Who is it?"

"I don't know." Terry put his headphones back on and jerked his head towards the library foyer. "It's some dude."

"That's incredibly unhelpful. Details would be appreciated."

"Tallish, dark hair."

"Is that all?"

"I'm a programmer. What else do you want?"

"You're really thick, you know that? Is he young or old? Handsome or not?"

"Older than you. Wearing a baseball cap."

She sat up sharply. "Is it red?"

"I'll tell him to go."

"No, don't." It came out too quickly, but she didn't care. "I know him." She switched off the computer screen, pulled her compact out of her desk, and popped it open. As far as the three-inch mirror could tell her, she was a complete wreck. She ran her fingers through her hair and smeared on some tinted lip balm, sighing. She ought to have showered this morning.

She hadn't seen or spoken to John since Frannie's wedding a month ago. His lessons with her father had been so infrequent and unpredictable, she usually missed seeing him. He hadn't been to church in ages either. Margaret stood and hurried towards the front of the lab, a strange clarity breaking over her.

She missed John. She missed his silence, his sarcasm, and the way he could laugh with his eyes, and how she knew exactly what he would say, even when he didn't say it. She stopped, pressed her back to the wall, and tried to think, hiding herself behind a large fake tree, her heart pounding as if something important were about to happen.

They'd spent a nearly perfect evening together after Frannie's wedding, driving around Milton and talking for almost two hours, instead of going home. He'd told her the history of the city and pointed out the older districts with the loveliest architecture. They'd argued and bickered, but in a pleasant way. When they finally turned in for the night, after he bought them both cheap milkshakes, John had given her a look that made her heart pound. If he was here now, to see her, did that mean he wanted to try again? To try *them* again?

Bloody hell. If they started down this road, there was only one ending. Did she want that ending? Did she want him?

She took a deep, steadying breath.

There was only one way to find out.

The man in the foyer wasn't John.

"Fred?"

Her brother turned, yanked off his hat, and flashed her his toothpaste-ad smile. "Hey Meg."

"Fred!" She pounced on him, throwing her arms around his neck. "You're here."

He twirled her around and pulled her into a bear hug. Every day, for nearly five years, she had waited, hoping to hear from him, hoping for some news that he was doing well, but as the days passed, she'd buried her hopes beneath the harsh reality of his absence. Now, she hugged him hard, trying to convince herself that he was here. Really and truly.

She pushed him back and studied his face, taking in the tanned skin, the bloodshot eyes, the hair that needed a wash and a cut, and the scraggle on his face. "Five bloody years and not a peep, Fred."

"Yeah, I know." He fluffed her hair, and she hugged him again, hard. "Don't be like that."

"Not one phone call, email, or text. What the bloody hell?"

He had the decency to look sheepish. "You're happy to see me."

"Of course, I am." She held on to him tighter. He was too skinny, too frail. She couldn't stay mad at him. She never could.

She finally let go, stepped back, and folded her arms across her chest. "Are you clean?"

"God, Meg, I'm an adult." He rolled his eyes. "Do I look that bad?"

"Bad enough. You need a trim, a shave, and a wash. Are you eating proper food?"

"There goes Mummy Megs, trying to fatten me up."

"Don't call me that."

He chuckled and poked her in the stomach. "What'll you do about it, huh?"

"Shut up, Fred." She pushed his hand away, holding onto it in both of her own. "Where've you been? I've worried and worried. Dad worried too. We didn't know where you were."

"I've been around," he said dismissively. "Everywhere and nowhere. You know how it is."

"Does Dad know you're in town?" She regretted the question as soon as Fred's face closed into a hardened sneer.

"You got something to eat around here?" he said, quickly changing the subject.

She shrugged. "I have some granola in my desk."

"Food, Meg, not sawdust."

"There's food at the house. I could cook," she offered.

He scowled and began to shake his head.

"You have to see Dad sometime," she insisted. "I won't forgive you if you don't at least pop in and say hello. Come on, Fred. Do it for me?"

He sighed, and grinned, a flat thing that didn't reach his eyes. "Sure, Meg. Let's go say hey to Dad."

Margaret quickly told Terry she was going home, and that she'd be back early tomorrow to make up for it.

"Okay." Terry looked over her shoulder at Fred, who was busy texting someone. "Who's this guy? You seem pretty happy to see him."

"He's nobody," she said, trying to sound casual. "We grew up together. We're just catching up."

"An old boyfriend?"

"No. He's nothing like that."

"Sure, whatever." Terry looked skeptical, and Margaret felt nervous, like she always did when people asked too many questions about her brother. It was none of their business.

"Please don't mention him to anyone. He's sort of a private bloke and likes to keep to himself. Forget he was here, okay?"

"My lips are sealed." Terry gave her a look before he strolled back to his desk. "See you tomorrow."

John jammed his shoulder against the window frame in his office, trying to crack the paint so he could open it. It refused to budge. He ran both hands through his hair and checked his watch. He needed some air—some *fresh* air. He grabbed his truck keys and hat, told Williams he was taking his lunch, and drove out of downtown Milton towards the St. Michael Cemetery. It took almost twenty minutes, but the view was worth it. From the top of that hill, he could see for miles, the city sprawled out at his feet.

He sat on the hood of his truck and breathed deeply. The current economic crisis was closing in on The Depot. The missing shipments and canceled contracts because of the strike the year before had hit hard. The recent housing crash only rubbed more salt into an already gaping wound. Any hopes he'd had to dredge up some new clients from the conference in Blanding were long gone. Still, he wouldn't go down without a fight.

He laid back onto the windshield and closed his eyes, listening to the birds and the wind and the leaves, ignoring the muffled noises of the city. The summer sun warmed his face. His thoughts calmed and immediately turned to Margaret. He knew now he couldn't get over her. It had been more than a month since he'd seen her at Frannie's wedding. Everything about that night made him hold on to a stupid, growing hope that something between them had changed. He thought about the setting sun shining through the trees on her hair, the gentle curve of her neck and shoulders, the laughing blue-gray of her eyes.

Untuck your tail, dust yourself off, and try again.

Williams had been right. He'd be a damn fool not to try again. He already had a lesson scheduled with Mr. Hale tonight. All he had to do was ask. The thought propelled John to his feet and back to the office with renewed energy.

Mr. Hale stared in shock when Margaret dragged Fred into their tiny kitchen. "Frederick?"

"Hey, Pops." Fred's greeting was like a challenge, and Margaret flinched at his tone.

She looked at her father, her eyes pleading. But Mr. Hale pulled his estranged son into a hug, startling them all. Fred stood awkwardly, hands hovering out to his sides as his father hugged him hard. Margaret let out a small breath and relaxed.

Mr. Hale let go and stepped back, studying his son. "How are you?"

"Why does everyone in this family feel the need to interrogate me? I'm fine."

"We love you," Margaret said, her voice low and placating.

Fred looked embarrassed and she smiled.

Mr. Hale turned back to the stove. "To what do we owe such an unexpected visit?"

Fred glanced at Margaret before dropping his eyes to the floor. "I heard about your mom dying. I'd have come sooner, but, you know, life happened."

"Who told you about Mum?"

"Dixon called me."

"You're a little late," Mr. Hale said, his face stern and pale.

"It was nice of you to come." Margaret said quickly. She took Fred's hand and squeezed it. "Really. We're happy to see you."

"Yeah, well, I thought maybe," Fred shrugged, "anyways, Maria and I weren't close, but I thought," his sentence trailed off and he frowned at his own awkwardness. "I am sorry."

"Thanks," she said. Her brother had never got on with her mother. But that was more her mother's fault than Fred's.

She turned to her father and tried to force a lightness into her voice that she didn't feel. "What's for supper, Dad?"

"I made lasagna."

"Pops cooking?" Fred grinned, but it was too sharp. "Now I've seen everything."

Margaret frowned. "Are we expecting company?"

"John has a lesson."

"I forgot." She looked from her father to Fred, a small panic tightening in her stomach. John was coming tonight, and he didn't know about Fred. She guessed they had another half hour before he arrived. Time enough to get her brother out of there and save her father the embarrassment of explaining him to John.

She forced herself to smile. "Dad only cooks five meals." She moved closer to her brother, counting on her fingers. "Lasagna, curry, tomato soup, roast beef with pan roasted potatoes, and baked chicken thighs."

"I make pancakes on Sunday mornings too."

"Fine. Six meals." She smiled at her father. "I bought him a cookbook at Christmas, but he hasn't opened it yet."

Fred laughed, and Mr. Hale looked at the floor, allowing himself a small grin. "When one lives alone as long as I have, cooking tends to be utilitarian."

"It's your own fault," Fred said and leaned towards Margaret. "Why do you live with him?" he asked, pulling a packet of cigarettes out of his pocket, lighting one. "It would drive me crazy."

"Fred, don't." Margaret hated being pulled between her brother and their father, like always. She looked at their father, the tension tight and obvious in the lines of his shoulders. "Save your fag for later, yeah?"

"Nah." Fred grinned and took a long drag. "Who's this John person?" He grabbed the one banana sitting in the fruit bowl. "A boyfriend of yours, Meg?"

"Did you ever finish your program, Frederick?" Mr. Hale interrupted, his voice too sharp.

"You mean that lame-ass excuse for rehab you dumped me in four years ago?"

"Fred—"

"It was for the best," Mr. Hale said.

"Bullshit. It was a hole in the wall where you could hide me away from all your stupid church friends."

"Please don't do this now." Margaret put a hand on her brother's arm, but he flung it off.

"No more, Frederick," Mr. Hale spoke firmly, looking more defeated than he'd looked since his wife died. "Please."

"What are you going to do?" Fred ground his cigarette on the table, ashes flicking across the clean surface. "Kick me out? Call the cops? Ruin your precious reputation?" Fred scoffed. "Poor Father Richard and his poor bastard son exposed at last."

"Fred," Margaret snapped. "Stop that."

"Look me in the face, old man, and tell me you don't wish I'd never been born. That you aren't ashamed of me."

"I am ashamed." Mr. Hale's shoulders slumped, his face pale. "Of myself."

Two sharp knocks at the door made everyone jump and turn towards the front hall.

"That's John." Margaret stood and grabbed at Fred's hand, pulling him towards the back door. She couldn't explain Fred to him, not now, not without humiliating her father even more and inviting John's merciless judgment.

"Come on." She dragged her brother from the room.

Fred paused and grinned back at Mr. Hale, sharp and unforgiving. "Fuck you."

♥

John felt a twinge of disappointment when Mr. Hale opened the door. Margaret must be working late. Again.

"All right, John?"

"Hi." John hesitated. The older man looked exhausted. A sudden outburst of laughter made John glance over his shoulder and frown. Margaret ran to the Hales' battered car parked a little down the street, dragging a strange man after her. John's frown deepened, watching the pair pile into the car. What the hell?

"Come in, come in. I apologize. Things are a bit of a mess."

John turned back to his friend and stepped inside, but his attention was fixed on the muffled sound of car doors slamming and the familiar squealing whine of the engine.

"Am I interrupting something?" He forced himself to shut the door behind him instead of staring after the disappearing vehicle. "I can go."

"No, please. I've made lasagna."

"Do you have a visitor?" John took off his hat. He tossed it and his keys on the table by the door.

"No, no, it's just you and I tonight. No visitors and no Margaret."

John nodded and followed Mr. Hale into the kitchen. He glanced at the mess of ashes, half-finished cigarette, and banana peel next to the fruit bowl. He ran a hand through his hair. He was missing something. Mr. Hale only smoked a pipe, and Margaret hated bananas. Someone else had been here. It was none of his damn business, but something about it made him deeply uncomfortable.

Like he was being lied to.

Chapter 38

"I don't want to go into Outwood Station pub this late, Fred." Margaret folded her arms and leaned against the car. "They'll want to see my ID, and I don't have my bag."

"It's just a restaurant."

"It's also the best bar on this side of town."

"Nobody in there gives a damn. They won't card you with me," Fred said, spitting the words out like a bad taste in his mouth. "Why do you always shit on my fun?"

"I don't like the bar scene. Besides, it's not good for you."

"Come on, Meg." Fred pulled his most charming smile, shifting seamlessly from frustrated anger to easy and relaxed. "Do it for your only brother."

She stuck out her tongue. "Only if you apologize to me and Dad."

"I didn't say anything he didn't deserve."

"He's your father."

"God, you can be a real b—"

"What? A bitch?"

"A brat." He winked and walked around the car to stand next to her. "If it'll make you happy," he said and slung an arm around her shoulder,

"I'm sorry."

"For being a right proper git?"

"Yeah. That."

"We're leaving the bar before midnight. Promise?"

"Don't ask for promises I won't keep." He grabbed her hands, and she let him pull her into the pub. The place was crowded with the after-work karaoke crowd.

"Bloody hell," she muttered. "Can't we go somewhere else, please? I hate karaoke."

He chuckled and collapsed into a booth close to the bar.

"I'd rather sit in the restaurant," she said, raising her voice over the increasing noise.

"What'll you have?" He studied the drinks menu, pretending not to hear. "Wine spritzer?"

"Bubbly water."

"Boring," he called in a sing-song voice. "Live a little."

"Someone needs to be boring and responsible. We both know it's not going to be you."

John sat at the intersection of Manchester Street and Outwood Lane, waiting for the light to change, his fingers drumming the steering wheel. His lesson with Mr. Hale had been mostly silent. The older man was too lost in his own head to deeply discuss anything, never mind the reading assignment. John spent the time mulling over his own troubled thoughts, while Mr. Hale smoked his pipe until the clock forced them both to give up.

On John's right, Outwood Station pub was teeming with people, inside and out. Thursday night was karaoke night. A familiar battered maroon car caught his eye. His hands tightened around the steering wheel, but he deliberately turned away and stared straight ahead. Why the hell was Margaret at Outwood Station at this time of night?

A horn blared behind him, and he swerved his truck into the crowded lot next to the pub. Something about this whole situation made him uneasy. His own angry curiosity got the better of him. Mr. Hale hadn't been himself tonight, and it had something to do with the stranger he saw with Margaret. Who was he? And why would Mr. Hale be so evasive?

He parked the truck and walked inside.

"John Thornton." The owner, Bill Sloan, stood behind the bar. He shook his hand. "How the heck are you?"

"Not great." John ordered a whiskey, neat.

"How's business?"

"Bad."

"Sorry to hear it. You want to open a tab?"

"This'll do." John glanced around the crowded room. Margaret was an adult and could handle herself. So why was he so suspicious? But he couldn't get the picture of her holding the stranger's hand—looking happier than John had ever seen her—out of his head.

"It's not your business," he muttered into his drink. Still, he stood there and searched the crowd until he finally spotted her in a small booth at the end of the bar, next to the restrooms. She was alone, fiddling with her skirt, looking uncomfortably out of place.

The strange man she was with soon stumbled out of the bathroom and staggered back to the booth. He sat and leaned in, whispering into her ear. She laughed, blushed a little, some of her discomfort melting into a fond, begrudging smile. The man leaned closer, and she gently kissed his cheek.

"Shit."

It was a date. Margaret was on a date with someone. *Someone else,* his mind screamed at him. John finished his drink too fast and tossed some cash onto the bar. He wasn't doing himself any favors hanging around here. But he hesitated when her date stood and headed for the bar. John eyed the skinny, curly-haired man as he pushed through the crowd. He squeezed in next to John and ordered another round of tequila shots.

John watched Margaret fidget some more. She twisted around to study the wall clock with a deep frown, picking at her sweater cuff. It was long past midnight. When she finally looked back towards the bar, their eyes met. Her cheeks turned red, her expression shifting from surprise to nervous embarrassment. At the same moment, her date finally noticed John was staring.

"Hey there, bud." The stranger gave him a stale once over. "Enjoying yourself?"

"Your date wants to leave," John yelled over the music. "Take her home."

"Mind your own business," the stranger said and picked up his shots from the bartender. "Quit eyeballing mine."

John shook his head in barely contained disgust and wove his way through the crowd towards their table. "Maggie."

"John?"

"*This* guy's your John?" the stranger slurred. He slammed himself down into his seat, laughing. "God, he's a stiff. You can do so much better, Meg." He winked at John. "With me."

"Do you want to leave?" John asked, focused on Margaret.

"I—" she hesitated, frowning at the table. "I'm fine."

"That's not what I asked." He didn't know what the hell was going on, but he didn't like it one bit. She was letting this shithead take advantage of her, like he had some prior claim. And maybe he did. The thought turned John's stomach.

"Hey, bud," the stranger sneered. "Take your lecture somewhere else. Leave us alone."

"Stop it." She glared at her date and shoved away the tequila shot. "I told you I don't want any."

"Maggie." John clenched his fists.

She finally looked at him, her face shifting instantly from discomfort to defiance, daring him to think what he liked about her. It pissed him off even more.

"You heard the lady." The stranger threw an arm around Margaret's shoulders and jerked her closer. He drained his glass and reached for her shot. "Fuck off."

She gasped. "Please stop," she said, dumping her drink onto the floor. "You've had enough."

"God." The man jumped up and shoved her aside as she tried to stand, marching towards the bar. "Forget you."

John caught her elbow as she fell backwards, but he was too slow. Her head made sharp contact with the exposed brick, and she winced, her legs trembling. She pressed her hand to the back of her head. When she pulled it away, there was blood on her fingers.

Crack! Crack!

John's ears were ringing. He steeled himself against the sudden memory of gunshots and the smell of blood and hazy blue glare of hospital lights.

Come on, Maggie, look at me.

"You're bleeding." He dug his handkerchief from his pocket and pressed it gently against the back of her head, his other arm circling around her shoulder. "Come on."

His decision was made; he was going to get her out of here. He'd failed her once before, and he wouldn't do that again. He helped her out of the booth and led her through the crowd, every step making him angrier and angrier. "Who the hell is that asshole, Maggie?"

"It's none of your business who he is." She glared at him and raised her chin. "He's no one."

"Liar."

It was the wrong thing to say.

"Let go." Her voice was hard and bitter. She wrenched herself free. "I don't need or want you here."

He stood there stupidly, his thoughts moving too fast for him to grab one and make sense of it.

I don't want your twisted version of affection. I never will.

He swore, turned, and walked away.

The dark expression on John's face cut Margaret like a knife. She'd hurt him again, and he couldn't hide it. As he turned away, she reached out to stop him, but Fred stumbled away from the bar, shouting at the owner, who watched him with a knowing stare, one hand on the telephone. Margaret felt panic roll in her stomach. She couldn't leave Fred, and she couldn't let John go like this. But her feet wouldn't move.

The front door slammed shut, the sound shaking her. John was gone. He hadn't looked back once. At the same moment, she heard her brother yell a series of foul remarks at the bar owner.

"Fred, shut up," she snapped and rushed over. "I'm sorry," she said to the owner, who grunted and hauled a protesting Fred outside.

Her brother sank to the ground still muttering. She pulled out her mobile and rang Mary Higgins. She knew she shouldn't bother Mary, but who else could she trust to understand?

I've got you.

She shook the memory away, guilt and shame washing over her. Maybe John would've tried, but she'd lied to him, and he knew it. He wouldn't understand why.

And he wouldn't forgive her again.

Between the two of them, Margaret and Mary managed to get Fred into the back seat of the car, before he completely passed out. He could bloody well spend the night there, Margaret thought bitterly.

It served him right.

"Thank you, Mary." she slumped down the side of the car and sat on the asphalt. "Really, you're a hero."

"Don't thank me." Mary looked solemn as she sat next to her. "It's only fair, after everything you've done for us."

"What a night." Margaret buried her face in her hands. "Every time I think things are going well, they manage to fall apart in the most spectacular fashion."

"What happened?"

And then, she was telling Mary everything about Fred, about her father's infidelity, her parents' divorce, Fred's failed military career, the drugs, and petty crime—everything.

"Are you all right?" Mary asked after she finished.

"No." Margaret rubbed her eyes. "Everything is wrong. I miss Bessie and my mum. Fred and Dad are already at each other's throats, like always. They can't be in a room for one bloody second. And there's Fred getting drunk and yelling at the bartender and—" she stopped, swallowing hard. "And John."

"Wait, John was here tonight?"

"He was, and I lied to him," Margaret said. "The icing on a

very wretched slice of cake."

"Why did you call me if he was here to help you?"

"I couldn't tell him. You know how he is, what he thinks of people like Fred. Look at how he treated your father and Bessie with their struggles. I couldn't tell him the truth."

"Whatever he thinks about my alcoholic family," Mary said, "he gave them more chances than anyone else ever did. He didn't have to."

Margaret bit her tongue, face flushing in sudden shame.

"I think," Mary said slowly, getting to her feet, "you should trust him. Bess would agree with me."

"She probably would, but I think it's a little late for that."

"Don't be so melodramatic." Mary wiped the dirt from the seat of her jeans and helped her up. "John might surprise you, if you let him."

"I hate surprises," Margaret mumbled. "What time is it?"

"Late. Or early. Pick one."

"I'll come by campus tomorrow with some coffee, as a Thanks-For-Helping-Me-With-My-Pissed-Brother."

"I won't say no, but I'll be at Marlborough Shipping until four."

"You will?" Margaret asked, bewildered. "But why?"

"I'm working on an independent project through the college of nutritional science. Mr. Thornton gave me permission to develop a nutrition and exercise program for the truck drivers. Dad and Thornton cooked up the idea ages ago, and I've been helping with the design for college credits. I profile the drivers and personalize an eating guide with a targeted exercise plan. When they reach specific goals, they earn extra home-time. It's kind of genius. It's a lot of work but Thornton's been supportive. He said healthy drivers get more done in less time."

Margaret was speechless.

Mary laid a gentle hand on her arm and held out the handkerchief

Margaret had dropped earlier.

John's handkerchief.

"He's a good man."

"I never said he wasn't," Margaret said defensively.

But that wasn't exactly the truth.

"Then why won't you give him a real chance?"

Margaret couldn't answer.

"Don't let your pride and your fear turn you into a liar, Marg."

Chapter 39

The car was gone when Margaret got home from work the next evening. A familiar sinking feeling settled in her stomach that she couldn't ignore. "He took it," she muttered.

"What's that, dearest?"

"Nothing, Dad. I'm going for a walk."

She'd left Fred in the back seat to sleep it off the night before, taking the bus to the computer lab. He must have found the spare key. Fred was always good at finding things he shouldn't. It was almost sunset before she found him on the north side of town, talking with a strange man. She felt her temper boil. There was only one reason to be on the north side railroad tracks. She marched up to her brother, ignoring the slimy man who made her skin crawl. "Frederick Richard Hale."

Her brother looked startled, and the man he'd been talking with slipped off almost instantly. "Meg, what are you doing?"

"You stole Dad's car."

"I borrowed it."

"For what exactly? A joyride to the drug dealer's side of town?"

"Shut up, Meg."

"I thought so." She grabbed his arm and towed him to the car, which was parked illegally in front of a fire hydrant.

"I'm making friends."

"I'm sure you are." She glared at him, a hard silence falling between them.

Fred unlocked the passenger door. He tried again to make small talk as she let herself into the passenger seat, anger and fear crawling over her skin. "You're using again, aren't you?" she interrupted.

Silence.

"You told me you were clean." She blinked back tears, her heart sinking. "You lied to me."

"I didn't," he cut her off, shrugging. "You just assumed."

"Where'd you get the money? Did you steal that from Dad too?"

He didn't answer, his knuckles turning white as he gripped the steering wheel tighter.

"Damn it, Fred. How could you?"

He shrugged again.

She took a deep, shaking breath. There was only one thing to do now. "You need to leave."

"What?"

"You're going to leave Milton." She made her voice as hard and cold as possible. "Today. You can't stay if you're using."

He started to make some excuses, but she raised her voice. "I won't let you do this to me or to Dad again. We've been through enough with you. I'll buy you a bus ticket and that's it."

"Listen, Meg. I'm trying, okay? I just need to get my head sorted out. Give me a chance."

"You've had chances; dozens and dozens and dozens of them. How many more do you need before you can see that you're killing yourself and us?"

"You know what, fuck you," he snapped, the car speeding up. "You don't know anything about me."

"I know I can't do this," she said. She was crying. "Not anymore."

"Fine," he shouted, and blew through a red light. He shook himself and smiled, the change in his mood almost eerie. "Look, Meg, I need a little money to get going in the right direction. Help me out."

"I said I'd buy you a bus ticket."

"Just give me the cash, and I'll take care of it."

It was a thinly veiled excuse. They both jumped when a police siren sounded behind them. The officer signaled for them to stop.

Fred swore.

"Pull over before you make this worse." She tugged his arm when he ignored her. "Pull over, Fred."

"I can't."

"Why not?"

"I'll go to prison, Meg. There's a warrant out for my arrest." He laughed, but it was a cold sound. "Meg, listen. I need you to help me. I can't go back to prison."

"Back?" Her ears rang. *Bloody hell.* Her stomach rolled with sudden nausea. He was asking her to cover for him. Again. And God help her, she was going to do it, like she always did. She was a bloody coward.

"Here." She pulled out her wallet and handed him all the cash inside. It wasn't much. "Promise me you'll leave town."

"You're the best—"

"You always say that," she cut in, her voice heavy and defeated. "Don't come back, Fred."

She wasn't sure if he heard her.

The policeman ran through the usual list of inane questions. When he asked for Fred's license and registration, her brother made a show of looking for it, relaxed, almost cheerful. The officer walked back to his vehicle, and Fred whispered, "On three."

One, two, three. She bolted out the passenger door, and he ran in the opposite direction. She ran straight into the policeman, hitting the pavement when he grabbed her, the asphalt biting through her jeans. She hoped it was enough of a distraction for Fred to get away. For now, at least. Tears streamed down her face as the handcuffs clicked into place, and the officer called it in. Margaret wept, finally seeing the truth in all its ugly reality. She couldn't fix her brother. Nobody could. She thought she could save him, that if Fred had a real chance, he would take it because he loved her. But he'd never wanted to be saved and maybe never would. He loved her, but not enough.

People don't change, Marg.

She cried harder as the spark of hope she'd always carried for her brother died. Bess had been right, and she almost hated her for it.

The phone rang, and John nearly fell out of bed, swearing as he hit his shoulder against the bedside table. He almost threw the phone at the wall but thought better of it. He snatched it up, flicked it open, and growled, "Someone better be dead."

"John?"

He pulled the phone away from his ear and looked at it. He took a half second to compose himself. "Margaret?" His voice rasped and cracked.

It was so stupid.

When he left her at Outwood Station with her date, he didn't think he'd have to speak to her again. Not this soon. He could still see the skinny stranger, arm flung around her shoulders, stumbling around, talking to her in a familiar way that made John's blood boil. He cleared his throat, shaking away the memory. "What's wrong?"

"I'm sorry to wake you," she said softly. She sounded worn and tired, and she was crying. "I need help."

"Help?" He shook his head, rubbing his eyes. "With what?"

"I'm in jail. My dad can't find out. He'll worry. I know I shouldn't even ask you but—"

"You're in jail?" He sprang to his feet and began to pace, a dozen questions running through his mind. "What the hell happened?"

"Please, John." She paused. "Will you please help me?"

He rubbed the back of his head, and checked his watch, sighing sharply. No matter how angry he was, he couldn't say no. "Give me thirty minutes."

The police station was a murmur of activity. Margaret kept her focus on her shoes, but John saw the tear stains on her cheeks, her eyes red, hollow, and glazed. Her jeans were ripped and blood-stained. She hadn't said a word to him or the police. He shook his head. He couldn't make sense of it. He turned back to the officer signing the appropriate paperwork. He knew this woman and several of the people who worked in this building. They wouldn't ask him questions out of courtesy, but he knew they wouldn't forget about him or Margaret.

"Your court date is set for the thirtieth, Miss Hale. Failure to show will result in the usual penalties. Do you understand?"

Margaret stared at a spot in front of her feet and nodded mutely.

"Do you have any questions, Mr. Thornton?" the officer asked him, clearly curious.

"No."

The officer shrugged and handed him the paperwork Margaret needed. "Her car has been impounded. She can contact us if there are any questions."

"We don't have questions," he said, and glanced around the room again, "and neither do you. Keep a lid on this, Jane. Please."

The police officer gave him a look, but she nodded. "I'll take care of it, sir."

"Thank you."

John guided Margaret firmly out of the station and helped her into his truck. They sat in the silent dark while his thoughts whirled, his grip on the steering wheel almost painful. This time the charge was obstruction of justice. How many times had this happened to her? And why? And why the hell had she dragged him into this and not the shithead she was dating?

She took a breath. "Thank you—"

"No." The word exploded out of his mouth, hard and cutting. "Don't thank me." He looked at her hard. "The only reason I'm here is your father."

"John, please." She fiddled with a piece of string on her shirt, twisting and untwisting it around her finger. "I know how this looks, but I promise it's not what you think."

"Then tell me what to think."

"I can't. Not without hurting someone else."

"Someone else." His stomach rolled. "That asshole you were with?"

"It's not my secret to tell."

"Keep your damn secrets," he growled. He turned the key in the ignition, put the truck in gear, and pulled out of the police station parking lot. "Next time, call your shithead boyfriend to come get you, and leave me out of it."

She gasped. The small sound was like a punch to the gut. His words had hit where it hurt. He wanted to feel satisfied, but all he felt was sick to his stomach.

♥

For once, John couldn't bring himself to walk Margaret to her door. She moved slowly, and when she stepped onto the porch, she paused and looked back at him. She was crying again. He waited until she turned, slipped the spare key from under the mat, and let herself in. The door closed. His mind jumped immediately to what needed to be done next. He would pick up the Hales' car in the morning before Mr. Hale missed it, but first, he had a call to make. He sighed and pulled out his phone.

"This better be good, Thornton," a gravelly voice said.

"I have a favor to ask, Chris. You're going to get an obstruction of justice charge. Last name is Hale."

"Are you asking me to make it disappear?" Chris Pollack sounded amused. As kids, he'd been a punk jock who made life miserable for everyone. As the county prosecutor, he was still a jerk, but damn good at his job. "That doesn't sound like you."

"I'd never ask that, and you know it. It's for a friend." John almost choked on the word *friend*. "I don't have proof but—"

"You think they're innocent?"

"I don't know if she is or not."

"She?" Chris suddenly sounded far too interested. "Is this your little girlfriend I've heard about?"

"I'm asking if you can help her."

"If it's a first offense, I can go easy on her, even if she's guilty as sin."

"Do it legally, or not at all."

"You got it."

"I owe you one."

"I'm going to enjoy every second of that."

John hung up and tossed his phone onto the dash. He turned his truck towards the highway and drove, the night flashing past, not caring where he went. The idea of Margaret lying for that shithead of a stranger, and being abandoned by him, made John feel physically sick. He picked up speed, driving until it was nearly morning, and he was almost out of gas. He stopped to fill his tank, turned around, and drove back to Milton.

♥

The moment the front door closed heavily, Margaret had slumped against the wall, sliding slowly to the floor. She stared into the dark, her eyes stinging, but she'd cried herself dry. She sat, playing John's stricken face over and over in her mind until she was sick with the memory. "Damn you, Fred." She slammed a fist against the floor. "Damn you all." She hit the floor again and again until her hands went numb. It was all too much; the shame, the regret, the desperation. She wanted it all to disappear, to erase the hurt and betrayal in John's face, and the razor edge of his voice.

"I'm sorry."

The night didn't answer. She stood, stumbled into the living room, and sank onto the couch. The house still smelled faintly of Fred, a lingering cigarette smoke smell. Somehow, more tears crawled down her cheeks again, and she cried herself into a numb, exhausted sleep.

SATURDAY: JUNE 21, 2008

When she woke, her head was pounding, her mouth dry. She burrowed further into her gran's old quilt and shut her eyes. She couldn't move.

"Margaret?" her father called from the kitchen. "I didn't hear you come in last night. Is everything all right?"

"Fine, Dad. I'm tired is all."

"Where's Fred?"

"He left town last night."

Her father didn't answer for a moment. Then, "Would you like pancakes or toast this morning?"

"I'm not hungry." She buried her head under the blanket. "You choose."

"I've got some good news." His voice moved closer.

She peeked out at his smiling face. "What news?"

He looked embarrassed. "I've decided to spend part of the next semester in Oxford with Mr. Adam Bell. The college has given me a grant. Isn't that lovely?"

She would've smiled, but she couldn't quite manage it. "You changed your mind."

"Thanks to you. I would like to visit my old haunts, and I might not get a chance again for a while." He paused. "You could come with me."

"I can't, Dad, but I'm glad you've decided to go."

The phone rang and Mr. Hale stepped back into the kitchen. "John? This is a surprise."

Margaret sat up sharply and pulled her knees against her chest, her heart pounding. What would John say? Would he tell her father what happened?

"Oh, yes. I understand," Mr. Hale was saying. "Take care."

She heard him hang up the phone and move around the kitchen, humming. "Who was that?" she called.

"John cancelled our lessons until further notice." Her father poked his head around the corner. "I think business must be very bad. This recession is hurting everyone. The Depot could be in real trouble, you know."

She sat, dazed and conflicted. John's business was struggling, yet he'd posted bail for her last night. He shouldn't have. So why did he? She pulled the quilt tighter around herself, as if to hide from all the bitter words and lies she'd flung between them like a wall.

The only reason I'm here is for your father.

Not her. She should've known.

"Dearest, may I ask you something?" Her father sat down on the edge of the sofa, dusting flour from his hands. "You don't have to answer if you don't want to."

She nodded.

"Do you think John is romantically interested in you?"

She couldn't speak, trying to swallow the lump in her throat.

Maggie, I love you.

"I suppose that's a yes." Mr. Hale took his handkerchief out of his trouser pocket, handed it to her, and patted her shoulder. "This explains several things."

"You," she hiccupped, "you knew?"

"Mr. Bell mentioned it first. And I've noticed John has a certain softness for you. I think he cares about you more than you realize. But if he hasn't asked you—"

"He did ask me," she blurted. "And I said no."

Her father frowned, speaking slowly, "What did he ask you?"

"Dad—" she broke off, the words choking her. "I don't think he cares anymore."

Her father pulled her into a protective hug and let her cry.

"I don't understand why I'm so upset. There's so much and I can't do it all. He's so angry with me, and I don't know what to do anymore."

Mr. Hale stroked her hair until she quieted and cleared his throat. "You've always seemed so much older and capable than other people your age." He squeezed her hand. "I think I've treated you too much like an adult instead of letting you simply be my daughter. That was a mistake." He took his now soggy handkerchief and replaced it in his pocket. "Allow me to give a little fatherly advice. Love covers a multitude of sins. Your pride is not worth your heartache."

He tapped a finger against her nose. "Trust me. I learned that the hard way."

She looked away, embarrassed and uneasy. They never talked about his affair or the divorce or Fred's problems. Her father's quiet admission was laced with a deep regret she hadn't noticed before. "I've ruined everything," she said finally, the words tasting bitter in her mouth. "John hates me again."

"Why would he hate you?"

"I lied to him. About Fred. I thought he wouldn't understand, so I lied, and he knows it."

"John is a good and reasonable man. He'll understand the truth." Mr. Hale stood and put his hands in his pockets, looking at her with a sad but kind smile. "But only the truth, Margaret Ann."

He walked back to the kitchen, and she sat, staring at a shaft of sunlight. She fiercely wished Fred had never come to Milton. But her behavior at Outwood Station wasn't his fault. It would've been so much simpler to tell John everything. To trust him. He valued the truth more than his own dignity, his reputation, or his heart. And she'd refused to be honest with him again and again for the sake of her own selfish pride.

"I wish I'd never met him."

But that wasn't the truth either.

Chapter 40

"Phone call for you, Master." Nick Higgins ducked into the office. "On line two."

John looked up from the mountain of paperwork covering his desk. Since Nick had moved from long hauls to local deliveries and office work, the two men had reached an odd truce. John no longer braced himself for what the older man might say or do next, and Nick worked his ass off. He was a good employee, and he kept his word.

"I got it." He picked up the phone. "This is John Thornton."

A brief silence. Then a throat cleared. "Thornton, it's Adam Bell. I'm calling with some difficult news."

John sighed. "What's happened now?"

"It's about Richard Hale."

"What about him?"

"He and I were at Oxford—"

"I know," John interrupted. "Get to the point."

"Thornton," Mr. Bell said softly, "he died last night."

"Died?" John sat for half a beat. Surely, he'd heard wrong. "Richard

Hale died?"

"In his sleep."

"Last night." John shook his head. That couldn't be right. "There's nothing wrong with him. He's not sick."

"The doctors are saying it was an aneurysm. Something about the flight overseas having brought it on, or something to that effect."

For a long moment, neither man spoke. Mr. Bell had been determined to visit Oxford and somehow talked Mr. Hale into joining him. The men weren't close friends, but they shared a love for England, Oxford, and Margaret. She'd encouraged her father to go, hoping time away from teaching might do him some good.

At the thought of Margaret, John stood and took two steps, the phone cord tugging the cradle into the scattered collection of stained coffee mugs clustered on the edge of his desk. He watched as one cup fell, almost in slow motion, shattering on impact with the concrete floor.

"Shit." He slammed a fist against the wall, the sting in his hand bringing his thoughts back into focus.

"I didn't know him well, but I am sorry," Mr. Bell continued, ignoring his outburst. "For dear Margaret's sake."

"Does Maggie know?" John demanded. First Bess had died, then her mother, then the shithead boyfriend left her, and now this; one sorrow after another fell on Margaret like rain, drowning everything in their path. "Have you told her?"

"I rang earlier." Mr. Bell sighed heavily. "I'm not sure what happened. She was on the line and then she wasn't. I was hoping you might have better luck."

"I'll find her," John said. He could always find Margaret. "I appreciate you giving me a call." He hung up and grabbed his keys and jacket.

"Williams! Slick!"

The two truckers appeared in the doorway so fast it was obvious they'd been eavesdropping and had heard most of the conversation. They both were uncharacteristically somber, following John as he marched to the machine shop where his pickup truck was parked. "I won't be back today. Slick, call the list of potential clients I've got on my desk. We need to hustle up at least half a dozen new contracts before the fifteenth, if we can."

"You got it, Master."

Williams cleared his throat. "You sure you want Slick to do that?"

"Williams, call the bank and set up a meeting for next week." John swung himself into his truck, ignoring his question. "One more thing." He hesitated. He hated asking his paid workers for favors, but Tucker Williams was more than just his employee. So was Nick Higgins.

"Master?"

"If my mother calls, tell her not to wait up for me."

"And if she asks why?"

"Be creative."

Williams grinned. "Sure thing."

"We'll hold down the fort. You find Margaret," Nick added and swung the truck door shut.

John checked the Hales' house first. "Margaret?" He knocked on the locked door, his mind racing. No answer. He crouched and pulled up the mat. The spare key was gone. He swore in frustration and knocked again, louder. "Maggie?"

Nothing.

"To hell with this." He took three steps back and ran at the door, slamming his shoulder hard into the weakest spot. It splintered at the knob where the wood was slightly rotten.

"Maggie?" he called, quickly searching the first floor. Her old quilt wasn't on the couch. He took the stairs three at a time and checked the bedrooms. Both empty. He jogged to his truck and drove across town to the computer lab where she worked. It was mostly deserted, but the tech on duty still let him in to check her desk when he explained why. There wasn't much to see except a faded polaroid of Bess Higgins on her bulletin board.

He snatched the picture free. He knew where she was.

When he pulled into the cemetery, he saw her huddling near the big oak tree. He grabbed the fleece blanket he kept under the seat and jogged up the hill, his boots slipping in the mud. She was soaked to the skin, staring blankly at Bess's headstone. He crouched next to her. "Maggie?" He unfolded the blanket and wrapped it around her. "You're freezing."

He grabbed her icy hands and breathed on them, trying to rub some warmth back into the skin. The wind blew her damp hair gently across her face. She stared straight ahead, eyes bright and glassy from unshed tears. How long had she been sitting out here?

She shivered as the wind picked up speed. John shrugged out of his jacket and pulled it over the blanket on her shoulders. "Come on, Maggie," he said, gently rubbing her arms. "Look at me."

The sun was starting to set. She needed to go home.

"I can't." Her voice was so soft and hollow, almost dead. "I can't stay there. No one's there anymore." She looked at him, tears spilling slowly down her cheeks. "My dad's gone, isn't he?"

He nodded.

"Everyone's gone. Mum, and Bessie, and Fred, and Dad, and—" her voice broke, her eyes widening with each name. "And John."

"I'm here."

"He's gone, and it's all my fault."

"No, Maggie." He held her face in his hands, his thumbs gently brushing over her cheeks. "That has nothing to do with you."

"But I told him to go, and he did."

"Your dad went to Oxford because he wanted to. It's not your fault."

She paled, shaking her head, tears gathering again, spilling over. "Dad." She stumbled to her feet, trembling. "He's gone too. He's gone."

Whatever had been holding her together broke, and she crumbled under the weight of the truth. John caught her and held her as she sobbed into his shirt, shaking with the unbearable, crushing loss. "I've got you."

He knew this kind of pain. If he could've spared her this hell, he would've. But the shadow of death couldn't be stopped, only endured. So, he waited, holding her up against the first onslaught. As suddenly as it had begun, the worst was over, and she slumped against him. "I want to go home."

He picked her up and carried her to the truck, moving slowly over the wet ground. The drive back to her house felt like moving through mud. He climbed the stairs and tucked her into bed, jacket, quilt, and all. He sat and pulled off her shoes. When he stood, she grabbed his hand. "Please, don't go."

He paused, hesitating.

"Please don't go again," she murmured and closed her eyes, already half asleep. "I'm so sorry. I didn't mean it. Tell John."

"I'm here." He waited for her to finish, but her breathing slowed into the deep steady rhythm of sleep. He squeezed her hand. "I'll stay."

When he was sure she was asleep, he fetched a spare pillow and a bed sheet from the tiny linen closet. He made up the couch and sat, staring at nothing as night fell. He couldn't make sense of it, but grief was like that. Thoughtless, numbing, overpowering.

Richard Hale was dead.

John leaned back heavily, scrubbing his face with his hands, the weight of the empty house settling on him. When his father had died, he had had Frannie and his mother, the Watsons, Dr. Donaldson, and even Mr. Bell.

Margaret had no one.

John moved slowly, pulled off his muddy boots, and tossed his hat, keys, phone, and wallet on the coffee table next to the shoebox of Margaret's photographs. Mr. Hale was proud of her pictures, always showing them off, but John had never taken the time to look at them before. He idly picked through them.

—Richard Hale, nose buried in a dusty book, pipe between his teeth—Bess Higgins, right before her accident, tired and smiling that smart ass smile of hers—Nick Higgins standing by his truck, laughing at Timmy Boucher who sat in the driver's seat—Mary Higgins and a blurred herd of children running around the Thomas Street Park—a flock of birds flying over St. Anthony's Cathedral, the bell tower cutting across the blue gray sky—Williams, sitting at The Depot radio, frowning—the Milton skyline—the oldest Boucher girl with a plate of cookies, looking proud—a wild, Helstone rose, growing in a chaotic mess over the gate—Frannie at her wedding, her smile wide and alive, and his mother, smiling back.

He paused, studying the photograph of his sister and mother. That conversation at his sister's wedding had given him hope. A stupid hope.

In my pictures I can always see the things I love.

These were the things and the people that Margaret loved. John stopped short when he saw the picture of the strange man from Outwood Station pub, sprawled out in the back seat of her father's car, sleeping. A fresh wave of defeated anger settled on John's shoulders, and he tossed the pictures aside.

I promise it's not what you think.

But what was he supposed to think when Margaret refused to tell him the truth? So much had happened, and none of it made any sense anymore. He had always believed a person controlled their own life, no matter when shit hit the fan. It happened to everyone. He sighed. He wasn't sure what he thought anymore. But he was here, and her dumbass boyfriend wasn't. Whatever happened next was up to Margaret, and it would have to wait for the morning.

TUESDAY: SEPTEMBER 2, 2008

A sharp, insistent knock came thundering through the stillness of the early morning. John scrambled to his feet, disoriented and bleary-eyed. "What the hell?"

Another impatient rap.

"Hold your horses," he grumbled and tugged on his shirt and jeans. He pulled the front door open and stared at a short, sharp looking woman, with viciously curled blonde-gray hair. She was glaring at him with equal surprise.

"Who're you?"

"Excuse me, sir, but I could ask you the very same question," the woman said. The waspish quality of her voice only emphasized her heavy English accent. "Where is Margaret Ann?"

"You're the aunt." He stepped aside, even as Margaret's aunt pushed her way past him. "Come on in," he muttered.

"Who are you?" The small woman was still speaking, moving

around the house like she owned the place. "I insist you tell me—"

"John Thornton."

"Oh." The woman stopped her flurry of movement and looked him over, sniffing loudly. "You're *that* man."

His frown deepened. He did not like this woman.

"Why are you here? Where is Margaret?"

Another knock interrupted them. John and the woman both turned towards the still-open door where Mary and Nick Higgins now stood. Nick nodded and took off his hat. "Morning, Master."

"Who are *these* people?"

"Friends," John growled.

Nick and Mary exchanged a look.

"We thought Miss Margaret might need a little company. We'll make something hot to drink," Nick said, and they slipped down the hall to the kitchen, leaving John and the aunt alone.

"I'm here for Margaret Ann. I'm her aunt—"

"I know who you are. Maggie's sleeping."

"Well," the woman seemed taken aback, "she can't stay in this dreadful place. I've come to—"

"She'll stay until she's ready to leave." He took a step, putting himself between the aunt and the staircase. "Come back later."

"Excuse me?" The woman stepped closer, but he didn't budge.

He straightened to his full height. "I said come back later."

"I'm Victoria Shaw, her closest surviving relative," the short woman continued, standing taller. "I don't care who you are, or why you're here, but I insist you leave immediately."

"No." John folded his arms, scowling. There was no way in hell he was going to let this woman anywhere near Margaret, but before he could open his mouth to say something worse, Mary returned from the kitchen with a steaming mug of tea. Nick followed, a cup of coffee in each hand.

"Someone should check on her," Mary said softly to John, deliberately ignoring the aunt, pleading with her eyes for him to let her by.

"Master." Nick said. His lined grizzled face was sad, like he knew John wanted to be the one to stand between Margaret and the rest of the world right now. Like he also knew John was trying to hold himself together. Margaret wasn't the only one who'd lost someone yesterday.

John's shoulders slumped and he nodded, letting Mary slip upstairs.

It didn't matter what he wanted anymore.

"I should go home," he muttered.

"Yes, you should," the aunt said. "My lawyer will contact you if any further communication is necessary."

John ignored her and the coffee Nick offered him. He gathered his things from the living room and left. He stood in the yard, barefoot, feeling helpless and angry, but there wasn't a damn thing he could do about it. He glanced up at Margaret's bedroom window.

"I'm sorry, Maggie."

He turned and left.

Chapter 41

Margaret stood at the foot of the Milton airport escalator, clutching one of her father's old books to her chest, like a shield or an anchor. Maybe it was both.

Once her Aunt Shaw had descended upon her, all the necessary arrangements were made in two agonizing days. Margaret didn't have the energy to say or do anything, allowing herself to be swept along in her aunt's path. It was almost nice to have someone tell her what to do and where to go. But she couldn't explain the incalculable relief she felt when Dale Dixon had turned up, unannounced, the same afternoon as her aunt's arrival, and refused to leave.

It was soon decided that after her father's funeral, Margaret would stay in England. Mr. Dixon offered to work directly with Henry Lennox and a local auction house to liquidate as many of Mr. Hale's remaining possessions as possible, as quickly as possible. After that, as executor, Margaret would be able to sift through her legal responsibilities under Henry's guidance. She had numbly agreed to it all, except for one thing.

"Don't sell the books."

"What will you do with them all?" her aunt demanded.

"I want them."

"It'll be such an inconvenience to ship them overseas."

"They're mine, and I want them."

Aunt Shaw had eventually conceded. Henry Lennox would return to Milton in person to sort out the selling of the house, and deal with the problem of Mr. Hale's extensive library then. Everything else had happened so quickly, and now Margaret was standing in the airport, waiting to fly home.

Home.

She frowned. Was London home anymore? Had it ever been her home? She'd spent her whole life longing for England, for a real home, and now she dreaded the thought of it. Going back meant leaving behind everything she'd grown to love since moving in with her father.

"Who, exactly, are we waiting for?" Aunt Shaw asked again.

"My friends." She hadn't seen anyone except Mr. Dixon and Aunt Shaw since Monday, but she was determined to wait until the last minute, if need be.

Her friends would come.

Aunt Shaw held her arm, a gesture part possessive, part comforting. Mr. Dixon stood nearby. Margaret had never understood what her mum had seen in him. He was unassuming and forgettable, but he had always loved her mother, and he was the only person Fred listened to. Margaret was strangely grateful for his large quiet presence now. She still didn't like him, and maybe she never would, but he was a good man.

"I don't think you can have many friends here to say goodbye to." Aunt Shaw declared, glancing again at a large clock. "We ought to go."

"They'll come," Margaret said. "You'll see."

Nick and Mary Higgins, and all the Boucher children, were the first to arrive. Lilly tried not to cry, and Timmy blushed when he gave Margaret a kiss on the cheek. She tucked her favorite Polaroid of Bess into Nick's shirt pocket, and the surly old truck driver brushed his eyes roughly. "You're a good girl. I miss your dad."

"Me too."

Some of her coworkers from the maths lab came next. Terry Hopkins gave her an awkward handshake, and Mina and Nabeel wished her good luck. Even Tucker Williams strolled into the terminal and swept her into a startling hug. He looked like he was about to say something, but he only grunted roughly, told her to take care of herself, and left.

When the first boarding call sounded over the intercom, Dixon gave her a crushing hug. "Take care, Margaret."

"You'll look after Fred, yeah?"

"I will." He took out a tissue and blew his nose. "Call if you need anything."

Mary hugged her fiercely. "Promise you'll come back?" she whispered.

"I don't know."

"Our flight won't wait, Margaret Ann." Her aunt stepped determinedly towards the escalator, but Margaret pulled her arm free when she caught sight of a familiar red hat. John walked through the sliding glass doors and glanced around. She hadn't let herself hope he'd come, but he was here. She slipped through the meandering crowd and met him halfway. "Hello."

"Hello, yourself," Frannie said, appearing at her brother's elbow. "Sorry we're so late."

"It's all right." Margaret said with a small, tired smile. "I'm really glad you came."

"Mama sends her best, and Watson too." Frannie gave Margaret an unexpected and sincere hug. "I'm sorry about your daddy," she said softly. "Really."

"Margaret Ann, the time," her aunt called sharply.

"You'll be staying in England," John said gruffly, half glancing at her aunt, "after the funeral."

It was a statement and a question.

Margaret swallowed hard and nodded. She held out the book in her hands. "This is for you." Her voice caught in her throat at the achingly familiar words.

How many times had a book passed between them?

"It's Dad's copy of Plato's *Republic*. I thought you'd like to have it." Her voice shook. "You were his good friend."

"And he was mine." John stepped closer and took the leather-bound book. "Thank you."

She nodded, blinking at the familiar sting of tears. There was so much more she wanted to say to him, but the words refused to come. He moved closer again, dropping his voice so only the two of them heard. "Will you ever come back home?"

She looked up. She could smell the faint hint of coffee, cheap soap, aftershave, and peppermint that always clung to him. She didn't understand his question. If he'd only tell her that *he* wanted her to come back, that he wanted *her* even though—

But why would he want her, after everything she'd said and done?

"Margaret Ann," her aunt called. "Our flight."

"Goodbye, John."

She was too exhausted, too numb and broken, to say anything else.

John watched Margaret step onto the escalator, his eyes fixed to the back of her head, hoping, waiting, willing her to look back one last time, to give him something, anything. The aunt disappeared first. "Turn around," he whispered under his breath. "Turn around and tell me you'll come home."

"Hey," Frannie tugged at his sleeve, "are you okay?"

He glanced down and she flinched back as she caught sight of his face. She frowned, confused, and turned sharply towards the escalator before looking back at him. "John, what—"

"I'm fine."

It was a lie, and he hated himself for telling it. He forced himself to turn towards the exit and walk away, leaving everything he loved behind. He didn't let himself look back again.

Margaret was gone.

It took less than three seconds for Frannie Watson to realize her brother was in love with Margaret Hale and had been in love with her for a while. It would've been funny too, except for the terrible look on his face after she left. John had never been in love with anyone before, never seriously dated, never showed more than mild interest. Somehow, Frannie always assumed he would never change, would never want or need another person. Not like that. But now that she saw the truth, it was the most obvious thing in the world.

Of course John was in love with Margaret.

Did Watson know? And why hadn't John told Margaret he loved her before she left? It would've been so romantic. Frannie sighed heavily. She turned to follow him, then stopped.

An envelope lay on the ground, near where he had been standing. She picked it up and turned it over. John's name was written on the front in a neat, old-fashioned cursive. It must have fallen out of the book Margaret had given him. Frannie knew she shouldn't open it, but it wasn't sealed, and she was curious.

Inside were three Polaroid pictures—a selfie of Margaret, smiling at a mirror, with the bright glare of the camera's flash reflecting off the glass, a picture of Mr. Hale, laughing over his pipe, and a picture of John from the Lancasters' New Year's Eve party the year before.

Frannie sucked in a small, sharp breath as she studied the polaroid of her brother. "She's in love with him too."

MONDAY: DECEMBER 1, 2008

Mrs. Thornton found her son asleep at his desk. Again. Even now, on the brink of failure, he worked harder than ever. She sighed and steeled herself as she thought about the coming days. Marlborough Shipping Depot would go under despite everything John had done to save it. She looked at the files, papers, and notes strewn across his desk. He'd shoved a stack of files to the side, probably in frustration, knocking several more to the floor. She quietly gathered up the papers and placed them back on the desk. Her hand paused over an envelope with John's name written in a soft cursive. She picked it up and glanced inside at the three photographs, her grip on the paper tightening in anger. Why would Margaret Hale give anything to John? Why couldn't she leave him alone?

"Good riddance," she muttered and tossed the envelope into the trash. She knew it was wrong to interfere. He would be angry if he caught her, but she couldn't stand seeing her son so worn, so defeated, and so unhappy.

"Mother?" John sat up, blinking sleepily.

"Come home, son."

He nodded and sighed. "I'm sorry."

"Don't you dare apologize. You did everything you could."

"I hope so."

She folded her arms. "We've done this once before, and we can do it all again."

"We don't have much of a choice." He rubbed the back of his head, and stretched, wincing. "I'm selling the Depot. I've got a decent offer from Greenspace Freight."

"I'm sure you do." She sighed and shook her head. Big carriers always hovered over the dying corpses of smaller independent shipping businesses.

"Mother, let it go."

"When will the sale finalize?"

"At the end of the month. I have a few things to negotiate." He ran a hand through his hair, making it stand on end. His father had had the same funny habit when he was thinking.

"At least I went down swinging." John sighed. "Between that and selling the house, we'll cover most of our debts."

"I'm proud of you."

"I know." He stood and groaned, stretching. He tugged on his hat, walked around the desk, and gathered up a stack of files. He needed a shave and a decent meal.

Mrs. Thornton took a deep breath to steady herself. Tears were useless. John would find his way. He always did. She frowned when he paused by the trash can, and bent, pulling out the envelope she'd thrown away. She felt a small twinge of guilt as he glanced at her, his face hard, and tucked the envelope into his back pocket.

"You're being a fool," she said.

"I didn't ask you."

She pressed her lips together but said nothing else. Maybe she couldn't stop him from loving that foolish girl, but at least Margaret Hale was thousands of miles away.

Chapter 42

Margaret could feel her cousin Edith watching her as they sat in the fine parlor in her aunt's house in Harley Street. It had been three months, and all Margaret wanted to do was read history catalogs, work tricky maths on every spare bit of scrap paper, and sleep. She knew she ought to try to be happier, but even the thought exhausted her.

"Henry." Edith was whispering to her brother-in-law. For the last two weeks, Edith had been conspiring with Henry and James to try and cheer Margaret up. Both Lennox brothers submitted to her demands, but Margaret had never noticed how silly her cousin could be, until she saw her behavior through Henry's sarcastic compliance.

"Migs," Edith said, louder.

Margaret looked up from the textbook she was flipping through.

"There's a New Year's Eve party at the Dodds' tomorrow, you know." Edith smiled. "I think you would enjoy yourself. Henry could take you if you like. He's promised to cheer you up."

"Oh." Margaret exchanged an awkward look with Henry. "I'd rather not, thanks."

"But it'll be so lovely, and Henry's being so nice to you. You've always been thick as thieves," Edith said, ignoring her. "A change of scenery is exactly what you need."

"If a change of scenery is all she requires," Henry interrupted, a hint of sarcasm in his voice, "then we could take a walk and skip the party altogether."

"Oh, yes!" Edith latched onto his suggestion instantly. "A walk will be just the thing." She quickly stood. "You must either walk with Henry and I or go to the Charlesworths' for tea," she said with a wheedling smile.

Margaret couldn't stand Mrs. Charlesworth and Edith knew it. "Fine." Margaret sighed and stood.

It didn't matter what she did.

Their walk was miserable and cold and mercifully short. But surprisingly, it did make Margaret feel a little bit better. When they returned to Harley Street, Henry awkwardly helped her with her coat. She hoped he wouldn't mistake Edith's efforts to throw them together as evidence of something more. Margaret shuddered, remembering that New Year's Eve when he'd tried to force something to happen between them. Her lips tingled, defying her best efforts not to remember John— how he'd kissed her and held her as if no one else mattered.

"Are you enjoying your time in London?" Henry spoke a little too forcefully as they made their way to the drawing room for tea.

She nodded and sat in the chair he pulled out for her. Edith poured the tea and handed it down. James had returned from work early, and he and Edith sat off to one side, chatting.

"Margaret, may I speak with you privately?" Henry asked quietly, once Edith's attention was fully occupied. "It's about your father."

They stepped out of the drawing room into a small, rarely used study. Margaret sat and took a sip of tea, looking at Henry warily over her cup. She'd forgotten he was still tending to her father's legal affairs. He briefly outlined the auction, the closing of Mr. Hale's bank accounts, and the lengthy process required to sell the Milton house. She had reluctantly agreed to put the beloved house up for sale. It made sense, but it still made her feel lost, like a ship without its rudder. Henry soon moved on to her father's stock portfolio. "Mr. Hale wasn't the cleverest of investors," he was saying. "He purchased several shares in a local shipping business in Milton, among other random businesses."

"You mean Marlborough Shipping Depot."

He nodded stiffly. "The business was recently purchased by a larger freight carrier."

"It was?" she asked, frowning. "When?"

"The sale was finalized yesterday."

"What happened?"

He briefly explained the Depot's slow sink into obscurity, like so many other small businesses. She listened in silence, her tea going cold. "Thornton could've sold his business for much more if he'd been cleverer about it," Henry finished. "It's a moot point now, I suppose."

"What do you mean?"

"He refused to negotiate about his drivers, insisting they be kept on the company payroll for the first year."

"John did that?" She stared hard at Henry. "For his drivers?"

"He could've walked away with far greater profits if he hadn't." Henry's face settled into a familiar smug expression. His lawyer face. "You need to decide, with your Aunt Shaw's approval, of course, what you would like to do with your shares."

Margaret set her tea on a small table and fiddled with her skirt.

"I would like to read all the paperwork myself before having that conversation with Aunt Shaw."

"Of course." He retrieved his briefcase and removed a large folder. "Lastly, a Mr. Adam Bell contacted our firm at the beginning of December. He's made over a large portion of his monies to you. All the legal details are here."

"Mr. Bell?" She stared at the folder. "He's giving me money?"

"To be held in trust until he passes away or until you turn twenty-five. It's a substantial amount." Henry handed the files to her. "You're quite a wealthy woman now, Margaret."

"Thank you, Henry." She blinked hard and stood. "I'm going upstairs. Bit of a headache."

♡

Margaret sat on her bed for a long time, hugging her arms around herself. She wished there was something more she could do. Marlborough Shipping Depot was the livelihood for so many of her friends in Milton. Without it, what would happen to them all? What would happen to John?

She pulled her father's battered suitcase from under her bed and opened it, smoothing out the canvas jacket inside. It still smelled like John. She knew she should've returned it that last day at the airport, but she couldn't. She set the jacket aside and took out her polaroid camera and the shoebox of her pictures. She hadn't touched them since returning to England. She didn't want to think about everything she'd left behind. She pulled the lid off the box, slowly took out each photo, and set them down, one by one, onto the bedspread.

This was Milton. Her Milton. There was beauty there even if it was often hidden under a layer of dirt and smoke. She sighed when she picked up Fred's picture. She still hadn't heard from him since he'd left.

I think you should trust John. He'll surprise you.

She should've listened to Mary, and to her own heart.

The door to her room flew open, and Edith swept in. Before Margaret had time to react, her cousin closed the door, and flounced down next to her, looking at the pictures spread out on the bed. "Oh, how wonderful," she said and picked up one of Mr. Hale. "These are quite lovely, Migs," she said softly. "I'll ask Henry to pop down to the shops and get you some more film. Won't that be nice?"

"What for?"

"Taking these silly pictures always did make you happier, and you can be happy again."

"Eds, you can't command me to be happy and expect it to happen."

"Margaret," Edith frowned prettily, "you've been moping about for weeks on end. You're not eating, and you're not sleeping. You hardly do anything at all. I understand you miss your father terribly." She laid a gentle hand on her arm. "It's been months."

"It's not only my father. Everything I've ever loved is gone."

"But you still have us. And Henry."

Margaret took a deep, exasperated breath. "I'm *not* in love with Henry. I never was, and I never will be."

"But—" Edith paused, blinking. "You're not?"

"No," Margaret said. "Never."

"But I had so many lovely plans for you, me, Henry, and James. It was going to be lovely—all four of us living in London, neat and tidy."

"I'm sure you'll recover," Margaret said flatly. She tried to smile. "I'll carry on eventually. I just need time, Eds."

"Couldn't you try liking Henry? He's so pleasant and polite, you know, and he fancies you. I'm sure of it."

"I do like him, but—"

"Not enough," Edith said with a sigh and a pout. She leaned closer. "Because you're in love with someone else. It's not Henry, but it is someone, isn't it?"

"I," Margaret blushed, "I'm not in love with anyone."

"That's a lie." Edith waited, expectant and resolute. "You've fallen in love with some vulgar American in that awful place."

Margaret didn't trust herself to answer. "Milton isn't awful," she said after a moment. She picked up a picture of St. Anthony's Cathedral. "It's my home, and I miss it."

"You miss Milton?" Her cousin sounded horrified.

"Not just the city, but the people there. And my father, my mum, Fred." Margaret almost laughed. "I might even miss Dale Dixon too."

"No, you don't." Edith smiled knowingly. "You miss your American, whoever he is."

"I do miss him," Margaret whispered. She'd wondered what John thought of the pictures she'd given him, but he hadn't contacted her. She thought she hadn't wanted him to ring, until he didn't. His silence hurt, adding a new pain to the gaping raw place inside of her that always seemed to ache.

"What are these?" Edith reached into the shoe box and pulled out a small stack of polaroids tied together with a dark red ribbon.

"Eds, please don't—"

"I bet they're your American, aren't they?" Edith giggled, holding the pictures out of reach. She untied the ribbon, tossing it at Margaret. Her mouth opened in surprise, and she murmured softly, "Oh Migs. This *is* him, isn't it?"

Edith carefully laid them out on the bed. A strange urgency tugged at Margaret as she studied them. She hadn't let herself look at John's pictures, had ignored them and hidden them from herself. But now she couldn't look away.

—John, sitting in the library at Helstone, reading, a glass of whiskey in his hand—John, standing in front of an auditorium at the business conference—John, ball cap pushed back on his head, arguing with Williams—John, holding the ground keeper's two little boys, laughing at the bonfire that final night in Helstone—John, bent low at the waist as an elderly woman adjusted his bow tie and shirt collar at Frannie's wedding—John, standing by his father's grave, the flaming sunset making him a dark silhouette—John and her father, looking embarrassed when she asked to take their picture, the first day she'd seen him after his disastrous proposal—John, bored and uncomfortable in his suit at the Christmas Dinner, drinking a whiskey—John, in safety glasses and earplugs, scowling as he took aim at the firing range—John, shirtless, working on his truck during his lunch break—John, leaning against a wall outside their classroom, looking intently over a paper, a pencil tucked behind his ear.

There were so many, each one a painful data point painting a picture of a terrifying truth she'd tried to ignore for three long years.

"He's a dish even if he is American," Edith giggled and handed her the last polaroid.

It caught Margaret off guard, and she stared at it, a hand pressed over her mouth.

"Migs, what's wrong?"

"I forgot about this one."

—John, dressed in a dark gray suit, standing on the landing above the stairs leading up to the loading bay at the Depot, the first day she'd met him.

"I can't believe I took this." She wiped her cheeks. She was crying again. "I don't know why I have so many of him."

"You're in love with him."

The hair on Margaret's arms stood up. "I think I started to love him even then," she said softly. She felt more tears on her cheeks. "I was falling in love with him from the very beginning, and I missed it."

"Does he know?"

"No."

Some part of her had known—from the moment she met him—that John Thornton was her home. And she had left without ever telling him the truth.

"Call him, darling. Tell him."

"I think it's too late."

Chapter 43

It was the end of the last shift. John walked through the building, turning off lights, making sure everything was in order. He stood and stared at the line of empty trucks. He breathed out a long, defeated sigh, took off his hat, and frowned at the faded stitched logo. It was the first company merchandise he'd made when he started. It was missing the 'u' in *Marlborough*. The printer had left it out, but he'd kept the hat anyway, out of pride or stubbornness—or both. John roughed his hair and settled the hat back on his head, feeling old. Pride and stubbornness couldn't save his ass now. Or his business.

Selling was the smartest move, but it still stung like a bitch. He'd taken a hit insisting all his drivers be retained, with benefits, for at least a year, haggling tooth and nail until he had his way. No one else would eat his failure, except him. He checked his clipboard one last time. All the keys had been turned in except one. He headed to the dispatch desk and grabbed the CB radio. "Master to Slick. What's your twenty? Over."

"Slick here. I was left hanging almost half a day for this shipment," the grumbly voice replied. "Get that stick out of your ass, Master. ETA five minutes. Over and out."

Six minutes later, Nick Higgins pulled into the bay. John frowned at him as Nick jumped from his truck. The older man smiled, flashing his crooked teeth.

"Where's Tim?" John asked when the skinny kid didn't follow Higgins out of the cab.

"Down with the flu."

The two men regarded each other for a moment. "It's been one hell of a haul, Master."

"Nobody's the master anymore, Slick," John said, annoyed by the handle the drivers had slapped on him since his first day as an owner-operator, nearly ten years ago.

"I'm too old to use your proper name now. I reckon you're still young enough to start over."

"Maybe." John sighed. "I don't feel like it."

"You'll figure something out."

"My skill set is pretty limited."

"Well, if you're ever in the position to take on drivers again, there's a whole list of us who'd be ready to truck for you." Nick handed him a dirty envelope stuffed with a few sheets of yellow lined paper. "I wrote down all the names with contact info. Just in case."

"Thank you." John stared at the envelope. He hadn't expected this, or anything else, from his crew. But they'd all given their best, up until the end. He tucked the envelope into his back pocket. "I wouldn't hold your breath."

Nick followed him to the office to help him lock up. "Have you heard anything from Margaret yet?"

"She's in England," John said gruffly. "She sold most of her dad's stuff at an auction, and now the house is up for sale too."

"You went to the auction."

It wasn't a question, so John didn't bother to answer. He'd gone. He was glad to have a few small pieces of furniture no one wanted, and an old tea set he didn't know what the hell to do with.

"She's not coming back," he said. He locked Higgins' truck key in the silver key cabinet. "There's nothing left here for her."

"Well, I thought she'd make it back to America eventually." Nick leaned against the office doorframe, hands still deep in his pockets, as John shifted papers around on his desk.

"Why would she do that?"

"To see her brother."

"Her what?" John's hand froze over a stack of files, and he glanced sharply at Nick, who was examining dirt smudges on the doorframe.

"You knew she had a brother, didn't you?" Nick said, feigning surprise. "Tallish, curly brown hair, real skinny; a loser called Fred."

"Her brother."

Nick's description matched the stranger from Outwood Station pub.

It's not what you think.

"That shithead was her brother?"

"He's a half-brother, the old parson's son from before he left the church. The whole thing's a huge Hale family secret, Mary says. The old man strayed and tried to fix it, but it blew up in his face. Seems the brother is nothing but trouble. He was dishonorably discharged from the military, into drugs and other petty crime. Car theft, I think." Nick sighed. "Poor Margaret covered for him the last time he was in town, so he wouldn't get sent back to prison."

I'm in jail.

"Holy shit," John breathed. It all made sense, and the sheer relief made him feel lighter and heavier. Why hadn't she told him?

"Margaret protects the people she loves like a mother bear. She'd never abandon them."

"Nick," John spoke as steadily as he could manage, "did Maggie tell you she'd be coming back?"

"She didn't tell me nothing." Nick strolled forward and picked up the three polaroids John had kept on his desk ever since she'd left. "Did Margaret give you these?"

John snatched the pictures out of his hand, and Nick chuckled, his eyes twinkling. "Thought so."

"Go home, Slick." John stuck out his hand and gave the old trucker a final handshake. "And good luck."

"I'm going back to Milton," Margaret said. She braced herself for her aunt's pointed disapproval and resistance, but she held her ground. Henry produced the appropriate documents, and Margaret smiled inwardly as her aunt complained about the inconvenience and the expense. Why would she want to go back to Milton to sign paperwork on a house? Why couldn't it all be done electronically?

"It's my house now, Aunt Shaw. I want to be there personally, and I want to see my friends again." She tried to sound immovable and stalwart. "Henry advised me to deal with it all as quickly as possible. My dad's books are still there too—"

"Not those dusty things again," Aunt Shaw interrupted. She pressed her lips together disapprovingly until they turned white.

In the end—after an endless supply of tea, biscuits, and gentle, unyielding persistence from Margaret, supported by timely compliments from Henry at appropriate pauses—her aunt gave in. "Oh, very well. If you must go, I'll book our flights for next week."

Margaret glanced at Henry, pleading with her eyes. Returning to Milton alone was her plan, but if Aunt Shaw was going to agree, the idea must come from him.

"Will you be attending the sale?" Henry asked, sounding almost bored. "That seems an unnecessary expense, Mrs. Shaw."

Mrs. Shaw considered this and said, "Well, I leave it all to you then, Henry." She waved a hand at him. "You can accompany Margaret and see that everything is done properly and quickly."

After her aunt left the parlor, calling for Edith and the housekeeper, Margaret slumped in her chair, exhaling deeply, almost giggling with relief. "You did it." She smiled gratefully at Henry, who was replacing the necessary paperwork in his briefcase. "Well done."

He studied her for a moment and nodded. "About the loan for Mr. Thornton." He pulled another folder from his briefcase. He'd been stiff and distant with her ever since she'd told him she wanted to return to Milton to help John Thornton. She'd been too much of a coward to admit her real reasons, but Henry wasn't stupid.

"All the necessary paperwork is here. I don't need to be present for this transaction, Margaret. Any reputable lawyer will do."

"I want you to be there. I want to do this right."

"This?" He raised his eyebrows, his voice stiff. "But I'm not part of *this*, am I?" He stood and regarded her. "You're in love with him."

It was a little bitter but frank and resigned.

"I am," she admitted softly. "It doesn't matter. He's not in love with me anymore."

"You're wrong." He buttoned his jacket and picked up his briefcase. "A man like Thornton doesn't give up what he wants, and he's always wanted you."

FRIDAY: JANUARY 9, 2009

Exactly one week later, Margaret sat at the bar in the Milton Palace Hotel, sipping her drink. She'd ordered a whiskey, neat. It wasn't quite the same as her first bourbon at Helstone, but the taste was still startlingly abrupt and warmly enticing. Just like John. She sighed and glanced at the clock propped up on the shelf next to an empty bottle of tequila. She had another half hour until she and Henry were supposed to meet John for a late lunch in the hotel restaurant. She'd insisted Henry set up the meeting, without mentioning her at all. If John knew she'd be there he might not come. And he might not accept her business proposal either. Still, she had to try. She studied herself in the mirror behind the bar. She ought to change out of her skirt and sweater into something more posh, more confident, more—

"Can I get you anything else?" the bartender asked.

"A different life."

"Sorry." He gave her a well-practiced look of disinterested sympathy. "We're fresh out."

"Too bad." She folded her arms on the bar and laid her forehead on top of them, taking a few deep breaths. "Be brave, Margaret Ann," she muttered to herself. "The worst he can say is no."

Or hell no.

If John didn't want her money, that was fine. And if he didn't want her either, well, then that would be fine too.

Liar.

She closed her eyes and whispered, "Please." It was almost a prayer. "Please say yes."

"Where's my order, Dane?" John called back into the kitchen. The cook ignored him, throwing the bird over his shoulder. John would have to wait, like all the other servers. He scratched his chin, three days' growth of whiskers itching like hell. The general manager of Outwood Station pub wasn't picky about facial hair so long as he shaved every few days.

"Move your ass, Thornton," the cook snapped. The bell rang and four plates slid across the counter. "Order's up."

John piled them easily along his arm, ignoring the cook's extra colorful muttering about the ungrateful wait staff. Short order cooks were always sweaty, impatient, and cranky as wet cats. But they were king of the kitchen, and John didn't have the energy to argue.

Everything was done now. The Depot was sold. The old house was on the market. His mother had moved in with Frannie and Watson for the time being, while John figured out what he wanted to do next. So far all he'd managed was a job waiting tables at Outwood Station pub during the week, working at the pub bar on the weekends, and his own shitty walk-up apartment. At least he had a job and his own place. There was a satisfying dignity in that. Not much, but it was something.

He delivered his orders and refilled drinks at tables seven and eight, glancing at his watch. He had two minutes left on this shift, and twenty minutes before he had to be at his lunch meeting with Henry Lennox.

The email from Margaret's lawyer had haunted him all week. It was full of high-brow legalese, but essentially, there was one final piece from Mr. Hale's estate Lennox needed to wrap up, and somehow it involved John. He had zero guesses what it might be. Besides that, he remembered the tight-ass Henry Lennox all too well, and he wasn't looking forward to seeing him again.

He started a fresh pot of coffee and headed for the door, waving goodbye to Bill Sloan on his way out. He untied his apron and tossed it onto the passenger seat of his truck. He didn't have time to change into fresh clothes. His black slacks and white oxford would have to do. He made it downtown with five minutes to spare, ran his fingers through his hair, combing it into something mildly presentable, and slapped the truck's sun visor back into place.

The Palace Hotel was the nicest place in downtown Milton, favored by big business executives and other New York money. John stepped inside, his body tense, feeling stupid and out of place. The restaurant was near the bar, and he'd only been there a few times. When he reached the bar door, he paused, looking over his reflection in the glass one last time. He swore and glared at a large coffee stain on his white shirtsleeve, near the cuff. That was never coming out. He sighed and rolled up both sleeves. *Good enough.* He looked up and promptly forgot what he was doing.

"Maggie?"

Margaret sat at the hotel bar, a small glass of whiskey at her elbow, her head resting on her folded arms on the bar top. He blinked, rubbing his eyes. Ever since Nick Higgins had spilled the beans about her brother, John had dreamed of seeing her again so many times, that, right now, he questioned his own sanity. He shook himself, dragged his hands over his face, and looked again. She was still there.

He let out a ragged breath. "I'll be damned."

John did the only rational thing he could do. He walked into the bar, sat down next to her, and ordered a drink.

Chapter 44

"What can I get you?"

"Whatever she's got. Neat."

The familiar gruff voice scratched over her skin and Margaret sat bolt upright. "John?"

He smiled slowly and stared at her. "Hi."

"You're here." It was a stupid thing to say, and her cheeks flushed hot. Of course he was here. Henry had invited him to dinner. "Hello."

"What are *you* doing here?" he asked. He looked so odd, dressed in a rumpled white oxford, black slacks, and sturdy black leather shoes.

"Having a drink."

"I meant here in Milton."

"Right. That." She glanced at the bartender as he set down John's drink. "Dad's house sold, and we're closing on Tuesday."

"We?"

"Henry Lennox and myself."

"I'm supposed to meet him for lunch." He picked up his glass, never taking his eyes off her, but he didn't drink it. "I'm late."

"No, you're not," she said, her cheeks and neck flushing again. "You're supposed to be having lunch with me, actually."

"You?" He looked at her hard. "Why?"

"I heard about the Depot." She closed her eyes and took a deep breath, willing herself to be calm. "I'm so sorry."

"It is what it is."

She nodded and glanced down, unsure of how to start.

He sipped his drink and cleared his throat. "So, where's Henry?"

"He—" she paused and glanced at the door. "I don't know where he is. He should be arriving any minute. I wish he would, as he could explain my proposal better than I can, I think."

"What proposal?"

"My proposal." She sat up straighter and reached for her leather shoulder bag tucked under the bar. "To you."

She pulled out several papers, chewing her lower lip, praying she could remember all the particulars. "Selling Dad's house has generated a lump sum of money that will sit in a bank account, earning a small percentage of interest," she explained. She laid the paperwork down on the bar top.

John picked it up, his eyes moving deliberately across the first page. For once, he looked his age, the years sitting heavily around his eyes, forehead, and mouth. She wondered if he was sleeping and eating properly.

"I can't do much with it, other than investments. Most of my assets are being held in trust by my Aunt Shaw until I turn twenty-five."

He made a small noise in his throat, his expression darkening.

"I want to invest in you—your business, I mean. I can't give you the entire amount from the house, but I can give you enough to start up the Depot again."

"No," he said and set the papers down.

"But you haven't let me finish—"

"Maggie," he interrupted gently. "Tell me about Fred."

She sat back, surprised. "How do you know about him?"

"Because Nick Higgins can't keep a secret to save his ass. He told me enough about it to make me feel like an idiot."

"Don't say that." She thought for a moment before finishing the last little bit of her own drink. "My parents tried to have children for almost fifteen years before Dad had an affair. I don't know the details, except that he left the church right after. Then I was conceived. I know they tried to carry on for a bit, for my sake, but they separated when I was five. Fred's mum had dropped him off one night, unannounced, and never came back. Dad hadn't told my mum there'd been a child, and that was the last of it. She never forgave him."

"But you did."

"Yes." She shrugged. "Eventually. It was never hard to love my father or my brother. Mum couldn't understand why I did." She stared at her hands. "Dad's mum took Fred for a time, hoping it would help, but my parents divorced when I was nine. Mum came to America a few years later, to study art in Boston, she said. She had a grant and everything, but I think she hoped an ocean of distance would make it easier to hate my father."

"How does Dale Dixon fit into this?"

"Did you meet him?"

He nodded. "At your mother's funeral."

"He's an old friend of Mum's from uni." She sighed. "She swore to me she never broke her marriage vows, not physically, but I don't know. It doesn't matter. I think she was trying to prove a martyr's point to Dad. But I always thought she betrayed him as much as

363

he betrayed her."

"What happened with Fred?"

"His mum is American, and he was born here, so he's American too. I don't know too much about his childhood, but he joined the US Navy when he was eighteen. They threw him out for drug abuse and car theft. He stole a commanding officer's private vehicle." She tried to laugh but it sounded so hollow. "Dad was here by then, and he reached out to Fred. He tried to help him, but things were always rotten between them. Everything got worse, with the drugs, no matter what we tried. I've stopped trying. The day you met him was the first time I'd seen him in years."

"Why didn't you tell me the truth?"

"I should have." She laid her hand on his arm. "I'm sorry I lied to you. The truth is, I was ashamed and embarrassed, and I know how you feel about people like Fred. I told myself you wouldn't understand, but I was wrong. I've been wrong about so many things, especially about you."

"Maggie—"

"But, about my proposal," she said quickly. "There's no obligation to me personally, and really, it's far more advantageous for me, since you'll owe me interest on the investment, and I want stocks as well."

"I don't want your money," he said.

Her heart sank a little.

"I've sold Marlborough Shipping. I'm a bad investment."

"Henry would disagree."

"Well, your Henry Lennox doesn't know jack-shit about it." He tossed back the rest of his drink and stood, as if to leave.

"John, wait. He's not." She grabbed his hand. "He's not *my* Henry, not like that."

John paused, an odd, conflicted look on his face as she continued to clutch his hand. "Did you get the pictures?" Her voice was shaking. "I left them in Dad's book. For you."

He didn't answer. Instead, he pulled his hand free and took out his wallet. Inside were the three polaroids. He set them on the bar, where they lay, slightly curled. "Why did you give me these?"

"I only take pictures of what I love, remember?"

"I remember."

"And do you remember the night I took this?" she asked. She slid a finger along the edge of the picture of him. It was her favorite.

"Should I?"

"It's from New Year's Eve." She forced herself to look up, her heart thundering against her ribs. "*Our* New Year's Eve."

"Ours?" He tilted his head, his posture stiff and defensive. He didn't quite believe her, and she didn't blame him. Not after all the terrible things she'd said and done to him.

"John." She looked down and covered her face with her hands, as if that could hide her from all the guilt and turmoil and heartache of the last three years. "I tried so hard to tell myself I didn't love you or want you, but I can't lie anymore. I wished I had said yes that day. That's why I gave you these pictures. That's why I'm here. I needed to tell you the truth."

"Maggie," he rasped, a rough, almost hoarse sound. She felt his hands on hers, tugging them gently away from her face. But she still couldn't look at him.

"I'm sorry, John, I—"

"Say yes now," he interrupted.

"Now?"

"Marry me now," John said, firm and determined. He tilted her face closer, his blue eyes blazing. "Today."

"You're not serious."

"I am." His thumbs brushed over her cheeks, wiping away her tears. "If you love me, then marry me."

Her eyes widened in disbelief. "You're serious."

Her mobile phone rang loudly from the bar top, making them both jump. She turned, dazedly, and snatched it up, an odd rushing ringing noise in her ears, a thread of hope winding through her. "How was your flight, darling?" Edith chirped. "Were you very ill?"

Margaret could hardly form a coherent sentence as her cousin chattered away. John wanted her. After everything that had happened, he was here, and he still wanted her. A strange confidence she'd not felt for ages sparked heat in her veins, and she almost laughed out loud.

"Eds, I'm sorry. I've got to go." She snapped her mobile shut and grabbed her things, stuffing the papers roughly back into her bag.

"Maggie." John was still there, still waiting. His hair was sticking out at funny angles, like it always did when he nervously fiddled with it. "Please stay. Please, I—"

"John," she interrupted. "It's nearly three." She grabbed his hand. "The courthouse closes at five."

"Wait." He almost tripped over his feet when she tugged him towards the hotel doors. He looked stunned and so bloody hopeful. "Is that a yes?"

"Bloody hell, yes."

She let out a happy little yelp as John yanked her against him, kissing her with all the fire and energy he had, his fingers threading into her hair. It was a hard, bruising kiss, all lips and teeth and tongues, fierce and possessive and presumptuous, the kind of kiss that takes and gives, stings and heals.

She didn't know how long they stood there tangled up by the bar. All she knew was she'd never felt more at home than in this perfect moment, pouring her passion, her trust, her love—her whole self—into this impossible man. They only managed to stop when her mobile rang.

She wrenched herself away, breathless and giggling. "It's my cousin."

"Let it ring." He snatched the phone from her hand, switched it off, and shoved it into his back pocket. He lifted her off her feet, kissing her again.

"But what will we tell everyone?"

"We won't tell them."

"My aunt will have a fit."

"I don't give two shits what Victoria Shaw, or anyone else, has to say about us."

"So tactful." She rolled her eyes, shivering as he pressed feather-light kisses along her jaw line. "I can tell you exactly what she'll say." She pitched her voice higher, and screeched, "Not *that* man!"

To her surprise and delight, John threw his head back and laughed, a deep, velvety, rumbling sound that vibrated through her. She'd never seen him laugh like that, like he was truly happy. She tried to wriggle free, but he held her tighter, as if he'd never let go, and smiled.

It was the smile he saved just for her—irritating, mischievous, and all too knowing—but hers all the same. It erased the tired years from his face and transformed him into someone entirely new, someone who belonged only to her. Margaret held his face in her hands, brushing her thumbs along his scratchy cheeks, studying him for a moment.

"I love you, John."

"Yeah?"

"I've always loved you."

"Lucky me," he said, brushing his nose against her cheek.

"Aren't you going to profess your undying love and devotion?" she teased. "It's only fair."

"I just asked you to marry me. For the second time."

"Tell me you love me anyway." She nudged his face playfully. "Go on then. Woo me."

"You know I love you."

"John," she grumbled, rolling her eyes, but he cut her off, kissing her again. She sighed contentedly, savoring the coffee peppermint taste of him. She could search the whole world for the rest of her life, but she'd never find a better man than John Thornton. She shivered when he let out a rough sort of growl.

"If you keep this up," she murmured against his mouth, "we'll never make it to the courthouse in time."

"Like hell we won't." He let her slide down and picked up her briefcase, grinning wickedly. "After you, Mrs. Thornton."

"Impossible man," she gasped, laughing at his cocky audacity, as he tugged her after him to his truck.

Chapter 45

Margaret lay curled on her side in her hotel room bed, tired and happy and deliciously sore, watching her husband's chest move in a steady slow rhythm. He was sprawled diagonally across the mattress, like a human puddle, fast asleep. She smiled softly. He was so tall he couldn't fit the queen-sized bed any other way.

Marrying John had been one of the easiest and oddest things she'd ever done. There were a few legal formalities in front of a pokey old judge with two overworked secretaries acting as witnesses, a signed paper document, dated, stamped, and notarized; in all of twenty minutes, Margaret Ann Hale became Mrs. John Thornton without further fuss or complication.

John had asked the judge to recite the traditional Anglican vows and held her hands in a grip so tight it almost hurt. His voice had gone soft and gruff as he said his vows, as solemn and sure as she'd ever seen him. She'd made her own promises to him in a firm, clear voice which neither shook nor wavered.

This man, and this life, was exactly what she wanted.

She smiled to herself and picked up the two polaroids lying on the nightstand. They were her only wedding pictures—one for him and one for her—taken by an obliging courthouse janitor. She didn't have flowers or finery or even a ring, but she had John, and he was more than enough.

He shifted in his sleep, and she studied his lanky, well-muscled frame. She inched closer to him, sighing in quiet contentment. He'd fallen asleep within minutes after they'd made love, utterly exhausted and spent. He hadn't been sleeping well, the lines on his face deeper than she remembered. He looked skinnier too. She reached over and brushed at his tousled dark hair, spotting a few errant grays. She loved his hair, soft, thick, and a wonderfully useful handhold, as she discovered tonight. If only they'd done this sooner, instead of the maddening dance of the last three years, he might not be so worn down.

"Oh," she gasped as a strong arm curled around her, pulling her closer. "Did I wake you?"

"You were staring."

"I was. You're quite lovely, for a man."

"Am I?" He shifted onto his side and propped himself up on his elbow, his eyes roving slowly over her. He grinned when she blushed. "Did you enjoy yourself, Mrs. Thornton?"

"Yes." Her blush deepened. "Ten out of ten, would recommend."

"Even when I made you cry?" His face grew serious, and he laced his fingers slowly through hers.

"You didn't." She had cried during their first time together, but it wasn't because of him, or the fumbling awkwardness, or even the small twinge of pain at the beginning. "I keep thinking how much time we wasted, and all the awful things I did and said to you."

"That's done, Maggie," he said. "It doesn't matter now."

"It does matter," she insisted, closing her eyes in shame. "I'm so sorry and I—"

"I'm sorry too. We made a mess, but it had a damn happy ending."

"Lucky us." She sighed happily. "Bessie would've been terribly smug about all of it. She told me once we needed to get a room and work out our sexual frustration."

"When did she say that?"

"The first year. She insisted I was drooling over you."

He looked immensely pleased, lacing his hands behind his head. "I wouldn't blame you for drooling."

"So smug."

"You gave me a ten out of ten."

"I did," she said with a nervous smile. "So, what about me? Do I get high marks, comparatively?"

"Compared to what?"

"To the others."

"Other what?" he repeated, clearly confused.

She squirmed, her face burning with embarrassment. She wanted to know what he thought, and some part of her desperately needed to know if she was enough for him, despite everything. It was silly and yet—

"The other girls you've been with."

He sat up, surprised, and she was suddenly terrified of his answer.

"No." He shook his head, his face stern, and pulled her closer. "I'm not going to bother answering that."

"But I'm your wife."

"Exactly. I married *you*, and that's enough for me."

"And as your wife, I deserve to know about your conquests. It's only fair, you know."

"Maggie, stop," he said firmly. "I've never had sex with anybody else. Just you."

"Wait." She stared, open mouthed. "You never?—is that a joke?"

"Don't laugh," he warned.

But she couldn't stop herself. She burst into giggles, the absurdity and intensity of her relief making it almost impossible to control her laughter. Every time she tried, she glanced at his face, and it set her off again.

"Shut up," he muttered, giving her a playful shove. "It's not funny."

"It's absurd," she gasped, holding her sides, still laughing. "John, you're thirty years old. How on earth did you manage celibacy all that time?"

"I'm twenty-nine," he said irritably.

"In twenty-nine years, you never had a shag? Not a single dalliance?"

"I'm not the kind of guy who fucks around," he growled. "It's too much damn effort."

"Too much *effort*?" She dissolved into laughter again.

He tossed his pillow at her, and she caught it, clutching it to her chest. "You are the most impossible man I've ever met. How did you manage?"

"The internet." He rolled his eyes. "I'm not a monk."

When she still didn't stop laughing, he pulled her mouth to his, cutting her off with a slow, insistent kiss. Thankfully, his lack of practice hadn't rendered him completely talentless. All her thoughts began to fade into a growing heated longing, but she pulled back, determined not to be distracted yet. "You weren't ever tempted, not even once?"

He looked sheepish. "Define *tempted*."

"I knew it. You *were* tempted." She climbed over on top of

him, forcing him to look at her. "Who was it?"

He made a noise, his embarrassment written all over his face. "Nothing happened."

"So, you just happened to almost bed some random woman for no reason other than the stars aligned?"

"No."

"Go on then," she teased. "Tell me who almost made it into your bed before me."

"Guess."

"It's someone I know, is it?" She was grinning again, matching his mischievous mood. This John was her favorite, all teasing and playful and enticing. Then the answer dawned on her.

"Wait," she half-shouted. "You almost had sex with Lana Lancaster? John Thornton, you did not."

He cleared his throat, trying to keep his face blank, but his lips twitched a little and she punched his shoulder. "Nothing happened," he said, reaching out to brush a feather light touch across her skin, as if he were memorizing each smooth curve.

"Did you snog?"

He frowned, dragging his eyes slowly away from her body to her face. "Did I what?"

"Kiss her?"

He nodded.

"With tongues?"

"Sure. We made out."

"Did you like it?"

He studied her for a moment and shrugged. "Yes."

"Did you touch her?"

"Clothes stayed on the whole time." He pulled her down onto his chest and kissed her collarbone. "But yes, I did."

A wash of something very like jealousy made her squirm. "Why didn't you shag her then?"

"Because I'd have to talk to her the next day." He rolled her onto her back, continuing his distracting attentions. "She's hot, but that's it, and I wasn't raised to treat a woman like a piece of meat."

"This explains so many things." She shivered, his mouth tracing over the little hollow between her collarbone and her neck. "No wonder she hates me."

"That's her problem."

"She better leave you alone after this," Margaret said, pressing an insistent kiss against his chest. "You're all mine now."

"Are you jealous, Mrs. Thornton?"

"Terribly." She ran her hands through his hair. "Tell me you were drunk, and I'll forgive you."

"I wasn't exactly sober." He nudged her cheek with his nose and kissed her. "Maybe I'll decide to be jealous of Henry Lennox, and we'll call it even." He raised his eyebrows, trying to look casual, but she knew instantly what he wanted to know.

"Don't be jealous." She trailed a finger along his lower lip. "You're the one who ruined my maidenly reputation tonight, John Seamus Thornton."

"I don't give a damn about your reputation," he grumbled. "I just want to know if that asshat ever laid hands on you."

"That's rude." She pushed his face, trying to sound disapproving. "If he did, it would've been with my permission." She shifted underneath him, enjoying the fiery look that blazed across his face as her body pressed against his. "Do you really want to know?"

He stared at her for a long time, then shook his head. "No."

"Why not?"

"Because I'll beat the shit out of him."

"John! You will not."

"I would."

She grabbed his face and kissed him, annoyed and a little pleased. It was utterly ridiculous, and yet she loved him more for it. "For Henry's sake then," she said, "you should know he never touched me. I'm not casual about sex either."

A slow stupid grin spread across his face, and she rolled her eyes. "Stop smiling like you've done something spectacularly clever. Surely you could tell I was a virgin?"

"I wanted you to tell me." His hands twisted in her hair. "I like being your first," he said in that grumbly way that made her shiver. He tugged her head to one side and began to kiss her neck, lightly at first, and then with more purpose.

"John, don't. You'll leave a mark."

"That's the point," he growled. "You're my woman now. Every single perfect inch of you is mine."

"You're ridiculous," she hissed, her skin tingling with this new delicious fire. Being Mrs. John Thornton came with many delights, as she was starting to learn.

8:47 PM

"Didn't your mother ever tell you it's rude to bite people?" Margaret murmured sleepily.

"She might've mentioned it." John had left several marks on his new wife after he discovered several specific places she particularly enjoyed. He'd given his full attention to each one. Most of them could be hidden with clothes. But a few couldn't.

He brushed his thumb over a bright spot on her ribs.

"That tickles." She squirmed back. "You're such a tease."

"You like it when I tease you." He let out a contented sigh as she ran her fingers lazily through the light dusting of hair on his chest, goosebumps running over his skin. He would never get used to having her here, naked and willing and his.

"When exactly did you and Lana have your little tryst?"

"Maggie." He sighed heavily. "Do we have to talk about this?"

"Yes, we do. Just this once and then never again."

"Fine," he grunted.

She let out a happy humming sound and wedged herself closer.

"It happened the winter you came to Milton, at their New Year's Eve party."

She looked startled.

"Lana kissed me," he said, tickling her. Margaret squealed and tried to wriggle away, but he didn't let go, grabbing her hands, tangling his legs over hers, until she was hopelessly stuck. "Right at midnight," he growled into her ear. "Sound familiar?"

"And you were a completely innocent bystander, were you?"

"You stuck your tongue in my mouth first, Mrs. Thornton."

"You let me do it," she struggled to free herself, "and you kissed me back. Quite vigorously, if I recall."

"I wanted to do a hell of a lot more than that."

"I know you did," she admitted, her face flushed pink. "I almost let you, but then Frannie interrupted."

"What?" He pulled back to look at her. "You would've let me stay over that night?"

"I think so." She was blushing again, and John swore. "Are you cross?" she asked.

"Maybe a little."

"But why?"

"You're telling me we could've been having sex for the last *two years*, and we didn't because of my sister?"

She blushed, shrugging. "Having sex once doesn't mean that we would've kept going."

"Trust me," he said, unable to resist running his eyes over her body again, his own responding to the sight almost instantly. She was so damn perfect. "You couldn't keep me away."

"Is that a challenge, Mr. Thornton?"

"Hell yes." He grinned, knowing he'd already lost.

He'd willingly lose every fight for the rest of his life if it ended like this. She leaned closer and kissed him with a newfound confidence. He let out a sound that was more of a grunting groan than an actual word. It was like New Year's Eve all over again, each kiss a small step in an intricate dance that would take them a lifetime to master. It was the only dance he would willingly practice. She kissed him slowly, a deliberate, focused, and possessive thing. He let her take what she wanted from him, exploring his body as thoroughly as he'd explored hers. She paused, her lips hovering over his.

He swore softly. "Don't stop now."

"Please stop swearing." She pushed him back into the pillows. "It's vulgar."

"Then make me say something else, Mrs. Thorton." He grinned, tugging her closer. "I dare you."

10:16 PM

"For someone with so little experience having sex, you're rather proficient," Margaret mumbled. She had buried her face against John's neck, languidly sprawled over top of him. She couldn't stop her lazy smile as he wrapped both arms around her. She wasn't sure she would ever stop smiling now.

They had nearly fallen asleep when the room phone rang. He swore loudly, reached across her, and grabbed the handset, barking out a sharp, "What?"

"International call for Margaret Hale," the hotel employee said, loud enough for her to hear. Then the line clicked over, and her cousin's shrill voice made them both wince.

"You'll have to call back," John said. "Maggie's not available."

Edith began yelling, and Margaret bit her fist to keep from laughing as her husband's face darkened in annoyance. It was odd to watch him change from sarcastic and teasing John, her husband and lover, into fierce and unmoving Mr. Thornton, a force to be reckoned with. She ignored the growing heat spreading through her body and grabbed at the phone; but John held her firmly against him, rolling onto his side, still keeping the handset out of her reach.

"She'll call you later," he said firmly. "She's busy." A pause. "Having lots of sex."

"John, don't!" Margaret's cheeks flushed hotly as she imagined the look on Edith's face. She struggled to get free. He moved the handset away from his ear as Edith unleashed a long scathing torrent of British insults about his mother and father, his character, and general behavior, loud enough that Margaret caught a few words. She snorted.

She finally shimmied loose, grabbed the phone, mouthing *rude* at her husband before saying, "Eds, calm down. I'm right here."

"Who the bloody hell was that, Margaret Ann Hale, and what the bloody hell is going on? Why is there a man in your hotel room?"

"It's complicated."

"No, it's not," John muttered.

Margaret pushed his hand away from the phone, waiting until her cousin paused for breath. "I promise I'm fine. I'll be back in London in a week, all right? Tell Aunt."

"No, you won't." John snaked his arm around her waist. "You're not going anywhere."

"You'll come too." She winked at him. "I need a man to carry all my things."

"If somebody doesn't answer my questions,"—Edith was shouting again—"I'll call the police!"

"Oh, don't be ridiculous."

"I demand an answer, Migs. Who is that with you?"

"Eds," Margaret bit her lip. But she was too tired to tiptoe around her family anymore. She'd made her choice, and she would stand by it. "Do you remember John Thornton?"

"Not *that* man? Don't you hate him?"

"Why does everybody keep saying that?"

"Are you actually *shagging* him? Oh my God, is *he* your mystery American?"

"Eds, breathe, please."

"He is, isn't he? Are you out of your bloody mind?" Edith was off again, and Margaret sighed, suddenly exhausted.

"Hang up," John said, slinging his arm over his face. "Please."

Margaret slapped the receiver back down and a gentle silence fell over the room. "I think it went rather well," she said after a minute.

"You shouldn't have said anything about the sex."

"You're a grown woman who can make her own decisions. And you're *not* going back to England."

"But we have to explain ourselves to our families, John. Eventually."

379

"Over my dead body." He pulled her closer and buried his face in her lap, his stubbled cheeks scratching the sensitive skin of her thighs.

"You're not going to die," Margaret kissed his shoulder, "but we need to work on your bedside manner."

"My manners in bed are fantastic," he grumbled. She chuckled and he lifted his head. "What?"

"I think I'd rather face my Aunt Shaw than your mother."

"I don't want to talk about my mother, Maggie." He crawled forward, pinning her underneath him. "I don't want to talk at all."

"You're insatiable," she scolded, trying to look unaffected. "There are other things we can do tonight."

"Like what?"

"I'd like a shower, and you need a shave."

"Shower sex sounds great."

"And then," she continued, ignoring him, "we could order in some supper. After all this exercise, I'm a bit peckish. Aren't you hungry?"

"I've waited thirty years for you. I can skip a meal."

His stomach growled loudly, and she gave him a superior what-did-I-tell-you face. "Perhaps we should skip the shower and start with food."

"I'd rather have you instead," he said, a wolfish smile on his face.

"Wait." Her skin burst into gooseflesh as he peppered a slow trail of kisses down her neck. "That's not fair."

"What's fair got to do with it?"

"John." She felt like she was drowning in him, his mouth, his smell, his skin, muscles, and hair.

Well, perhaps food could wait.

11:21 PM

For the first time in twenty years, John could finally relax. His wife was curled into a ball, his arms lazily circled around her, her hair tangled between them. His eyes drifted shut, sleep beckoning.

"What a strange day it's been," Margaret said, her voice thick and slow and sleepy.

"Good-strange?" he asked, only half awake, "or bad-strange?"

"A little of both."

He cracked an eye. "How was it bad?"

"It's a bit vain but I should've liked a wedding dress," she said, smiling slowly. "You're also complete rubbish at proposing."

"You said yes anyway."

"That's the strangest bit, you know? I never thought I'd marry anyone, you least of all." She scooted closer. "But marrying you is the best thing I've ever done. I wish I'd said yes the first time. Everything would've been so different."

She sighed softly and they lay there in the velvet silence long enough for him to almost fall asleep again.

"John," she said, hesitantly. "I wish my mum had met you."

He sucked in a slow breath through his nose, suddenly wide awake. He couldn't see her tears, but he could hear them in her voice. "Don't, Maggie." He brushed her hair away from her face and kissed her wet cheeks. "Don't cry."

"Sorry, I know you're tired. You should sleep."

"Do you think your mom would've liked me?"

"I don't know." Margaret forced a laugh through her tears. "I never knew what she liked. Besides, I wouldn't even know how to explain you or us."

"Try." He began to cover her face with small, light kisses. "Come on, Maggie. Flatter me."

She thought for a minute. "I suppose you're a bit like that bourbon we had at Helstone with Mr. Bell." He felt her smile. "You're a punch in the mouth at first, but quite lovely once you get used to it."

He grunted. "Lucky you."

"Do you think your father would've liked me?"

Her question startled him, and he stared hard at her in the sudden flush of silver moonlight pouring through the window. Her eyes shone, gentle and sincere.

"Yes." He finally said and rolled onto his back, staring at the ceiling. Talking about his dad never got easier. "He would've said you were too good for an asshole like me."

She made a sharp sound of protest, sitting up so she could see his face. "That's a terrible thing to say."

"But it's true." He reached up and cupped her cheek with one hand. "You're too damn good for me."

"Bollocks. I'm not good enough—"

"And you think I am?" He let out a hard breath. She stared at him, her face full of concern and tenderness. He couldn't say anything with her looking at him like that. "Maggie." He pulled her into a tight hug, burying his face in the crook of her neck. "I love you."

It was the only thing he could say.

It was the only thing that mattered.

"And I love you." Her arms tightened around him. "So very much."

"Why?"

The painful word fell between them. He hated the rough, frightened edge in his voice, booming out in the silvery dark room. "I'm a shit human being."

"You are not." She sat back, holding his face in her hands. Something shifted in her eyes, as if she suddenly saw all the things he wanted to say but couldn't say out loud. "I love you because you're you." She brushed his hair out of his eyes, sliding her fingers slowly, delicately, down along his jaw, stopping at his mouth. "Because you're all mine."

Then she leaned in and kissed him, hungrily, tenderly, an intense, sensual enjoyment of his mouth. Every muscle and nerve in his body responded to the honeyed taste of her. "I wouldn't change you," she said. "Not for the whole world."

He let out an odd choking noise, his grip on her tightening. For the last three years he'd watched everything good in his life steadily fall apart, until he had nothing left. But somehow, she was here, loving him at his lowest, kissing him like she wanted only him, making love to a wreck of a man—failures, faults, and all.

None of it mattered now.

As long as this fiery woman was his, he'd always manage to get back up again. For her, he could do anything.

Chapter 46

John blinked and rubbed his eyes, scrubbing the sleep from his face. The sun slanting through the white sheer curtains told him it was late morning. He couldn't remember the last time he slept past five a.m. He grabbed his watch from the bedside table and swore loudly.

He rolled out of bed, sorted through the discarded clothing that littered the floor from the night before, and snatched up his belt, shoes, and black pants. He smirked when he found his boxers slung over a lamp and grabbed his socks and undershirt from the corner. Where was his shirt? He glanced around the room twice before he looked back at the bed where Margaret lay curled in a tight ball. He grinned, dumped his clothes into an armchair, and climbed onto the bed, rubbing her cheek with his. "Thief."

She groaned, and hid her face in the pillow, his white oxford almost swallowing her whole.

"Maggie." He chuckled when she tried to shove him away, burrowing deeper into her cocoon of covers. "I need my shirt."

"No," she mumbled. "Get off."

"Take it off?" He slowly and happily began to loosen the fabric, button by button, planting sloppy, open-mouthed kisses along her chest and stomach as he went.

"Stop it," she grumbled, wriggling back, and kicked at him. She yanked the covers high over her head, leaving her legs exposed.

He turned his attention to her thighs until she sat up, scowling at him. "Good morning, Mrs. Thornton."

"What time is it?" She yawned, pushing a tangle of snarled curls out of her face.

"Almost ten."

"Why are you awake at ten on a Saturday?"

"I have to work." He tugged at his shirt. "I need this."

"Right now?" She blinked owlishly, as if words didn't quite make sense, folding her arms around herself.

"After I shower."

She nodded, yawning again. He stepped into the bathroom and flicked on the shower. He didn't have a razor or a toothbrush, so he made do with the scant hotel toiletries. She was still dozing on the bed when he finished. He watched her for a moment, drying his hair with a towel.

He had a *wife*.

John tossed the towel into the corner and quickly dressed, his mind racing through the inevitable consequences of last night. He didn't regret a single moment. His mother was going to be pissed, but that was another problem for another day.

Margaret stirred and rolled over, watching him sleepily as he pulled on his boxers, socks, and pants. "Where are you going?" she asked, frowning.

"My shift starts at eleven."

"Tell them you got married."

"One of us has to make money." He sat on the edge of the bed, tugging on his undershirt. "And I'm the one with a job."

"I could get a job too." She rubbed her eyes, her frown softening. "Can't you beg off? It's only one day."

"No." He grabbed her hands and pulled her into a sitting position. "I would if I could." He slid his shirt over her head, the sight of her body yanking him to a stop. "I want to stay."

She smiled softly and leaned into his touch. "Then stay."

"I can't."

"You can." She pressed herself closer, kissing him.

He shivered, trying to pull his focus back to getting his ass out the door. He still needed to swing by his apartment, brush his teeth, and shave, but—

"Surely you can spare me twenty minutes, Mr. Thornton?" she whispered against his neck.

John swore.

He could be late. Just this once.

"We're going to have a lot of explaining to do." Margaret ran her hand through her hopelessly tangled hair, watching with growing amusement as John hurried into his clothes again.

"I know." He finished buttoning his white shirt and tucked it into his trousers. He sat down on the bed next to her, pulling on a strange pair of black shoes. She shivered, a small ball of heat curling in her belly. She was so used to seeing his jeans, plaid, and work boots, but she rather liked this more formal version of him. She'd already put him behind schedule, but if he didn't leave soon, she'd make him very *very* late.

"When do you get back?"

"The restaurant closes at ten-thirty, but the bar stays open until two. I'm staying late since Bill let me off early yesterday."

She groaned and leaned her head on his shoulder. "I hate Bill."

"He's the reason I have a paycheck."

"I have money too, you know," she huffed. "I'll miss you."

"I get a thirty-minute lunch break," he said with a sly smile. "And another one for dinner."

"But you have to actually eat."

"I skip meals all the time." He tugged her onto his lap. "I'll survive. Especially if you're on the menu."

"We didn't have any supper last night."

"Your fault, not mine." He kissed her. "I won't die."

"I'm not letting you go until you eat something." She forced herself to slide off his lap, pulled on her knickers and bra, and rummaged through her bag.

He waited, buttoning his shirt cuffs.

"Here." She smiled triumphantly, holding up her discovery.

"Granola?" His voice flattened as she handed him the package. He gathered his wallet, penknife, and keys, throwing the granola at the bin. "I'm not five."

She grabbed it off the floor and followed him to the door. "Eat this," she commanded, tucking the snack and one of their wedding polaroids into his shirt pocket, "or else you'll be spending your lunch and supper breaks alone."

"No, I won't." He bent down and kissed her slowly, lingering until she pushed him away with a groan. He grinned, twisted a key off his key ring, and gave it to her. "Our apartment is on Draper's Street, Unit 427. Meet me at one?"

She nodded, still clutching his hand. "Promise me you'll eat something proper today."

He laughed, a low, gravelly rumble that sent little shivers running along her spine and kissed her one more time. "I promise."

The Draper's Street apartment was tiny and a bit shabby. Margaret put her luggage by the door and glanced around at the neat stack of cardboard boxes along one wall. John barely had any furniture except for a single coffee table, his favorite armchair, a nightstand, a chest of drawers, a lamp, and his giant bed. He didn't keep any clocks in the apartment or wall calendars. She sighed, smiling to herself. When he wasn't working, he didn't like to be on any schedule except his own, but they needed at least one clock and a shared calendar. For her sanity.

She collapsed onto the bed and buried her face in his pillow, breathing in the intoxicating blend of cheap soap, coffee, aftershave, petrol, and peppermint that was uniquely his. It was ridiculous how much she missed him. They'd taken shameless advantage of his lunch break, leaving a mere five minutes for him to bolt down the sandwich she'd brought him. She sat up, dug the remaining polaroid of their wedding out of her bag and set it on the nightstand. In it, she and John were laughing, looking stupid and happy and lost in their own perfect bubble of bliss. She hated to end it, but they couldn't ignore the real world forever.

"Be brave, Margaret Ann." She switched her mobile on, flinching as it nearly exploded, the notifications ringing out in a constant barrage—twenty-nine missed calls, forty-eight texts, and eight emails. She took a fortifying breath and dialed the one person she trusted to keep his head.

"Good afternoon, Margaret." Henry Lennox had the decency to sound a little bored. "Are you all right?"

"I'm perfectly fine."

"I take it Thornton has accepted your proposal?" His voice was stiff and guarded. He knew. Of course, Edith must have told him about last night's awkward phone exchange.

"He did, yes." Margaret smiled to herself. "Henry, I need to ask you a confidential financial question." She took a deep breath. "What happens to my money held in trust if I get married?"

"Married," he repeated. "Did you actually marry him yesterday?"

"Please answer the question."

"Of course." He coughed, but his voice quickly morphed into a more professional tone. If nothing else, Henry Lennox was an impeccable lawyer and bloody good at his job.

"Your trust is currently overseen by your aunt until you are twenty-five. There are no instructions concerning your eventual marriage from either your father or your mother."

"All right." She held back a sigh.

"But," he paused uncomfortably, "but unlike your parents, Mr. Adam Bell included a specific clause stating that should you marry before your twenty-fifth birthday or his demise, you would be granted immediate access to the inheritance he's left you."

She swallowed. "All of it?"

"Yes."

They were both silent for a moment. Henry took a breath and said, "I hope you are quite certain about this."

Margaret looked back at the polaroid of her wedding. This was her life now. She'd fought hard for it, for three awful years, and she wouldn't trade it for the world. "I am."

"I see." He let out a sigh. "Are you happy?"

"Very happy."

"Then I'll draw up the paperwork for the transfer of your funds."

"Please do." She sighed, almost giggling in relief. "Thank you, Henry."

He murmured something stiff and polite. She disconnected the call and flopped onto her back. They would be all right—more than all right. She slid off the bed and rummaged through John's boxes until she found a pencil, a pad of paper, and his old-fashioned address book. With her money and budgeting skills, John's clear head and work ethic, and a little bit of support from the right people, they could start over again. She selected the first number and dialed. "Mr. Bell. This is Margaret Thornton."

"Well, well, well," Mr. Bell chuckled. "I hope this means you've found the little nest egg I've left you, goddess mine."

"I have. Thank you. You shouldn't have done that."

"My dear woman, I delight in doing exactly what I shouldn't. Your happiness pleases me. Now, to what do I owe the pleasure?"

"I have a business proposal for you."

"Do you indeed?" She could hear his wicked grin. "Tell me everything."

Chapter 47

John knocked on the large wooden black door. He took Margaret's hand firmly in his and she glanced at him, trembling. "This is utterly and completely mad, John Thornton," she whispered as Frannie's housekeeper ushered them into the large home. "Your mother's going to bloody murder both of us."

"Let her try."

All too soon they were standing face to face with his sister and his mother. Frannie Watson's easy smile grew wider when she saw Margaret. She was studying their joined hands with a happy intensity. "John-John, what's going on?"

She sounded so genuinely pleased that Margaret smiled back.

"I'd like an explanation as well." Mrs. Thornton looked up from her book. She sat on an impossibly flowery-patterned sofa, flanked by two side tables spilling over with vases of fresh flowers and greenery. "I see you've returned, Miss Hale."

"Mother." John stepped slightly in front of Margaret, his arms folded, in a stance that dared her to disapprove of them. Margaret held back a smile. He expected a fight, but he had no intention of losing.

"How was church?" he asked.

"Where were you?"

"Busy."

"You may as well sit down," Frannie said easily, seemingly ignorant of the silent battle of wills in front of her. "I'll have some coffee made in a jiffy."

"What is *that* girl doing here?" Mrs. Thornton asked, her sharp tone cutting across the tension in the room.

"You already know," he replied.

"Did you think I'd bite my tongue while you let her hurt you again?"

"Mother—"

"John," Margaret interrupted. "It's all right." She stepped closer, placing a gentle hand on his back.

He hesitated. He wanted to say more, but he waited for her.

"Mrs. Thornton," she took a breath, trying to slow her racing heart, "I understand why you're angry, but I'm not here to hurt anyone. I was wrong and stupid and foolish. I love John, and—"

"A girl's love is like smoke," Mrs. Thornton interrupted coolly. "It vanishes when the wind changes. My son isn't a toy; he's a man. And he deserves so much better than you."

"That's enough." John stepped between them, his voice sharp. "You say what you want to me but leave Maggie alone."

Margaret swallowed hard, and Frannie tugged at her hand. "Come on. Let's fetch that coffee," Frannie murmured.

Margaret followed her. She'd expected a tongue lashing, but she didn't expect the blow to cut so deep. The voices from the parlor grew louder. The kitchen door swung gently shut, muffling the sounds, and Frannie let out a whoosh of breath. "I'm so sorry. Are you all right?"

"Yes." Margaret dashed her hand across her face, shifting awkwardly under Frannie's compassionate scrutiny. "It's fine. I knew it would be awful, and I thought I was prepared." She tried to laugh. "I guess not."

Frannie nodded apologetically. "Would you like a beer? You look like you could use one."

"Yes, please." Margaret sighed and sat. "I promised myself I wouldn't cry, no matter what she said. Fat lot of good that did me."

"Mama will flay you alive if she thinks you deserve it." Frannie pulled two cold beers from the refrigerator and handed one to Margaret.

"Maybe I do deserve it," Margaret said. "She loves you both, and I treated John like rubbish. I know I hurt him."

Mrs. Thornton's anger was understandable, but her words hit Margaret where it hurt the most. She didn't deserve John. She never had. So why did he still want her?

"I was so awful to your brother."

"He didn't die," Frannie said, waving a hand dismissively. "Although he did punch a hole in his office wall after you turned him down."

"He did?" Margaret blinked, a twinge of guilt twisting her stomach.

"Don't tell him I told you. Watson said he nearly broke his hand." Frannie rolled her eyes. "My brother is a tad melodramatic."

"Oh." Margaret's cheeks grew hot. "But he was all right?"

"Right as rain after Watson fixed him up."

"Frannie, can I ask you something?" Margaret said, desperate to talk about something else, something normal. "Why do you call your husband by his last name?"

"Because his first name is John." Frannie rolled her eyes again and took a sip of her beer. "It's kind of a mood killer when your husband and your big brother have the same name."

They shared a loaded look and then burst out laughing. There was an easy openness to Frannie that Margaret had never noticed before, and she was grateful. When they finally caught their breath, Frannie said, "I'm sorry for what Mama said to you. You won't get an apology from her, but I hope you'll take mine."

"Thank you. I'm sorry too. I've misjudged you terribly, you know."

"Water under the bridge." Frannie smiled and leaned in conspiratorially. "So, are you and my brother dating or what? I need all the details."

"Sort of." Margaret blushed. "It's still new."

"He loves you."

"I know he does."

"And he does deserve you," Frannie said. "John deserves to be happy for once, and you make him happy."

"I hope so."

They sat in silence for a moment, sipping their beers. "I wonder what they're saying in there," Frannie mused, hopping to her feet. Margaret had to smile. She seemed so untouched by her mother and brother's moodiness. She must have learned how to swim in her own sorrows or drown.

"Your mother's probably trying to convince John why Lana Lancaster would've made a much more suitable wife than me."

Frannie snorted. "I knew he liked you better than—wait!"

Margaret realized her mistake the exact moment Frannie set her beer down so fast it nearly tipped over.

"Did you say *wife*?"

"You married her!" Frannie burst through the parlor doors, Margaret on her heels.

John sighed and swore under his breath. This couldn't get any more awkward.

"They got married on Friday." Frannie was almost shouting as she swept him into an exuberant hug. "It's so romantic and perfect." His sister twirled around and flopped into a chair, her hand pressed over her heart. "Just like a fairytale."

"It wasn't a fairytale," he muttered. "The after party was much more exciting."

Frannie laughed, and Margaret blushed furiously.

"You married her?" His mother demanded, ignoring Frannie and Margaret, her eyes fixed on John.

He nodded.

"When were you going to tell me?"

"I don't know."

"Did you plan on lying to me about her?"

"I wasn't going to lie. I just didn't want to tell you." He folded his arms. "Yet."

"Oh, Mama, let him have his way," Frannie broke in. She looked pleased with herself. "He wouldn't have let us plan anything even if he *had* told us."

"No." Mrs. Thornton shook her head. "No more."

John and Frannie exchanged a look and a silent sigh. He knew convincing his mother to forgive him and Margaret would be difficult. There would be other days—better days—to deal with this train wreck. He stepped over to the sofa, bent down, and kissed his mother's cheek. "This is my decision," he said. "You *will* respect it."

His mother didn't move.

John straightened and nodded to his sister. "Thank you, Fran. We'll see ourselves out."

Margaret followed a step behind him, her thin arms wrapped tightly around her middle. He reached down and took her hand, leading her back to the truck. "I'm so sorry," she said, resting her forehead on his chest. She was trying not to cry. "We should've waited."

"No, my mother was out of line, not us. She'd be pissed no matter when we told her."

"Are you sure?" Her voice quavered. "I don't want to make a row between you two. She's not very nice, but she's still your mother."

"She'll come around." He wrapped her in a hug. "We might have to jump through a few hoops."

"We'll probably have to name a baby after her."

His mouth suddenly went dry. He leaned back and stared at her, a slow grin spreading over his face. "A baby?"

"It's something people do to placate their fussy relations—"

"But Maggie," he interrupted, "you could be pregnant right now."

She stared at him, wide-eyed, and shook her head. "I am *not*."

"We didn't use anything on Friday. Or yesterday. Or today." Her face reddened and his smile widened. "You could be."

"Which would be very inconvenient and—" she broke off, her face drawn and anxious. "We can't have a baby now, can we? Not with the reopening of the Depot. We've only been married three bloody days."

"We'd make it work." John nuzzled into her neck, breathing her in. "I like the idea of you pregnant."

"John-love, please focus."

"Maybe I'll knock you up right here, right now."

"We're outside and it's the middle of the day," she scolded, slapping his hands away as he unbuttoned her coat. "It's freezing—" she broke off with a gasp when he slid his hands under the hem of her blouse. "Oh no, John Thornton."

"Come on, Maggie." He pressed her against the truck. "Play hooky with me."

"We can't shag in your truck like a pair of teenagers."

"Says who?" He yanked the door open and hoisted her inside.

"We're parked in front of your sister's house," she hissed. "What would she think if she caught us?"

"That her brother is one lucky son of a—"

"No swearing," she interrupted, slapping her hand over his mouth. She shuddered as he pushed her hand away, planted a long line of kisses down her neck, tugging her coat from her shoulders. "John, I can't get pregnant now."

"Why not? I want kids."

"I do too but—" she shook her head, grabbing his hands as he began to unbutton her blouse. "But what if I'm bad at it?"

"Bad at what?" He paused, his grin melting away when she finally looked at him. She was flushed a light pink, her hair spilling in a mess of brown curls over her shoulders, but her expression was sharp and almost anguished.

"Maggie, what's wrong?"

"What if I'm a bad mum? Like—like mine?"

"You won't be," he said firmly and laid his hand on her cheek so she couldn't turn away. "You're beautiful, kind, and smart as hell. Our kids will be the luckiest kids on the whole damn planet."

"Do you really believe that?"

"I don't say things I don't mean."

She hesitated for a moment. Her grip on his arms tightened and she tugged him closer, kissing him with a new fierce determination.

"Maggie?"

"Just shut up and hurry before your sister sees."

Chapter 48

John paced the floor of their apartment, glaring at the clock Margaret bought two days after they were married. It was long past ten, and she was still out visiting Mary Higgins and the Bouchers kids. He was supposed to be working on the contracts from Mr. Bell's lawyers. He was tempted to call it a night but without Margaret in the bed, he couldn't sleep. It shouldn't have surprised him how fast he'd come to depend on her simply being present. He slept better, ate better, and worked harder—all for her and their family.

He kept pacing, scowling at the plastic drug store bag sitting on the counter. Inside was a box of pregnancy tests he'd bought earlier that day. Her period still hadn't come, but she insisted they had to wait another day or two. He rubbed his hands over his face and swore under his breath. A sharp knock came at the door, interrupting his thoughts. He yanked it open and frowned in surprise at the woman standing in the hallway.

"Mrs. Shaw."

Margaret's aunt wasn't a tall person, and yet she managed to give the distinct impression that she looked down upon everyone she met. She sniffed. "So, this *is* your doing."

"Can I help you with something?"

"I would like a word with you."

He hesitated, then sighed and motioned her inside. Family was family, even if they were a royal pain in the ass, and this woman was his family now, for better or for worse. Margaret's aunt marched into their tiny apartment and turned slowly, absorbing everything she saw, from the threadbare couch to the dirty dishes piled in the sink. Her distaste was palpable. John leaned casually against the countertop, waiting.

Finally, she faced him. "Where is my niece, Mr. Thornton?"

"Not here."

"What exactly have you done to her?"

He grinned at the absurd question. "I'm not sure what you mean."

"My daughter told me you and Margaret were together recently." The word *together* was spoken with enough venom to kill a horse. "I've come to put a stop to your unwelcome interference."

"Okay." He bit his tongue to keep from laughing.

"You're not to trifle with her. Or—"

"She's an adult," he interrupted. "If you really had any say in her life, why are you here telling me off?"

"Margaret is grieving," Mrs. Shaw sputtered, turning red. "She's vulnerable, and you've taken advantage of her youth and sensitive nature. I know all about your failed business, and I know that you currently support yourself as a waiter, in a bar."

"That's none of your business."

"Margaret's wellbeing is my business. Sir."

He opened his mouth to reply but was cut off by a sharp gasp.

"Aunt Shaw, what are you doing here?" Margaret stood in the doorway to their apartment, keys still in the lock, looking tired, bewildered, and angry. She glanced from her aunt to John.

He shoved his hands into his back pockets and shrugged.

"Margaret Ann, I've come to bring you home. We're leaving this awful place as soon as you pack your things."

"No." Margaret shut the door firmly. "I'm not leaving."

"I can't allow you to throw yourself away for," Mrs. Shaw threw a disdainful glance at John, "for *that* man."

"Allow me?"

"You need guidance." Her aunt patted her arm in an awkward, but motherly gesture.

"Don't touch me, please." Margaret jerked her arm away. "I'm not a child, to be brushed aside, or placated, or dictated to. You shouldn't have come."

"It's my duty to look after you."

"By barging into my home and ordering me about?"

"Your real home is in England."

"England was never my home."

Mrs. Shaw drew herself up and glanced at John again. "Whatever you've done with this man, you're forgiven."

"I wasn't aware I needed forgiveness," Margaret said dryly.

John winked, and she smiled. "I'm not going back, Aunt. He's my home now."

"*That* man?"

"Yes, *that man*. Why is it so hard to believe John is what I want?"

He squirmed a little, a flare of pride itching under his skin as Mrs. Shaw glared at him. He was tempted to end this and throw the interfering woman out of his home, but this was Margaret's fight.

"You told Edith you hated him," her aunt was saying. "That

his manners were vulgar, his morals outdated, his personality brusque and unforgivably offensive."

"And I'm standing right here," he growled, annoyed. "Geez."

"Aunt Shaw, please stop. I said so many things I shouldn't have."

"Dearest," Mrs. Shaw's voice turned surprisingly soft. "You're not yourself. How is this what you want? You could have so much more."

"Do not mention Henry Lennox."

"He's a good man—"

"But he's not John," Margaret snapped, tossing her backpack onto the counter. The force of the backpack knocked the plastic bag over the edge, and the box inside clattered out onto the linoleum, landing at Mrs. Shaw's feet.

John swore under his breath as she grabbed the bright pink and purple package, staring at it, her face turning an ugly gray. So much for keeping that a secret. Margaret sighed and buried her face in her hands. "Margaret Ann Hale." Her aunt sounded eerily calm. "How long have you been sleeping with this man?"

"It's Thornton now, not Hale." Margaret looked up and pulled the box from her aunt's hands. "And it's quite normal to have regular sex with one's husband."

"Your husband?" Mrs. Shaw turned from grayish white to an awful shade of reddish purple. "And he's," her voice dropped to a hissing whisper, "he's already impregnated you?"

"It's none of your bloody business." Margaret laughed, her shoulders slumping with sudden fatigue. "But yes, he probably has. If he hasn't yet, he will eventually."

"Did he force you?"

"Stop." John stepped between the two women and scowled darkly at the fuming aunt. "We're done now."

Mrs. Shaw sniffed and drew herself up, furious and silent. John knew he looked smug, but he didn't care. She'd crossed a line, and this conversation was over. He followed her to the door, closed it behind her with a solid thud, and turned the lock.

"That was bloody awful." Margaret blew out her breath and flopped onto the couch. "I'm sorry."

"I'm the one who let her in." He sat down next to her, and she snuggled against him. He wrapped an arm around her shoulder and kissed her hair. "Your family sucks."

"So does yours."

"Except Fran and Watson."

"They're lovely," she agreed. "My cousin Edith's quite nice too."

He snorted. "I'll have to take your word for it."

"Why did you buy these?" She held up the box of pregnancy tests.

He shrugged.

"You do realize that now my entire family will think I'm pregnant within the hour."

"Your period's late."

"Only a day, and that happens sometimes."

They looked at each other for a long moment. She reached up and brushed his hair out of his eyes. "Shall I take one now, and set your mind at ease?"

"Please."

"Fine. Help me up."

He stood and pulled her to her feet.

"Don't follow me, don't pace like a caged animal," she scolded, poking him in the chest, "and don't get your hopes up."

He slumped down into his armchair and sat for the longest four minutes of his life, one leg bouncing up and down with nervous energy.

He sprang to his feet, his heart plummeting into his stomach, when she opened the bathroom door with a strange little smile on her face.

He wasn't ready for this.

What person in their right mind was ready for a kid?

She held out the white stick. "I was right."

"There's a line."

"Pregnant is two lines."

He frowned at the single pink line. "Are you sure?"

"Yes." She laughed and gave him a playful shove. "You can always try again, you know."

"True." He grinned, tossing the test in the trash. He picked her up and slung her over his shoulder. "How about now?"

"That's not how it works," she said. She laughed as they settled onto the bed. "Besides, I would like to have you to myself for a bit."

"But soon."

She studied him for a moment. "Are you sure?"

"Hell yes."

"All right." She kissed him softly, smiling. "Very soon."

Epilogue

Margaret Thornton arrived in Milton, Connecticut on a gloomy winter's day, the sky cold and gray, the brilliance of fall long faded. The city was still as dreary and weary as it appeared when she'd first arrived here. That first sad day she'd stepped from the Milton airport was so long ago it felt like another lifetime. She shivered as the wind forced its icy fingers down her neck in a rude greeting. She smiled, hunched her shoulders, and walked to the waiting line of taxis.

"Where to, lady?" The cab driver chewed on a toothpick, eyes looking past her.

"The hospital." She pulled her old, battered camera from her rucksack and loaded it with the film box she'd saved for this trip. She blew dust from the viewfinder and waited as the cab lurched through the tangled streets about the airport. There was one building she was looking for, and when it rose, straight and familiar, the bell tower cutting across the smoky sky, she snapped its picture. She never grew tired of St. Anthony's Cathedral. She smiled at the photograph as it developed. She was always improving, but sometimes a shot worked no matter the lighting or the angle. She'd missed Milton.

When she reached the hospital, she was turned away at first. "Visiting hours are over, and Mrs. Thornton isn't accepting visitors who aren't family," the nurse said, with a look of patient apology.

Margaret sighed. "Will you be so kind as to tell her that her daughter-in-law, wishes to see her?"

The nurse raised her eyebrows and nodded. "We'll call you if she changes her mind."

"Thank you." Margaret scribbled her number on a scrap of paper and handed it to the nurse. Some things never changed, no matter how hard she tried.

♡

The Watsons still lived on the east side of Milton, in a gated community where the houses were managed and manicured within an inch of their lives. It made Margaret miss the soft chaos of her own home in Blanding, South Carolina. The older housekeeper showed her up to the sumptuous guest room Frannie always kept ready for her. Margaret dumped her bags on the floor and sat on the bed. She dug an old polaroid from her pocket and propped it up against the lamp. She sighed, running a fingertip over John's barely smiling face. She'd only been gone half a day, and she already missed him.

Frannie was out running her four boys to their various sports games and Watson wouldn't be home until long past supper. Margaret grimaced at the sudden thought of food. Flying always made her queasy. What she wanted was a good, strong cuppa, the way her father used to make it, with scones, butter, and jam.

"Anything is better after a cup of tea," she murmured, missing him. She eventually made her way to the kitchen, and poked around in the cupboards until the cook, a grumbling old Irish woman named Kathleen, appeared. The older woman frowned, flapping about, a little flustered. "If you need anything, I can see you get it, miss."

"Do you have tea? English breakfast?"

"Certainly, we do. Miss Frannie keeps all that. Should I make up a tray for you and send it up?"

"Nonsense. I'll wait." Margaret chuckled. Frannie's extravagance always amused her, especially compared to John's practical simplicity. When the tea was ready, and several scones sliced and plated, Margaret finally relaxed. "Thank you, this is lovely."

"Miss Frannie said you were to have everything to your liking," the older woman said stiffly. She looked like an old chicken with its feathers ruffled in annoyance.

"Thank you," Margaret said. "I should like tea every morning, if it's not too much trouble."

"It's no trouble," the woman said with a grudging smile.

TUESDAY: DECEMBER 3, 2019

It was quite late in the afternoon before Margaret could return to the hospital. She'd left her work conference for the day and found Frannie Watson sitting alone in the hospital waiting room, staring at her hands. Margaret watched her sister-in-law for a moment, her heart heavy.

"Fran?"

The young woman lifted her head and stood, looking relieved and exhausted. "Margaret Ann. You're a sight for sore eyes."

"And a sore heart." Margaret hugged her tight, and Frannie leaned on her shoulder, crying quietly. "Don't cry, Fran. It's all right." She held her sister-in-law until the wave of grief passed. "Here." Margaret held out a well-loved handkerchief. "How's your mother today?"

"She sleeps most of the time." Frannie wiped her face. "The doctors say she won't last much longer."

"What can I do to help you?"

"You're here and that's enough." Frannie folded up the handkerchief. "John should be here."

"He should."

"Mama won't budge, and neither will he." Frannie's voice hardened. "I'm so tired of this stupid argument between them."

"I know." Margaret took the handkerchief and ran a finger over the initials stitched into the corner. When she first married John, the fight had seemed simple. Mrs. Thornton was angry at Margaret for her treatment of John and wouldn't forgive her. Then, after Margaret finished her undergraduate studies in statistics, she and John had moved their little family from Milton to Blanding, with no intention of coming back. Margaret had hoped time and distance would heal the breach between mother and son. But grudges and bitterness piled up, one after another, into an immovable wall of Thornton stubbornness. She sighed. "They're cut from the same bullheaded cloth."

"Don't I know it." Frannie shook back her hair, squaring her shoulders. "I'm done crying about it. If they want to be stubborn, that's their business."

"Go on home, Fran." Margaret gave her elbow a loving squeeze. "Leave your mother and brother to me."

"Good luck." Frannie chuckled darkly. She shook herself, suddenly looking lost, her eyes filled with tears. "I never thought my mama would die. Isn't that stupid?"

"It's not stupid. She's your mother, and you love her."

"I'm sorry we dragged you into this."

"Don't be. I never gave a fig what your mother thought of

me," Margaret said with a wry smile. "Why would I start now?"

Thorntons were all stalwart and stubborn, Margaret included. This was something she had to do, for herself, but mostly for John. He had lost part of his family for Margaret's sake, and he was about to lose his mother for good. It felt so cheap to beg for peace at the end, but she had to try. There wouldn't be any more chances.

Margaret sat quietly while Mrs. Thornton slept. The older woman looked peaceful, even as she lay there, her life slowly being eaten away. She'd developed pneumonia after her latest round of chemotherapy and couldn't shake it. Margaret shuddered at the sound of her struggle to simply breathe. It was dark when Mrs. Thornton finally opened her eyes. "Miss Hale." She stared at Margaret with a severe dignity that was almost comical. "Why are you here?"

There was none of Frannie or John's soft southern lilt to Mrs. Thornton's voice. It was clipped and rough, almost defiant of the disease slowly killing her.

"How are you today?" Margaret asked, ignoring her rude question.

"Alive."

"Do you want me to leave?"

"If you want."

"You've never cared for what I want."

Mrs. Thornton's dry chuckle quickly turned into a thick racking cough, shaking her frame.

Margaret stood and held a cup of tepid water to her lips after she caught her breath. "Hannah, please call John. He should be here with you while he can."

"Why don't you call him yourself?"

"You're his mother. He loves you."

"And now he loves you, Miss Hale."

"Loving me doesn't change his love for you." Margaret set down the cup a little too hard. "You still haven't forgiven me for that, have you?"

Mrs. Thornton didn't answer, but she didn't look away.

"I didn't steal him from you."

"You broke his heart."

"I did break his heart," Margaret admitted, feeling the familiar pang of guilt. The passing years had softened it, but it never really went away. "I'm not asking you to like me." She took the older woman's hand, feeling tears of frustration sting her eyes. "John will never forgive you if you don't let him say goodbye."

The silence hung between them, Margaret holding tight to her mother-in-law's hand, despite the bitterness in the older woman's eyes.

"I've always liked you," Mrs. Thornton said at last. "You're exactly the kind of woman I admire—passionate, fierce, strong. You've got iron and steel in you, and John needs that."

Margaret stared at her. "Then why hold a silly grudge for ten years?"

A strange look settled on Mrs. Thornton's face. "Jonnie's death almost killed my boy."

Margaret sat silent. John never spoke much about his father, but she knew he still had nightmares. Not often, but he never talked about them.

"I couldn't stand seeing him hurt like that again, his heart and spirit crushed."

"Oh, Hannah—"

"I wanted to hate you, but I was wrong." She closed her eyes, as if exhausted by the bitter confession. "I wanted him to be happy, and he is happy with you."

"I hope so." Margaret squeezed her hand. "Can we be friends now?"

"Friends?" Mrs. Thornton opened her eyes and stared at her with a razor's gaze. "I'm dying."

"Well, you're not quite dead yet."

"You're a stubborn thing."

"Very much a Thornton, aren't I?"

Mrs. Thornton almost smiled. "I suppose you are."

WEDNESDAY: DECEMBER 4, 2019

Margaret spent the next day in meetings and lectures, taking notes, smiling, chatting, checking her phone for updates from Frannie, and trying not to show how exhausted she felt. More than once, she ducked into the bathroom when her stomach refused to keep down what little she'd eaten. The conference would last two more days. She ached for her children, for John, for her own simple, happy life, unable to shake a weary listlessness she hadn't felt in almost ten years.

When the day finally ended, she took a moment outside the Watsons' house and stared into the overcast sky, trying to see the stars that lay hidden beneath the thick covering of clouds and city lights. The stars were never bright in Milton. She sighed and turned back to the house. She wanted to go home.

She let herself in through the back door, shivering. She paused in the mud room and listened to the unexpected swell of voices, an achingly familiar deep baritone drifting down the hall. "John?"

She rushed into the kitchen where her husband sat at the table, a cup of coffee in one hand, his long legs stretched out in front of him. He stood and swept her up into a warm hug so tight it almost hurt.

"Bloody hell." She hugged him tighter, breathing in the familiar smell of home—cheap soap, coffee, aftershave, petrol, and peppermint. "I missed you."

"I missed you more." He pulled back and brushed the hair out of her face. "You're freezing, woman." He pulled out a chair for her, scooted his own chair closer, and poured her a fresh cup of coffee. "Drink up."

She made a face and shook her head. "Maybe just tea, yeah?"

"I can't get her to eat anything sticking," Frannie teased. "It's always tea and toast. And don't think I haven't heard you puking out your guts every morning."

"Puking?" He scowled at her, his worry cutting a stern line across his forehead. "Maggie?"

"I'm fine," she interrupted firmly and laced her fingers through his. "My stomach is never happy when I fly, and you know that. I'll be all right soon enough. I'm just tired."

"You shouldn't have come."

Frannie and Margaret exchanged a look, and Frannie set down a steaming cup of tea before excusing herself.

"One of us had to do something," Margaret said once they were alone. "She's dying, love."

He didn't answer and she studied him quietly. He was a scrupulously honest man, but he still hadn't admitted his mother's declining health out loud. But he wasn't an idiot.

She sighed. "How are the boys?"

"Alive."

"Are they behaving themselves?"

"They miss their mother."

"Have you slept at all?"

"Not much." He never could sleep well when she was gone.

"Impossible man."

They fell into an easy silence, watching each other over their cups.

Talking would come later. Right now, being together was enough.

♡

John swore. He stretched out on the floor of Margaret's bedroom, grumbling under his breath, a blanket tossed carelessly over him.

"There is a bed, you know."

"You try being six foot four and fitting into that tiny-ass bed," he said, turning onto his stomach. "My feet hang off the edge."

"Frannie would buy you a king if you would come visit her."

"I hate Milton." He punched his pillow, reshaping it. He was too old to sleep on the floor. He sighed heavily, staring at the ceiling. "You knew I'd come this time."

"Yes." She sounded sad. "Your mother is dying, John."

He made a grunting sound in his throat, not trusting himself to answer. They lay there in the dark until he heard her sigh. She rolled out of bed, pulling the blankets after her, spreading them out on the floor next to him. She tossed down the pillows and settled herself against him. "Better?"

He wound his arms around her and pulled her close. "I hate it when you leave."

"I've only been gone three days."

"Three days," he said, nuzzling into her neck, "and I hated them."

"You're impossible."

"I'm an asshole."

"You're not." She laid a hand on his cheek. "You're hurt and sad and your mother is dying, love."

He grunted, already half asleep. He didn't want to talk about his mother anymore tonight. "I love you."

"Lucky me."

THURSDAY: DECEMBER 5, 2019

Frannie and John stood in the hospital waiting room. Margaret watched them silently. "She doesn't have much time left," Frannie said, her hands fluttering about her, as if she could soften the tension hanging in the air. "I think she's been waiting for you, John-John."

He yanked off his hat and ran his hand through his hair, his mouth set in a stubborn line. He tucked the cap into his back pocket and followed his sister down the hallway. Margaret stayed behind, waiting patiently as her husband finally said goodbye to his mother. She prayed he would forgive her.

She paced as she waited, her mind wandering to her own parents, both passing before they made their peace. She would give almost anything for one final goodbye.

A door slammed and she looked up. John marched out of the hospital room, his face dark and haggard. He stormed past her and headed for the exit. Frannie appeared a moment later, tears streaking down her cheeks. Margaret gave Frannie a quick hug before hurrying after her husband. She stepped through the automatic doors, blinking as the sunshine broke through the clouds for a moment, warming her skin. John leaned against one of the concrete pillars, looking up at the skeleton trees. "Did you talk to her?" Margaret asked gently, reading his anger and hurt in every line of his stiff posture.

He nodded.

"Does she want to be alone when she goes?"

He nodded again and her shoulders slumped.

"I'm so sorry, love."

"Me too." He took his hat out of his pocket and tugged it on. She slid her hand into his and they walked out into the chilly mist. He

413

helped her into the truck and drove away from the city. When they reached the St. Michael Cemetery, she stepped out into the cold silence, the city noises muffled by the mist and fog.

Hannah Louise Thornton died quietly that evening, without fuss or inconvenience. John held his sister while she cried. Margaret took care of most of the arrangements as quickly as possible, but there was little to do. Mrs. Thornton had it all planned. The funeral was a small family affair two days later. John didn't cry, not for his mother or himself or even Frannie. Margaret wished he would, but it just wasn't his way.

When everyone else had gone, John and Margaret lingered. His parents' black gravestone stood in stark contrast to other pale granite stones surrounding it. He pushed at the freshly turned earth with his shoe. Her heart ached for him. She took his hand in both of hers and kissed it.

"The Thorntons all hated my mother," he said, his voice rough.

"Why?"

"She always did what she thought was best, no matter what anyone said or thought."

"That sounds familiar."

He shrugged.

"At least your parents had each other, yeah?"

"Not really. Thorntons are all fucked up, especially them."

"Don't say that." Her voice was edged in steel. "Your mother loved your father, and you know it, even after everything that happened. He loved her too, and you and Fran, in his own way."

"Is that why he blew his brains out?"

"John Thornton!" Margaret bit her tongue and he looked away, folding his arms in defiance of her silent reproof. "There was love there," she said, once she had hold of her temper. "It was just all twisted and broken and very human. Your mother loved you, and you loved her, in your silly, dysfunctional Thornton way. She knew that." Margaret watched the hard lines of his shoulders slowly soften. "You Thorntons love fiercely, consequences be damned," she said with a smile. "It's what I love most about you."

He nodded, once, then pulled her into a rough, fierce hug. "Do you want to see Bess?" he asked.

She nodded.

They walked slowly up the hill, hand in hand, to where the familiar old oak tree stood sentinel over the grave of Bess Higgins. Margaret brushed away the wet leaves and placed her hand on the cold stone. John stood quietly. The sting of their grief would never fully fade. They'd both lost so much in this place.

"Fran said you went to see my mother," he said. "Before she died."

"I did." Margaret took his hand again. "We made our peace."

"Did she actually forgive you?"

"Not in so many words, but yes, I think she did. She told me she liked me. She even apologized."

"How the hell did you manage that?"

"I made her a promise. It's silly, but I think she was pleased."

"What kind of promise?"

"To name our baby after her."

He raised his eyebrows. "Are we making another baby?"

"We already did, love," she said, pulling a plastic pregnancy test from her coat pocket. "It's entirely your fault too."

"Shit." He took the test and studied it. "When did this happen?"

"Mr. Thornton, in the study, with his bloody-high sex drive."

"Specifics, Maggie."

"I was trying to grade papers and you," she poked him in the ribs where he was the most ticklish, "were extremely horny and romanced me into making love to you on my desk."

"Good for me," he said, a wide, stupid grin splitting his face. "You're sure this test is right?"

"Two lines means pregnant, love." She rolled her eyes and turned towards their truck. She smiled when he caught up to her and wrapped her in a bear hug, nuzzling along her neck with wet, warm kisses.

"Are you happy?" she teased.

"Hell yes." Another man probably would've said something sweet or romantic, but this was John, and he did things his own way.

She waited expectantly, until he said the only thing she ever wanted him to say. "I love you, Maggie."

"John," her smile suddenly turned into a small frown, "what do we do if this baby's another boy?"

"We keep popping them out until we get it right."

"That's not funny—"

"You promised my dying mother a granddaughter."

"Four grandchildren is plenty, even if they are all boys."

"Thorntons never make promises they can't keep," he said, his grin widening. "And I want a daughter, something fierce."

"You know, your silly farm boy accent gets rather thick when you're pleased with yourself." She sighed. "You're lucky I love you so much."

"Damn lucky."

MONDAY: JUNE 29, 2020
EIGHT MONTHS LATER

Hannah Maria Thornton was born on a sunny summer day, and Margaret laughed when she saw her daughter for the first time. The little baby girl had a shock of fluffy black hair, and a very stern, inky black pair of eyebrows perched over her bright blue eyes. "Why do all my children look exactly like you? It's unfair."

"Too bad for her," John said with a yawn.

"What does that mean? You bloody well know you're still fit and quite handsome. Even if you are forty."

"Almost forty," he grumbled. "My face on a woman is ugly as hell."

"She's beautiful."

"Your fault, not mine." He shifted their daughter to one hand, and pulled Margaret closer against his side, a mischievous look on his face. "She's perfect, like her mother."

"Flatterer." Margaret tucked the blanket back where little Hannah had kicked it loose around her feet. The baby wrinkled her little red face, trying to cry. "Give her here, love."

"She's fine." He tucked the tiny baby against his chest and leaned back into the mountain of pillows, his feet hanging off the edge of the hospital bed. He closed his eyes and sighed.

"She needs to eat, John."

"You got her for nine whole months. She needs her dad."

"You mean *you* need her," Margaret teased. "There'll be plenty of time for daddy snuggles after I feed her."

"There's time right now. She likes me."

Margaret shook her head, pulled her camera out of their duffel bag, and snapped a quick photograph. John would hold their daughter every moment he could in the hospital. It made going back to work a little easier. When the picture finished developing, she tucked it into his shirt pocket. He would put it on his desk next to their wedding photo and the picture of their three boys.

"You're such a baby hog," she murmured.

"You love me."

"I do." She looked at him for a moment. She leaned closer and kissed him. "You're my home."

the end.

acknowledgements

This book is a small miracle. It's imperfect, messy, and very dear to me, and so many others, without whose support and encouragement, *Where North Meets South* would never have come this far. Years of work, endless conversations, lots of love, and dedication have been poured onto these pages.

First, thank you to my husband and my parents.

Dan, thank you for giving me space to create, brainstorming with me when I'm stuck, and teaching me ever so many tips and tricks of editing and formatting. You believed I could do this long before I believed you. You took my dream and made it yours, and I cannot thank you enough. I love you.

Dad, thank you for never forgetting to ask how my writing is going. I know you love me and are proud of me, even if this book isn't exactly your kind of book. You have always been in my corner, cheering me on.

Mom, all those years ago, when I spent my days singing and telling myself stories, I'm not sure you thought we'd end up here. Thank you for being the first person who saw the glimmers of who I'd become and loved me through it all.

Second, thank you to a few creatively minded friends, some old and some new, whose encouragement has helped me keep going. Philip and Olivia Vogel and Holly Epperly—you've been here for the long haul of my writing journey. Beth Blake and Fleur Smith—your friendship means everything.

Third, thank you to my writing friends, The Millers. You are an enthusiastic and generous group of people who became my friends at a time when I felt I had none left. You were the first to read this book, the first to love it, and the first to believe in it. You read this story over and over (and over) again, giving priceless feedback.

Tom Schachner, the most unlikely of friends. I'm so thankful we met. And I'm glad you're still here.

Theresa "Merry" Hewitt, you deserve a line all to yourself. You brought the Millers together and were always so persistent and vocal in your belief that I ought to publish For Real. I hope this book carries your memory for a long, long time.

Diana K. Cooper, who helped edit massive portions of this text without complaint, as we nit-picked our way through the grammar and punctuation rules of English, both American and British. You're a gem. Never change.

A very special thank you is due to my favorite (and only) daughter, Autumn, who helped rethink the title of this book and spent hours with me as I tweaked the cover design until it was perfect. You're the best, sweet girl.

And lastly, I must thank a stranger I've never met—Vanessa D. Anderson—who returned this manuscript to me after I thought it was lost. Without your kindness and generosity, I would've lost part of my soul. This book is yours too.

about the author

ROSE JOHN SHEFFLER is a Catholic writer and teacher who sometimes wishes she'd been born in England, near Bristol or maybe Oxford. A lifelong Anglophile, she lives primarily in her head with her characters, but her body resides in Louisville, Kentucky in a beautiful Victorian home with her philosopher husband, three children, a pet rock named Roy Moss, and three typewriters.